BLUE AVIARY

A Novel

RICHARD L. QUINN

North Carolina

Blue Aviary
© 2023 Richard L. Quinn. All rights reserved.

No part of this book may be reproduced in any form or by any means, electronic, mechanical, digital, photocopying, or recording, except for the inclusion in a review, without permission in writing from the publisher.

This is a work of fiction. All of the characters, names, incidents, organizations, and dialogue in this novel are either the products of the author's imagination or are used fictitiously.

Published in the United States by BQB Publishing
(an imprint of Boutique of Quality Books Publishing, Inc.)
www.bqbpublishing.com

Printed in the United States of America

978-1-952782-87-9 (p)
978-1-952782-88-6 (e)

Library of Congress Control Number: 2022947959

Book design by Robin Krauss, www.bookformatters.com
Cover design by Rebecca Lown, www.rebeccalowndesign.com
Cover artwork by Richard Quinn

First editor: Caleb Guard
Second editor: Allison Itterly

for Sarah

ACKNOWLEDGMENTS

First of all, allow me to express my undying gratitude to my female family and friends who allowed me glimpses into the female psyche. Admittedly, I am not certain when the learning began . . . but I do know it never stops, nor should it. A special thanks to my niece, Dr. Jennifer Towns PhD, who aided me in my early attempts to clarify the trauma experience.

A special thanks to Thomas and Emily Cusson, who produced valuable marketing materials for *Blue Aviary*.

And to Norma Brown Dalessio and Claire Hughes, who both gave the book an early read. Your generous encouragement proved vital to the completion of this work.

And most importantly, the hugest thank-you of all to the best technical support, my dearest friend and dearest love, Laura Betters Smith. Without you, *Blue Aviary* would not have come to be. I love you.

CHAPTER ONE

The air is cool September mornings up on Trumpet Hill. Dampness settles in shadowy places. The early hour promises warmth. A sun-drenched day begins to reveal itself through the big hemlock that lays its lower branches just above the aviary hard deck. Pigeons race in an orbit around the Bowden farm. They test the limits of their trespass, flying just above neighboring fields and yards. I came early this morning to spring the flyway gate. In a frenzy of beating wings, twenty birds escape the aviary confines. I settle into a familiar hollow along the rock wall to watch the flock pass between me and a splash of orange morning sky.

I am happy here these days, this little farm nestled deep within the Catskill Mountains watershed. Down below, Esopus Creek guards the eastern flank. It winds its way beside a two-lane road that mirrors it for a stretch, both of them cutting channels through the thick green forest of southeastern New York State. The creek rolls through hamlets buried quietly in the pines, past Kingston, the seat of Ulster County, all the while collecting the tithes of a hundred lesser tributaries trickling down from up above. Near Saugerties it pours its Appalachian ginger brew into the mighty Hudson River.

Some mornings I ascend the mountain to an outcrop just beneath the clouds, where the Village of Saugerties appears as a loosely assembled clutch of chalky buildings, strewn up and down the Hudson's west bank. But I must go early to catch first light, to see my world in its entirety from the top of Trumpet Hill. A sprawling patch of mountain green wraps the Bowden farm and extends for a mile or more in every direction. There are people. There are fallen-down barns and built-up barns, a milk cow, a fattened-up pig or two . . . all that is familiar to me. As far back as I remember, I have looked upon this swath of green and all that thrives within it to be my neighborhood . . . my *nearby earth*.

The pigeons stall in flight with each pass above the aviary. They anticipate a breakfast of cracked corn and scraps from the kitchen. When no call comes, the flock continues on its way, lost in one moment behind the woodshed and the barn. The birds rise to clear the treetops that lend cover to a brook, and a teepee showing its age. It teeters on a dozen spindly legs. We played there, Zach and I, and almost daily the flight of the birds turns my head to that place.

The tight flock swings south over Jolly's pond. If rumors are to be believed, the pond is an abyss that harbors demons in its depths, demons that devour small children, toddlers eaten and just as quickly forgotten . . . because none truly went missing, none that I ever heard about. Even Ol' Jolly himself, who dug the hole in the earth decades ago, scoffed at the rumors, calling them sensational and ridiculous.

There will always be mornings that tempt me from my room with my notebook in hand. This day is one of them. I am Sydney Bowden, a woman of twenty, by now. I am a little tall and a little lean. I am smart, a little. I've been told I am a little pretty, but I don't hear that often enough. Grandmother always said my hair was a little auburn. I get that from my father, who got it from her.

I was precocious even as a toddler. But I was indeed a child then, and far too young to fathom the complexities of added burdens in my life. As I grew older, I was declared gifted, and assessments of my intellect were bandied in hushed tones.

That might have been the extent of it. Cautious journeys were undertaken to measure my mental acuity. They continued for a time but failed to unearth the grail.

It was my father, when I was seven, who made sense of it all in his own way. "Genius assumes great things, darling . . . postulating life on Neptune and a dependable way to get there by morning," he said to me. "Gifted requires proficiency at the piano by age six."

I thought about it and said, "I don't play piano, and I'm seven."

"Aye," he offered in his best pirate's voice. "It must be good to know you can do it if you choose." But that was my father, and he often left me wondering if my shoes were on the wrong feet.

Suffice it to say, I knew some things at seven. I knew postulating meant guessing, and I knew if I were proficient, that meant I would be good at something. So, my vocabulary alone might have been ahead of the game for my age. Perhaps to prove his point, a week later an old upright piano appeared against the wall opposite the front windows.

Chronology, I've determined, is not always so easy for a child. In my world, even an eternity has to start someplace. I recall the very day I became a living, bleeding person, and it had little to do with genius. I was sitting in the front seat of Grandmother's big car examining my knees for fresh skins and scrapes. Upon inspection, I discovered jagged circles of dried blood crusting like mud pies and lifting loose at the edges. Even at my earliest emergence into consciousness, I was counting my blessings.

I cannot be certain why I was not forced into the kid seat in back. While Grandmother's boat of a car bucked over potholes and broken pavement, I grappled to get hold of anything that might safely secure me aboard. We laughed all the way to the garden store at the top of the hill. A stick-figure rendering, done in blue crayon, preserves the occasion, depicting Grandmother, the tiny woman dangling from the helm like a shrunken boatswain. To this day the picture hangs on the wall above my bed. It was a day to remember, and I have done that—the two of us, Grandmother and me, hunting petunias for her garden.

I adjust my position on the stone wall, remembering those days of my childhood when I sat in this very spot near the aviary, scribbling pieces of a story, waiting for the kitchen door to rattle open and then go quietly closed. It was the sound that signaled Beepah's arrival. It was a familiar noise then, and remains a comfort all these years later.

Beepah is how I knew him, the man fifty years my senior. He took care of the farm, the gardens and the birds, and brother Zach and me. Beepah was not a name ordained by a christening. That name was Benjamin Bowden. Beepah was the name I bestowed on him when I was but one or two. By challenging phonetic norms, or some such thing, Beepah is the name I gave to my father. I refused to be taken to task or corrected. Either way, it stuck, and all other names lost favor . . . at least with me.

Every morning, Beepah raised his eyes skyward. The birds recognized Ben Bowden heading toward the kennel gate, swinging a scrap pail in one big hand. Their reaction was immediate. They'd adjust their flight and began descending to the aviary hard deck. Mass hysteria ensued when news leaked that breakfast was arriving. The birds would push and bump their way through the trap gate.

Rare mornings might even deliver a stranger to the mix, a bird with unique plumage, nervous and uncertain, questioning the impulse to enter. I might have seen him and recognized him as an outlander, but I rarely inspected the coop like Beepah did. Outlanders were welcome in the aviary. Other times it was a weasel that stirred a calamity and put the flock on edge. I recall those mornings when a successful raid was evident by the carnage confronting Beepah. Uneaten flesh lay stringing from disjointed bones. Bloody feathers lay in a matted tangle, stirred into the dirt floor where a sacrifice played out in the black of night.

Beepah had an uncanny sense of when things were amiss. He would stand just inside the kennel gate peering upward through the hemlock branches until the chilly air above quieted. He'd pull at the coop door, step inside, and let the door slap shut. Those mornings the sun played on him through the grid of chicken wire. Part of him was in shadow and some of him in the coolest morning light. He studied the scattered bones and feathers and quietly calculated there were two carcasses ripped and torn apart. Those he would deliver to a common grave back of the barn when his chores in the coop were done. There would be no ceremony for them, but the task was filled with unpleasantness. It had to be done. Rotting flesh on the aviary floor would only attract more scavengers.

Some mornings, and without a word, Beepah knew I was there, sitting in the shadows of the hemlock, or basking in the early sunshine that pushed fingers of light through the wrought iron kennel fence. I would watch him patiently and often in silence while he inspected the coop for interlopers and assassins.

Beepah was tall, six feet and something. Sinewy might best describe his build. Some mornings were greeted with a smile, a broad one. He was good for that. The bloodbath in the coop denied his smile that day. He removed his baseball cap and scratched at his thinning hair. His eyes came up to me finally. "Morning, Syd," he said.

"Morning, Beep."

"What'cha writing?"

I put a hand on my notebook and gave it a moment's pause. Beepah was always respectful of my notebooks, encouraging me almost daily, ever playful in his inquisitions. Some days I revealed my literary endeavors. Other days I would clutch my notebook tight to my chest and Beep would laugh a little, acknowledging the deepest secrets I held.

"I was thinking about Grandmother. We still talk some mornings."

"Yeah, I miss her," he said, his eyes drooping again. "She's been gone a long time. I'm surprised you remember her so clearly. She died when you were little."

"We planted flowers in her garden that last summer. I was writing about that day. I remember you told me she had to sleep in the cold building at the cemetery until the ground thawed enough to bury her. The school bus still stops near that awful place on its way. I thought about Grandmother lying in the cold in her blue dress. I must have cried every day until spring."

Beepah stabbed his toe against the kennel dirt. I could tell he instantly felt bad. The little gesture was enough of an apology for me after so many years, and him unaware of the sadness his words had stirred in me back then. We saw the world differently, Beep and me. I dare say, he might have even considered it a comfort for me to know where Grandmother passed the rest of that winter. Only now am I beginning to recognize the small differences between a hole in the ground and an icy bed above it. Cold places both.

"We lost the Goochie Doll," Beep identified one of the chickens, dead in the coop. The Goochie Doll was a good egg layer, but more spectacular for her name alone. Beepah was good for naming animals, just like our neighbor Ol' Jolly. It seemed like half the time they were in competition. Chickens were included, and pigs and geese and goats. Even pigeons earned a moniker if they stayed long enough. Beep often reminded me that every creature deserves a name, and he kept busy imparting names on any new arrivals. Even counting the pigeons in the rafters, I could name most of the birds. I knew them, but deaths in the aviary rarely moved me to tears any longer.

"I wasn't sure who they got," I admitted, offering a sad frown for the Goochie Doll. "I didn't look at it for very long."

"Any stragglers?"

"Jolly was out back tossing pellets by the pond," I said. "He gets a few birds to drop by. Buddy and Beebo were noisy. Did you hear them?"

"Crazy goats," Beep grumbled. "That's trouble, those two."

"The geese fight them for food," I said. "Ol' Jolly throws pellets on the water so the geese get their share. The goats won't swim for them at least."

"What was Jolly thinking, bringing those bad seeds aboard? Noah himself would have kicked their asses off the ark," Beep said with a smirk. "Anyways, Jolly's pellets bloat the pigeons. They sit up in the rafters all day like they ate a box of rocks. I ask you, what good is a pigeon if he can't fly for my amusement?"

Beepah went to the coop door. He reached above it and took down the call can. He gave it a shake. The familiar rattle stirred the quiet morning air. Sure enough, seconds later three stragglers arrived on the hard deck acting indignant and confused. They pushed their way toward the wire entry trap, then the three, reluctant to join the flock inside the aviary, dropped to the churned earth inside the kennel to battle the chickens for food. He tucked the call can back above the door. "Goats," he grumped. "I caught those two bad sores on the kitchen table a few days back because somebody left the backdoor open." He gave me a punishing glare. "In they walk, the two of 'em, jump on the table and kick over the sugar bowl. They're grazing in ambrosia when I come in. They're lickin' up sugar like they died and gone to billy goat heaven."

Right away it became clear to me, Beepah was inventing a new tale and trying it out on me before he took it on the road.

"I swear, Syd, to top it off, the two of 'em had found the

motherload on a chokecherry bush. Goat turds dropping out of their ass-ends like caviar on a biscuit," he said. "Purple goat turds falling on the kitchen table right where you sit at dinnertime."

"No way!"

"I swear," he said again, this time throwing his right hand in the air to attest to the truthfulness of the tale. "Hey, I wiped the table off. It's all good. I doubt you'll even notice. It's still a little purple though, but everything fades with time." He enjoyed teasing me, leaning down as if to pass his eyes over the very spot on the table where the goat turds landed. "Those chokecherries stain like blood." He gave a shrug. "If I'da had a gun, I'da shot those two scabs."

Beepah slung the scrap pail at arm's length, scattering egg-shells and moldy bread crusts and corn cobs from dinner the night before. He stepped back inside the coop and gave the feed bucket a few kicks until it popped open. He scooped cracked corn into the scrap pail, then tossed handfuls to the dirt floor. Pigeons descended from the rafters in a cloud of dust and pin feathers. Chickens were roused from nesting boxes along the back wall. They bounced down the pyramid of roosting poles like puffed up ballerinas.

"I chased them goats off," Beepah kept on, talking through the chicken wire. He stopped his corn dispensing long enough to chuck the two bloody chicken carcasses into a heap near the kennel gate. Then he cast a smirk in my direction. "I swear, Syd, what an outrage, those two. They jumped off the table and ran across the yard high on sugar. What a couple nitwits."

Beep shook his head and laughed at the thought of it, real or otherwise. I was left to believe it was only possibly true. But then, to challenge his recounting of the tale only meant he may relinquish a portion of it to absurdity and swear to the rest. I chose to let this one die on the vine, especially since it was clear he fingered me for leaving the door ajar, which would have been slanderous had he uttered it aloud.

Beepah removed the blocks from the swing door. A half dozen laying hens strutted toward the scratch yard. Leading the way was a foul-tempered rooster who went by the name Cowboy, although he never answered to it. Ol' Cowboy used his head like a battering ram. He hit the swing door at top speed and tumbled into the kennel scratch yard before his landing gear was fully deployed. Beepah referred to the maneuver as, "Cowboy's ass over tea kettle three-point landing." Beep said it was unique in the animal kingdom.

Cowboy skidded to a stop in the loose earth. He stood in the sliver of light that sliced through the hemlock branches. His eyes went instantly into frantic search mode, seeking anything familiar. When he caught sight of me sitting on the rock wall, the orange feathers on his scrawny neck bristled. His eyes burgeoned indignation the moment he realized I had arrived in the scratch yard ahead of him.

The old rooster had been a fixture in the aviary and the surrounding kennel almost as far back as my memory allowed. He arrived with the first brood of chicks, a dozen infant egg layers in a shoebox with head holes cut out. The yellow and orange noggins that poked through twisted with excitement and curiosity. Cowboy was among them, an interloper of the highest order, defying the gender-specific order for girl chickens only.

The crotchety old bird had outlived several generations and had grown into the aviary's crabbiest resident. He even chased me in his earlier years, pecking at my legs and hands while I battled to fend him off. Nowadays, he wakes me. Each morning at sunrise, his garbled baritone stirs me from sleep.

Cowboy got his name because of his bravado and nothing more. At the very least, it was a name designed to shield me from

Beep's clumsy explanations about the bony chicken's appetites, and we're not talking cracked-corn casserole here. One morning, when I was small, I witnessed the crazy rooster riding a hen around the scratch yard. I was perplexed at the sight, all chickens being equal to me in those days. But this behavior was worth inquiry. So, I braved the question, "Beepah, what is he doing to her?"

Beep's eyes quickly located the scrawny rooster astride a little red hen. She was doing her best to toss the brute face first into the kennel mud. The crazy rooster only dug his spurs in deeper. Beep pushed his baseball cap high on his forehead and gave his tangle of hair a scratch. "He's a cowboy all right," was all he said. The name stuck.

Early on, Beep discovered my willingness to rise with the sun. When I was four, he began taking me with him when he went out to work on chores before breakfast. I would often sit an hour or more in the quiet when the air was warming. Beep had a gift. He could lie about any number of things and swear to them.

"There's Neptune," he once said, pointing at a star still twinkling low in the horizon to the west. "Neptune is really a planet, not a star. If you lay in the meadow after the sun goes down and look into a clear sky, you'll see it. It's blue."

It was some years later I learned that nobody has ever really seen Neptune, not with the naked eye anyway. Rather than dismiss Beep's certainty in the matter as heretical, I simply developed a healthy dose of skepticism. By then, Beep's brainwashing had established a foothold in me. It wields influence to this day. I still lay in the meadow looking up on clear nights. I harbor hopes that Neptune is there, that I will someday see its blueness shining down on me.

CHAPTER TWO

The dilapidated kennel, built years before, was designed to hold a dog. Beep worked tirelessly to ready the enclosure with new posts and wrought iron fencing. Little Tilly arrived for my brother Zach's sixth birthday. She was a roly-poly bundle of a little yellow lab. The very first day, Zach threw her into Jolly's pond to teach her to swim. Instead of struggling to save herself, she loved the water. She used her little club of a tail like a boat tiller, and that's how she got her name, Tilly. She quickly endeared herself so completely to the entire family, imprisoning her in the kennel was never a real option, so she slept in Zach's bed every night.

Instead, the kennel became a place for the birds with the addition of a coop. First there were chickens. Chickens, after all, legitimized the little farm. "We're a going concern," Beep said of it once the members of the first class of infant egg layers began to fulfill their God-given purpose. First there was one egg, then a few days later maybe two or three. It wasn't long before the Bowden farm was in full production. Eight, ten eggs a day almost filled my little cane basket.

The pigeons came a year later. It was Zach who first imagined a place for pigeons. He put the idea to Beepah one morning while standing at the kennel gate eating a dirty carrot yanked fresh from the garden. If I recall, it was a Saturday, Zach's favorite day by far. I was five or so, and there to collect eggs at Beep's insistence. I scissor-stepped across the bales of straw, shooing chickens from their nests. I gathered the warm eggs in my basket or Beep's baseball cap.

"I was just out there checking my rabbit trap," Zach said. He pointed with his carrot toward the garden out back, as if Beep needed a reminder as to the whereabouts of the infamous rabbit trap.

Beepah was always inquisitive. "Get anything?"

"Just this toad." Zach clutched the fat amphib in his hand opposite the carrot. He raised it over his head for inspection. "He jumped in there in the middle of the night. Toads like the dark. Anyway, he's the biggest toad I ever caught. I might keep him for a pet. A toad's a toad," he said, giving a shrug. It was a small victory by Zach's standards, and his frustration showed. He kicked at the iron gate. "A rabbit would make a good pet."

Beepah used a pitchfork to move old straw to the scratch yard where chickens churned it up in their hunt for cracked corn and bugs. "Rabbits are generally gentle creatures," Beep said. "Their talents are limited. They don't fetch or herd cattle. They're lousy swimmers too. I tried to teach one myself when I was about your age. It didn't end well."

Zach was familiar with Beep's teasing and this time it bothered him. "I don't care about that stuff. I don't need a rabbit that can swim. That's just dumb anyway," he grumbled.

Beep laughed and jabbed at Zach again. "It's a good thing you think so," he said. "It's not easy sorting the smart rabbits from the less gifted. Much like people in that regard."

Zach snapped off a bite of his dirty carrot and chomped on it until it was chewed fine enough to swallow. I could tell his mind was grinding over Beepah's digs. He chomped off another bite and crunched it in his teeth. All the while, his eyes surveyed the kennel and the coop. At last he spit the carrot chunks to the ground, inciting a rush of hungry chickens. "You know what this chicken coop needs? A whole bunch of pigeons, that's what," Zach declared.

Beep leaned on his pitchfork and cocked his head to watch the last of the orange sunrise drain from the morning sky to the east. He smiled. "You might be onto something, Zach boy," he said.

I remember clear as day how Zach's simple suggestion started things rolling and how a lowly chicken coop became an aviary. Quickly there was progress made. One afternoon I came home from school to discover an odd contraption mounted on the roof of the coop. It was an entry trap. Pigeons could learn to enter the coop through the trap, but they could not exit. It was an ingenious idea. Beep said he saw it in a sporting-bird magazine.

After church that day, Beepah loaded Zach and me into his old Chevy van. Zach sat up front, and I slid into the back seat behind Beep and off we went. All the way down Trumpet Hill, Beep explained what he had learned about pigeons and his rationale for driving into the big town of Kingston on a Sunday.

"Here's the plan," he said. "Parking lots are empty on Sunday, except if there's a concert, or a flower show, or something." Then at a red light, and complete with hand gestures, he said, "We swoop in there and set up the trap and haul off with a load of city pigeons while the townsfolk are still scratching their behinds." There was no talk of legal entanglements. The purpose was to capture pigeons, pure and simple. Jail times were barely discussed.

The plan got Zach's attention. "Like Vikings on a raid!" he jumped in. "Only they don't use traps. They chop up all the boys and haul off all the girls. Go figure that, Sydney!"

"The cattle raid of Cooley!" Beep blurted out of the blue. His sudden outburst even incited his own laughter. "Your grandmother told me the story many times. Cooley . . . that's where her people come from. Your grandmother lived there until she was ten. She had a way of telling a story, the dear woman," Beep said.

"She sang to me at bedtime," I said.

"She had the sweetest Irish lilt till her dyin' day," Beep said. "It seems the Queen of Connacht became jealous of the Cooley bull, the most magnificent bull in all of Ireland. She sent her army to steal the beast away," Beep said. "Ah, but there is a hero to this tale: a boy named Connell."

Zach spoke up. "Hey, that's my name!"

"Yup, Zachary Connell Bowden. It was your grandmother's idea. In her story, it's Connell who drives off the army with nothing but a slingshot. He saves everybody, and the family bull too."

"I got named for him?"

"Yes, you did, Connie boy." Beep reached across and gave Zach's sandy brown hair a scrub with his knuckles. Beep rocked back in the driver's seat and wheeled the old van off the highway and onto a quiet Flatbush Avenue. The van rolled past a gas station guarding the entrance to the town. Zach's excitement was palpable. It was that very kind of derring-do, accompanied by bold talk, that had become Zach's modus operandi and Beep discovered the willing spark in Zach over his first seven years of life.

The morning of the great pigeon raid might have been a story onto itself. But alas, we were not confronted by an angry mob of townsfolk seeking to waylay our planned plunder. None gave our raid the simplest notice. Strangely, after Beepah's old van rolled to a stop in an empty parking lot, I stood with my eyes pointing skyward. My head turned to engulf the enormity of the universe in one swift pirouette. Suddenly, I passed from almost invisible to very conspicuous.

Zach was quick to point out the obvious, all of it said to frighten me. "Look at all those windows, Sidney!" he blurted. "Just because it's Sunday doesn't mean there's not people up there watching everything you're doing. If they catch you stealing pigeons, they'll put you in jail!" He cupped his hand to his mouth and brought it near my ear. "And girls don't get their own cage neither," he warned me. I did my best to ignore him.

Beepah stood for a moment studying the building tops with his hand shading his eyes. He walked to the rear door of the van and swung it up and open. He removed the wire mesh contraption he had fashioned for capturing pigeons and set it on the pavement a few feet away. He raised the mesh door and strung a string from the trap to the van's side door. I crawled back into the van. It seemed a more secure perch. Based on Beepah's stories, I suspected a rain of pigeons was about to descend from the building tops to our little spot in the world.

"Hold this," Beep said to me, and he handed over the string. He went to the back of the van again and retrieved a can of cracked corn and held it out to Zach. "Scatter a handful around the trap. Not too much. Just let them see it."

Zach came prepared. "I got corn in my pockets," he said. "I'll use my own." He reached into his jeans and hauled out a fistful of cracked corn and scattered it on the pavement. All the while his eyes were trained on the building tops. "Most of it goes in the trap. I caught squirrels this way before." He swirled another handful inside the wire trap.

It took only a second, maybe two. The first pigeon dropped from an almost invisible flock strung from one end of the towering eave to the other. And, whether the bravest or the hungriest, he dropped in with barely a beat of his wings, almost skidding to a stop near the trap. Zach backed his way slowly toward the van where Beepah leaned quietly against the open side door. He watched as the awakened flock took flight overhead, circling more cautiously in its descent.

Zach poked his head into the van. "Give me the string, Sydney." He snatched it from me before I offered. "I did this with squirrels, even a skunk once."

Sure enough, the flock descended almost like a swarm, piling onto the pavement, muscling toward the trap door. Each was ravenous, desperate to get a fair share. Zach truly was a pro at catching animals. He waited just long enough. He gave the string a yank and held on tight to keep the contraption closed.

Beep made the few steps to the trap and snatched it up. He held the wire door closed in his big hands and hurried to the back of the van. He pushed the trap inside and tossed an old army blanket over the contraption to keep the birds quiet. After that, he pulled the tailgate door shut and slapped his hands together. The entire operation took less than five minutes. It was slick. It was stealthy, as much as daylight and a disinterested citizenry allowed.

We talked about the raid during the ride back home. Even though he had instigated the entire operation, Beepah suggested it was unfair to the birds, who had no say in the matter. They could have chosen freedom. They could have remained high up under the eaves. They were betrayed by human behaviors they had been conditioned to trust. People tossed breadcrumbs in the park and popcorn on the sidewalk in front of the movie theater. Beep said it was generosity without consequence until we showed up.

I think often about that first raid, its cruelty perhaps. I went only twice more during the year that followed, in part because Beepah and Zach would go off quietly on Sunday mornings and return a few hours later with a basket of birds. Even at an early age the practice weighed on me a little, but I was too young to truly measure the worth or the cruelty of it. I waged little skirmishes against the practice. Zach did his best to make me cry, and sometimes he succeeded. Beep took me on his lap on those occasions. "You can let the birds out in the morning," he would promise. "If they come back, they're welcome to stay another day."

Like Beep promised, there were many mornings I sprung the entry trap. Out they went, led by a handsome male Beep dubbed

Ralph Loren "Because he has sex appeal," Beep said. Ralph led the flock all around the place, over the forest rim and out over Jolly's pond, and almost always with his little coffee-colored mate as wingman.

My repugnance for the raids did not diminish during the year or two that followed. I won't deny a healthy militancy had reared its head in me, prematurely perhaps. But my efforts were rewarded with compromise, and after a time, the raids on the city pigeons ceased. The population in the aviary became self-sustaining. Mating dances were at a healthy frenzy, and when spring arrived, a rash of babies hatched in the rafters overhead.

CHAPTER THREE

It was dark and I was dreaming of sleep. Dreaming of sleep is not the same as sleeping. If you're sleeping and dreaming of sleep, you have settled into a doubly deep abyss, pleasant and lingering. I stared up at the ceiling, noticing the cracks.

I remember one morning when I was six. It was a moment of discovery, where dreams and reality mingle. I pushed my cheek against the pillow and rolled my head just enough to allow one eye to open a sliver.

A glint of blue light settled on the lower sash of my window. Cowboy crowed in his emerging baritone. It was early sunrise on a late summer morning. It struck me then, I was dreaming in color, because sunrise is often yellow, or orange, or even blue, but that night I had laid awake, awaiting its arrival.

Sunrise on a Friday, Zach's second favorite day. Friday was special to Zach for only one reason: it was next door to Saturday, a day without school, without church, especially in the summer. It was a day designed for turtle hunting and hiking to the top of Trumpet Hill. There were even apple wars with kids down the hill. We were blessed with a wild apple tree that produced ammunition to support just such a war. Apples grew green and hard, and almost each had a worm. The tree was wild because of its location, not its ancestry. It stood hunched over and twisted in a meadow just beyond the stream. According to Beepah, it might have been planted by Johnny Appleseed himself. That would make it very old indeed, if it were true.

I slid from my bed and went out into the faint light in the hallway. I was hoping to be first to announce Friday's arrival. Zach's door was open. I could hear him breathing as I crept across the floor. I put my hand on his shoulder and gave him a gentle shake. He rolled a little, opened an eye just enough to catch the glint of light coming in beneath the shade.

"What? What?" and he jerked awake.

"It's almost Saturday," I whispered.

Zach curled his arms around his pillow and pushed his head in deeper. "I'm sleeping, Sydney."

I put my mouth near his ear. "Are you double sleeping or only sleeping?"

"Scram!"

Grasping the concept of double sleep was no small task when I was six, but especially not for Zach, even though he was older. I silently forgave him and made my way back into the hallway. After all, who chooses to abandon sleep only to dream of it? I was certain Zach was already clawing his way free of the pleasant and lingering effects of double sleep, and would soon, in the wee hours of morning, be his happy, obnoxious self.

I went down the hallway to the big room with its bold beams and a pale green ceiling vaulting upward to a peak above the bed. I often lay there alone when I was younger, staring into the empty space above. Mom and Beep slept there, although there were nights Beep snuck off to sleep in the basement. Who knew why? As much as I knew, it was just Beep's way. I climbed up on the foot of the bed and bounced my way to the gaping space between them. There was room aplenty. I was convinced the giant bed was built for no less than three people, and big people at that.

Mom rolled over and kissed my cheek. She put her arm over me and pulled me close. A heavy thud shattered the quiet and when I looked, Beepah was gone.

A gasp escaped Mom, and her head jerked from the pillow. "What the fuck, Ben?"

Beepah's tangled patch of hair poked above the edge of the bed. He saw me and offered little more than a stunned expression. "I fell out of bed," he admitted with much reluctance.

It was not the first time. I'd heard about it plenty. It drove Mom to distraction. Doctors at the veteran hospital referred to his frequent animations as a sleep disorder, at least that's what I heard at breakfast one morning. This particular episode left him pulling his way up from the floor, groggy and confused. Mom never did explain the VA's diagnosis, at least not back when I was even smaller. But even I suspected the occasions precipitated his trips to the old basement couch.

Mom's head flopped back down. "Jesus, my luck," she muttered into the pillow.

"I had that fucking dream again, Angela, if you care," Beepah said. "You know . . . where I jump off the bridge." He peered above the edge of the bed, his head clearing enough to recognize me there. "Oh, good morning, Syd," he greeted me with some surprise.

"You guys both said the "f-word.""

"It doesn't count, Syd. I didn't even know you were there. Besides, I got that nasty habit from your mother," he grumbled. He pushed himself up a little and sat on the bare floor rubbing his knees. He was annoyed that his precarious position at the edge of the bed had caused him to be flung to the floor yet again. "Christ, Angela, I was holding on by my toenails, if you give a damn."

Beepah falling off the bed happened plenty. In fact, I even witnessed it one other time. I was certain Beep fell out of bed only to make me laugh, and it worked. He poked his head up and showed the world his best bewilderment, and I laughed. But this time the inflection in his voice attributed blame, and Mother was the culprit. In his mind, it was Mother who forced him to the precipice at the edge of the bed, where peaceful sleep was not possible for him, especially when dreams invaded his nights. I realize now that Beep was troubled even then.

Mom's head popped up from the pillow again. "Nobody put you over there, Ben," she snapped at him. "You did that to yourself."

Beepah's hand inspected the crown of his head for blood. "I don't know why I have that dream. It wasn't the worst of it," he said. "In my dream, there's four of us, standing on a footbridge— me, Hoby, John, and Dick, maybe . . ." Beep shrugged, suddenly unable to summon the rest of the names. "There was fire all around, both sides of the river, napalm ripping everything. I was watching it, like watching a bad movie. We weren't even supposed to be there. We should'a cleared out hours before. We got trapped." His eyes grew wide with the memory of it. "I went ass over teakettle into the river. What a shitstorm."

"You said shitstorm!"

My outburst seemed to bring him from his trance. Talk about the war was rare. Nam, he called it. And I heard the word *shitstorm* from time to time, from Beep or one of his friends. I was rarely allowed to say it. Shitstorm and plenty of other bad words were reserved for grown-ups. Sometimes the only way to know for sure was to throw it out there. Zach was good for that. "Shitstorm! Shitstorm!" Zach sometimes tested correctness without warning.

Beepah's hand continued to search his scalp for blood. He found none and finally gave up the hunt. "When I came up, I was swimming beside a water buffalo, believe it or not," he said. "There was a little band of fighters just downstream. They were onto me . . . bullets splashing all around. The river was pulling me down. There was a leather strap stringing from the buffalo. His horns were tangled in it, and I grabbed hold and he dragged me into the bushes." Beep gave his head another scrub with his hand and crawled up from the floor. "I would've drowned or got shot, or washed down into the jungle with all the fire. Anyways, I laid there on the riverbank for a couple hours until the boys found me." Beep shrugged.

"You got saved by a buffalo?"

"True story," Beep declared with a raised hand, then he bent to rub his bruised knee again. He grumbled and limped to the bathroom across the hallway. He stood in front of the mirror twisting his body to explore for contusions. "You kicked me," he sang out after peeling his boxers down to expose the red welt on his hip. "This footprint on my butt is all the proof I need."

Mom laughed. "Justified ass-kicking," she said.

He leaned back through the doorway. "Did you kick me out of bed, Sydney?"

"What happened to the buffalo?"

"Oh, he ran off into the jungle before he gored me to death," Beep said, which made me laugh too.

Beepah hobbled back to the bed and snared me by the foot. He twisted it and gave it a thorough inspection. "Nope," he said finally. "There is no way this little foot made this giant bump on my butt. It had to be this clodhopper here . . ." and he grabbed Mom's foot and gave it a twist. "We're sleeping in the teepee tonight," Beep said. "Dress warm."

Mother declined immediately. "No thank you. Can't." She jerked her foot from his grip. "I have prep work for my trip. I'm not even packed. Anyway, I'm not spending my Friday night scratching the lumps out of that patch of mud in the woods." She rolled over again, driving her face into the pillow. "You do it. You'll be safe stretched out in the mud. You can't do any bridge jumping out there," she said and laughed again.

"Okay, then," Beepah conceded, slapping his hands together to seal the deal. He grabbed me by the foot again. "It's you, me, and Zach, and a pack of dogs," he said.

He headed for the bathroom again, then turned back one more time. He showed a pensive face to the shadows playing on the window to the west. "We ran upon the buffalo in the jungle," Beep recalled. "He was sprawled in the dirt, snorting up a cloud of dust. There was a bullet hole behind his ear oozing blood. He was dying for sure." Beep aimed his finger and made a popping sound with his lips. "I could have ended it just like that. Pop! The boys said no. Too many gooks around. We just wanted to slip out of there without getting skinned alive." He knocked his knuckles against the doorjamb and shrugged. "We left him there. It still feels like unfinished business."

Mother rolled to her elbow. "You never told me that story."

"I save those tall tales for the boys at group," he said, slumping into the bathroom. "They eat that stuff up."

I thought about it often during my childhood, Beep's story about a buffalo that saved his life in the jungles of Vietnam. He didn't return the favor by ending the suffering with a bullet to the head. Neglecting it inspired an occasional leap from a bridge into rushing water. It made me sad for the buffalo, but near as I could tell, nobody else died that day. I was left to find the message, if there was one. It may have been just another colorful yarn. Beep was good for those.

——

The first time Emily Lipton showed up at the school bus stop with her son Jason, was a day in early September. Emily was pretty and about thirty-five, the same age as Mother. Over the days and weeks that followed her arrival, I found out from Beep that Emily was a dental hygienist. She was almost always dressed in her pure white hygienist dress or white scrubs. She had brown hair that she pulled back for work. And she had round breasts she pushed way out. That much even I noticed.

It was easy enough to see that Beepah liked Emily Lipton. She stood very close to him while they talked. From the start, Beep's unease was apparent, but once he became comfortable with the behavior, he allowed her aura to engulf him. Even I could tell it pleased him.

Jason Lipton was older than Zach and me. He was in sixth grade. In fact, he was the oldest kid at the bus stop, a couple grades ahead of Zach, although his size defied his age. He was short in stature, with fair skin and shaggy blond hair faintly tinged with red.

The two of them arrived from Philadelphia during the summer and settled into the old Rubin Smoran house at the bottom of Trumpet Hill Road. In disposition alone, Jason was the exact opposite of his mother. While she was ready with a smile, Jason was sullen and abusive. Beepah said it was his uprooting from Philadelphia that was his reason for attacks on the younger kids. To me, it was cruelty, plain and simple. Jason Lipton was just mean.

Beepah stepped in on occasion with his form of gentle diplomacy. "Jason, leave the kids alone," Beep would say and shake his head in disbelief. There was nothing physical. Jason never directed his wrath toward me, but from the beginning his very presence put me in fear. I rarely left Beepah's side at the bus stop when Jason Lipton was nearby.

The effects of Beep's castigations did not last for long. Jason did little more than turn an aggrieved face to Beep with an expression both sanctimonious and threatening. But when Emily showed up, Beep turned most of his attention to her. In fact, since the first morning Beep saw Emily Lipton, his enthusiasm for trips to the school bus improved.

"I got a divorce," she admitted boldly. "I lost my job when Dr. Boyle retired, at least temporarily. I couldn't wait around for another fresh face out of dental school to pick up the slack. So I threw a dart." She shrugged. "The first one stuck in the map near Juarez, Mexico. The second one landed on the Outer Banks. So I flipped a coin. That's how I ended up here."

Beep dismissed her logic with a laugh.

"I got a job with Manny Lapeer. It turns out everybody in town knows Manny Lapeer, even though he pronounces his name 'Leaper,' and for no apparent reason that I know. Anyway, I sent for Jason. He hasn't quite forgiven me yet," she said, this time with a wry laugh. "The rest is history." She threw up her arms in an apparent moment of distress. "Do you know anything about garbage disposals?"

Beepah had been silent, entrapping the cloud of her breath with his own, catching the flavor of her coffee. "I've installed them. I've unplugged a few," he said with some authority, suddenly inspired by the plan she was hatching to take advantage of his good nature. I could see him doing his best to conceal his willingness.

Emily looked at her watch. "I have to go to work," she said. "Maybe tomorrow? It's Saturday. Do you mind? I don't have to work until ten. The Leaper has a Chamber of Commerce meeting. Can you take a look at my kitchen sink?"

"The Leaper. That's funny."

"Oh, I call him that all the time. I think it quiets his aggressive tendencies." She added a flirt with her eyes. "It makes him a more interesting man. So, can you help? My neighbor says you're handy with all sorts of things." She tossed her head back with another laugh.

Beep nodded. "Ah, yes, Gracie Campbell," he said. "I built her a set of stairs five years ago and I've been reaping the rewards ever since." He scratched at his head with his cap, contemplating the task. "I'll throw some tools in my truck. We'll have a look."

The school bus arrived with lights flashing as it crested the rise in the road. It rolled to a stop and the doors sprang open. Jason Lipton muscled his way to the front. He climbed the steps and disappeared toward the back of the bus.

Emily watched with disappointment on her face. "Oh, that boy," she said. "I wish there was a way to salt his tail. He's a bully like his father. He got in with a bad bunch. He resents the move here. He's a constant worry for me."

Almost always the last one aboard, I scurried out from between Beep's legs and climbed the bus steps. I spun around. "Bye, Beepah!" I called out.

When I turned back to wave again, Emily Lipton was making her way up the gravel driveway toward the Smoran house. Beepah watched her through breaks in the hedge that ran the length of the property. By the time he reached his truck, Emily had crossed the porch and disappeared inside. I settled into a seat halfway back and caught sight of Zach across the aisle talking turtle hunting with one of the Sullivan boys. The bus rolled into the low road along Esopus Creek.

School dismissal began a good afternoon. We made the quick ride to Trumpet Hill on the bus and walked the mile up the hill. Zach ran ahead after collecting turtle bait from a hiding place behind the Sullivans' garage. In fact, it was a small bucket with rotting chicken parts from the Sullivans' kitchen and a flattened squirrel harvested from the edge of the road. Zach and Booger Sullivan spent the late afternoon hours hurling rancid chicken parts secured to the end of a clothesline rope into the middle of Jolly's pond. They were not new to the game.

Beneath the depths of Jolly's pond lived the lone denizen, gruesome, without a soul, capable of dismissing a toe from a foot, or the whole of the foot itself, should he choose. Zach had sworn utter destruction on the beast and had spent entire summers honing his skills toward that very end. He had designed a tight-wrapped wire-mesh cage to secure the bait. A long length of rope tied to a tree above the banks of the pond ensured the giant snapping turtle, left unchecked, would not devour the entire contraption.

There had forever been concerns about Jolly's pond. Superstitions flourished. The depth was never determined, at least to a collective neighborhood's satisfaction. Ol' Jolly himself, who had years before created the abyss with a steam shovel or some such machine, once hazarded a guess at the depth. "Somewhere near fifteen feet, if memory serves," Ol' Jolly said with an ounce of certainty. But, by exaggeration alone, the depth doubled by midday, and by week's end the great crevasse in the earth was virtually bottomless. "The devil lives below," became the mantra designed to frighten children and keep them from the gloomy depths. The fear tactic didn't work on Zach.

I sat on the sloping bank with my notebook and a box of crayons creating images destined to live forever, of course. They were pictures of my brother Zach hurling his baited rope into the middle of Jolly's pond and watching it settle quickly into the deep. He and Tilly and Booger Sullivan sat on the bank with their feet anchored in mud, waiting for Satan himself to break the surface with his hellish barrel roll. That was Zach's wish. That would be success, to see it, to bear witness, to one day bring him ashore, to out-clever the devil himself.

———

Inside the tree line at the southerly end of the Bowden farm, a brook twists its way through spindly birches and maples, heading deeper into the woods. It gurgles with innocence, like soft voices, spilling over jagged rocks on its cascading course toward Esopus Creek below. In the early evening, lights burn inside homes on

Trumpet Hill. Birches rustle in a gentle breeze along the brook. Our teepee stood out there just beyond the tree line.

Beep announced a campout the very morning he fell out of bed. Zach and me spent an hour after school hauling firewood. We stacked it inside the teepee along the back wall. We cut saplings for skewering hotdogs and marshmallows, and Zach even rolled out his sleeping bag to secure his most preferred spot next to the hatchway door.

Even before daylight began to fade, Beep let Zach start the campfire. By dark we were sitting on stumps around the circle of stone with hotdogs skewered on willow sticks. The scene made me laugh a little, as usual as it had become.

"What's funny?" Beep asked me from across the fire.

"This morning you said we were sleeping in the teepee. Mom wouldn't come. You said it was you and me and Zach, and a pack of dogs. Now I get it," I said, holding up the plastic-wrapped hotdogs. "It made me laugh, that's all."

Zach was quick with an insult. "That's dumb, Sydney," he said, then he laughed.

Beepah rolled his dog to the underside. "Did you land that turtle yet?"

Zach tossed his head, undaunted. He was cooking hotdogs for two, and he pulled a hot one from his stick and pitched it to the teepee floor. Tilly pushed it around with her nose until it cooled enough to eat. She snatched it up in one bite, dirt and all, and came looking for more.

"That turtle comes up to the top sometimes," Zach said. "He's gotta breathe, you know. He makes a splash and the water gets stirred up. If I could only get a hold on him right then—"

"I've seen him do that," Beep said. "He's a big one, all right. Be careful with that rope. He'll take you down and stick you in the mud and eat you when you're nice and tender."

"He bit the rotten chicken once," Zach said, disappointment clear enough. "You gotta pull the rope just right or he drops it and won't come back for a week sometimes."

"I drew pictures," I said.

Zach wrapped a half-cooked hotdog with a bun and pulled it off the willow stick. "Sydney draws good, I'll say that much," he said, filling the entire bun with ketchup. "Too bad there wasn't no turtle to draw."

It was a rare compliment coming from Zach. It might have been the heat from the fire, but I felt my face glow with pride. Either way, I did what Zach did and slipped a bun around my hot dog.

"I'm not a big mustard girl," I told Beepah, and he squeezed ketchup up and down the dog for me. "Why doesn't Mom like sleeping in the teepee? What could be better?" I asked. "She says she likes it, but she only did it once."

"Some people need a soft bed," Beep explained. "Your mother is like that. Me, I like getting back on the ground now and then, down here with all the other crawly things." Beep slapped me on the knee. "Your mother got domesticated. It happens, like catching scabies," he warned, leaning close with a whisper. "Don't let it happen to you, Syd. Once you get it, it's hard to get rid of, and it itches worse than ants in your pants."

"Nope, not me! I'm a crawly thing like you . . . permanent!" I declared my allegiance. "How about you, Zachary?"

"I'm crawly!"

We went on that way for another hour. I ate my hot dog and four roasted marshmallows, and I made bold declarations about the comforts of teepee living. Beepah told a story about a man who followed a flock of geese all the way to the South Pole. Zach burned his thumb and insisted it didn't hurt much. A blister bubbled up. He said little more about it. He rolled out his sleeping bag near the flap door of the teepee and squirmed his way down inside. He lay on his back looking up into a night sky that hovered just above the treetops.

Beepah dropped his sleeping bag on the dirt floor and rolled it out beside Zach's. He kicked off his boots and stuffed himself down inside. I was reluctant to let the night end. I scratched at the embers with my stir stick, sending sparks skyward. They swirled in the heat and departed through the smoke hole at the very top of the teepee. I was bundled in heavy pajamas and a knit cap pulled down over my ears. Mother had insisted on the cap, and it did keep me warm.

The fire was all but gone. No flames remained to light the space inside the teepee. The night was pouring in to douse the last embers and fill the void. I dropped a small log over the last of the dying embers, sending a legion of sparks twisting upward.

That forced a bark out of Beep. "Syd! Put the stick in the fire! Get over here!"

I chucked the stick into the circle of stones and scampered through the scant light toward Beepah. I dropped my bottom down near him and squirmed myself deep inside his sleeping bag. I settled into a warm place and yawned. My hands came up under my chin and I turned sleepy eyes toward Beep.

"Do you think this teepee will be here when I get big?" I asked.

Zach scoffed. "Teepees don't last forever, Sydney," he said. "Indians lived a hundred years ago right here in this spot. You don't see teepees standing around. Anybody knows that much."

Beep was less cynical. "We take care of it . . . it might last awhile," he offered up a little hope.

It had been three summers and then some when Zach first conceived of the idea of the teepee. I was almost too small to remember events that happened back then. My memories of the teepee construction are spotty at best, and without discernible evidence to the contrary, it is still standing. Beepah called it a ragged combination of tarps and long poles all wrapped together and tied with rope. To me, it was a miracle, the truest reflection of our childhood. Everything before my memory had been enlivened belonged to its own eternity. The teepee is part of that.

I nestled down into Beep's arm and rolled my sleepy eyes to the heavens. Stars shined between streaks of clouds moving on a light breeze. If I craned my neck enough to the north, I could see Mom passing windows and turning off lamps. My eyes were so heavy, not even the stars could hold them open.

"What are stars for?"

Beep was half asleep himself. "I expect they're all patron saints of something." He gave his nose a rub with his sleeve to fight the chill. "I hear you can even buy a star nowadays. That transaction takes some chutzpah. Catch a falling star and put it in your pocket," Beep mumbled out a song in his gravelly, sleepy tenor. "It might burn a hole in your shorts. Learn to count stars, Syd. You might hit upon some magic number. You might find a patron saint for your mother . . . maybe for good ol' Zach over there, or maybe even me, if there is one up there."

With that, Beep dropped off. Lying there, I thought hard about forever—my forever and Beepah's forever. They were not the same. Mine had only begun, seconds ago by cosmic standards, and yet my forever was destined to go on without a seeable end. Beep's forever was old. It had a past and a future. He could look backward or forward and see the beginning and the end of it. His was a very short forever, pervasive by design, and yet diminishing, and destined to trouble me.

CHAPTER FOUR

The following morning me and Beep made it to the back porch before the earth began to warm. It was Saturday and a glorious sun had crept above the horizon to send feelers of colored light through the treetops to the east. Soon enough the warming air would bake the dew from the grass. But that had not happened, not yet, and I was aboard Beepah's shoulders for a ride above the heavy grass that would keep my pajamas dry. We didn't wake up Zach. No doubt he would come running when he shook the cobwebs from his head and recognized the smell of Saturday in the air.

Beepah stomped his feet and delivered me to the porch floor. When he pushed the door open, I ran inside and got sight of Mom filling the coffee pot at the kitchen sink. I hurried over and stood near her. Just like me, she was dressed in pajamas. I rolled my head far back and pushed my knit cap above my eyes. I gave her pajama leg a tug.

"I slept in Beepah's sleeping bag."

Mom smiled. "Was it warm?"

"Yeah, real warm."

"What did you guys see for animals?"

"I watched for bears, but Tilly keeps them away," I said. "Tilly can smell a bear a mile away. That's what Beep says. Anyway, bears are black, so you can only see them in the daytime. I fell asleep."

Beepah kicked off his wet boots and sat at the kitchen table. "Zach got up to pass water sometime in the night—"

"Beepah, you mean pee?"

"Yeah, pee," he said, annoyed at the interruption. "He saw a pack of raccoons by the creek. They're troublemakers, especially when they show up near the chicken coop. Even Tilly doesn't mess with coons . . . nasty little buggers."

Mom turned off the faucet. She reached down to push my cap above my eyes again. "And where is that beautiful boy?"

"Mom, boys are ugly, especially Zachary. Girls are beautiful."

"Thank you, sweetheart," Mom said, cupping her hands around my face. "I'm going to assume you're talking about me."

"Yeah, you . . . and Mrs. Lipton's beautiful."

I pulled off my knit cap and my hair erupted in a giant electric solar burst. "I'm drawing a teepee picture," I announced. "I thought about it all night in my sleep." I scrambled for my crayons and my perch at the kitchen table, snaking into my chair and pulling my drawing pad to the ready. I drew out a brown crayon and created a prelude to the teepee drawing. It was completed in only minutes, not my best work. I scrolled across the top in bright orange letters, "Zachary Passing Water," lest I forget. It was not flattering in any regard.

I barely noticed the accusatory look Mom was giving Beep. "Is that right, Ben? Is Mrs. Lipton beautiful?"

"She's pleasant enough," Beep said, a little annoyed. "That reminds me. I'm going down to her house this very morning," Beep said, as if he had just then remembered his commitment at the bus stop on Friday. "I guess even beautiful women get their drains plugged on occasion. I told her I'd give it a look-see."

"Well, aren't you the Good Samaritan," Mom said, turning on the water again to rinse the sink. "I've never met the woman, but I did hear she's pretty."

I kicked in my two cents. "I see her all the time. She's pretty," I said.

"If you drop the kids at the bus one day—say, any Tuesday—she's usually there," Beep said.

"Oh, you know her schedule. That's rich."

Beep shrugged, annoyed yet again. He pulled on his boots, realizing coffee was not ready, and pushed himself out of his chair. "I know she's there almost every day. That's what I meant. Pick a day and you'll meet the woman. She's pretty, only slightly pretentious. You know the type. You might even like her."

"Well, you can't do it today," Mom said. She delivered her dishes from the night before into the sink with the appropriate amount of clattering. "I've got a strategy meeting at the office with my team. Who knows how long that will take? You'll have to stay with the kids." She straightened at the sink. "You haven't forgotten I'm traveling tomorrow?"

"Oh, that's tomorrow?" he feigned surprise. "Singapore?"

There was true distain in her voice, and she made no attempt to hide it. "Geneva, Ben," she said. "Singapore is in the spring. It happens every year."

"We'll miss you, won't we, Syd?"

I immediately consoled her. "Yes, Mom, we'll miss you. I dreamed about an Indian girl making a fire in her teepee. I'm drawing her for your trip. She looks just like me, so you won't be sad."

"That'll do it," Beep concurred while twisting at the doorknob. "Sadness averted."

He went out then, flashing a smile and pulling the door shut in his wake. I watched from the window as he went across the porch and down the two steps to the patio, his eyes fixed on the teepee nestled in the trees just beyond the open field. The sun reflected gold off the maple tops. The teepee poles, gathered and bound at the smoke hole, were in full light. Tilly came bounding through the deep grass when she caught sight of Beep on his way to the coop.

There was still no sign of Zach. He would feel the sun splashing through the open flap door soon enough. He would come running, eager to make a day of it.

Beepah's dusty green pickup rolled along the gravel driveway in front of the Smoran house. It was nine or close to it. The truck slowed to a stop near the porch and Beep killed the engine. He got out and closed the door quietly. He went to the back and dropped the tailgate to haul out the wooden toolbox filled with plumber's tools. He came around to the passenger side. "Come on, boss. Let's get this done," he said.

I slid out, dropping the last two feet into loose stones. My eyes surveyed the old house. I had never been there, not inside at least. The paint on the outside was gray and failing, curled in places like the Dead Sea Scrolls, enough to exaggerate the age of the place. From the driveway, it appeared gloomy inside too, although a dim light burned in the kitchen. I gathered my drawing paper, crayons, and my pencils, and I followed Beepah across the porch to the kitchen screen door. He knocked. I stepped back. Jason Lipton was standing just inside the screen door in his bathrobe. He was drinking orange juice from a clear glass.

"Morning, Jason," Beep greeted him. "Is your mother here?"

Near as I could tell, Jason was angry even on good days. He took a small swallow of orange juice. A few minor run-ins with Beepah at the bus stop had unchangeably set his attitude in stone, and he was not about to miss a chance to offer up a snarl, if it came to that. To Beepah it came down to making a situation better or making a situation worse. It was a delicate matter with Jason Lipton, who stood expressionless for a tense moment.

Beepah held his smile as best he could. "She asked me to help—"

Jason cut him off. "My mother says I should let you in."

He pushed the screen open with his foot and held it that way until Beep wedged it open wider with his big toolbox. I became a barnacle on Beepah's pantleg. He stepped across the threshold. I followed close behind with my drawing pad clutched tight to my chest for protection. Beep quickly surveyed the kitchen and rested his toolbox on the old linoleum floor. I went up on my tiptoes to see over the rim of the sink. It was a swill of thick, smelly water that looked like pea soup clear to the top.

"What's with the kid?" Jason asked, which only encouraged me to shrink a little more.

Beepah had a high tolerance for belligerence, not that I had often witnessed the need for it. He almost always showed generous patience with Zach and me, so I expected the same treatment for everyone. But with Jason, his irritation was getting difficult to hold in check. "She's my helper," Beep said. "Is your mother here?"

"She'll be down. You like her, don't you? My mother, I mean. I see you guys talking at the bus," Jason said.

I didn't know his intent, but even at six, I felt the challenge in his tone. His words sounded threatening. Don't get me wrong, I felt safe with Beep, but I was not with him every waking moment. In those days, everything this new kid said sounded threatening. I watched him pull a girl's hair until her scalp bled, and all she did was call him a jerk, which was pretty much a universal appraisal by then. I heard him once say he had a gun. He said he would kill one of the Campbell grandkids. Jason Lipton's threats were unpredictable and scary because they were not all hot air. That much I knew.

Beepah plucked a plunger from his big toolbox. He let the rubber end settle slowly into the swill. "Is there a reason I shouldn't like your mother?" Beep asked finally.

Jason came across the room toward the sink and boldly angled his mouth upward toward Beep's ear. "She don't need you is what I mean," he said in a low tone. He let the empty glass roll from his hand, splashing into the swill, sending the soupy mix cascading down the cabinet front. "She's got somebody already."

His boldness caught Beep by surprise. Jason Lipton was a sixth grader, nothing more. Beep was a full-grown man. He was twice his size, even bigger. He could have squished him. That was my first thought, and I truly feared he might.

Instead, Beep turned to confront him. "I'm here because your mother asked me to fix the sink," he said, still stunned. "If you're the man of the house—"

"I'm talking about my father," Jason said, almost spitting the words, suddenly driven to bitter anger. "He's coming up here pretty soon. You'll see."

"I don't know your father. I hope you guys get all that worked out. In the meantime, since you're not about to move your dead ass to unplug the sink, back off," Beep said, turning his back on Jason once again.

"Morning, Ben," came Emily's cheerful voice.

Beepah was fuming. He could not bring himself to turn and greet her. Instead, he rocked the plunger into the drain hole and gave it a mighty push. Dirty water slopped over the rim of the sink and onto the floor. Some of it landed on my shoes. A few drops even found Jason's moccasin slippers. Beepah's boots didn't matter. He was dressed for work.

"Sorry," Beep said, finally willing to turn his eyes to Emily. "It could get messy." Then he offered without further hesitation, "I was getting to know your son a little better."

He put his hand on my head and urged me into the beam of light coming through the window over the sink. I got my first look of the morning at Emily Lipton. Her auburn hair was loose of its usual clips. It cascaded in waves to her shoulders. She was dressed in her hygienist white dress. The dress was so white, in fact, it added considerable light to the room. It was open at the neckline enough to plunge past at least two unbuttoned buttons on its way to her round breasts. She walked close to Beep and looked up at him, exhibiting her trademark immodesty. Beep noticed.

"Her mother's off to Geneva tomorrow morning," Beep explained my presence. "Big strategy meeting at the office. All the muckety-mucks will be there."

"Very important people, muckety-mucks. Just ask 'em," she countered. They laughed quietly at that. Emily appeared to enjoy Beep's laugh. She looked up at him, testing their familiarity. Her hand touched the back of his arm, and she briefly turned her eyes to the foul sink. "What's the verdict?"

"Oh, guilty, of course."

She admitted the sink had been plugged for weeks. She hadn't found the time to deal with it. "I don't know any plumbers, but I'm getting real tired of ignoring my dirty dishes." She lowered her gaze cautiously toward the sink. "Oh my god, it's awful. I'm so embarrassed." She covered her nose and mouth with her hand to fend off the unpleasantness. "You're a godsend, Ben," she said, her words coming slightly garbled through her clenched fingers. They laughed again.

"We'll get it cleaned up," Beep assured her. He gently eased the plunger out of the drain hole and brought it carefully to the surface of the pea-green water. An air bubble followed and sent another wave of putrid water over the rim of the sink. Beep quickly urged Emily to safety with an outstretched hand. The white dress was spared. "Syd's got a big project for Angie's departure tomorrow." He looked down at me to encourage my agreement. "It's a drawing, right, Syd?"

I acknowledged the teepee drawing with a nod.

"I might be an hour, unless the disposal is crapped out. I'll rig the drain to work," he said, shrugging off the time estimate. "Can Syd sit at the table?"

"Sure, she can." Emily hurried to the table and uncluttered it, removing a bowl and cereal box, milk, sugar, and a wad of napkins Jason left behind. She placed the entire collection at the end of the counter farthest from the sink. Then she spun back around, retrieved the milk, and delivered it to the refrigerator. Lastly, she switched on a lamp on the wall just above the table. "How's that?" she asked me, smiling impatiently. She took a look at her watch with the same urgency. "I have to go," she said.

I broke free of Beepah's pantleg and walked to the table and climbed into the chair that faced the sink. I scanned the kitchen and surrounding doorways for any signs of Jason. He had mysteriously disappeared when Emily arrived in the kitchen and there was still no sign of him. I hoped he would stay away all day, if not forever. I smiled at Emily Lipton. I liked her and so did Beep, which made Jason's nasty disposition even more perplexing.

Emily rolled a sweater over her arm. She disappeared to the dining room and returned with a small bag. "Thanks, Ben," she said, rooting in the bag for her keys. "If you need anything, Jason is in his room."

Beepah considered the news of Jason's whereabouts with newfound contempt, his friendly tone scuttled by the mere mention of his name. "We won't be long," he said.

Emily went out the back door and across the porch in a hurry. The screen door clattered shut and I heard her yell something like, "See you at the bus stop!" As loud as it was, I wasn't certain what she had said. I followed the sound of her but heard nothing more until her car started. A moment later, her Bronco rolled past the back door. Beepah craned his neck to catch a glimpse of her through the rolled-down window and she was gone.

I had always felt safe with Beep, but when I looked at him from across the small distance, I could tell he no longer regarded the old Smoran house a safe place for me. Sharing the space with Jason Lipton filled him with unease. The confrontation in the kitchen gnawed at Beep. He listened for threatening noises coming from upstairs. He kept a watchful eye beyond the darkened dining room to the foyer, where the staircase descended into faint light. But the staircase was just out of view, and the dimly lighted entrance was a great distraction to him.

Despite it all, Beep went about his business. He hauled buckets of the dirty water from the sink to the toilet in the bathroom just off the kitchen. He dismantled the trap beneath the sink and manhandled the disposal until it gave up a stubborn chicken bone, the culprit in the entire matter.

I never did open my drawing pad in the old Smoron kitchen. Instead, I slid from the chair and crept through the dining room and into the foyer. I stopped in the silence and scanned the small entrance. It was cloaked in faint light. There was a coat closet along one wall, and the door was slightly ajar. There was a withering bouquet of roses in a vase that rested on a console table against the opposite wall. A shotgun leaned precariously in the corner. It was much like the one Beep kept in a locker in the barn.

My eyes tracked to the front entrance and the two narrow windows that looked out on a tangle of brush. A morning that had shown itself to be bright with promise moments earlier appeared dreary, almost sunless.

A gloom descended from the upstairs, and when I turned my eyes to the staircase, Jason Lipton was there. Watching me! Fright took hold like never before. He had made half the descent unnoticed. He stared at me, peering out from beneath eyelids half drawn, and he smiled the most grotesquely evil smile.

His voice came out in a whisper, forced and graveled. "I'm going to kill your father," he said in a low tone. "You won't never know when. Someday I'll just do it."

I felt the blood flush from every vital part of me, until the world threatened to go black and send me to the floor. Instead, I bolted from the foyer and went in a dash toward the kitchen. When I arrived there, Beep had just emptied one more bucketful into the toilet off the kitchen.

He took one look at me and the empty bucket slipped from his hand, banging to the floor. Beep dropped to a knee. He took me by the arms, and I watched his face go pale. "What is it, Syd?"

I didn't speak. I only motioned to him to follow, and I led him over the hardwood floor in the dining room and into the dim light of the foyer. My eyes quickly returned to the very place on the staircase where Jason Lipton had stood. He was no longer there . . . returned to his bed perhaps. A low and irregular mumbling emanated from a place down the upstairs hallway. Voices . . . a television, most likely.

Beep leaned down. "What say we get out of this creepy joint?" he whispered, feeling the sudden chill of the place. "I just have a little clean up."

I wanted him to see one more thing. I pointed to the corner near the closet, just as I turned to peer through the faint light. There was nothing to see. The shotgun was gone! The closet door was closed. Jason had been there. In the moment I bolted from the foyer, terrified and in search of Beep, Jason had descended the steps to get the gun.

I led Beep by the hand into the living room and toward the kitchen. He pulled me to a halt in front of the fireplace to examine the photographs on the mantle. One stood out, at least to Beep. He picked it up like his hands were dirty from work, barely pressing his thumb against the dusty glass. I craned my neck upward to see what had grabbed his attention. It was a photograph of Emily Lipton in a bathing suit sitting high up on the backseat of a big red convertible. At the bottom was the notation, "Parade Day." The picture was years old, by the look of it. She was much younger. She had the same smile and the same auburn hair. She was pretty. She wore a sash draped from her shoulder to the opposite hip.

Beep pulled the photograph close to give it a lengthy look. "Huh, Miss Philadelphia," he muttered in a whisper.

CHAPTER FIVE

It was Sunday morning. We sat on the front porch steps and watched for the limousine to arrive. It was to take Mom to the airport, and it showed up at breakfast time. The limo was a perk Garland-Price provided for traveling executives. Garland-Price was where Mom worked. As limos go, this one was not especially long, just big and black and clean. It rolled to a stop under the cherry trees that spread their branches over the driveway.

The engine purred. The trunk lid clicked open and slowly eased upward. A big man with slicked-back hair sat in the driver's seat. He stepped out into the driveway dressed in a long and impeccably pressed black suitcoat. He smiled at the three of us sitting on the steps. Tilly was sandwiched between Zach and me . . . she at least, not understanding the commotion. The big man went to the back of the limo and disappeared behind the raised trunk lid. Beepah delivered one suitcase to the back of the car and the big man deftly placed it to the trunk floor.

Mom came out the front door dressed in sweats and sneakers. "Traveling clothes," is how she described the outfit. Her cropped hair was tucked behind her ears, and she wore no makeup. She was in a hurry and frazzled. That was normal behavior. She traveled often, and we said good-bye often. She always complained about the flight to Geneva. She had experienced it a dozen times in my lifetime alone. Over the years it changed little—ten hours, some flights with a brief stopover in Paris. But to her, the stop in Paris was little more than a tease. By her own account, she had rarely seen it in daylight, and even then, only from the air, staring into a sprawl of lights as the plane descended into Charles de Gaulle Airport.

She kissed me on the cheek and Zach on top of the head. "Take care of your father," she said, already off the porch and on her way to the limousine. She hurried down the driveway carrying a small bag over her shoulder. "I'll carry this one," she said, waving the big man off.

"We have plenty of time, Ms. Carmichael."

I already knew what the driver had yet to figure out. My mother did not like driveway good-byes. Amidst the flurry, she did manage to rise to her tiptoes and touch her cheek to Beepah's. "See you in a few days," she said.

Beep said nothing at first. He pushed his hands into the back pockets of his jeans and forced a smile. The moment was clumsy for him. He never managed to detangle it, to make it smooth and affectionate and free from spite. Things he might have said began to feel repetitive over the years. "Have a safe trip," and, "Let us know when you get there," were well worn. Instead, he pulled one hand from his pocket and wrapped his arm around her neck to gently pull her closer. "The kids miss you," he said to her.

The sting was immediate. She pulled back and looked up at him. He had chosen an odd time and an odd place. His words were delivered without limits. It was not about missing her for the ten days she would be in Geneva. It was about missing her always and forever because she did not love us enough.

When she looked down again, she found me hugging her leg and crying. She turned back to Beep and this time she sounded angry. "You could have taken them to church, Ben," she hissed. "You know how much I hate this."

"The kids have to say good-bye to you, Angela," Beep said. "They need to know you're coming back."

"Well, of course I'm coming back, Ben. When have I not?" She found Zach still sitting on the porch steps. She waved at him. "Bye, Zach," she said.

Zach waved. Running into the driveway sobbing was not about to happen. He waved again, choking back tears when the big man opened the back door of the limo. Mom slid in, tossing her bag to the seat beside her. The big man closed the door. We watched the limo back out of the driveway and roll down Trumpet Hill Road. Zach wiped his nose with a swipe to his sleeve and walked back into the house.

That Sunday was the first day when I realized my mother and father did not love each other. It cut me in my heart because I loved them both. I turned to my bedroom and my notebooks. I scratched out a drawing of my father and mother with angry faces, saying good-bye in the driveway under the cherry trees.

During the days Mother traveled, Beepah did not stray far from the Bowden farm. Zach regularly disappeared into the woods with neighbor kids to whittle a new bow or fashion a trap from vines. Suppertime was fun, more hotdogs and marshmallows on the open fire. We slept in the teepee three nights in a row, then scrambled to get to the school bus, still wearing dirt from the teepee floor.

In early September, a road crew tore up the mile of crumbling pavement and laid down a thick black layer of asphalt all the way from Esopus Creek to the cul-de-sac at the top of Trumpet Hill Road. In the span of five days the crew of eight men and one woman managed to transform the carnival ride down the cracked and cratered hillside into a rue de fleur fit for any rat-drawn pumpkin carriage imaginable.

After the polishing was complete and Trumpet Hill gleamed, there was asphalt left over. The crew chief appraised the driveways that emptied onto the fresh, new road and determined the driveway at our very own farm to be among the neediest.

The crew chief jerked his thumb over his shoulder in the direction of the road and made an offer to Beep straight away. "We can get down a finish just like that there." He would sell the resurfacing for a next-to-nothing, bargain-basement price, and if Beep paid in cash, he would generously slash the price in half. In other words, the cost of the job would be a steal.

Beepah stood on the front porch with his arms folded across his chest admiring a perfectly unblemished Trumpet Hill Road. On the hillside, just beyond the slowly hardening flow of tar, the rest of the crew had removed their boots and were cooling their feet under the elm trees. Zach sat on the porch steps. He was dressed in ragged cut-off jeans and nothing else. He had been drawn by the pungent smell and burning heat of hot tar, and he spent much of the day chasing back and forth across the freshly blackened road to test his tolerance for pain.

While the crew chief kept extolling the merits of a sleek new driveway, Beep got a look at Zach. The sun had baked his shoulders to a crimson red and his feet were caked in tar. Beep's forehead creased with concern. "Stay off the road, Zach boy," Beep ordered. "Fire walking is not a healthy pursuit, especially for tenderfoots."

"Well, I ain't one of them," Zach said, slumping up the porch steps and dropping into an old wicker chair.

The crew chief wrapped up his sales pitch. "We can be outa here in three, four hours," he said, holding an expectant stare toward Beepah.

Beep smiled. "My darling wife will be pleased," he said with cunning anticipation. "There won't be a pothole left to swallow her when she arrives home." He stepped down from the porch to shake the man's hand. "Let's do it," he sealed the deal.

The next day, with the road and driveway completed, the roadwork equipment began to vanish from the hill.

During the days Mom was in Geneva, shingles were applied to the barn. The building had stood for a handful of years. Beep built it about the time I was born, or so I was told. It was functional. Tarpaper covered the entire roof, but it had been left ragged and torn by a hard wind and rain in August. As Beep said, "She sprung a leak, so she's gettin' shingles."

Louie King showed up to help finish the job he and Beep had partially completed in the spring. Louie's old Dodge pickup coughed and screeched its way up the new road and swung into the Bowden driveway. Louie cut the engine. The door growled open and he slid out onto new pavement. He slammed the truck door and the rusty hinges ground out the same unpleasant noise in reverse.

Louie was a fat man with Popeye arms and shrapnel for teeth. I never saw him without his engineer's cap. It was pulled down over a mop of gray to the very brink of his ears where a pencil stabbed the tangle of hair. He wore dirty bib overalls. Louie was a friend to Beepah, a Vietnam vet who showed up at group meetings at McCutchen's Bar and Grill. Beep said group was for men who had trouble dealing with life, men like Louie King.

As Beep's appointed wait person, I was sitting in the big rocker on the porch in the early chill for Louie King's arrival, as if he was the pope or something. I was anticipating what might come out of his mouth. He had a penchant for bad words. Sometimes he used funny words. I wrote those down, and the bad ones too, adding them to the list of big and bad words in my notebook. Sometimes, if he smashed a thumb with a hammer, what came out of his mouth was doubly shocking. It was Zach who told me once, "Bad words let you know they're bad. It don't matter if you heard them before or not."

Beepah stepped out onto the porch. He tipped his coffee cup

toward Louie as a greeting and dropped his shoulder against a porch post.

Louie's head swiveled back and forth as he inspected the new driveway. He looked to the porch and offered Beep an approving nod. "Slicker than thigh-high patent leather" was how he described the shiny, new driveway.

That was it? I'm sure my disappointment showed. I could not detect a single bad word in the lot, but just in case, I wrote them all down. Later, I would check for spelling.

Beep almost cracked a smile. "I thought I heard your truck, still purring like a kitten," he joked.

"Like a cat's tail in a stump grinder," Louie countered. "Fuck me!"

There it was, the first reliable bad word of the morning, but that one was on my list many times over. I was waiting for something more deliberately foul, and chances were always good with Louie King around. "Most of the boys will protect your delicate ears, darling," Beep once said to me. "But Louie King is not that way."

Louie walked with a profound swinging gait. His left hip was destroyed years before when a bullet tore apart the head of his femur and shattered his pelvis. Beepah told us stories about Louie and some of the other boys who showed up at McCutchen's.

Louie got hurt during the Battle of Khe Sanh, is what Beep told us. "I didn't know Louie back then, but I was there. It was ugly."

Beepah was careful when he talked to me about the war. My questions were innocent enough back then, questions about killing and dying and bombing.

"Was God on our side or their side?" I asked him.

"God can't be too happy with any of us when it comes to that shitstorm." Beep eyed me, then said, "I'll tell you when I know."

Beepah and Louie worked the entire morning before stopping for lunch. I had taken up residence at the picnic table under the shade of the maple trees that straddled our property line and Jolly's field. I made a drawing of the barn and Beepah on the roof banging on shingles with the air hammer. Louie King drove the tractor and maneuvered the bucket filled with bales of shingles to the spot where Beepah was working. In four hours, the north side of the barn roof was almost shingled from the eave to the peak.

I had disappeared unnoticed for a time but returned to the picnic table with a basket of paper plates and bologna and bread. Beep climbed down the ladder and threw a leg over the picnic table bench. He took a paper cup from a small stack near the cooler. He filled it with cold water from the thermos and drank it down. Then he did the same thing again.

"It's warm up there," Beep said. He pulled off his cap and poured the last gulp of cool water down the back of his neck.

"Like diggin' latrines at Kow Pu in one-twenty heat," Louie said. He spun the thermos around and drew a cup. "I got there just in time to pull shithole duty for a month."

I couldn't help myself. I laughed. "Cow Poo . . . is that a real place?"

Louie scratched his head through his hat. "Maybe it was Cow Pie. It don't set off no bells no more."

Tilly came by for a handout. Zach was right behind, crossing the yard to investigate the lunch offering. He slung his legs over the bench and grabbed a slice of bread with his dirty hands. He wrapped the bread around a bologna slice and gobbled half of it. He dropped the rest on the bench for Tilly. She nabbed it like it was trying to escape. "Who made lunch?" Zach inquired with one cheek bulging out.

"I didn't make it, Zachary. I brought it from the kitchen."

That was explanation enough. Zach took another and assembled it the same way. He pushed it in to fill the opposite cheek.

"Thanks for lunch, Sydney," he said, popping right up and heading back across the yard.

Beep hollered after him. "Where you off to, Zach boy?"

Zach turned and backpedaled, hoping a hasty retreat would spare him from clean-up duty or some other misery. "I'm digging a new rabbit trap behind the garden," he said.

"Say hello to Mr. King."

Zach took off at a trot. "Hi, Mr. King!"

Louie smiled and slapped together a sandwich. "That boy is busier than Wrigley's goat."

The escapades of Wrigley's goat meant nothing to me. It sounded like another nonsensical Louie King story was about to be hatched, and although he had me snickering the entire morning with his foul words and silly stories, my disbelief registered with him yet again. It compelled him to launch his lengthy dissertation in the matter of Wrigley's goat and the 1945 Chicago Cubs. I knew little about baseball and nothing about the Cubs, but apparently, according to Louie King, the Cubs lost the World Series that year.

"The curse ain't been lifted to this day," Louie said finally, "and it's all because of that whorish goat."

Finally, whorish indeed! It was worth the wait! Zach was right about bad words. They pretty much declare themselves. It would take me a while to track down the word in *Webster's*. I held suspicions whorish was an unfair indictment of the goat, and I was right. As it turned out, the poor beast was nothing of the sort, certainly not in his public persona. But the word whorish won a special place on my bad-words list.

Beep said nothing to encourage a less vulgar tone out of Louie. With Louie, the damage was preordained. Beep inhaled the end of his sandwich, then spit it to the ground in a fit of laughter. "Jesus, Louie, that's a tall one, even for you," Beep said. "My dad died a broken-hearted Cubs fan, but I bet even he never heard that version."

They kept up a running dialogue the balance of the afternoon. Louie sat on the tractor and delivered a bucketload of shingles to the south side of the roof. And when Beepah straightened to ease the stiffness in his back, the air hammer fell silent. When standing upright he could gauge their progress and check the sun above the treetops to estimate the time of day.

And late in the afternoon Ol' Jolly arrived with his big green tractor. It rolled between maple trees, growling and churning its way over rocks and mashing vestiges of rotting stumps in its path. He pulled up beside the smaller tractor Louie was aboard. Ol' Jolly cut the engine and threw a big leg over the tractor fender. He flipped his thumb in the direction of the mysterious tarp-covered package resting on the ground near a crabapple tree. The package was smack-dab in the middle of the backyard and had been there for three days. It arrived sometime while we were in school. It was neatly wrapped in a blue tarp. Beep said it was a special delivery, a surprise for Mom, and he warned us not to go near it.

"That the birdhouse?" Ol' Jolly asked.

"That be her," Louie said. "Could be fancy, the way they got'er wrapped."

"Let's have a look," Ol' Jolly said, beginning the burdensome task of dismounting the big tractor and delivering his massive body to terra firma.

Louie did the same, and the two men stood near the ladder waiting for Beepah. It occurred to me just then that Zach would not forgive me if I did not alert him to the great unveiling of the mysterious blue-wrapped present. I took off at a full run across the yard toward the garden. Zach was still there, dirt to his shoulders, mindlessly digging to China with his bare hands and a stick.

"Zachary!"

Zach's face was camouflaged in mud. He backed his arm out of the hole and looked up to see me coming to a screeching halt. "See this, Sydney?" he said. "I put this trap right where rabbits sneak into the garden. They hop right over this hole. One of 'em will fall right in. You wait."

I grabbed a breath. "They're unwrapping the big, blue present!"

Zach jumped up and the two of us raced back across the yard. We stopped beneath the crabapple tree where Beepah was cutting the straps that held the wrapping in place. The three men unpeeled the blue tarp and let it fall to the ground. There it was! A little house standing all by itself! It was four sided with a small window on each side. There were no doors. There was no way in or out. I had seen the likes of it before. Beep called it a *cupola*, and I wrote that word in my notebook.

In the hour that followed, Ol' Jolly hooked chains to the little house and raised it high up to the peak of the barn. Beepah pulled it along a temporary slide until it arrived at the exact middle. Then he kicked out the slide and let the cupola settle into place. There was plenty of work to be done to anchor it and make it watertight. Beep retrieved a rooster weathervane from his bench inside the barn. He climbed back up and screwed it to the top of the cupola.

Ol' Jolly departed on his tractor with Beep's thanks. The rest of us stood in a close little bunch like carolers, belting out the praises of the new cupola with the rooster weathervane. Suddenly, I could barely wait for Mom to come home and see it for herself.

"It's magnificent," Beep said. "Isn't it magnificent?"

"It looks like ol' Cowboy," I said in response, and it did look like Cowboy, except the weathervane had a fancier tail and more feathers on its neck, and it wasn't as scrawny as Cowboy. But those were barely noticeable differences. And the best part was I could look out my window when Cowboy crowed in the morning. I could see him and the weathervane as the sun came up.

The next morning, I went out with Beepah before school. I wouldn't waste a minute by sleeping late. Zach was different. To Zach, school days did little else but invite sleep. I climbed to the highest straw bale and sprung the flyway trap. Out went the birds, Ralph Loren leading the flock over Trumpet Hill Road, turning south to see the new cupola for the first time.

Beepah switched on the radio above the door. Paul Spriole's smooth voice delivered the morning news at the six o'clock hour: "A helicopter was ordered to land or risk being shot down when it flew into the no-fly zone surrounding the White House . . ."

A new noise reached my ears, interrupting Spriole's newscast, as if the radio went dead. But it was not Spriole. It came from a distance, perhaps from across the pond. I had heard the sound before, a shotgun blast. Beep flinched. He looked to the tree line until his eyes found the faintest puff of smoke. Out over Jolly's Pond, Ralph Loren's wings stopped beating. He began to tumble toward the glassy surface.

". . . The craft was a mosquito-type small craft, shadowed in its descent by a flock of Marine aircraft to a landing area near the National Mall. No weapons were found. The pilot was identified only as a retired Sikorsky engineer. He was taken into custody for questioning. The first family was not in the residence at the time of the incident."

Ralph Loren's nose dipped downward, a crippled kamikaze aiming its final ounce of might against the middle of Jolly's Pond. Ralph's splashdown created little more than a ripple. In seconds the surface returned to glass. He had rejoiced in flight, Ralph Loren. He was gone so quickly, floating dead on an ocean just beyond the fence at the edge of the yard.

Beepah took the call can from its spot above the door. He

stepped back into the scratch yard and began to shake it. The birds arrived in clusters of two and three. They dropped to the aviary roof deck agitated and confused. A shotgun blast had shattered the tranquil morning. It had happened before. A shot rang out and a bird fell from the sky, but this time was different.

Ralph Loren's death was more than a mindless game of pigeon shooting. Ralph's killing was purpose driven. During the days since Beep and me departed the Lipton house, I had said nothing about Jason's death threat from the staircase. Oh, I imagined all sorts of calamity, but still, I had attached no real dread to any of it. The confrontation quickly turned surreal to me. At the very least, once my breathing and heart beat returned to normal, my mind managed to assemble Jason Lipton's words into little more than a sixth grader's idle threat.

Nor did I tell Beep about the disappearing shotgun in the foyer. Even to me, the story sounded more Nancy Drew than plausible, and when all was said and done, I barely considered Beep's life hanging in the balance. Near as I recall, I feared for me, and only me. I had dared myself to venture to the foyer to challenge my fear. I discovered the shotgun there. The gun had not been far from my thoughts, even during the completion of the barn roof on Sunday. And now this, as though I'd willed it by obsession alone.

Tears welled in my eyes. I could no longer see clearly. Ralph's death rekindled my fear. It was Jason Lipton who pulled the trigger. Jason Lipton shot Ralph. I was certain of it. I could think of no one else with such malice in their heart.

"This is Paul Spriole wishing you safe travels," came the sign off. "And in words inspired by Little Jimmy Dickens, don't let the bluebird of happiness fly up your nose."

"Stay out of the woods," Beep said to me. "You and Zach stay out of the woods."

By early afternoon there was no sign of Ralph Loren's body

floating on Jolly's pond. Something must have discovered him adrift and made a meal of him. Perhaps a raccoon moving about after sunrise caught sight of Ralph's splashdown and waited for the promising clump of feathers to ride a faint breeze into the shallows. More likely it was the big snapper, always lurking in the mud many feet below, rumbling to the surface, grabbing a breath and Ralph's lifeless carcass in one smooth barrel roll.

I picked dandelions along the grassy banks in the afternoon. Zach and Tilly came to the pond. Zach pulled his wagon with his contraption for catching turtles, along with the bucket of rotting bait. He was itching to ply the big snapper with the decaying squirrel. Landing the big turtle had been Zach's obsession the entire summer and time was running out. Soon enough the monster would disappear into the mud to hibernate for the eternity of winter.

Zach dropped down beside Beep on the grassy bank. "Maybe ol' Ralph sunk," was Zach's suspicion.

Beepah surveyed the pond. "Maybe," he said. "I came down to fish him out and bury him back of the barn. He floated on the pond all morning. Now he's gone. I guess I missed my chance."

"Maybe he only got winged. Maybe he swam to shore and walked home. Did you ever think of that?"

Beep smiled in appreciation of Zach's optimism. "I never saw a pigeon swim. Like you said, he prob'ly sunk. Either way, the snapper prob'ly got him."

"Dirty snapper!" Zach growled. He flung a stone to the middle of the pond and watched the tsunami spread in all directions. "If that snapper ate ol' Ralph, he won't be hungry for squirrel guts."

"Not likely," Beep said and shrugged. "I don't know for sure who brought Ralph down, but the turtle's just a turtle. That's what turtles do. You'll see him come spring. He might be ten pounds by then. Maybe even bigger."

"If I catch him, I'll squeeze out one of his babies for a pet, then I'll throw him back."

Zach's plan amused Beep enough to illicit a little laugh. Zach's idea sounded perfectly plausible to me . . . if the turtle was a girl and if she laid an egg, and if she had a husband lurking nearby. Even I knew that much at almost seven.

———

Louie King stopped by when he finished driving the forklift at the lumberyard. He came to retrieve tools and gloves left behind on Sunday . . . or so he said. His old truck bucked its way up Trumpet Hill and choked to a stop in the driveway. The screeching driver's door announced him and moments later he appeared near the barn. Beepah was standing at the peak atop the new roof, straddling a stack of cut shingles.

"How goes it?" Beep shouted down.

"Can you piss in a cup from up there?" Louie shouted.

"What now?"

"I need a fresh sample."

"Did you molest a crossing guard or what?"

"It's my kid," Louie said, averting his eyes and staring off toward the pond. "She got nailed for driving drunk last night."

Beep scratched his head with his hat. He came down the roof to the ladder and stepped over. When he got to the ground, he worked his hat over his head again to loosen a word of encouragement or comfort. He found none. He pushed his hands into the back pockets of his jeans and walked near Louie. He could read the distress on Louie's face. "What is she, Louie, seventeen?"

"Just turned," Louie said, his eyes dampening. "She just got her permit. I bailed her out and dropped her at school. It took all the money I had."

"What about Carolyn?"

"That drunk bitch," he said. His chin fell against the rolls on his neck. "Sorry," he added, visibly displeased by his own rough talk. He blew a stream of spit through a gap in his teeth. "The judge should give her hard labor, as much trouble as she's been. Maybe they can teach her a trade. Don't send her home until she's rehabbed, I'd say." Louie kicked a scrap of shingle toward the tractor with his good leg, then hopped in a small circle on his bad one. "Anyways, whatever they do, I got no money for her."

Beep pulled a wad of bills from his side pocket and stuffed it into Louie's bib overalls. "I don't know how much this will help. I was meaning to give it to you anyways. I'll do what I can. Just let me know."

Louie's eyes dampened, and the money Beep gave him only made it worse. He took out his jackknife. "Can I whittle my mark on this here barn?" he asked with a smile that failed to cover his pain.

Louie took two hours carving away at one of the stanchion posts opposite the big barn door. When he was finished, he folded his knife and pushed it back into his pocket. He stepped back and cocked his head to inspect his work. His words read, "LK helped build this barn, Sept. 10, 2001."

That day was a Monday. The next day the Twin Towers fell in New York City.

CHAPTER SIX

I remember this day well. Outside the Archer School, the scene was panic. When news of the Twin Towers collapse spread, parents descended on the school like a horde of Huns. Tires scraped against the curb on the narrow street out front. Horns squawked their urgent protests. Minivans became roadblocks. Parents struggled with calm. They sprinted on the sidewalks. They crossed the schoolyard at clumsy and unrehearsed gallops. The country was under attack! And their children might well be the targets!

But of course, as a child and a student, I was told none of this, forced by omission to relegate all panic into the hands of capable and battle-hardened grown-ups. There was little plain talk about the events in New York City. Teachers shooed us along the hallways. I heard the great urgency and fear in their voices. I suspected something bad had happened, but the details remained unclear to me.

"Come on, Zach!" Beepah growled, his voice barely audible over the chaos. "Stay close to me. The truck is right up the street."

"Do we get the day off school?"

"Yup."

I looked up at Beep. "How come?" I asked him.

The question incensed Zach. He snapped at me, "Never mind how come, Sydney. If God wants to give us a day off, it's his business, not yours."

Beep was watching a familiar black limo weaving its way

through the traffic collecting at the curb. The big man's head was visible through the driver's side window. There was little doubt, Mother had arrived. The limo rolled quickly to a stop and the back door opened. Mom stepped out.

The mass panic that occurred when the planes struck was still fresh, but when word broke that the buildings had begun to crumble and fall, the ongoing frenzy demanded even greater urgency. Mom's face was rigid with resolve. Her eyes found us on the busy sidewalk. She ran toward us, ducking other parents up and over the curb. She was on us quickly, pulling me and Zach to her, squeezing our heads like she tested melons for ripeness.

"I saw it, Ben. Oh my god," she said, barely able to take a breath. In fact, she appeared close to fainting in the first moments after finding us. Then with one more look, she seemed assured we were safe, at least for the moment. "They had it on a loop in the terminal, every television, over and over again. There was so much smoke and fire. We were barely on the ground before the first one hit. Then they announced Kennedy was closing. They diverted all the air traffic someplace else. I couldn't get my luggage. I couldn't find my ride. Thank God for Martin. He didn't abandon me. We got the hell out of New York. We might have been the first ones out of the city once we found each other."

"Who's Martin?"

"Martin's my driver," she snapped at the interruption.

"Oh, I didn't know he had a name."

"Don't be an asshole, Ben." She turned and gestured to the big man and watched as Martin muscled the sleek, black limo into an open space at the curb. "The kids can ride with me," she said, her hands still cradling our heads. She gave us a twist and aimed us down the sidewalk toward the limo.

There was still an ongoing rush of anxious parents. We shuffled our way through the crowd. I heard Beep shout something after us. It sounded like, "I've got errands," but it fell flat. Either Mom cared little or didn't hear him. She opened the door and we scooted across the Limo's backseat. Mom slid in and pulled the door shut. It made a muffled whoosh that shocked my ears and caused them to ache. The limo inched away from the curb and rolled up Holland Street on its way to Trumpet Hill.

The hysteria at the Archer School was quickly left behind. Home was a few miles away. Martin said he was scheduled to return to New York City in the afternoon. He seemed concerned about the trip. He said the towers falling would make his own ride home difficult, but he must go. He had a wife there, in the Bronx. There were grandchildren, too, three little girls in a brownstone four doors down. "I see them every day. I'm afraid for them," Martin said.

Mother got her first look at the new asphalt. The silky ribbon of black climbed the hill in front of the limo. She appeared excited by the upgrade. "You didn't tell me about this," she said to us, while reveling in the smooth trip up Trumpet Hill Road for the first time.

Martin dropped us at home. Mom stepped out onto the new blacktop. Gone were the potholes and the cracked and broken pavement. She had witnessed the decay over the years. She sucked in her cheeks and gave the entire driveway a thorough inspection. Even Martin noticed the improvement. He returned to the limo after delivering one small suitcase to the porch.

"It's amazing what a few days away can do," he said of the driveway. "I hope the airlines locates your other suitcase, Ms. Carmichael."

"Thank you, Martin . . . and thank you for sticking by me."

"Good day to you," he said, then slid in behind the wheel.

Except for the brief ride to Trumpet Hill, I knew little of Martin. But even I heard the concern in his voice. The limo backed out of the driveway and rolled down the hill. I watched it go, recalling a trip or two into New York City when I was four or five. My recollections were vague, but I remember marveling at the tallness of the place. Standing in the driveway in the shadows of the cherry trees, I found myself praying for Martin and his wife and grandchildren. I prayed no buildings fell on them.

As I found out in the hours that followed, there was little chance the buildings fell on Martin's grandchildren. They lived in the Bronx. Mom said the buildings were falling in Lower Manhattan, and the man on television showed a map of New York City. Martin's family was a good distance from the disaster. Nonetheless, once the video began rolling in my head, it was slow to relent. The big plane flew into the tall building and fire came shooting out the other side. The building fell to the ground. I watched the earth explode over and over. Thick smoke rolled out and buried people. Maybe Martin's family was spared, but it troubled me deeply, knowing somebody's grandchildren must have died.

Mother insisted I not go outside to play that day. Zach, she said, would stay in the yard. He could venture no farther into the woods than the teepee. Me and Mom talked about Geneva. She poured herself a drink from one of the bottles Beepah called "hair of the dog." I had never seen her drink from those bottles early in the day, but the chaos and the fear she witnessed that morning must have shaken her to her core.

"It will calm me," she said of the dog-hair drink.

And, near as I could tell, it did calm her, several times before dinner.

"Geneva is a beautiful city," she said, reflecting. "It's right up against the Alps. It's the most incredible sight, watching the mountains rise to meet the plane. I got there just as the sun slipped through."

Sometimes Mother talked over my head. She was very aware I was bright enough, but I had not yet learned everything about the Alps and about the world at large. After all, I was barely seven. There were times I was forced to bring her back to matters of common importance. "Did you show my Indian girl picture?"

She smiled. "Of course, I did," she said, her eyes catching sunlight as she peered beyond the front room windows into the eerie stillness of early afternoon. "I met a man on the plane ride from Paris to Geneva. His name was John Goff. He teaches art classes at a private school in Greenwich Village." She looked at the television and her smile shrunk away. "Not far from that horrid scene," she said, as she watched the rerun of the plane crashing into the building yet again. She swallowed painfully. "He saw your drawing." Her cheeriness returned quickly. "He wanted to know how old you are, and I told him you're going on seven. He said your drawing was wonderful. He wants to see more of your pictures."

"I have a hundred pictures!"

Mother tipped the glass to her mouth and rattled the ice cubes. She set it to the coffee table and poured more dog hair. "We'll have to go through your drawings and find your very best to send to John."

"What does he look like? Was he handsome or old?"

She gave that faraway look again and smiled, considering the limited options. "Handsome, I guess. I don't often notice such things, not as a first impression." She took a sip of the amber-colored dog hair, then stuck her finger in the glass and gave the potion a swirl. "I had just woken up. It was a peaceful trip. I unrolled your drawing for the first time and John saw it from across the aisle. He thought it was very good." She gave me a playful tap on the head. "We talked for the half hour it took to land the plane. He said he was in Geneva to capture sketches of old buildings. Renaissance architecture, he called it. We walked off the plane together. He had a big artist's valise and a small bag with a week's worth of clothes."

I was stricken with pride, of course. Here was a man with high praise for my crayon drawing, and he was an artist like myself, a fellow traveler. I could not appraise Mother's truthfulness regarding John Goff's appeal. It was clear from the start she liked something about the man because her eyes went a little glassy when she spoke of him. Yet, given her scant description of the man, I was compelled to invent him from the ground up.

If the truth be told, even at age seven, I had not begun to put shape or color to any notion of handsome. Over the next few years, John Goff's name was destined to arise out of the blue at times. I took it upon myself to secretly lavish masculine attributes on the man, should one avail itself.

It was well after dark when Beepah came in through the back door. He clumped his way through the kitchen to the front room. We were huddled together under a blanket, the three of us and Tilly. We were eating popcorn and watching *The Lion King* for the twentieth time. Zach never tired of it. I was certain he wanted a lion for a pet and was only disappointed none showed up near his traps.

Beep rubbed Zach's head with the heal of his hand. "Zach boy," he said.

Mom turned her cheek against the back of the sofa and rolled her eyes up. The dog hair had indeed relaxed her. She was barely awake until she recognized the voice. "Where have you been?" she asked of him.

"I stopped by Louie King's," Beep said. "His daughter had some trouble. Some of the boys showed up. You know how it is. Airplanes knocking down buildings makes them a little jittery."

Mother ignored him. "What did you spend on that driveway?"

Beep laughed and bent down to deliver a kiss to the top of her head. "I knew you'd be pleased, Angie darling," he said with a bit of Grandmother's lilt in his voice. "No more mother-grabbing sinkholes, roller skating with your children, garage sales on Saturday . . . a good thing all around, and believe it or not, it was practically free."

Mother rolled her eyes again and nodded off.

During the next few minutes, Beep baited Zach into leading us to his rabbit trap behind the garden. He rousted Mom and made her come along. We kicked our way through damp grass in the dark—me, waggling the flashlight at any suspicious shadow. Mom caught sight of a dim light shining from the barn roof, splashing in faint yellow squares over new shingles. She grumbled about expenses. Beep suggested she drank too much hairy dog.

"It's a cupola," I enlightened Mother. "Ol' Jolly calls it a big bird house, but it's a cupola, all right. I looked it up . . . and it's got a big ol' statue of ol' Cowboy himself right on the top."

My description brought Mother's familiar disbelieving look. "Jesus, Ben," she growled.

"It was never my intention to immortalize that bedraggled rooster," Beep said and laughed. "Wait till you see it in the morning light, Angie darling. It's almost as pretty as you are. You'll appreciate it when you're off the sauce for a few hours."

We reached the hole in the ground without falling in it. Zach waved us all into a small circle. He snatched the flashlight from me and shined it into the hole. I knew in that very moment, no matter what disasters befell the world at large, no matter what calamity threatened our little farm and our very lives, God loved Zachery. He loved me, and he loved Mom and Beepah too, even if they didn't love each other most of the time. Zach shined the flashlight into the rabbit hole just as he had done night after night for the entire summer. There, on a bed of clover at the bottom of the hole, were two baby rabbits. They were gray and white, with floppy ears, and noses twitching as they feasted on clover without a care in the world.

After all the time he had given to his obsession, Zach had won at last. Never mind these two rabbits looked nothing like the native rabbits that plagued the garden each year just as the crops were ripening. Zach was not suspicious, not a bit. He named them Bumper and Thumper on the spot, not that it mattered. They looked to be identical twins. Zach put them in the dog crate in his room until a proper hutch could be built. We lay awake most of the night pushing shoots of clover through the mesh-covered door, me beside Zach on a sleeping bag spread out on the bare floor.

Beep slipped into the room in early morning. He put his hand on me and I woke, seeing the rabbits and realizing I had been dreaming of them. Thoughts of falling buildings had abandoned me for the entire night. When I slept, I dreamed of baby rabbits eating clover.

"I'm going out to the birds," Beep whispered.

My eyes squinted into the soft gray light of morning. "I'll go," I said, encouraged by Cowboy's crusty baritone.

Zach was awake and registered an immediate complaint. "I didn't sleep a wink," he said while pushing more clover through the crate door. "I can't go to school today. These rabbits need me to take care of them."

Beep pushed the hair from Zach's forehead and gave him an apologetic look. An arm fell across Zach's eyes to cover his disappointment. "Sorry," Beep said, standing in the gray morning light. His socks glided him quietly over the plank floor toward the door. He stopped there and looked back at us. "Yeah, I'm sorry, but you two can't go to school today. I'll need help building a hutch for those rabbits."

The pigeons flew that morning. A silver-colored male with white wings led the way, an interloper who arrived after ol' Ralph nosedived into Jolly's pond. The newcomer hung out high in the hemlock for days, bobbing in courtship whenever a female showed up in the scratch yard. The truth was, he fancied ol' Ralph's widow, and made a big pain of himself until she relented and invited him inside the aviary. Beepah named him Tux because his white wings looked like formal shirt sleeves.

It took only one day to understand why Beep kept us home that Wednesday morning. In truth, we stayed home Thursday and Friday too. The rabbit hutch was built in a day and proved a great diversion. There was no talk of buildings falling and people dying while saws and hammers created a racket. The destruction in New York City caused fear and uncertainty. Beepah was determined to keep us close, and he got to blame the entire crisis on the mysterious arrival of the rabbits.

CHAPTER SEVEN

Those days came and went, as did that year and the year after. Ours was a world forever in transition despite my ignorance of it. There was great distrust among the nations. There was revenge, both sought and achieved. I heard it at the dinner table. I horned in on conversations never meant for my ears while sitting in the backseats of cars or up front in Beep's truck. I listened to "the mood of the masses," Beep called it.

Even Paul Spriole, who spoke to me and Beepah each morning on the radio in the aviary, often referenced car bombings in Afghanistan and rockets striking Israel as Armageddon's messengers. He continually encouraged prayer and soul searching with endless prognostications. "Warming along the Eastern Seaboard," the radio crackled. "And by the lunchtime hour, local temperatures rise into the high sixties, in the low forties during the overnight. Rain, as expected, arrives during the early morning commute. This is Paul Spriole reminding you to pray for the survival of a desperate world. Oh! And enjoy your day."

The gloomy attitude adopted by Spriole drove Beep to distraction. At least he said it did. Nevertheless, he continued listening for some months until Spriole's ratings plummeted and producers forced him to fold his tent. They replaced Spriole with the bubbly weather girl. "This is Amanda Newfeldt wishing you all the sunshine in the world . . ." Upon hearing that each morning, Beep stuck his finger down his throat to gag himself.

At nine, I was privileged to learn certain truths. One simple truth had nagged at me for a time. One morning I caught Beepah scattering scratch feed and came right out with it. "Where did Zach's rabbits come from? You can tell me. Did the Tooth Fairy drop them in Zach's hole in the ground?"

Beep stopped his work and laughed. "Tooth Fairy? You're talking God, yes?" he said, giving me a playful glare. "I'm sure he had a hand in it . . . roundaboutly, at least."

Beepah seemed willing to share the miracle of their arrival, but he never gave God full kudos. By the time I uncovered at least a partial truth, one of the two, Thumber or Bumper, had died in childbirth. At least that's how Beep described it. All he found was a half-prepared nest and a bloody mess. "A tubal pregnancy, maybe," is how he struggled to explain the unfortunate circumstance. One of the unsettling parts to that scenario, when Beep finally got around to telling the tale, both Thumper and Bumper were thought to be girls, perhaps even twin sisters.

"Do you remember what day we found them in the hole?"

"The day the towers fell down," I said. "Who doesn't remember that?"

"I went off alone. Your mother was gone ten days, and she wasn't overly friendly when she arrived at the Archer School," he said. "I took it personal. She was afraid for you and Zach. I get it. But it took me all day driving around to get over it." He shrugged. "I've never quite understood your mother. Usually, when she treats me like that, I head for McCutchen's to piss and moan to the boys . . . whoever will listen."

"You and Mom argue sometimes. I've seen that since I was little."

He stuffed his hand into the pail and drew out more cracked corn. He threw it at my feet. "We're talking about rabbits, know-it-all," he grumbled.

"Just pointing out the obvious, is all."

"I stopped by McCutchen's early in the afternoon . . . after your mother snatched you guys away from me at the Archer School. Some of the boys were there, feeling really agitated about the Trade Towers." Beep stopped slinging scratch feed to explain. "They get spooked when something wildly out of sync happens. It's the Nam thing. I feel it sometimes. Anyway, instead of drinking beer all day, I got in the truck and drove all over the state looking for rabbits."

"Me and Zach saw a rabbit just like them at the fair in Goshen," I said. "I swear we were staring at the lost triplet to those two. In fact, we named him Dumper on the spot and laughed about it the rest of the day." I went to my fat notebook and flipped through drawings near the front. There it was, Bumper, Thumper, and Dumper all in a row with the caption "At the Goshen Fair." I held it up and turned it toward Beep. "See, I captured the moment," I said proudly.

Beep peered through the chicken wire, swaying this way and that to get a fix on the three rabbits.

"Zach never questioned how the bunnies got in the rabbit hole, not even then," I said. "He still credits God. I always thought maybe it was the Tooth Fairy, until Dumper showed up at the fair. Anyway, Zach stuck with it, miracle or not, he never stopped believing. You know what the tag on Dumper's cage read?" My finger traced along the penciled script at the bottom. "Miniature Belgian Flop Ears," I read. "Really, Beep? They're not even American."

Beep choked on that one. It was a guilty laugh. "There must have been a run on rabbits that day," he said. "Those two were all I could find."

I recalled the moment with a laugh of my own. "Dumper had a pink ribbon, best in breed or something," and I shrugged. "The easiest way to win best in breed is to show up alone. They give ribbons for everything. I should get one for keeping my mouth shut all this time."

"Yes, darlin', best in breed . . . that's you, all right," Beep said, dropping his hat on a straw bale to signal me it was time to gather eggs. "Remember, Syd, you're sworn to secrecy. It's Zach's miracle."

Beep took me with him to McCutchen's around lunchtime that same day. My visits there were rare enough, but so often Beep allowed me to stay out of school because school was boring at times. While Zach was frequently issued detention for the same crime, I continued to be lauded as a prima donna by classmates and teachers alike, who were just as pleased to hear I might have come down with scabies or any deadly infestation that quarantined me for life.

"Time spent in school can be time wasted," Beep declared often, much to Zach's delight. And he often railed against the administration for its failure to place me in a stimulating learning environment. To counter the dull effect, Beep kept me home to paint the shed, or clean the coop, or go for lunch at McCutchen's.

McCutchen's was a ten-minute ride from the Bowden farm. I walked in behind Beep and Tilly and went up the two steps to the dusty plank floor. Overhead, the plaster ceiling had partially crumbled years ago. I could see to the roof boards, and the unlighted area in the attic had been cleaned and secured enough to diminish the likelihood of a further plaster collapse. A single fan turned with lazy indifference. Shoe prints defined traffic patterns over the dusty floor. "You could track Bigfoot in ballet slippers," was Louie King's nonsensical appraisal of the dusty terrain inside the place.

McCutchen's was in need of almost everything: fresh paint, cleanser in every corner, a broom. A fire burned in the old wood stove. The stove stood near a gap in the wall between the end of the bar and the door to the men's room. It spit ashes to the charred planks and offered far more heat than the place required for comfort. The front windows allowed little light. They were caked in generations of tobacco tar from way back when smoking indoors was allowed. Blackened orange ribbons of the ooze covered much of the glass, glacial in their descent to the sill in years past. They still remained, distorting the shapes and colors of cars passing on Main Street. And of course, the smell of the place was driven by the menu of the day mingled with the menu of last month, depending on air quality. Nonetheless, McCutchen's boasted a devoted clientele.

Tilly dropped down in the dust beside a chair and Beep dropped into it. "This is Syd," Beep gave the introduction, although I had been to McCutchen's often enough to recognize some of Beep's friends. Most had showed up on Trumpet Hill a time or two to aid in the completion of one project or another.

There was a collective, "Hey, Syd," from the boys at the big round table.

Beep waved me to a booth beneath a window along the back wall. I slid in with my drawing tablet and crayon box. I opened the tablet and lowered my head into my work, encouraging invisibility as much as possible. In spite of my efforts, the waitress Jin came right over with a glass of ice water. Beep had told me she was Vietnamese. She was slight, fifty, maybe even considerably older. She was friendly. She almost always had a cheerful smile.

"King Louie," Beep greeted with a nod.

"Morning," Louie said, even though morning had officially slipped away just minutes before.

Beep rocked back into a comfortable place and tipped his cap to the guy across the table. "James," he greeted him.

"Ben."

"How's Dolly?"

"She's back to work," James said with a generous dose of

enthusiasm. "She's sprouting hair and everything, getting her energy back."

I had not met James. He was not quite as regular to the big round table as some of the other regulars. I heard about Dolly at the dinner table. Beep said she was James's wife and she was sick with cancer. Dolly was a teacher. I never did learn where she taught school, but she marched on Main Street in all the big parades. "That's Dolly," Beep pointed her out on Memorial Day. She was a slight woman, and cancer had likely diminished her even more. She wore a pink headscarf and a determined smile.

James went on to describe her recovery in some detail, and one by one, the rest of the boys inquired about her improvement. James looked bravely positive about his wife's recovery. It struck me then, her illness must have taken a great toll on him. He slumped far down in his chair, and the whole of him was colorless, faded gray at best.

Beep looked over the table at Collin Jefferson, who had pushed his chair halfway to the wall. From there he rocked backward to teeter on hind legs. He once said it was to avoid back shooters. He was a little man, but sturdy. He sported an orange beard. A puffy fringe of orange hair bushed out from beneath his army-fatigue hat. His entire persona was elfin. If ever there was a living, breathing leprechaun, Collin Jefferson was it.

"He's always scheming up something," Beep once said of Collin Jefferson. "He's a happy sort."

I had seen the man more than once at McCutchen's or near the barn when he came to consult with Beep about one pressing matter or another. He was comical when he chose to be, and was always on the hunt for a story or a joke to cheer the boys. He was, without question, the best embellisher of the truth, or lack of it, that I had met in my nine years, and I had encountered a few.

"Hey, Jefferson," Beep said with a nod. "Did you shoot that dog yet?"

The boys at the table chuckled at that. It was a running joke, the precarious predicaments of Jefferson's dog, Patch, who some of the boys had never encountered, and at least a few even questioned the canine's very existence. Collin Jefferson needed little encouragement to bring everyone up to speed. Beep was an instigator in that regard. The boys expected little else.

Jefferson let his chair legs drop to the floor. He folded his arms over the table and slowly shook his head while his face creased with concern. "That old dog is living on borrowed time," Jefferson said finally. "The Pillson woman hauled us into court again."

In response to Jefferson's theatrical show of stress in the matter, there was a smattering of laughter at the table and "What for now?" and, "What the fuck, Jeff?"

According to Jefferson, Millie Pillson told Judge Harry Whispers she went out to the back of her house in the early morning to pull rhubarb for a pie. Patch snuck up from behind, ripped off her housecoat, and ran off down the road dragging the garment in the dust. The mongrel left the poor woman disrobed and shivering in her garden without a stitch. Jefferson immediately raised his hand to take the oath. "I swear to God," he assured the boys, his eyes closing in a rare moment of sanctimony.

It was classic Collin Jefferson fare, and the boys responded again with chuckles. It was the very kind of tall tale Beep related at dinner sometimes. It was destined to be the beginnings of a monstrous lie or the gospel truth, depending on your gullibility. I took the orange crayon from the box and began to create the halo of hair on paper. When Jefferson raised his hand to swear to the truth, I did my best to capture the moment, all the while following the story amid the swirl of voices and clatter drifting on the ether cloud inside McCutchen's.

I pushed myself along the bench to get near enough to hear. I caught sight of an old man sitting at the bar. He swiveled on his stool, listening intently from across the small dining room. I'm certain he was too far away to hear much of the story, but he appeared amused by Jefferson's animations. Jin stopped scratching out a lunch menu on the chalkboard. She pushed a grilled cheese and a pickle on a small plate across the table toward me. We shared a smile. Minutes later she returned, this time with more beers. She deftly delivered glasses and bottles around the big table with all the grace of a butterfly, only quieter.

"Lawyer Rupert Wayne Dooley . . ." and of course, there was a murmuring of recognition with the introduction of Rupe Dooley. Jefferson raised his voice a decibel. "You all know Rupe Dooley," he said, surveying the faces. "He'll verify my version of events."

I took artistic license and abandoned Jefferson's fatigue hat and picked up a green crayon. I gave him a Kelly green bowler with a gold buckle. I put his feet on the table, crossed them at the ankles, and curled the toes of his shoes. I dare say, changes to his persona were managed so cleverly, the tweaking was barely noticeable.

Jefferson said Rupe Dooley called Sheriff Micah Nash to the stand, and Jefferson's head popped up to quickly poll the boys again. "You know Micah, right?" and of course, all the boys nodded their familiarity with the congenial Black sheriff.

Jefferson's voice was about to climb another decibel, and he began twisting at his orange beard to conjure the story just ahead of its telling. "Micah Nash visited every house on Bridge Street that day. Not a single soul would admit to seeing Millie Pillson stripped to the feathers, naked as a jaybird in the presence of St. Patrick his-self," Jefferson said.

By that time, McCutchen's lunch service was well underway. The tables were filled with office workers and a crew of young men smelling like hot tar. Louie King ordered a plate of onion rings and called it his lunch. Then he passed the plate around the table until it was empty but for crumbs. I confess to being enthralled by Jefferson's tale, and not a bad word was employed in the telling, which Beep once said was a credit to Jefferson himself. Even with its growing infusion of embellishments, the story remained harmless enough . . . except for Millie Pillson. An ounce of truth or otherwise would leave her damaged by the tale.

Tilly was a frequent and welcome guest. She made the rounds, pushing her nose into any accessible crotch to earn a scratch behind the ears. I managed to remain inconspicuous. I spent the entire hour creating the crayon rendering of the orange-haired, leprechaunish Collin Jefferson, sitting with his feet atop a pot of gold, regaling a crowd of lunch-goers at McCutchen's Bar and Grill with the endless contrivance as to the fate of his dog, Patch.

According to Jefferson, there had been no answer at the door of John Jacob Plum. The elderly Plum lived directly across Bridge Street, and upon closer study, Plum's front porch provided an unobstructed view of Millie Pillson's garden.

"Sheriff Nash spent the better part of that day gumshoeing up and down Bridge Street, when he once again found himself standing at the door of John Jacob Plum. This time the old gent Plum comes to the door at last," Jefferson said. "Nash puts it to him straight away."

Jefferson slowed his delivery to summon the gravelly tones of the amiable sheriff, Micah Nash. "Two mornings ago—that would be this past Tuesday—did you see the Jefferson dog forcibly remove the housecoat from Millie Pillson, the lady across the road?"

Jefferson said the elderly Plum rocked back on his heels and rubbed his chin for a lengthy moment. He considered his complicity in the matter. Finding none, he planted his feet firmly on the porch and cleared his throat to speak. Just then, Jefferson rose from his chair and raised his finger to the heavens. "Did I see it!" Jefferson mimicked old Plum. "Why . . . I took a picture!"

The old man at the bar nearly fell off his stool. There was little doubt, not until that very moment, had he heard one syllable of the outlandish tale from his distant vantage. He had been entertained by Jefferson's contortions alone. But when the small lunch gathering hushed for an instant and Jefferson's voice rose an octave, the old man's stool teetered on one leg, threatening to toss him to the dusty floor.

Anyone inside McCutchen's who had taken the slightest interest in Jefferson's antics had become suspicious the story would not end anytime soon. The epic tale itself was encroaching on the final moments of their lunch hour, and the very idea that Jefferson's bolder oratory might be signaling the approach of a climactic end heartened some.

But not so fast. Jefferson was not finished. He dropped back into his chair and recommenced. "Sheriff Nash passed the photograph to Lawyer Dooley, who introduced it into evidence. Judge Harry Whispers studied the photo at length. He looked first to Millie Pillson, who was sitting at the table up front. He even looked through a magnifying glass at a plump Millie Pillson running down Bridge Street."

Jefferson smirked. "Whispers announced to the courtroom, 'Good god, woman! You're naked as Eve!'"

That brought a laugh, and Jefferson paused for only a moment. "Judge Whispers looked over his glasses and panned the entire courtroom. Then he threw up his hands and yelped in his loudest judge voice, 'Where's the damn dog?'"

Jefferson left that to settle over an audience simmering with anticipation. The end was near. They could almost taste it. He let his chair rock forward and he tugged his fatigue cap over his orange rim of hair.

"The courtroom went silent, except for old Plum, who was sitting in the back. Plum decided Judge Whispers was pressing him directly to explain the photo's glaring omission, so Plum stood up. 'I'm not a photographer,' he cried out. 'I used to be a plumber! My wife is gone now ten years. In all those years I have watched the woman parading through her garden in her housecoat. The one morning she runs naked past my porch, I get a visit from the sheriff.'"

Jefferson's eyes widened. "When Whispers heard that, he was moved by the injustice of it. He slammed down his gavel and declared, 'Case dismissed!'"

I laughed at that. The story was over, or at least he had chanced upon an ideal stopping place. Even tucked up under the window, I laughed. The old man at the bar, who had nearly dismounted his stool at one point during the tale, might have laughed the loudest. Jin even laughed a little and shook her head, declaring the tale a Jefferson classic. She went back to her menu and wrote *goulash* right under *chili* on the chalkboard.

Beep rocked forward in his chair. "Christ, Jefferson, that's a ten-mile train." He reached across to slap Jefferson's arm. "Good one."

"So, Bowden," Jefferson said, returning to quieter tones and not quite prepared to put a wrap on things. His chair legs knocked against the dusty planks. "I haven't shot my dog. He's been reassigned. There's a pretty widow living three houses down. She paces her porch some mornings." Jefferson laughed. "I better save that one for another day."

Jin hurried over to mop up the big round table. She called Jefferson a world-class bullshitter in her unique, well-groomed, barroom English, and she giggled freely. All the while Jefferson held his right hand skyward to doubly swear his steadfast allegiance to the silly tale.

Beep's chair growled against the rough floor and he stood up. He tossed some money on the table. "All set, Syd?" he called to me.

Tilly pushed herself to her feet with a groan, stretching long and hard. When Louie King stood up, she jammed her nose into his privates, Louie's being perhaps one of the more familiar crotches near the table. It caused Louie to fold a little at the knees. He straightened with a grimace. "There was a time I looked forward to that much attention," Louie remarked, scratching Tilly behind the ear.

"I never knew you to have a dog," Beep said, muddying Louie's meaning, which was likely Beep's intent.

I tore out the drawing of Collin Jefferson from my notebook and slid from my seat in the booth under the window. "Here, Mr. Jefferson," I said, holding the picture toward him. "I didn't hear all of your story, but it was still good enough to make me laugh."

Jefferson took the drawing with much surprise and looked it over for a long while. His smile broadened, chasing his mustache high up his cheeks. "Will you look at this, Bowden," he said, turning his big grin toward Beep. "Look at that . . . how pretty is this?"

"Sorry, Mr. Jefferson," I said. "I didn't think of that, but if orange is pretty, you sure are."

Jin scurried over to mop up the table again. She took the crayon drawing from Jefferson and quickly retreated to the bar. She went up on her tiptoes and boldly displayed the rendering among all the bottles of dog hair on the second row above the cash register. I bubbled with pride, and I'm certain I went red-faced when Beep's arm circled my head and pulled me close. He planted a kiss on my forehead.

"Come on, Tilly girl," he said.

We left that day after the lunch crowd cleared out. The old man was still perched on the stool, nursing a glass of beer. Jin gave the old oak slab a swirl with her bar rag, making a big wet half-moon around the old gent. I found out from Beep his name was Doc Dockery, which would suggest he was a doctor, maybe retired like old Plum the plumber. Or was Doc short for Dockery? The old man turned once and offered a little salute to the big round table. The boys acknowledged him.

I didn't go to school that day. I went to McCutchen's Bar and Grill, ate grilled cheese and pickles for lunch, and I drew a picture of a leprechaun by the name of Collin Jefferson that hangs above the bar for all to see. Beep was right; time spent in school can be time wasted.

CHAPTER EIGHT

By ten years old I had created a man of great character in my imagined love, John Goff, and by then I wanted more than the fantasies I had created. I recalled picnics and rendezvous in the meadow beyond the stream. On winter days, we lay on our backs near the big brick fireplace in the front room and shared stories and drawings, but those I had fashioned or only dreamed about. During the years that followed the first utterance of his name, I filled fifty pages in a notebook dedicated exclusively to him. The images of the man were well formed and they grew and changed, as did the rhythms of my childhood.

I dreamed we kissed once. I don't remember the year, but I recall all other aspects of the occasion vividly. It was on the steps at the Archer School just before I boarded the bus for home. John was scheduled to depart for an art show in Geneva. He would be gone for days, the very ten days Mother would be gone. Pure coincidence, I told myself. I assured him I would wait, and I sent him off with the grandest drawings in my collection. He was destined to return to me with citations and blue ribbons awarding my art, and I would display them on my bedroom wall.

It was the kiss on the Archer School steps that might have signaled my departure from childhood. It was the one kiss that appeared in a dream. Upon waking, it was the first time I was left desiring more. I did not invite the feeling, nor did I encourage it, but there it was. A warmth overtook me entirely, body and soul. I determined it to be the surest sign I was growing up. Yet, John Goff remained, perhaps diminished . . . just perhaps.

Mother escaped into New York City at predictable intervals. She stayed a day or two, "Whatever it takes to get my work done," was how she described the importance of her visits. Once at supper she mentioned John Goff by name. She even suggested she may see him during an upcoming trip. I had not heard the name in some months. It was so rarely uttered over the months, I began to imagine I had won the battle for his affection, if only I had been open about it. But then, our affair had been born out of secrecy, and what good is a secret once it's blabbed out at the dinner table in front of the whole family?

"I might see John Goff in New York," she said, pushing an asparagus spear around her plate with her knife. She pinned it down by the throat and lopped off its head, then speared it with her fork. "It's been a while."

To say the least, I was suddenly mortified. It was one of the boldest things I'd ever heard, either that or the cruelest, or the incredibly dumbest. I jumped in to protest. "Mother, really!" I said, completely stunned by her passive declaration in front of God, Beep, and everybody.

She teased her lips with the morsel on her fork, dreamy-eyed the entire time. "It would be nice if you had a drawing I could show off, dear. I've been invited up to his studio in Greenwich Village on Sunday. Believe it or not, I've never been there. He always speaks highly of your work, even when you were a little girl."

I looked from one end of the table to the other. Not an ounce of righteous indignation was tossed into the mix. There sat Beep, saying nothing. Not a single utterance escaped his lips. Not the slightest hint of heartbreak, nor jealousy, nor even curiosity showed on him.

Even Zach let the moment pass without notice. He was gripping a chicken leg in both hands, and he spun it over his teeth like it was an ear of corn. "This chicken is better than the one in my bait bucket," he declared, then laughed as if he offered up something profound instead of stupid.

It was building in me. I could feel it rising from a place deep in my gut, gurgling up without intent or benefit of forethought. What I was about to scream barely belonged to me. I had been completely willing to give up John Goff, and yet Mother clung to him relentlessly.

"My mother and my father! Don't either of you care?" I cried out.

In the dead-silence of the aftermath, a scarlet ooze washed over my retinas, rendering me blind but for the color red. Just as suddenly it began to leach away, I could see again. My face cooled. I was stunned to realize my outburst had garnered not the slightest notice. My voice had not registered a single decibel. Zach dropped the gnawed chicken bone to his plate and sprang in for another. He snatched one from the platter and dragged it back to his lair to devour. Beep frowned, watching Zach plow a greasy trail across the table while Mom remained dreamy eyed over John Goff.

They had not heard me. I had not said it. Instead, what came from my mouth was a stream of profoundly patronizing drivel. "I finished a drawing of Jolly's pond yesterday. I was sitting on the rock wall in the scratch yard just when the sun came up through the trees. The geese were on the water, making trails through yellow pollen. Colors are at their best in early morning," I said, my protest collapsing to nothing.

————

All said, Mother must have heard me. Within a week she arranged for me to accompany her to New York City. We took the train out of Kingston and followed the Hudson River due south, cutting through the forested lowlands at the base of the Catskills. A two-hour ride into the city of tall buildings. We talked the entire trip.

She insisted on holding my hand as though I was five and was preparing to strike out on an unaccompanied scamper down the center aisle of the train. I only protested the hand-holding a little. I told her I intended to engage with humanity, not forever distance myself from it.

She scoffed at that. "How worldly of you, dear," she said. "I can't help but want to protect you." She forced a smile and squeezed my hand tighter. She missed my point of course, if I even had one. I often found myself in competition with the woman and her pretentiousness, which frankly, only served to encourage my own. I informed her that I intended my remarks to come off as simple existentialism, and she eventually got around to it. We talked about an itinerary, about shopping and dinner at the Columbo just off Central Park.

Mother said, "I have a nine o'clock meeting all the way downtown in the morning . . . bankers and attorneys. Corporate is sending a couple bigwigs. At least I might know them. I don't know what I was thinking," she said apologetically. "But the meeting should go quick. You'll be all right at the hotel for a few hours. They've got a great spa. I'll tell them to expect you."

She said if all went well, she planned to meet a friend. "We're going to the Metropolitan Museum for lunch," she said. "You'll be amazed." She turned her eyes to the window and watched as the train rolled through Harlem. It was a mind-numbing stretch of red-brick project houses exposing their backsides to the train's gloomy faces. "The bank is not sending a car for me in the morning," she said. "I don't know what loser plans these meetings, but I'll have to take a cab both ways."

Oh dread was all I could think. *A cab both ways.* But saying it out loud would have been too much sarcasm, even for me, and I even decided not to protest the handholding any longer. She seemed determined. When she said she planned to meet a friend for lunch. instantly I thought of John Goff. I knew none of her friends, not really. In fact, I was not certain she had other friends. John was the only one she ever mentioned, at least the only name that found my ear.

I heard little else she said after that. The friend she spoke of had to be John, and my brain questioned whether her affair with him had lasted longer than mine. Did she make this trip often, boarding the train to fulfill plans for a secret rendezvous? Did they stroll Central Park together? Did they kiss at Rockefeller Center during the same Christmas tree lighting I watched on television once? At the very least, I should have been informed. I could have looked for them mingling with the crowd, embracing in the frosty air. I might have taken my first look at the real John Goff. Come to find out she had denied herself nothing in all those months of silence and had managed to keep me entirely out of his life.

Late in the morning the train rocked its way to a halt. We emerged from the darkness of the platform below into a cavernous Grand Central Station. Mom knew her way and stayed close beside me as we scurried to the doors adjacent to Forty-Second Street. We walked into a cool October day. The wind pulled us almost to our knees until our keels aligned and we fell against each other for support. We found the hotel courtesy van. "That's it," she said. "The Hilton."

Try as I did, I could not forgive her the entire day and well into the next. Even as we climbed the stone steps from Fifth Avenue to the front doors of the Metropolitan Museum of Art, I could think of little else. I was about to come face to face with John Goff himself. It was a face sure to exhibit recognition when his eyes found Mother. I would catch him smiling. I began to search faces, to find a man sturdy and handsome, a man of an appropriate age, I suppose, though I had never truly considered it.

And there he was, standing almost at the top of the steps,

holding the railing to brace against the gusting wind. I stopped cold. There was a man with long, unruly hair thrashing about his face in a brutal wind that threatened to dislodge his glasses. He wore a brown leather jacket zipped to the folds of skin on his neck. He was lean, even thin. No, he was skinny. He wore high-top tennis shoes and tight jeans. His spindly legs fought mightily to hold himself at anchor against the gale. He must have been of an age like Beepah, ancient, closing on sixty, if he was a day. By the cut of him, he was my size. The very sight of the man betrayed my every single expectation, except for the smile of recognition . . . and there it was.

I was frozen to the spot while Mom hurried up the steps to greet him. He put his arms out and held onto her to keep from flying off like a runaway kite. They kissed, not the peck-on-the-cheek kiss I once received daily from Grandmother, but something longer and wetter. Suddenly, the very idea was truly repulsive to me.

I slowly climbed the steps while a wave of forgiveness spilled over me. Mom could love John Goff all she wanted. My feelings for the man could not be fleeting fast enough. In forgiving her, the discomfort I might have felt confronting the man was lifted. My thoughts turned briefly to Beepah, to my knowledge, unaware Mom was kissing another man. The realization was destined to complicate any warm feelings, but not so much that day.

I reached the two of them at the top of the steps. John must have sensed my arrival because he managed to part the tangle of hair enough to get his first look at me. His pucker diminished immediately. He swiped the hair across his head once more and his smile returned. "You're Sydney. I've seen your picture," he said, pushing out one hand and clutching my mother with the other. "I'm John Goff."

Whatever feelings I developed that day were genuine, not

pulled up out of the dust to fill pages in my notebook. John Goff proved to be charming and affectionate toward Mother. To me he was guarded and polite. He must have known I had a father at home that I was not seeking to replace. He was sensitive in that regard, not engaging in efforts to win my heart. Instead, I walked among breathtaking displays in relative solemnity. We visited art in all its glory, its simplicities, and complexities, and there were moments I witnessed John Goff's true reverence.

He pulled his glasses to the end of his nose to study the white marble statue of *David*. His eyes passed over it for a long moment. "The original is in Florence," he said finally. "It's too valuable to travel. Magnificent thing, perfectly magnificent." He pushed his glasses back into place. "Isn't art a feast for your senses? Your drawings too, Sydney. We see it all so differently. Even a replica like this one, it's hard to deny it's . . ." He stopped his gushing, unable to summon untried words of praise for the figure.

How they passed the evening after dinner at Columbo's remains a mystery to me. I could only imagine, but I suffered mightily not to. When the cab dropped us at the Hilton, we slid from the back seat and into the teeth of a gale-force wind. We scampered through the big doors and into the lobby. At the elevator John leaned in to kiss me on the cheek, closing in on me with his windblown tangle of hair and his crooked glasses. His lips landed somewhere north of my ear. It was a clumsy maneuver on his part. When he pulled away, I could tell he was less than pleased by the effort.

"I won't be long," Mother said to him. She stepped into the elevator ahead of me. "I'll meet you." She kept up her direction, pointing at the blue neon sign across the lobby that read, "Lounge."

John leaned over to offer a silly wave like he was sending a toddler to daycare. He struck out for the lounge just as the doors went shut. We rode the elevator to the thirty-second floor. Most of me was grateful she accompanied me. Part of me resented the need for it. In the room she scurried around, turning lights on and off in a full-out military sweep of the place.

In the end, she kissed me on the cheek. "I'll have a nightcap with John," she said. "I see so little of him. He's such a dear friend." She kissed me on the cheek again and left.

Everything was neat in the room. Sometime during the day, maids had dressed up the place. The two giant beds were made. There was fruit and wine and fresh flowers. There were extra towels for the spa and the pool folded neatly on the beds. The place was plenty big enough for a family of eight, and suddenly I was feeling very alone.

I stood near the huge expanse of glass, washed in the blue glow of night. I looked out on a million dancing lights and remembered being small. Back then I could spend an hour in the late evening stretched out in the meadow grass beside Zach, peering into a clear sky just as the stars awoke, the two of us, me and Zach, counting stars the way Beepah taught us. Here, adrift in New York City's blueness, there was a lifetime of stars to count, each star the patron saint of something, no doubt.

I undressed in the blue, hoping the eyes of the world had not discovered me as I had discovered them. I pulled on pajamas and rolled the covers back and forth to cover me. I stretched out in the middle of the wide bed, stricken by the enormity of the manmade universe of stars beyond the windows on the thirty-second floor.

I lay in bed contemplating the day just spent. It became clear to me my perceptions of life and loving were destined to change with the dismissal of John Goff from my world. He was there for some years to help define my emotional limits. Those days were filled with tears and laughing and whatever fantasies John prevailed on me. They were playful, but contrived, and after a time, they were no longer enough.

Two hours later I was still awake. I heard the keycard trip the door lock, and I heard the slightest whoosh of the door over the carpet. Mother's voice came to me in the breath of a whisper. "She's asleep," I heard, and I was comforted that she had arrived safely. When the door went silently shut, I caught sight of them standing in each other's arms in the blue light of night. I quietly buried my head beneath my pillow, determined not to emerge until morning.

When morning did come, I rolled my eyes up cautiously to find Mother asleep in the big bed across the room. Her face was a perpetual smile, at least in the short term. That notion brought a tiny burst of laughter because that thought reminded me of something Beep might say had he been there to see the dear woman for himself. The moment brought me fully awake. I realized, over the course of that night and in my dreaming, I had indeed said goodbye to John Goff.

We came home on Sunday. Mother said goodbye to John the same way she had said hello to him the day before. By then I had become less indifferent to their practice of indiscriminate smooching. I believe John was more sensitive than Mother in the matter. His pucker lost much of its enthusiasm whenever his eyes found me watching.

We waved to John and stepped onto the train at Grand Central Station. I had witnessed a piece of Mother's secret life, and she had been willing to allow it. I realized it was never truly up to me to pass judgment or assign its worth. In the end, I felt deep gratitude. I had survived childhood, or so it seemed. In the process, I had named several patron saints while lying in the big bed. Mother's was among them. I assigned her the light at the top of the Empire State Building, because from there, a big piece of the world might be visible in the blue.

The sun was bright by mid-morning. The wind blew out of the east, freshening yet another day. Beep once said to me, "Patron saints have nothing to do all night except keep an eye on you. Anyway, it's mostly an honorary title." Given my preoccupation with the man throughout much of my childhood, perhaps it was John Goff who was my patron saint. Stranger still, perhaps I was his. I held Mother's hand all the way back to Kingston while the train rocked her to sleep.

CHAPTER NINE

It was a Friday, the night Ol' Jolly died. In the front room, his darling wife was about her annual task of knitting children's mittens when a monstrous quake roared up from beneath the earth to shake the dwelling loose of its anchors. Just as it began, it ceased. Not a handful of seconds spanned the whole of it. When the rolling ceased, she scurried to the kitchen only to discover her husband of fifty years sprawled in a heap at the bottom of the stairs. It was not an earthquake after all. It was the death of Ol' Jolly himself.

That night, Beepah stood at the door to the gymnasium looking forlorn. He was easy enough to spot, taller and grayer than anyone in the place. He wore the lost old man look he had perfected over the course of my lifetime. He used it appropriately to garner sympathy or solicit aid and support. I was dancing with classmates in the middle of the gym floor when he appeared at the big double doors.

He surveyed the complete junior high population until our eyes settled on each other. He breathed a sigh. We had arranged for him to pick me up, but his arrival was a curiosity. He was early by at least an hour. When I broke from the pack and went to him, he greeted me with a diminished smile. There was a sorrowful look to him. His eyes scanned the gym, and he acknowledged a teacher or two with a nod of recognition. Finally, when the music stopped and the low buzz of appreciation faded, Beepah quietly came out with it.

"Jolly died," he said.

I was shocked at the news. I looked upon the Jollys as ancient and not long for this world, but Ol' Jolly's eventual passing was nothing I dwelled upon. "I'm sorry," I said, feeling little emotion, but certain I should. It took only a few seconds to think of Ol' Jolly and the place he held in my heart. I threw my arms around Beepah and cried into his shirt.

"I offered to drive Nanny to the hospital," he said. "Who knows how long I'll be? I figured I better get you first."

"How?"

"He fell down the stairs," Beep said and shrugged. The weight of the loss had not yet fully registered with him either. "It was probably a heart attack. We won't know until . . . well, who knows? It took every man who showed up just to get him out the door and down the steps to the ambulance. He sure was a big man, and he was a good neighbor. He was always there to help." Beep held up his wrist and looked at it as if he wore a watch. "We better go," he said.

Some of us had stashed our shoes under the bleachers when the music started. I retrieved mine and hurried back to Beep in a dash. I waved goodbye to my friends. On the short ride home, Beepah regaled me with stories about Ol' Jolly, about how the big man read Zach stories for the entire six hours it took me to be born, and how he became embattled with local entities and denied public access by placing concrete barriers across the road. That memory made Beep laugh. "He spent a night in jail for that one," he said.

Beep reminded me I was not yet in the world when Jolly dug out the earth to create Jolly's pond. Within a few years there was a burgeoning fish population. There were ducks and geese and a giant snapping turtle lurking in its depths. If ever there was a creation built for a boy, Jolly's pond might have been it. And this from a man without children, no heirs at all.

I recall a conversation with Beep only days before Jolly died. I brought a sandwich to the pond in the afternoon and dropped down on the grass next to him. I handed him half of the bologna and cheese with my fingerprints squished into the bread from holding it too tight. Beep took it and thanked me for it and bit off half. He sat for a time, content to watch Zach throw a line into the shallows a few feet off the bank. Beep had a peaceful look on his face.

"You know, Syd, not everybody likes this pond. Some people even think it should be filled up with dirt. They say it's a danger in the neighborhood." Beep pushed more of the sandwich into his mouth, bulging out his cheek. He tossed a crumb to the grass for Tilly. "You know what I think? I think Ol' Jolly saw Zach coming when he dug this pond. I think he was divinely inspired to dig it. That's what I think."

"He had a vision."

"I know this much," he said. "This very spot right here helped mold that boy."

———

With Jolly's passing, the world was destined to change. Normal shifted yet again. Nanny Jolly would never recover fully after the death of her dear husband. She sat in her chair near the front windows surrounded by half-knitted mittens. She had lost the ability to fashion thumbs out of yarn, and so a dozen thumbless mittens lay scattered at her feet.

I reflected on my time there, standing in that warm place where I had spent so many pieces of days when I was small. Since my earliest incarnation, back before Beepah stayed home with us fulltime, I knew the smell of Nanny Jolly's kitchen. I remember sitting in my diaper on the kitchen plank floor, sharing my bottle with a squealing little pig. He came to live in the far corner behind a folding fence. He simply appeared one morning, and of course, we became fast friends. "Panfry," Ol' Jolly dubbed him.

Every morning little Panfry pushed his wet snout through the fence in pursuit of my breakfast bottle. When I stuck the nipple in his mouth, he sucked mightily until the plastic bottle was empty, and it collapsed. I suppose I was indignant. After all, it was my own dear mother's breast milk, and Panfry was a pig. Eventually, and to my good fortune, he got fat and won a transfer from the kitchen to the hog pen out back where he spent his days with his brother Fatback. I saw little of him after that. Besides, he and Fatback mysteriously disappeared the following spring. To this day, I dare not tell Mother it was her own breast milk that made little Panfry fat enough for the butcher.

I had come to the Jolly kitchen to examine the bloodstain left on the pinewood floor when Jolly tumbled to his death. Beep warned me that Jolly bled from a gash above his ear. Nanny covered the red puddle with a braided rug before neighbors arrived on Sunday. None of them seemed to realize they were grinding Jolly's blood into the kitchen floorboards whenever they crossed the braided rug. When they had all departed, I lifted it for a cautious inspection. I could feel the sticky resistance against the rough wood floor. Much of the blood had been wiped up. What remained had hardly begun to dry in the two days since his death.

I took a scrub brush to it. I was obstinate in my efforts, peeling the rug free of the floorboards and hauling it out the back door. I was armed with the brush and a bucket of cool water. I scavenged rubber gloves from beneath the kitchen sink. At last I was on my knees, as prepared as I might ever be, when the foulest of smells hit me. Perhaps my familiarity with Ol' Jolly himself made my revulsion ten times worse. My belly began to twist. Then, to complicate matters, I threw up right in the middle of the sticky swill seeping into the floor.

In the end, if there was to be such a thing, I managed to convert the bloody stain, the size of a small pizza, into the random image of a fluffy pink cloud. Admittedly, it was considerably larger, with swirls created with my scrub brush. It was far more pink than red, assuring that with the passage of time and the proper dose of exorcism, it might not smell so foul.

I told Nanny Jolly goodbye and said I would stop down the next morning after I sent the birds out to fly. "Be careful near the stain on the floor, Nanny. It might be a long time drying."

She smiled at me, her eyes peering over her glasses, lost in a hunt for my face. She dipped down and retrieved two mittens from the floor. One was blue and the other orange with black trim. She looked up again and found me. "Here, dear," she said, handing me the pair. She leaned in and cupped her hand to her mouth. "They don't have thumbs," she confided, amused by her deception in the thumbless-mitten matter.

I pulled them on. They each had a hole for a thumb to exit. I popped my thumbs out and tested them for flexibility, wiggling my bare-naked thumbs nearer her face. "I think you're onto something, Nanny," I said. "Can you make me a pair of white ones for Christmas?"

She scanned her giant yarn basket and came out with an answer right away. "Yes, dear, white mittens for Christmas."

Mom arrived home Monday night to attend Ol' Jolly's funeral on Tuesday morning. She grumbled about the inconvenience of it all. Her work schedule was frantic, and Jolly's death could not have come at a worse time. But then, appearances are everything, was how she put it. Beepah even slept in the big bed on Monday night. Whether they shared physical comforts or simply talked into the night was undetectable to the world beyond the walls. Beep did not fall out of bed. They were pleasant enough over morning coffee, and neither of them betrayed confidence.

No sooner had she come home late Monday evening, she was to depart after the funeral on Tuesday. Martin showed up in the shiny limo to haul her back to New York. Her group, Garland-Price, was to meet with the Marsh-Gainer Group for a working lunch. She informed us all she could not miss it. She got into a snit with Beepah in the driveway over her running start out of the church ahead of Jolly's coffin.

"You hauled ass," Beep said. "That was awkward."

She turned on him immediately. "What do you expect of me, Ben? I gave Martin a time to be here. How was I to know your long-winded shaman would blab on for an hour? I swear!" she blasted him, swinging her purse and catching Beep on the shoulder with it. "That's why I drove my own car, Ben. So I could get the hell out before some other Chatty Cathy had a tongue in my ear. I was doing my best not to disrupt things," she kept on. "You and the children didn't have to follow me. For chrissake! When did your time become so valuable, Ben?" She managed to open the limo's back door. She flung her briefcase across the seat and turned on Beep again. "You try and deal with these assholes in New York! Do you think they care if Ol' Jolly is dead? I can assure you, Ben, they don't give the world's tiniest fuck!" She pinched her thumb against her forefinger like she was mashing a mosquito. She shook it in Beep's face to illustrate the minuteness of the world's tiniest fuck. "It took all I could do to move this meeting! They expect me there!"

Beep grimaced during her entire tirade, realizing he'd opened his mouth and stepped in a pile of unpleasantness. Then he turned around and stepped in it again with the other foot, as if once wasn't good enough. "I'll go down and throw a little dirt on the ol' boy," he said, looking at his watch for effect. Then he added, "If it's not too late, I mean." And he gave his watch yet another look. "It's the least I can do. He's been a good neighbor."

Mother went up on her tiptoes and put her lips near Beep's ear. "I bet it's a big hole in the ground, plenty big enough for both you and Jolly too," she said. "And get rid of that silly watch. I bet it doesn't even work." True enough, the old timepiece was nothing but an occasional accessory to his one brown suit.

By then she was heading toward me and only rolled her head back to issue one more painful promise. "I'll bring flowers to celebrate," she declared. She went directly from that final bit of cruelty to a happy grin and a wave to Zach on the steps.

"Gardenias!" Beep snapped, expressing his sudden preference in flowers. "I like gardenias," he assured her again when she refused to acknowledge him further.

She draped her arm over my shoulder to deliver a warm squeeze. "I'm going to try to get home by late Friday," she said. "Take care of your impossible father."

She kissed me on the forehead while I was thinking about Martin. The two of us shared an awkward smile, and suddenly I was brimming with empathy for the man. He had been helpless in his efforts to ignore Mother's tirade, and he got an earful of it. I found myself hoping she would get into the limo to aid and abet Martin's getaway. When another clumsy smile passed between Martin and I, I was certain I was shouldering the humiliation for the entire family.

Mom passed the driver's window and patted Martin on his jacket sleeve. "Sorry," she said. She slid into the backseat and pulled the door shut. I could not see her through the blackened windows, but I'm certain she was sighing with relief. It occurred to me then, after years of observation, there was a purpose to their angry good-byes. Driveway battles set the stage for apologies and forgiveness. It was foreplay, and as near as I could tell, it accomplished every element required to occasionally deliver her to the basement upon her return home. But then in actuality, what did I know?

CHAPTER TEN

I was to turn twelve in early September. That event alone might have rattled the world at the end of a quiet summer, but what happened only two months earlier was destined to shake every living creature on nearby earth. Jason Lipton got a car, and not just any car. And the chain of events all began early in the morning on the fifth of July.

I went to the barn when the light above the side door clicked to life, casting its dreary yellow glow into the maples nearby. I picked up the empty grain pail and headed for the barn. I scooped a pail of cracked corn and set it to the floor near the door. Zach and Booger were there, moving in the dim light, preparing to depart in the coolness of early morning.

Booger was always anxious, but when he saw me, he tried to come out with something clever. "Come on Zee-man! The trout are havin' heat stroke already."

Zach gave Booger a rap on his backside, then leaned his pole against the workbench and dropped down on one knee. "Hold your pickle, Boogerboy," he said. Zach popped the door to Beep's little refrigerator under the work bench. He shuffled a few beer cans around and snagged a coffee can. The plastic cover was punched full of breathing holes. Zach set the can on the workbench. "We'll need these," he said.

At first Booger offered little more than a sheepish look. "Oh, yea, I forgot the bait," he admitted finally.

I leaned near his ear. "Don't worry, Booger. These are magic worms. I caught them myself in the mist near Jolly's pond. It was two nights ago. It was the perfect rain for night-crawling. Remember?"

"Yippie for you, Sydney . . . and you would know," Booger growled.

That happened just before sunrise. It was early afternoon by the time I decided to step out into the sunshine to greet the most glorious day ever, ninety degrees and the gentlest breeze. There was not a single worry, not a hurt or an ounce of sadness. Of course, should any one of those concerns poke out their ugly head, it might have been seen as an omen.

I thought of that very thing while on my way down Trumpet Hill, and just passing the Campbell home. In that moment, and right in front of me, a sleek black automobile whipped its tail into a ninety degree turn and peeled off the road. It disappeared behind the hedge that ran the length of Emily Lipton's driveway. I watched for a moment, but the car did not reemerge. So there, well hidden, it must have remained.

I found the behavior curious, to say the least. Without another thought, I darted across the road and into the trees. I made my way clear to the trail down the mountain to the place where a stream emptied through a long culvert into Esopus Creek. I clawed my way up and out of the ditch and hurried through the tall grass to a familiar hiding place we had discovered during the apple wars. The falling-down Smoran barn leaned badly toward the Esopus. I peered around a collapsing barn timber. Across the field, I could see Emily Lipton standing on her porch with her arms folded. She watched a big red convertible with its top down roll up the driveway.

I saw them then, Zach and Booger, snaking their way through the tall grass, inching slowly toward Emily's porch.

I gave them a sharp "Psst!"

The man in the convertible stepped into the driveway. The

movement caused me to shrink a little behind the barn timber. The man screwed his shorts up an inch or two. He pushed the car door closed without a decibel of noise, and took a few steps around the front of the big car. He wore black socks almost to his knees and a sleeveless undershirt, the kind of shirt Beep once referred to as a *wife-beater*. I watched it happen, all of it, but it made not a sound. I could almost make out his face, enough to realize I didn't know the man. But there appeared to be a smile there. Zack must have heard my *psst,* because he quickly motioned me to stay put. I ignored him, of course. I flopped down and squirmed my way past the corner of the barn and through the tall grass until I popped up between the two of them.

"Wha'd I miss?" I whispered.

When he saw me, Booger punched Zach in the arm. "What the fuck, Zee-man? We can't catch a break," he hissed at my arrival.

Zach threw his arm across my shoulders. "Stay down, Sydney. You wanna get killed?"

When my head finally poked up again, I watched the man complete his circle around the red car. He walked to the edge of the porch. Emily's arms never unfolded to greet the man. Instead, she appraised the red behemoth parked right in front of her, while he extolled the vehicle's virtues like a pushy salesman: the workmanship perhaps, or the roominess, or the perfect paint job—but then, I heard none of it.

What I did hear clearly was a screen door clap shut. Then "Dad!" came a loud and high-pitched voice. Its enthusiasm rode the gentle breeze clear across an entire field of wild wheat and grasses to reach my ears. One second more and Jason Lipton bounded to the edge of the porch and cleared the four steps in one mighty leap. He landed in a patch of grass near the driveway. They embraced each other with plenty of back-slapping and joyous laughter.

So, now, we knew. The man Jason identified as his dad was indeed none other than the infamous Willie Lipton, the one man Emily was quick to disparage at the school bus stop over the past few years, such was her disdain for the man. Yet, Jason expressed his devotion to the man with a firm embrace and a kiss on the cheek.

Willie walked to the edge of the driveway and looked out toward the hedge. He pulled a white handkerchief from his back pocket and flapped it open. He raised it high over his head and whirled it in a circle. Almost instantly, an engine roared to life. An exhaust cloud rolled up and over the thick green hedge. The beast of a car appeared at last, fishtailing in a tight half-circle in the grassy field. Then it was on the asphalt again, screeching tires, growling engine, aiming its wrath up the Lipton's driveway, gathering might for a full-frontal assault. It appeared in the sunlight at last. It was not black after all, but midnight blue.

At last, the beast could not be restrained. It defied the reins that held it and came charging unchecked, fishtailing almost out of control, spewing gravel clear across the road and into the ditch.

Two hundred feet up the long driveway, the machine skidded to a stop. It stirred a voluminous cloud of dust left in its wake to slowly settle into the convertible's red leather seats.

Booger Sullivan raised his head from the crook of his sweaty arm. "Fuck me. I almost shit in my shorts," he said.

Zach muffled a laugh. "What do you mean, *almost*, Boogerboy?"

We laid there, baking in the brick-oven heat for another half hour, until we had all added a few shades of blister-red to our skin tones. It was dangerous to be there, yet dangerous to move, if Booger was to be believed. Booger had heard some gossip, second or third hand, of course. To Gracie Campbell, the purveyor-in-chief of such news, Willie Lipton was a killer, and Gracie's word was good as gold to Booger.

"They could kill us all and peel outa here in those two cars and go hide out in Philadelphia before anybody finds our lifeless, sunburnt bodies," was Booger's gruesome assessment of our dire situation.

Zach said the car was a Ford Mustang, but he couldn't tell the model year from so far away.

Booger agreed. "Yup, mustang."

Just then, the mustang started up again. Jason was in the driver's seat. Willie was the passenger. Jason slipped it into reverse and the car responded with a jerky beginning. It swung up the road squealing a little, as if Jason was that quickly familiar with the car. I heard the shifting gear respond with another screech. The mustang disappeared up Trumpet Hill in a flash of midnight blue.

When the mustang's jet wash dissipated into harmless turbulence and diminishing noise, and the giant dust clouds that helped conceal us drifted just above the tall grass, the three of us took our leave. After all, while Jason and Willie were off for a test drive, there were fewer eyes to find us lurking in the tall grass, and there were fewer killers near the Lipton porch. We squirmed backward in retreat until we found ourselves in the shadow of the old barn at last. Once there, we could get off our bellies. We felt safer in the shadows. We caught a breath, then headed for the trees, keeping the cover of the barn at our backs. We made our way to the trail up the mountain. Zach and Booger headed off to collect their fishing gear near the Esopus. I headed home, back up the mountain, back where there was no talk about getting killed.

The following day, I was in the pickup truck when Beep wheeled it into the Lipton driveway. When he stepped out of the truck, Emily came out onto the porch and gave a wave and smile. She wore shorts and a halter top. Her skin was olive and I had never seen quite so much of it. Not that she was modest by any stretch, but I rarely saw her dressed in anything but her white hygienist clothes. She came down the two steps in her bare feet and stopped in the soft grass just at the edge of the gravel.

She twisted a little to peer through the open window. "Hi, Syd," she said to me.

I had my knees pulled up and clasped in my arms. My feet were dusty to the ankles. I planted them against the dash. "Hi, Emily," I said, exercising my right as a soon-to-be twelve-year-old adult for the first time.

She was onto me immediately. I had never called her Emily before that day. She reached through the open window and patted me on the knee. "That's right. You're about to have a birthday yourself," she somehow remembered. "Congratulations," she said as though she was welcoming me to womanhood.

I'm sure I smiled sheepishly. "Not until September," I said.

"That's right. Last year your father brought a birthday balloon to the bus stop. I remember that."

Beep gave the mustang a thorough visual inspection. "Zach told me about it. I had to stop and see it for myself." He spun around, then jerked his thumb back over his shoulder. "There's one dangerous machine," he concluded with his head cocked in anticipation of things to come. "Sure is pretty, though."

"Oh, it's pretty," Emily said, her arms folding across her chest. "Sonny Jim Pitcher wouldn't steal an ugly car."

Beep issued his usual brand of humor. "Sonny Jim Pitcher? An orange juice spokesman?"

She laughed. "He's Willie's partner in crime," she said, rolling her eyes. "Of course, If you ask him, he runs Philly's north end like he's the mayor or something. He drove the mustang up here, and thank God he was here to take Willie Lipton back to Philly where he belongs. Jason went right up to Sonny Jim and gave him a hug. He calls him Uncle Sonny. It breaks my heart."

Beep climbed back into the truck and pulled the door shut. Emily came around the front, hobbling over crushed stone and grimacing with each step. She stood at the driver's door finally and stretched enough to peer through the open window. "I should have wore shoes," she grumbled, smiling bravely through the pain. "If there is one reason I left Philly, it's Sonny Jim Pitcher. He runs drugs and money. I'm sure I don't know the half of it." She gave a sideways glance toward the mustang. "Carjacking is one of his sidelines. He gets kids involved. That's how Jason ended up here with me. It was this or juvie." She thumbed the mustang with disgust. "Once upon a time that mustang led a pristine life, but it's dirty now."

Emily said the visit lasted less than an hour. "Sonny Jim had a big shit-eating grin just to piss me off," she said, expressing her repugnance. "He makes my skin crawl. Willie spent a lot of the time near the front porch, talking me up about reconciliation." She yelped at the notion. "Yeah, right! Like that's gonna happen. Finally, the two of them got into the Monte Carlo and headed back to Philly. They left the mustang, of course. Willie made a big show of that."

"Zach said there was a big red car," Beep recalled.

Emily threw her head back. "Oh, yes, the Monte Carlo."

"I believe I saw that car in the photograph on your mantle. I got nosey the day me and Syd fixed your kitchen drain. You were sitting high in the saddle, on top of the back seat in a bikini, no less. Miss Philadelphia is what I remember."

"I'm sure it was a little more than a bikini, Ben, please," she said, recalling her days as a Philadelphia beauty queen, and all these years later, sounding a little embarrassed by her preoccupation at the time.

Beep nodded his surrender. "We all see what we wanna see, I guess."

"It was thirty degrees and raining. A fireman came down off his firetruck and wrapped me in his fireman coat. I should have married the guy. It might have changed my life for the better."

"What was that, ten years ago?"

"More like twenty, but thanks," she said and shook her head. "I can't believe Willie kept that car all these years. He said, 'the only reason I bought that car is because you look so damn good in it.'" Emily rolled her eyes, mocking Willie's words. "Anyway, that's what he said yesterday. Twenty years too late, if the truth be told."

That was it, the whole story, at least as much of it as I could ingest. It was easy to see that Emily was still nursing the pain caused by a broken marriage and a life she could never condone. In all those years, she was never able to forgive the man for whatever misdeeds he had perpetrated on the world at large, and on her and his own son.

Beepah let me in on some of the details the next morning in the aviary, but they had talked quite a while, in and out of the truck. I believe he chose not to tell me everything. No doubt there were more nefarious details. I knew very little about cars and theft and all the complications surrounding the mustang, but whatever the details, they were unsettling to Beep. Emily did not want the mustang there, and yet, there it stayed.

"She needed to tell somebody," was how Beep described their exchange. "As usual, I got in the barrel and stuck my nose through the blow hole." He tapped me on the rear with a gentle warning. "Don't talk about this, Syd. Some things are better left alone. Jason Lipton and his father are probably two of them."

———

The mustang was visible on the hill almost daily after that. Screeching tires imperiled neighborhood ears, sometimes far into the night. Most people on the hill were aware of the feud that continued to fester between Jason Lipton and Beep. The squealing tires were surely for Beepah's benefit. Beep said little. The burnt rubber stripes were evidence enough, if neighbors dared complain.

As for those of us at the bus stop, we were pleased. Jason rarely showed up anymore. With his absence, there was less to fear. Often, after we'd gathered in the coolness of September mornings, the dark-blue mustang came charging to the end of the gravel driveway, growling and skidding to a stop. The little kids retreated in a cluster.

I watched the mustang roll slowly onto the main road and coast past us. Jason often showed a threatening face from behind the wheel. I did my best to present a firm jaw. At twelve, I had come to fear him less, and I wanted him to know it. There was an added comfort when Zach was nearby. Zach had grown tall and fearless. He rarely concerned himself with Jason Lipton, and for Jason, Zach's indifference alone was torment enough.

There came a day in late September, Zach had earned an hour of detention. I rode the bus without him and headed up Trumpet Hill on foot. Halfway up was where Jason Lipton slowed the mustang, squealing the tires a little as it pulled up beside me. Without a look, I knew it was him.

The mustang lurched, then squealed again, inching forward. "Hey, Syd, wanna ride?"

I had not conquered my fear, after all. It rose in me yet again. I didn't want to be afraid. I wanted to confront him bravely. In that very moment, I realized not a word had passed between us in five years. I was a little girl then, back when my eyes found Jason Lipton standing in the pale light on the staircase. His words had lived in me since that day, pitching me into fits of terror. When I woke from the nightmare, his words stirred anguish in my very soul. *I'm going to kill your father.* Those were the words I heard.

The fear never left me, although I struggled to dismiss it. It was an illogical kind of fear. After all, it was a threat spoken by a mere child barely bigger than me at the time. Still, I feared his very presence would render me speechless even though I never tested the theory when he was around. Even this time I had not summoned a single word to offer up, nothing clever, nothing brave came to me. I slung my backpack to my other shoulder and quickened my pace, hoping to reach home before he said anything more that might test my ability to speak.

The mustang lurched again. Jason drew hard on his cigarette, then flicked it into the brush across the road. He blew a big smoke cloud that rolled out the open window. "Come on. I'll take you on a ride to the top. I'll show you what this car can do."

I stopped finally. I had yet to reach the Jolly's driveway. That meant it was a long way to ours, and I refused to let running be an option. I would have to speak. I let my eyes pass the length of his car while I collected a thought, hoping I had the power to say it, hoping above all else it didn't sound stupid. When our eyes met, I did my best to meet his piercing glare, and I said it. "I know you can leave black stripes all the way from the top of the hill to here."

He laughed at that, and rightfully so. It sounded stupid. "I bet your old man likes that," he said.

I started walking again. "He never said," I managed.

"I hear he drinks a lot," Jason said with a laugh. "Remind him I shoot pigeons. Sometimes even bigger things. Tell him to stay away from my mother." He slammed the pedal to the floor and the mustang fishtailed almost into the ditch.

The burning rubber raised a noxious smoke cloud into my face. I hurried up the hill to our driveway and sprinted under the cherry trees, then up the two steps to the porch. The door closed behind me just as the screeching tires began their angry descent back down the hill.

A week after that encounter with Jason, Zach came home late from school. It was a Friday. I watched for him through the front window. He walked up the hill alone, carrying his pail of turtle bait from behind the Sullivans' garage. The front of his shirt was soaked in blood. It ran from his nose unchecked. When he appeared in the driveway covered in blood, I hurried to the door and met him on the porch. He set the bait pail down and pulled his shirt off over his head. He wadded it up and pushed it against his nose.

"What happened?"

"I took one in the nose from Jason Lipton," he said, talking through blood-clogged nostrils. "It got me bleeding, is all."

"What started that?"

"He stopped his car in the middle of the road," Zach said with a shrug. "He came over and grabbed me by the shirt, so I popped him one. That got him going and he punched me back." Zach pushed his nose in the air so I could see up inside it. "One good thing . . . I can't smell this." He raised the bait pail toward my face and laughed a gurgling laugh.

I retched a little, if only to amuse him, and I peered up into his busted nose. "It looks like it hurts," I said.

"Where's Beep?"

"Gone for chicken feed, I guess."

"Grab a towel," he said. "Meet me at the stream."

I went back through the house and fumbled in the bathroom for an old towel. I went out and across the grass at a trot. Zach was in front of me. He set his bait bucket near the barn door and strolled off toward the stream, turning back once to beckon me onward with a cheery, bloody smile. When he got to the stream, he kicked off his shoes and stripped down to his underwear. He sat on a rock and let the icy water wash over his feet.

I handed him the towel. "You look like holy hell," I said, giving his nose a more thorough inspection. I cocked my head and peered up into the bloody darkness. "He sure nailed you," was the best I could offer.

Zach scooped up a handful of water and splashed it in his face, then he dropped the towel between his legs and into the stream. He put it to his face and worked it over all the tender places. When he removed it, the damage was still evident but less repulsive.

"I popped him first, a good one too," Zach said, summoning as much pride as he could, smiling to expose teeth smeared with blood. "He's cleaning gobs of blood out of his new car right now . . . either that, or he's got a big, fat lip. Serves him right. What an asshole."

I watched the water tumbling past his ankles, soaking the towel and stretching the length of it over rocks and a tangle of branches. Blood rinsed free and twisted in the current, the water fading to pink for the briefest moment, then to the purest clear.

"You should tell Beep."

He bathed his face in the towel again, then pulled it away to inspect for blood. "I thought about it. The last thing I need is Beep fighting my fights," he said. He slapped the towel into the water and finished mopping up his face. He put his finger to his nose and pushed it up for me to get another look inside.

I gave him my professional appraisal again. "It's gross," I said.

He blew his nose into the towel and dropped it at his feet to rinse. "Anyway, it would only make things worse. Beep's a man, and men can't go around slapping the shit outa kids, even assholes like Jason Lipton. Beep would go to jail for it."

My head dropped a little. "I didn't tell him either," I admitted.

"What?"

"Last week, Jason stopped me on the road on my way home

from the bus. He tried to get me to ride in his car." My eyes followed the last of the pink water disappearing over the rocks. "I mean, he asked me and I told him no way."

"Stay away from him, Sydney," Zach said. He jumped up from the rock and waved his finger at me. "Stay away from Jason Lipton." He slung the towel over a tree limb and stretched it out to dry. "I'll tell you something . . . if anything happens to you, he'll have more than Beep to worry about. I might kill the asshole myself."

CHAPTER ELEVEN

Somewhere I heard, Normal is a town in Illinois. So, depending on who you ask, normal is a place, not simply a tolerable level of global static. But there was peace at home, as much as we could expect. Mom and Beep spoke mostly in guarded tones. Beep slept in the basement almost every night. In fact, the ping pong table had been permanently folded and stowed away to make room for an old bed he hauled home from a thrift store. The addition of the bed gave the basement a certain permanence, as far as bedrooms go. But even that new arrival did little to prevent Beep from tumbling to the floor on occasion, and the concrete proved an even more malicious adversary.

Mom arrived home late on Friday. Come Saturday morning, I was at the table sipping milk when she slipped into the kitchen from the catacombs where Beepah slept. The basement door eased open with the slightest whoosh of air, then clicked shut with an echo from the stairwell. Her stealth amused me, as if bedding down with Beepah was an affront to normal rather than a vital ingredient to it.

Her hair was tousled, but rarely enough to betray her whereabouts or her purpose for descending into the basement on a Friday night. Her slippers went quietly over the tile floor toward the counter. The coffee pot was on a timer and was just gurgling to completion. She swept the hair over her ears and took a cup from the rack.

Only minutes before, Cowboy's first crow of the morning

brought me from sleep's abyss. The old rooster was only clearing his scrawny throat. Even that woke me, so tuned I was to his vocals. Some mornings Cowboy's crowing was little more than proof of his belligerence. He wanted out of the coop to fulfill his secondary purpose in life, his gravelly crowing meant to wake the dead.

Some mornings I loved the old bird. This was not one of those mornings, and I was slow to accommodate him. I had lain awake half the night anticipating Mother's arrival. She still managed to slip in while I slept.

I sat quietly in the early coolness following her soft footsteps slip across the hard kitchen floor, all the while reluctant to wake completely. I allowed the hood of my sweatshirt to keep my sleepy face in shadows.

"Morning, Mother."

"Oh, good morning, sweetheart," she said, surprised while stifling a yawn. She poured a cup of coffee and collected it from the counter with both hands. She shuffled across the floor to the table. She set her coffee carefully in place and slid into the chair across from me. "Have you been out to the birds?"

I shook my head inside the hood, as if she noticed. "I was thinking about Nanny and Ol' Jolly," I said. "I never wrote much in my notebook, but I found a drawing from way back when I was a kid. They both look like ripe tomatoes, both of them . . . except he's wearing bib overhauls. I forgot to dress her. I gave her a belly button. She has a big smile and a basket of eggs. I guess that's how I saw them back then."

"The poor, dear woman," Mom said.

"Did I tell you, Ol' Jolly cracked his head when he fell down the stairs? He was bleeding until the ambulance came. Anyway, there was a puddle of blood. Nanny covered it with a braid rug before people came on Sunday. The whole thing got sticky and smelly. I went on Sunday to wash the floor."

Mom was put off, nearly lost for words. She covered her mouth with her hand and managed to mumble through her fingers. "Oh dear, they left that to you?" she said.

I ignored her feigned concern. Instead, I held up my hands to show off my mittens. "Nanny made these."

She looked at the mittens with my thumbs poking out. We both snickered quietly.

"I think they're cool," I said.

She took a timid sip of hot coffee and set the cup back to the table. "I can't believe your father left that for you."

I reminded her, "Beep doesn't like blood, especially peoples' blood," and I shrugged. "It's from the war."

"Even so, wiping up Jolly's blood didn't give you nightmares? It would me," she admitted. "Anyway, it must not. You're a brave soul, aren't you?" She cocked her head, attempting to peer inside my hood to meet my eyes, but to no avail. She rocked back in her chair, mildly frustrated. "I peeked in on you last night. I got home so late. Sure enough, you were sleeping like a baby."

I might have told her I laid awake most of the night expecting her to arrive. Instead, I said, "I must have been dreaming about you, Mother, and here you are." And as near as I could tell, my sarcasm went unnoticed.

"I was exhausted. I slept in the car all the way home," she said. "Poor Martin. He's been driving me back and forth to New York forever."

I decided to hold off on comments about poor Martin. After all, there were no fights in the driveway at midnight. The good man escaped to the sound of a purring engine, and if he listened really hard, fairy music filled the air. "Are you finished in New York?" I asked her instead.

"Of course not," she said, grumbling. "I think preliminaries are done. I can barely tell anymore." She clicked her fingernails on the table. "I'm thinking about taking some vacation time at Christmas. I might even take my children to Hawaii . . . you know, someplace tropical."

I began to ease my face out of the shadows. "I've never been someplace tropical," I said, pulling the hood back completely to announce the obvious glitch in her plan. "You'll never get Beep to go. He never goes that far from home."

She took another cautious sip of coffee and shrugged. "We'll go without him," she quickly announced. "Somebody has to stay behind and feed the chickens. Better him than you, my darling."

Beep did not fare so well with Ol' Jolly gone and Mother ping-ponging between Trumpet Hill and Lower Manhattan for meetings and dinners and other important affairs. Occasionally, she slipped into the basement upon her return and slept with Beep. Coffee time the next morning could be mystifying, for me at least. The talk was friendly. Other times she went weeks without venturing to the bed in the basement. "Conjugal visits," I once heard a prison warden on television call them. The visits were rewards for good behavior, although I never knew what sacrifice was made to earn one. All I knew was they became rare indeed in the Bowden basement, near as I could tell.

I think Beep was sad in those days. He kept up with the birds, often beating me to the kennel in early morning. He greeted me cheerfully when I arrived. But his mood often faltered when news came on the radio. He even pined for the days of Paul Spriole's gloomy signoffs to bolster his depression.

He continued to visit Emily Lipton, but even I could not unscramble the nature of their friendship. Visits with Emily genuinely cheered him, at least for a time. If the truth be known, Emily was sharing time with Sheriff Micah Nash. The sheriff's car often appeared in her driveway and sometimes stayed for an hour or more. Emily even stopped visiting the bus stop, and Beep quickly became aware of the sheriff's influence over her.

Beep filled the void by visiting McCutchen's Bar and Grill. Zach and I often arrived home after school to find him gone. He stumbled in, often after dark.

One night I looked for Zach after a basketball game. He was nowhere to be found, not in the gymnasium or out front of the high school. I suspected he had departed with his friends, assuming Beep would be there to collect me for the ride home. I'm sure he believed that very thing. I searched for Beep's pickup truck up and down the street. He was not there waiting like he always had been before. I even tried to phone him. I pulled my phone from my back pocket and punched in the call. That was a waste. Beep rarely carried his phone.

That night, I began the three-mile walk home, expecting to meet Beepah somewhere along the way. The street and sidewalks bustled with rowdy students under the lights. People were overjoyed. The Raging Rams won. There were packs of kids singing the familiar fight song. Horns blasted. The night was cool and festive. When I turned the corner along Esopus Creek, the glow of the streetlights diminished little by little. Darkness poured in to fill the void. I was alone then, but for the occasional oncoming lights splashing over the pavement. When lights assaulted from the front, I stepped from the asphalt, searching the slender shoulder for good footing.

A car made the turn at my back. The headlights shot a beam wildly across the road, then jerked it wildly back again. It settled into a steadier track, bathing the road out front in yellow light. I could see again and welcomed it.

As the car approached, the beam of light crawled the length of me, up my legs and up my back, until the whole of me was in the spotlight, my own shadow stretching out in front of me for an entire football field. The engine slowed, and I knew in that instant who it was. I had heard the sound before. The mustang!

I picked up my pace. The car slowed. I stepped into the gravel to let it pass. When the mustang had almost come to a complete stop, I turned to confront Jason Lipton smiling at me.

"You shouldn't be out here alone, Syd," he said. "You never know who's driving around after a ballgame. Come on. I'll give you a ride."

Car lights appeared over the rise. I prayed it was Beepah's truck. If it were him, I would not feel compelled to make this decision. As it approached, I could see it was not a pickup truck, and when the mustang headlights hit it, there was a flash of green. My heart sank a little. It was not Beep. The car slowed to clear us and sped off, leaving the road behind me in total darkness again. The mustang's tires screeched. Smoke swirled into a tangle above the asphalt, then all fell silent again.

I looked far up the road to the top of the rise where flashing lights would signal the school bus arriving come early Monday morning. But for now, home was two miles away and it was dark. Jason Lipton's offer sounded genuine, but I expected he was good at that when he chose to be. "Hornswoggled" was how Beep referred to the deception. I considered all the things that could go wrong. He was sure to say awful things about Beep. I could get my hair yanked until it bled. That one would be tough to explain to Zach. I thought hard about Jason's past behaviors, and I wanted my fear to end. I wanted to find an ounce of good in him.

"Okay," I said.

I hurried around the back and through the burning-rubber cloud that lingered. I opened the door and slid down into the leather seat. He looked at me and smiled. He stomped on the gas.

The rear tires screeched again. The mustang fishtailed. I closed my eyes and held my breath until he eased up on the gas. The mustang rolled into a smooth track along the creek.

We were at the bottom of Trumpet Hill in seconds. He barely slowed when he made the turn. The mustang growled its way up the hill with the sound of Bruce Springsteen blasting out the windows loud enough to rock the world. It was the purest mix of raw terror and exhilaration I had ever felt. All I could wish for at that moment was a longer ride.

We blew past the Bowden farm doing eighty. I managed to look past Jason. Beepah's truck was not in the driveway. At the top, Jason cranked the wheel and stood on the gas long enough to create a giant black donut where he had left so many over the months since his birthday.

I said nothing, but he must have sensed the excitement the ride stirred in me. He pointed the mustang downhill and pulled it to the curb. He turned off the lights and cut the engine. He leaned over and pulled my head to him, mashing his face into mine, snaking his tongue past my lips and into my mouth. It felt strange, but it was the taste of his cigarettes that forced me to try and pull away. I was trapped against the back of the seat, and he came at me again, this time without hesitation, driving his tongue into my mouth, pushing his hand past the buttons on my shirt, searching, squeezing the flesh inside. There was little there. Mother called them buds once when she surprised me fresh from a shower, but it was Jason's frenzied search that disturbed me most—his hand pawing inside my shirt. I felt suddenly defenseless. The feelings were frighteningly strange, and my shirt was flimsy armor. It did nothing to protect me. For the first time in my life, that barrier had been breached.

There was a burst of light. Another car was coming up the hill at a good clip. The engine was growling. The headlight beams were bouncing on the asphalt, then sun-bursting against the mustang windshield.

Jason squirmed down in the seat. "Get down," he said, pushing on the back of my head, forcing me below the dashboard.

I felt the sting of humiliation as he attempted to pretzel me toward the floor. I was slow to react to whatever threat he was sensing. Finally, it came to me. I was underage by a considerable margin, me being only twelve. And getting caught with a twelve-year-old with nothing but boob buds could cause enormous damage to his reputation.

I was not only frightened. I was angry. I refused to shrink beneath the dashboard to preserve whatever was left of his withering libido. Of course, in that moment, little of that sophisticated analysis truly found me. Instead, I pushed back against his hand.

He snatched a handful of my hair. His message was clear, strained through clenched teeth. "Stay down, you little bitch," he snarled. He jerked his hand from the back of my head and gave the ignition key a frantic twist just as the new arrival made the circle around the cul-de-sac. The mustang revved quietly, then eased away from the curb. Jason hit the lights and the mustang rolled down Trumpet Hill.

I was silent. I owed him nothing. We had not become friends in the course of that moment. I had said nothing to him except one simple word when I accepted the ride. *Okay* put me in his car. *Okay* gave him a free pass into my mouth and inside my shirt.

A minute later he slowed to a stop along the road in front of my driveway. He seemed agitated, wrestling with the gear shift, and twisting his neck to peer through the trees toward the top of the hill. No headlights showed, but he was eager to make his getaway without being seen again.

He grabbed me by the arm before I could escape. "We'll do this again. You can be sure of that," he said. He gave me a shove when he released me, tossing me toward the door. "Someday we'll be alone again. You'll see."

I jumped out and raced up the driveway toward the front steps. I heard the mustang door close with a dull thud. I heard music playing, first quietly, then louder, something almost operatic, a crescendo drowning out the fairy music and the other sweet noise in my life. When I climbed the steps, I could see the mustang over my shoulder. It slipped away into the night making not a single sound of its own.

CHAPTER TWELVE

The birds began returning to the aviary flight deck just as Beep arrived at the kennel gate. There was excitement in the rafters when he opened the coop door. A few pinfeathers floated down like snow. He reached over the door and switched on the radio. Paul Spriole was back on the airwaves after wandering for forty days and nights in a jobless wasteland. He'd been credited, after all, with collapsing the station's happiness index or some such gauging mechanism. Beep's foul mood some mornings was proof of that.

The producers brought aboard the bubbly Amanda Nufeldt. In Amanda's world it was warm and sunny. Traffic moved at a comfortable pace, and very few bad things happened in the world without generous compromise. "An exchange of rocket-fire near the Syrian border ended with no confirmed deaths," Amanda reported. "In other words, both sides missed and nobody died," she gushed.

In other words, according to Beep, we were riding on the Good Ship Lollipop, searching for Whoville all over again. "Come get these eggs, Syd." He turned his cap to receive the eggs and dropped it to a bale of straw.

I took it to mean everybody was getting fresh straw and he wanted the eggs out of the way. I slid from the freezing rock wall and stood, rubbing my tail to bring life back to it. The numbness departed and pain set in like fire for a moment. I retrieved my notebook and headed for the coop door, giving ol' Cowboy a nudge with my boot. He was already in the scratch yard, having rolled in from Neptune or somewhere and landing in this strange world. He tumbled in as he had every morning of his adult life, yet he cranked his neck in utter dismay upon arrival. His eyes bugged in their efforts to discover one single recognizable feature. Finding none, he strutted across the yard, stopping once to crow.

"We'll get snow tonight," Beep said. "I can feel it. I wouldn't need Spriole to tell me that. I'm changing out these nests to give the birds more cover."

There was a clean place on the straw. I dropped my notebook there and went along shooing stubborn hens and gathering up the eggs. There were seven eggs in all. I felt their warmth through my mittens when I placed them in the baseball cap. Barring a complete reversal of the polar vortex, it would be the last morning I would bring my writing to the rocks until spring. My fingers grew colder each day, and it was impossible to write, even wearing Nanny's thumbless mittens.

I was destined to spend those early hours during the approaching freeze scribbling in my notebook and thinking of Mother and Beepah and Zach. It had been some weeks since Jason Lipton kissed me with his tongue. I had not told Zach, nor anyone but Grandmother. After a time, I vowed to be silent. Telling Zach was not an option. I feared for him because he was fearless for himself. I had already helped him clean the busted nose he received from a run-in with Jason. This one would be worse. Zach would take it upon himself to protect me or seek retribution. I was certain of it.

Grandmother's opinion and advice mattered deeply to me. With her, it was never necessary to explain. There was no psych testing to untangle whatever perversions were festering inside my head. Grandmother was far gentler in her approach, but she often took eons delivering a quiet message, sometimes while I slept. I waited, patience being a virtue, just not one of mine.

Jason's promise still loomed clearly. He had assured me we would do it again. I continued to anticipate the moment with worry. I learned nothing in the brief passage of time since he plowed my mouth with his tongue. It was impossible to expect the next experience would somehow be less repulsive. In fact, the foul taste lingered. Even the blue mustang rolling past, belching smoke, enlivened the unpleasant memory.

"Don't fret," Beep once said to me. "Spring will come again. It almost always does."

I stepped into the scratch yard and looked overhead. Pigeons straggled back from their morning flight, popping through the trap gate. Chickens made their way out the swing door to the scratch yard where Cowboy was down from his morning bellowing and looking for a ride.

Paul Spriole's voice came loud and clear over the radio, spewing news about a capsized truck near the west end of the Wurts Street Bridge. "A tractor trailer overturned early this morning, spilling frozen hams almost to the banks of the Hudson River. Crews are on the scene cleaning up the carnage, tossing hams into bucket loaders and highway department dump trucks. Traffic is at a crawl, thanks to rubberneckers slowing to peruse dinner options."

I went out the coop door. "Bye, Beepah, if I don't see you," I said.

"You'll get to the bus?"

"I'll go down with Zach."

Beep's pitchfork rattled through the nesting boxes. In my wake his shout of pure joy rose up from the aviary. "Spriole's back! Ham dinner tonight!" he shouted after me.

Beepah was right. Spring did come again. Winter passed with only minor incidents. Christmas came and went without a visit to someplace tropical. Hawaii was barely mentioned, but the promise from Mother of destinations tropical was extended, meaning simply, someday we would go. She herself disappeared for a week in early February without fanfare. Beep said she was in Italy for work. A week later she exited the shower and stood in a towel in front of the mirror. She had tan lines from a bikini I never saw. I could only surmise, somewhere in Italy it was sunny and warm in February.

Beep began spending more time at McCutchen's Bar and Grill. "The boys need my council," was how he once put it to Mom. She scoffed at that, but otherwise protested little. When he came home, he went straight to the basement to sleep. There were nights he did not come home at all. His truck appeared at Emily Lipton's house frequently during the winter, often after a snowstorm or when Jason was mysteriously absent. I only found out later Jason was spending more time in Philadelphia. The why of it was far beyond my scope, but his absence was a comfort.

I spent hours stretched across my bed, writing letters to Grandmother and praying to the Tooth Fairy for guidance. Both were beacons of hope and wisdom to me. Grandmother may have spoken to me on the matter of Jason Lipton. Her message arrived simply over the passage of time, gently urging me to be patient but vigilant while Jason disappeared from my life to pursue one of his own. I hoped for such a thing, while the recurring memory washed quietly from my thoughts.

I grew an inch during the winter and my breasts began to show promise. Mother had not seen me naked any time in recent memory. She did tell me once to give my breasts a chance. She picked up the hair dryer and switched it on, then off again. She pulled a part in her wet hair and grumbled at the gray roots.

"Gravity took mine after you were born," she said, pushing her left breast upward draped in the towel. She let it freefall. "Count your blessings, dear."

I knew she was getting ready to head for New York. It was the middle of the week, and she was about to go off with her briefcase and a small bag of clothes and catch the train out of Kingston. I could watch for Martin. If by chance he showed up with his shiny black limo, the trip was on the up and up. If not, it was a ruse and John Goff was about to be visited. I no longer made queries unless she encouraged them, and candidness from her was rare.

"I have meetings," she said, switching off the dryer again. She pulled another part in her hair and scowled. "I might see friends," she confided. "There's an art show at the college."

I decided her comment was encouragement enough. Besides, I was certain she was referring to John Goff. "How is he?"

"He's wonderful. I'll tell him you asked," she said, still pushing her hair around in search of signs of early aging. "You and I should go down there soon and walk the campus in Greenwich Village. It's a beautiful place, only a building or two. It's been a couple years since we visited New York together. John always shows interest in your drawings. He could be patronizing, I suppose, but I don't believe that. I'm no judge of talent, but I know people. I believe John sees real promise in your drawings. We'll be talking colleges in a few years. He could be valuable to your future." She slapped me playfully on the shoulder. "We'll go bra shopping," she teased.

I offered a sheepish smile. "That's a big train ride for such a small brassiere," I said.

That made her laugh. "We'll make a weekend of it. We can see a show, have dinner at Columbo's. We always enjoy that."

I was pretty sure who the *we* was, because I had only eaten at Columbo's once and that was two or three years ago. I remembered the name, but it held no fascination for me. This time

promised to be more memorable, with John Goff ogling my new
training bra from across the table at Columbo's. In fact, from the
Theater District to Saks Fifth Avenue, all of New York would soon
know of my physical inability to fill a cup-less Wonderbra. Then,
they tell their friends, and so the excitement builds.

It was early morning. The sun was in the trees, breaking into scattered patches of light over the barn roof. The birds were
waiting to fly. Zach had not tumbled from his bed to greet the
middle of the week with disdain. I doubt Mom knew the hour
when she offered to drop us at the bus stop. It was a full hour early.
She was trying to be motherly in her offer, but I saw the truth in
her eyes. She was hoping all the while not to be bothered.

She threw her arm around my neck to pull me closer. Her
cheek brushed mine. "Bye, sweetheart," she said.

In that moment I knew how much I loved her, and I knew how
difficult it would always be to tell her so. I did not cry when she left,
not since I was a little girl. Nor did I show grand emotion upon her
return. What I do know, always upon her arrivals home, a breath
came out of me . . . a breath suffering for release from a place near
my heart. "Bye" was all I managed.

"Love to Zach and your Beepah. I can't believe they're not up.
I forget sometimes, you're the early riser in the family." She pulled
on one glove, then dug for her keys in her purse. "Keep your phone
on, dear. I'll call if I'm delayed. Otherwise, I'll see you Friday," she
said, putting her hand to my cheek.

Martin never showed up with his shiny black limo. Mother left
in her white BMW for the drive to the train station in Kingston.

Saturday morning was thick with sunshine and colored sky.
Just as the sun breeched the horizon to the east Cowboy cleared
his pipes. His boisterous medley scattered the deer grazing in the
backyard and brought groggy neighbors grumbling their way into
a new day. I descended the steps in the hour straddling dawn and

went across the kitchen to the drone of Beep's television humming upward through the floor. I sipped milk and watched the world through the backdoor window. The sky began to shed its color. There was light enough to watch the deer grazing, ever vigilant in the morning mist. An owl flew low over Jolly's pond, returning to his hollow lair high in a rotting oak.

In those days of late March, spring's musty air invaded every space. Even near the kitchen door I could smell mold and fern spores that rode in through the cracks on a wisp of wind. Grass was greening. Finches and jays were busy in the sparse light. I thought just then it was time to return to the rock wall with my notebook. Grandmother would be pleased to feel the earth thawing around her. Suddenly, I was eager to draw her a picture to remind her of spring.

The coffee pot gurgled to completion. Beep's footsteps were on the basement stairs. The door clicked open, and he walked into the kitchen scratching his head. "Morning, Syd," he said. He went to the coffee pot and poured a cup. "The basement toilet is backed up," he said, as if it was simply a fact of nature finally fulfilled. "Of course, I don't see it until I'm standing ankle deep, pissing in my boot."

"I'm wise to you, Beepah. That sounds like something Louie King would say just for its shock value."

He ignored me. "There's too much water in the ground and no place for it to go, so it comes out through the toilet. I'll have to move my headquarters to the big bed for the foreseeable future. Your mother probably misses me anyway." He snorted a little laugh. "I'll get the septic pumped out. It happens every year."

"Did she get home last night?"

"She rolled in about ten, the poor woman," he said. "She works too hard."

Beep dropped his cap on the table. He pulled out a chair and sat down. "We should go up to the top today." He nodded almost skyward toward the top of Trumpet Hill. "I was up there last week. The beavers are busy as ever. I only saw one, but there might be babies by now."

I slid into the chair across from him. "You know Zach. He likes baby anythings."

"He sure did when he was a kid," Beep said, giving his head one more scratch for good measure. "But there is no such thing as a domesticated beaver. I hope your brother has learned that by now. The first thing they do is chew off the post that holds up your porch. They're moody buggers too. They got no time for fun and games. They'll fight you tooth and nail."

I laughed quietly, certain enough that Beep's dismissal of beavers as good pets was right up there with the likelihood of befriending a snapping turtle. Zach had considered both during his childhood. "I can't go," I said. "Me and Mom are making macaroons."

Tilly came down. I heard her nails clicking out their clumsy cadence on the back stairs. She came across the kitchen floor and charged at Beep, her club of a tail flailing in wild, happy circles. Beep swung around in his chair and got hold of her ears. He scrubbed her all over with both hands and gave her his morning baby talk. "Did you hear us talking about you, Tilly girl? Did you? Did you? Huh?"

Tilly responded by rolling on her back with her feet in the air, squirming with delight. Her arrival was a sure signal Zach would not be far behind. It was Saturday, after all.

Beepah turned Tilly loose. "Macaroons for who?"

I shrugged. "For you guys, who else?" I rolled my eyes for effect. "It's girl time. We agreed before she left on Wednesday. It's a mother-daughter thing . . . get it?"

He gave Tilly a nudge with his boot and twisted himself in his chair. "Oh, that," he said, as if he had the vaguest notion.

I didn't bother to tell Beep it was a promise she had made, and I had thought of little else for the three days she was in New York. My longing for her had always been my best-kept secret. The explanation for making macaroons was simple enough, accomplished without the slightest exaggeration or deviation from the truth.

The sun broke above the treetops at last. The Cowboy weathervane atop the cupola pointed due south into a mild breeze. It promised a warm day in early spring. The birds were out to fly. I left the trap gate open the entire morning. They could come for cracked corn or forage on their own. They could chase after the pellets Nanny Jolly scattered near the pond. They could disappear to seek out new and friendly places. My efforts to grant them clemency, permanent or otherwise, were genuine, but none chose freedom that day. I determined that some found their freedom in the aviary . . . or at the very least, they had responsibilities that tethered them to the place.

Zach and Tilly appeared in the scratch yard. Tilly took a run at ol' Cowboy just for fun. The crotchety chicken reared up and threw his talons in the air, then strutted another lap around the yard with his neck feathers bristling like a moth-eaten boa.

Zach brought plenty of bluster. He talked about the giant turtle and his renewed interest in pursuing the monster for the entire summer. "When I have time," was his new caveat to the practice. He wore cutoff jeans and unlaced work boots. He kicked around in the kennel mud for a few minutes, then snared a rake from a hook near the coop door and began scratching at the soft kennel floor. Then he stopped scratching the ground for a moment. He leaned on the rake. "I wanted a pet beaver when I was a kid," he said. "It took me years to get past that."

Beep cleaned the watering trough with a spray hose, and he didn't hesitate until the last of the bird poop was washed away and disappeared in a stream beneath the back of the coop. He tossed the hose to the ground and turned off the spigot. Then he rubbed his chin whiskers with the back of his hand. "Make yourself a beaver hat. It's safer," Beep joked.

"I'd have to kill a beaver to make a hat."

"That's the preferred method," Beep said with a laugh. "I know you're not a killer, Zach boy," he said. "It's one of your finer qualities. Anyway, beaver hats went out of style a few centuries ago, sometime after the great flood or the invention of television. Trappers started layin' around all winter watching reruns of *Davy Crockett* and ignoring their traps. I guess there is nothin' entertaining about makin' hats. Anyway, trappers got soft."

What a load, of course. I could tell Beep was amused with himself. He looked up into the hemlock and filled his lungs with early spring air. "I tell you what, get the tractor and move a couple heaping helpings of this old straw out to the garden. We'll take a run up there later . . . unless you got other plans." Beep stooped to get through the door and shooed all the hens from their nests. "Nothing grows green beans like good old-fashioned chicken shit, and this old straw is covered in the stuff. And Syd needs her beans, don't you, Syd?"

Zach laughed. "You hear that, Sydney? This chicken shit is all for you because you're full of it."

Mom came out the back dressed in jeans rolled up at the ankles. She had on a red flannel shirt and rubber boots. It had been a while since her last visit to the kennel, maybe a year or two. She stood proudly on the sloppy earth and tapped the boot heels together. "I found these in the garage," she said. "I think mice lived in them all winter." She had a coffee cup she sipped from until the smell of the coop overwhelmed her. She dumped the coffee on the ground near Zach and laughed. "There you go, Zach, coffee for the birds."

Beep greeted her through the chicken wire. "Sleep well?"

"Oh God, I'll never catch up."

"We're heading out for beavers," Zach said. "I'll bring you one. You coming, Sydney?"

"Can't."

"We're making macaroons," Mom jumped in. She smiled at me, pleased with herself just for remembering. She sipped at her empty coffee cup and looked me up and down. "You'll need a complete costume change, dear, and a bath to wash off the war paint." She was only half kidding, of course. "Good lord, Benjamin, you're raising a chicken farmer."

"Salt of the earth, that girl."

She ignored Beep. "You can't bring the coop into the kitchen, dear. I recommend a full body scrub."

"That's right, Sydney, and wash your hands. We don't want chicken shit in our cookies."

I laughed at that, then struggled mightily to hold my tongue. I shot a threatening smirk toward Zach.

The doorbell rang that Saturday afternoon. Mom sent me. I swung the door open to discover Alexandra Su Bien. She was tall, with silky black hair that fell below her shoulders. It was shiny like Martin's limo. Oh, and she was beautiful. Even I knew beautiful when I saw it, and there it was, standing on the front porch in all its glory.

Alexandra Su Bien worked with Mom. I had seen her in the office at least once, but I rarely went there and never stayed long. The only time I ever stayed longer than ten minutes was on Take Your Daughter to Work Day when I was eight. That was the last time Mom took me to the office. I drew lots of pictures and stayed out of the way. I remember Alexandra from that day. She was wearing a business suit with her jacket folded over a chair and the buttons on her shirt undone well into her cleavage. Back then, that meant she was hard at work. She didn't have a daughter with her, so I assumed she had none. She looked younger than Mom. At that time, I didn't notice her beauty, but I admit I was in awe at the sight of her when she stood on the porch in a free-flowing skirt with a flower print bodice fitting snugly over her silky skin.

She had a briefcase she switched to her other hand, suggesting it was heavy. "Sydney, right?"

I was half covered in flour, so it was no wonder she had to guess my name. "Hi," I said.

"Is your mom home? I have some papers for her."

I pulled the door open and beckoned her inside with a wave.

She stepped over the threshold and I led the way. We were seconds from the kitchen doorway when it occurred to me suddenly that an announcement should precede our arrival in case preparations were in order. So, I bellowed it. "Mother! Miss Su Bien is here!"

Despite my efforts to save her, Mom was caught slightly off guard. She spun in place while her hands fumbled for her apron. "Oh!" she said. "I thought it would be later."

Alexandra stepped into the kitchen. Her skirt twisted freely in the flour-filled air. "I'm sorry," she said. "Brett insisted we go to the shore. His family is driving down from Boston. I've been running errands all morning. I should have called." She leaned in and kissed Mom on the cheek. Then she took a step back and her eyes brightened with delight. She laughed a little playful laugh. "I've never seen you in all your dusty domesticity," she said.

Mom wiped the flour from her face. "My mouth tastes like sour pickles, and there's flour down my shirt. It's beginning to feel a little pasty in here," she joked. "But we have macaroons. I'll fix a box for your in-laws."

I excused myself, as if they noticed. I ran upstairs to my bed and added "dusty domesticity" to my list of words and phrases. These words I knew, of course, but never had I heard them work so well together. I even tried to recreate the moment, standing in front of the big mirror, the moment her lips gracefully made the words amidst a pattering of laughter. "Dusty domesticity. Dusty domesticity," and I watched my lips contort. I decided, at least secretly, Alexandra Su Bien was the most beautiful woman to ever grace our kitchen.

The two of them sat at the kitchen table and talked for half an hour. The papers Alexandra delivered proved to be an assembled written plan for their trip to Singapore, come a week from Sunday.

"Almost every department contributed to this," Alexandra said. "And if you ask the right people, it's a big deal."

They laughed at that while I quietly contemplated another ten-day absence for Mother. I had lived through several and only remembered one or two. If there was reward at all, it happened upon her return. It was never the bobbles nor the traditional beads and sequined silk gown still feeding moths in my closet. I was not designed for dresses like that. Instead, Mom told me stories of her trips when prodded. They were never elaborate stories, but I made them so in my notebooks when I was young. The stories painted pictures in my imagination. I clung to them and sometimes even reproduced them in crayon.

When all had been discussed, Mom handed her the box of a dozen macaroons at the front door. She went up on her toes and kissed Alexandra on the lips, then looked at me and laughed, as if embarrassed. "That was a kiss for luck," she quickly explained the affection. "Can you believe this? I'm flying east, and Alexandra is flying west."

Alexandra laughed and rolled her eyes. "Who gets to No-wheresville first, thanks to our clueless travel planners."

"It's not like Singapore is nowhere."

"But getting there? Please," Alexandra said in disgust. "It's an experiment, or something."

"They have a package for Geneva."

"Dah," Alexandra droned. "FedEx! Hello!"

Mom sounded pleading. "You have all week to fix this, Alex . . . so please . . . why not send us in the company plane? At least we could ride together. Think how much we'd get done."

Alexandra laughed again. "Ten days, that's why. The bigs can't be without their precious plane for ten days. They might need to go someplace important."

"Well for chrissake," Mom griped. She slapped her hands together and a flour cloud flew out. "They can dump us in little Shanghai and take a junket to Bora Bora. They probably got girlfriends there."

Alexandra playfully cocked her head. "Or boyfriends," she suggested.

The two of them had a good laugh. There was no more kissing, but they did touch hands again. Alexandra picked up her briefcase and stepped out to the front porch. She turned around, and her eyes flashed at me only for an instant. "I'll see you at the Mandarin," she said to Mother. She went down the two steps to the driveway and walked beneath the cherry trees. Her flowered bodice melted into the clusters of red and white blossoms when the sun splashed through. I lost her in the mosaic.

I watched her car roll away, then I turned to Mother. "She's pretty," I said.

Mom's smile was fixed on her face, warm with expectation, I suspected. "Yes, sweetheart," she said. "I suppose she is."

"What's the Mandarin?"

"It's a restaurant. Alexandra and I had dinner there. It was just last year, but it became a special place for us."

She was all mushy-eyed. For the first time ever, I realized how much I truly envied her secret life. It played out in snippets I collected like scratch feed. There was never enough to explain a life or assemble one on paper, but always I was left to puzzle over the woman.

The bloodstain on Nanny Jolly's floor faded over time from soft blood-rose to a darker coffee blend. The smell that permeated the Jolly home for the entire winter softened at last into air less pungent, even returning to comforting in its familiarity.

I set the plate of macaroons on the counter near the stove and went to the front room to kiss Nanny Jolly on the cheek. She was knitting, of course. She had managed to create one long tube of a mitten that stretched to the floor where there was a considerable stack without thumbs. She simply depleted a yarn skein of one color and tied on another. "I like going around and around," she explained, "Instead of back and forth."

"Can I make you tea, Nanny?"

"So nice of you, dear."

I put water on the stove and set it to boil. I stayed with her for an hour. She knitted almost the entire time, stopping once to nibble a macaroon and declare it delicious. The tea went cold. I rinsed the dishes and set them out to dry, then pored over her stack of thumbless mittens for a random pair. There would be no need for mittens until winter returned, but I was not certain she would be there and the thought of it saddened me.

We said good-bye and I went out the back. The sun had set, but it was not as dark as it appeared in the lamplight when peering through the window near Nanny's chair. I could see clear to the edge of the woods from the back porch. I walked there, thinking how much I would miss the place when Nanny Jolly was gone. I recalled times with Ol' Jolly near the pond, tossing feed for the animals. I passed the pen where a dozen piglets grew fat over the years. One by one, they mysteriously disappeared when spring arrived. Ol' Jolly invented plenty of names for them. There was Jerky and Fatback and Hamhock . . . and of course, little Panfry.

"Where's Jerky?" I recalled asking one spring.

Ol' Jolly leaned back and smiled. He rolled his hand in circles over his big, fat belly. "Piggy Paradise," he told me. Then he told Zach that Hamhock went to Hog Heaven. Even at age four or five, I figured them to be different names for the same fun place, and I don't recall ever asking again.

It was much darker in the trees. I crossed the stream and stepped onto the trail. Someone was coming up. A flashlight beam waggled a jagged course up the rocky terrain on the path. I watched it approach. Neighbors were often out at night, but few ventured over the rough path in near total darkness without some urgent business. The flashlight was helpful, but it was never an easy trip, stumbling over the rocks in the dark. When the light was within a few feet of me, it stopped.

I was unnerved but did my best to conceal it. "Who is it?" I asked of the light.

The blinding beam settled on my eyes and froze there for a long moment. I struggled a little to ward it off with my hands in front of my face. It swung away finally to find another place, pressed beneath a chin. The light put the blood aglow. The patterns on the face were grotesque and revealing. There stood Jason Lipton!

"Hey, Syd," he spoke finally. "Chance this." The light rose from his throat to paint a pink outline behind his teeth. "Dark out," he said.

There was no hiding my fright upon seeing the distorted face before me. The chills my sudden fright produced threatened to take me to my knees. "Why are you up here?" I managed.

His features went dark again. He lowered the beam of light to a cluster of rocks near his feet. "I come up here sometimes," he said. "I see you through the backdoor, walking around in the kitchen. I see your brother sometimes. Whenever I see him, I want to punch him in the head." The circle of light danced around the path until his foot found a rock to kick. "I know where your room is. I can see you from right over there," he said, gesturing in the near blackness toward the teepee.

He was bold in his admissions, and that made his very presence more frightening. I undressed in that bedroom every night, sometimes in front of that window in plain view of the birds and the rabbits. I had always felt safe there. Suddenly the thought of him standing near the teepee as I prepared for bed left me feeling very naked and cold. But as bad as it was, his hatred for Zach troubled me more.

"What do you have against my brother?"

"He's got a big mouth," he said. "He should learn to keep his mouth shut before he gets hurt bad." He continued to stub the toe of his boot against the stone until it broke loose from the hard path. He gave it a kick and sent it rolling into the underbrush. "If I tell him something, he don't listen. Then he tells me to stay away from you . . . like he can make me. I punched him in the nose for that one. He'll catch on sooner or later."

"Zach doesn't talk big. He's just not afraid of you, that's all."

"Yeah, well, he should be. He's a slow learner. It's too bad for his stupid ass."

I turned and walked away, up and around the south end of Jolly's pond and near the teepee. I stopped there to peer upward along the edge of the barn roof to see my bedroom. Jason was right. When standing near the teepee door my bedroom window was in full view. He must have been watching me for months and I had never given it one moment of concern. It was my safest place, my room, my aviary. There was where I dreamed. There was where I composed letters to Grandmother and consorted with the Tooth Fairy. I cracked my window most nights so Cowboy's bluster rang clear come morning. That would all change. How could it not?

I felt his arm go around my neck from behind. My knees buckled from the terror of the moment. I couldn't scream, and by the time I thought I might, he had covered my mouth with his other hand. I began to kick to free myself, but before I knew his intent for certain, I was sprawled on the canvas floor inside the teepee. He was on top of me, pressing his hand over my mouth, chanting the evil mantra, "Don't, don't, don't," imploring me to silence.

His breath came into my nostrils—a vile, choking breath. Its paralyzing rot threatened to still my heart and lungs. He pulled his hand away enough to force his tongue into my mouth while he fumbled at my crotch for a zipper. I felt his hand pushing inside my pants, pulling at my tangle of hair, and driving a finger inside me. At first one finger, then more, until I was no longer certain what was tearing at my insides.

His attack ceased just as quickly. Something happened. I think he ejaculated in his pants. I knew about ejaculation, although I had never witnessed one firsthand, except for an animated version in health class. That one drew giggles. This one, not so much. He jumped up and rearranged whatever was going on in his pants. He kicked the flashlight across the teepee floor, then went searching for it in the dust. When he found it, he clicked it on and shined it in my face. He could see I was hurt and crying with fright.

"Sorry," he said with surprising contrition. He lingered, maybe wanting to say more, or thinking I might say something to mitigate his brutal assault. When I said nothing, he left through the teepee door and staggered back toward the trail as if he was drunk. I heard his stumbling retreat for a long while. It echoed in the quiet of an otherwise peaceful forest.

When the noise of his clumsy descent washed into silence, I lay there only a few minutes more. Amazingly, I found myself concerned I might be discovered. I surmised, any sane person stumbling across me on the teepee floor in the chill and the dark would expect an explanation. I quickly decided that would be awkward in the moment, so I picked myself up and went toward the house. My thoughts were a tangle. My pain had turned to numbness so quickly.

Mother was home. She was sitting in the front room with the paperwork Alexandra delivered in the early afternoon. It was scattered in piles on the coffee table. She had a glass of dog hair with ice nearby, and her eyeglasses teetered precariously at the end of her nose. She peered over her glasses to study me for a moment. I was disheveled, completely disheveled, and I hoped she would say nothing. After all, it was not a new look for me. She dismissed it, if she even noticed. She dropped her pen into the stack of papers and raised her glass to her mouth. She took a drink and set the glass back. The television droned the news, but it was enough to distract her when she spoke. "How is Nanny Jolly?" she asked.

On my way to the house, I had considered telling her the entire truth about the horrifying attack in the woods. Instead, I found myself calculating the amount of blather it would unleash, the number of counselors, all the dos and don'ts. Nurses and doctors poking and prodding me. There might be lawyers with all their stupid questions. "You said it was dark. How can you be sure it was Jason Lipton? Could it have been a stranger passing in the night?"

Ships pass in the night, you dolts, was my silent response to all of it . . . *and no, I don't want my vagina reexamined again for abrasions. And if hours of television drama taught me anything, a witness is not allowed to slap a stupid lawyer.* Even the short list of disqualifiers was enough to encourage my silence, at least until my head sorted the heinous details from the simply clumsy. Jason Lipton had accomplished both.

I finally managed, "Nanny's in her own world. I think she's happy. We had tea."

The television had Mom's attention. "Oh, that's good," she said.

The light was dim on the stairway when I slipped away to my room. I pulled down the shade and stripped off my clothes and left them in a heap on the floor. There was blood in my underwear. I had even bled through my jeans. Mom had not noticed. I showered, letting the spray wash the blood from my thighs into the swirl of water at my feet. I remembered Zach and how bravely he washed the blood from his nose at the stream. We watched it swirl and disappear in the icy water . . . and even though that was his blood, and this was mine, I had always felt there was little difference.

The thought of Zach brought a warm feeling. In moments clarity began to return. The numbness that engulfed me while I lay alone in the aftermath on the teepee floor began to abate. Hurt returned—emotional hurt and physical hurt—bringing along all the authenticity of the pain stinging my insides. In a while, the water at my feet ran clear, but I was certain, feeling truly clean again was a long way off.

By the time I fell asleep, many truths began to find their way back to me. Come morning, Beepah would be in the aviary, and the birds would be out to fly. Mother would be preparing her paper stacks for high-level meetings on Neptune. Zach would be asleep in his bed as I slipped quietly down the back stairs. Come morning, ol' Cowboy would crow to wake the world. It would be warm, And if not tomorrow, maybe Tuesday.

CHAPTER THIRTEEN

I spent much time in my room during those days of early spring. I thought about what had transpired and where to place blame. The window shade was always drawn. The darker hours were of greatest concern, when my imagination was in complete control of perils in the night. I often went to the window during daylight hours. I parted the blinds just enough to peer out into the backyard. All things appeared ordinary. The small tractor might be parked at the garden gate, and patina-clad Cowboy inched back and forth atop the cupola, encouraged by a tiny breeze. It often pointed southeast toward Jolly's pond and the vacant pigpen across the way.

Mom departed for Singapore on the following Sunday, just as she planned. The black limo arrived and Alexandra stepped from the back seat, her long legs proceeding the rest of her into the driveway. Aside from all else intriguing, upon seeing Mother, she flashed a wide grin. To them it was no surprise. Mom said Alexandra had successfully rearranged their flights. They would make the entire twenty-hour flight together. They were dressed for comfort in similar attire: sweatpants and loose-fitting T-shirts were the uniform of the day. I had never seen my mother so happy upon departing. Even Martin appeared relieved there was no squabbling in the driveway.

She waved frantically. "Bye, Zach! Bye, Syd!" Even when Beepah stepped out onto the front porch and saluted her with his coffee cup, she could not curtail her enthusiasm. "Bye, Ben!" she said.

I stood beside Zach in the grass under the cherry branches and watched the two of them slide into the backseat of the limo. Martin carefully delivered Mom's bags to the trunk and quietly closed the lid. I could hear the click of the trunk latch above the teenage giggling coming from the backseat.

"Bye, kids," Martin said to Zach and me.

He gave Beep a casual salute and slid in behind the wheel. Mom rolled her head against the seat back just as Martin closed his door. I did not see her again through the blackened windows. The limo backed slowly into the road and drove away. I could not help but imagine the two of them, dressed in their loose-fitting clothes, as far from business casual as they could retreat. I imagined the twenty-hour pajama party all the way to Singapore, and the prospects of enjoying the company of Alexandra Su Bien left me feeling painfully envious.

Hours later I found myself standing beside the big bed in Mother's room. I could see the woodshed below, and I could clearly hear the chatter of the little tractor through the slightly opened window. Zach was busy behind the garage, tossing scraps of split wood into the trailer. There were already plans for a teepee fire later. It had become tradition after Mother departed for days and days of business elsewhere in the world. I rapped on the glass with my knuckles, but the tractor chewed up the noise and spit it out with its own sputtering. Zach was unaware.

There was a green book on the nightstand. I had seen its like before. It was very official in appearance. "Garland-Price Annual Report," it read. I picked it up and flipped through. Near the front was the list of officers, and there was a photograph of Mother. *Angela Carmichael, Vice-President, Sales and Marketing*, was the caption. She was listed fourth down from the top. Near the bottom was a photograph of Alexandra Su Bien. Her hair was a bit shorter. Her smile was beautiful as ever. "Legal" was all it read.

The corner of a single photograph peeked from beneath a candle dish. I tipped the dish and took the photo from the night-stand. It was a picture of the two of them, standing on a hillside above a long stretch of beach. Mom wore a bikini with a flower top. Alexandra's was bright canary yellow. The two were locked in a friendly embrace. Far in the background was a small community of gazebo structures and a scattered fleet of motorboats and gondolas. The ocean behind them was a swirl of greens and blues. At the bottom of the photograph was script in black ink. It read simply, "Remember us, cool in the Canaries, 2007, Alex."

There it was, the mysterious Italy trip Mom took in February. Beepah did say it was work related. Alexandra's inclusion might have been the perfect legitimizer, if not the sole purpose for the excursion. There in the photo was the bikini that helped create the tan lines so evident upon her return. She had stood in front of the mirror fresh from the shower, looking healthy and happy, uttering not a word about the trip. I could often parse her behaviors. At the time, I secretly credited John Goff for her happy demeanor and the tan. Little did I know it was Alexandra Su Bien the entire time.

I took the book and the photograph back to my room and set about the entertaining, if not obsessive task of discovering their secret hideaway. I took to the internet, and I took to the collection of old *Britannica* encyclopedias gathering dust and spiders in the loft over the garage. I had not visited the loft for some months. I followed the dusty footprints to the window and peered into the side yard.

The only window in the loft was tucked under the gable end and looked out on a hedge and little more. The room was cluttered with boxes of Christmas ornaments and anything else native to attics. Most of the junk was pushed under the eaves and had lived there undisturbed longer than me. The best feature was an escape hatch in the floor that once became part of our pirate ship, "Argh!"

I spent two hours in the loft that day reading near the dusty window and under the glow of an old desk lamp.

Zach sent Tilly to retrieve me from my room before he left for the teepee. Tilly had no trouble sniffing me out. She pushed her way through the crack in the door. I gave her a scratch and left the encyclopedia on the plank floor. Tilly's hair was damp from a light mist, but by the time we left the house it had turned into a soft rain. Even from the porch I could see the fire glowing through the teepee wall and bathing branches above the smoke hole in dancing orange light.

I had not ventured inside or anywhere near the teepee since my encounter with Jason Lipton. In fact, I was grateful for Tilly's company. We pushed our way through the wet grass. The rain was a mere sprinkle, but my clothes were damp by the time I poked my head through the teepee doorway. They were there, Zach and Beep, sitting on stumps with hot dogs secured on sticks over the fire. I laughed at how normal the scene had become over time, and their company removed the trepidation I felt after a week of self-imposed exile from the place.

Tilly rushed to Beep and shook off her rainwater. I dropped Mom's sleeping bag on a tarp near the stack of firewood opposite the door. I sat down on the stump between the two of them and picked up a stick with a burnt end. I held it over the fire until it burned a little more to incinerate all germs. Then I plucked a hotdog from the plastic wrapper. I ran it through from stem to stern and returned it near the flames.

Zach was a little incredulous at my mysterious absence. His eyes followed me the entire time. "What the heck were you doing, Sydney?"

"Schoolwork," I said, a rebuff clear as mud. "We're studying the Canary Islands."

Beepah shooed the wet dog away. "I thought you were at Nanny Jolly's," he said.

"I went down when Mom left," I said. "Halfway through the morning and poor Nanny is still in bed. I got her up and helped her find something to wear. Mrs. Campbell picked her up to go to the church. They were making pies."

Beep nodded at the sleeping bag I had dropped beside the firewood stack. He pointed with his stick. "Where'd you find it?"

"In the loft. It's Mom's. She slept in it . . . maybe once," I said with some sarcasm and shrugged.

Beep acknowledged the sleeping bag with clumsy indifference. "Good thinking," he said. "You're too big to sleep with me. That's for sure."

Zach laughed. "That's right, Sydney. You're a girl now."

It suddenly became a painful and embarrassing moment for me. After all, Beep didn't say I was too old, or too sexually mature, or even somehow too weirdly irresistible to lie next to him. He simply said I was too big, which I believe was no more than a complaint about available space in his sleeping bag. But then, any one of those personal hang-ups fit the bill.

If the truth be told, I had long since abandoned Beep's sleeping bag. I remember my eighth birthday when the rusty army cot mysteriously showed up in the teepee. "I got it for your mother," Beep explained the rickety old cot upon arrival. "Even that amount of luxury is not nearly enough to lure the woman out," he said, his frustration in the matter always evident.

I opened a bun and used it to pull the blackened hotdog free of the stick. I squeezed out some ketchup and set the bottle back on the stump. "What do you guys know about the Canary Islands?"

"They're for the birds," Zach said.

Beep considered it, then said, "I think they're in the Atlantic

Ocean." He dropped his stick over a stone and proceeded to dress up his hotdog with relish and mustard. "I never went across the Atlantic," he said, reminiscing with sudden, but noticeable pain in his voice. "I had two trips across the Pacific, one going and one coming back. I was only supposed to be there a year. But unforeseen circumstances forced me to re-up for a second tour. I spent almost twenty-one months in Vietnam—twenty months, nineteen days, and a wake-up is how we counted time back then, and that was enough for me."

Beepah talked that way sometimes. Often, all it took was the slightest mention of an upcoming trip to Neptune, or the smell of smoke on the wind. Painful memories came alive in his brain. Then he would stop short and tell us little else. Dr. Campion worked with Beep for a time, referring to memories of some tragic events as "suppressed." But then Dr. Campion died unexpectedly, and somehow Beep slipped through the cracks. He must have decided he had beaten the system. He was cured. Eureka!

"The Canaries are off the coast of Africa, but they're sort of part of Spain," I said. "It's warm and sunny all year. I guess it's a good place to get tan, if you want. There's a place there called Forever Spring . . ."

"Sounds like dish soap," Beep said.

Zach pitched his enthusiasm into the mix. "I heard the beach is loaded up with naked girls," he said. "Course, I did hear it from Booger Sullivan, and what's he know?"

"All I know is, I'm tan from the neck up," Beep said. "I used to turn blond in the summer sun, back before I turned gray. I'd look like a freckle-faced lobster if I was to drop my drawers in the sand. Besides, watching naked girls all day long could sour me on the experience, but I don't say that with any certainty."

"I'm not sour on it," Zach piped up. His laughter exposed

his sudden excitement at the prospect of seeing an entire beach crawling with naked girls.

Beep rubbed the smoke from his eyes. He pushed himself up from the stump and stretched. "That's enough for me," he said. He took the few steps to his sleeping bag that was rolled out near the hatch. He laid it open and kicked off his boots. "You two yokels don't stay up too late. There's school tomorrow." He got on his hands and knees and squirreled himself into his bag. "And don't get Zach all juiced up with stories about naked girls. Everybody knows school and naked girls don't mix. That's been my experience." Beep laughed. His head dropped into the crook of his arm and in minutes his gentle snoring was stirring up little dust clouds over the tarp-covered floor.

I had listened to their playful banter about girls. I tried mightily to find one normal feeling. Even the familiar smells inside the teepee had turned foul. I struggled to dismiss the terror that began to settle on me. A vapor wafted through every crack and crevice to putrefy the air inside. The smell of Jason Lipton's breath began to choke off my wind. My stomach was rolling. It threatened to spill out. I sprang to my feet as the panic swept over me. "I can't be here!" I tried to explain, straining to get the words out. "I can't be here anymore!" I stumbled toward the hatch.

"What the hell, Sydney?"

"Take Tilly," Beep said, barely moving and never opening his eyes.

Tilly heard her name and scampered through the hatch. She bounded into the deep grass. I followed her. She stayed close to me, sensing my unease and my sudden sadness. I knew in my heart the teepee could never again be a warm and safe place for me, and I vowed Beep and Zach could never know why. I was certain it was only my silence that would protect them.

Tilly and I crossed the lawn near the garden and I cast a look overhead. There were stars, a whole cluster of stars. I prayed that among them there was a patron saint for me, and in my grief I cried.

In the morning, Zach and I talked our way down Trumpet Hill. The panic that overwhelmed me the evening before had departed, at least for a time. My ability to breathe was miraculously restored sometime in the dark of night. Thanks to Beepah, the birds flew overhead, and ol' Cowboy's voice rang clear as church bells a full hour after sunrise.

"You guys weren't no fun last night," Zach said. "Beep's asleep at seven thirty. You and Tilly bail on me at eight. What a conspiracy of lightweights."

"I had a bellyache."

"Well, it's like I said last night, Sydney. You're a girl now."

The dark blue mustang rolled to a stop at the end of the Lipton driveway. Jason saw us and turned up the hill in our direction. The car growled its way slowly, then screeched when it stopped near us. Jason lowered his head and gave the two of us a look. The engine revved. He shifted into reverse and inched down the hill beside us. "Hey, Bowden," he said. "How about I give your sister a ride to school?"

Immediately, I knew it was a test and it came down to this: Should I tell Zach about the teepee attack? Jason was probing. What did Zach know? If Zach knew about the attack, Jason would be forever on guard. If Zach knew nothing, it was a free pass to rape me all over again. I had not considered the horrible dilemma. I got hold of Zach's arm and squeezed it until my fingernails buried into his skin. I leaned in and whispered to him, "Don't let go of me, Zachary," I said. "Don't ever let go of me."

Zach kept his cool. He barely slowed. "We're catching the bus," he said.

"To bad the bus left already," Jason said. He touched the gas pedal and the mustang lurched backward. "Did you guys camp out last night? I could swear I saw fire in your teepee. I thought about coming by to juice up the party. I figured your old man was there. I got no use for him."

Zach slowed. He looked Jason in the eye. "We'd throw your girlie ass in the creek," he said. Then he turned to me and laughed. "Come on, Sydney! Let's get the bus!"

The mustang smoked and fishtailed its way up Trumpet Hill, and me and Zach took off running the last hundred yards to the bottom of the road. We arrived just as the bus was cresting the rise. The bus lights flashed, and Zach began laughing again.

"See that, Sydney! There's the bus!" he said. "Jason Lipton is a dirty, rotten, no good, butt-fucking liar!"

He got me laughing. He got me laughing so hard I could barely raise my leg to clear the first step into the bus. There were some days I loved my brother more than other days. That day was one of those days. Jason Lipton, a butt-fucking liar indeed.

———

I arrived home in midafternoon to sunshine and warmth. The house was empty. I decided quickly Beep was meeting with the boys in group therapy down at McCutchen's, or he was off running errands with Tilly in tow. Either way, they were not around. I slipped into my room and secured my pirated photocopy of Alexandra Su Bien in my notebook. Then I went to Mom's nightstand and placed the Garland-Price Annual Report where I had discovered it the day before. I tucked the photograph of her and Alexandra carefully under the candle dish, just as it had been.

I went through the quiet house. The pickup was plainly visible, parked out back near the barn. I went out to search for

Beep and Tilly. The chickens in the scratch yard acknowledged my arrival. Their voices reached me in gentle murmurings of fleeting curiosity. There was little other noise. I went to the barn and stepped through the side door. Buddy and Beebo were inside. The two hooligan goats were wildly chewing away at the grain bin, attempting to eat their way through the plywood cover. I shooed them off. They went across the yard toward the Jolly farm at a full gallop, giggling all the way. There was still no sign of Beep.

I went out through the tall grass. Trees moving on the slightest breeze made the only sounds. I went past the teepee and across the creek on the stepping stones that stood high above the shrinking trickle coming down the mountain. When I stepped down onto the soft forest floor, my steps began to churn the leaves in a smooth, sweeping cadence.

Beep's head appeared just above the fern fronds that lined the trail. He must have heard the dry leaves rustling at my feet. He pushed his head up, craning his neck until our eyes found each other. I hiked myself up to the trail to find him sitting on a big rock that was partially embedded in a clump of maples. His shotgun lay across his legs, and he seemed intent on watching the thick swath of ferns for movement.

As I approached, quiet seemed appropriate. "Beepah," I whispered.

"Hi, Syd," he greeted me without turning again. "Anybody up at the house?"

"Mom's not home yet. I think Zach's at Booger Sullivan's."

"Come sit with me," he said, patting the rock above his knee.

I climbed up until I could see past the maple trunks along the trail down the mountain. I dropped down on a blanket of damp moss and felt the coolness work its way through my jeans to my skin. Beep returned his gaze to the shade in the undergrowth. He was still for a long while, though he had welcomed me to join him with mild exuberance.

"Have you seen anything?" I braved.

"Not for a few hours." His eyes were fixed on the dancing shadows.

It slowly occurred to me the behavior was out of character for Beep. He rarely came to the woods with a gun, and when he did, the outcome was preordained. A turkey would gobble around Thanksgiving time, and he would charge out to harvest the bird and haul it home. He might have even gutted it along the way. Then he would string it up above the back porch in the coolness of autumn and let it cure for a day or two. He made it clear to me it was an occasion that thoroughly amused him because the swinging carcass aggravated Mother so completely.

This day was different. He had been sitting on the rock for hours, he said. It struck me just then that he was not hunting turkeys. "I don't think the turkeys are down here," I said without any particular reason other than a sudden twinge of worry. "They might have moved up the mountain."

"Do you remember my friend, Collin Jefferson?" he asked out of the blue.

"The leprechaun man," I said with momentary relief. "He told the story about his dog and the neighbor lady. I drew a picture at the table in McCutchen's."

"Your picture is still there to this day, stuck above the bar under glass. It's a big honor," Beep said with a bit of a snort. "Not too many of the guys have forgot Jefferson." He scraped at the soft moss with the tip of the shotgun barrel. "He shot himself, you know?"

"No, Beepah! When?"

"Oh, it's been a year or more. I was sitting here thinking about him, is all."

"I remember him. He was a happy man," I said, overtaken by the news, yet struck by a moment of disbelief. "He always seemed so happy."

"He lost his kid in Iraq . . . blown up, I guess," Beep said. "Anyway, it put ol' Jeff on a bad skid." Beep rested the gun barrel in the crotch where his boots crossed, one over the other. "He told me once God screwed up by passing him over in Vietnam. He figured it should have been him killed in the jungle, killed and forgotten. If he got killed in Nam, his son would have never been born. But Jeff survived Nam, and his kid got blown up in Iraq."

Beep shrugged. He closed one eye and looked down the length of the barrel and gave his boot a tap. The words did not come easy for him just then, and when he spoke again, he strained to speak with some measure of clarity. "I think about that when I think about you and Zach . . . about keeping you safe. It's an odd kind of fear I have. Maybe they'll send me back, but then I wake up and realize it's over. Over there, it's over. It's over, over there."

A year had passed since Collin Jefferson shot himself in his woodshed. Beep never told me, not a word. Now this sudden burst of candidness. Psychotic episodes, the veteran's hospital once referred to his occasional bouts of odd behavior and depression. It was a diagnosis that made its way all the way to my notebook a few years back. I was not at all sophisticated in my understanding of the malady back then. As the years passed, recognizing an episode, no matter how rare or benign, concerned me more and more deeply.

All the boys at group had issues. It took me some years to realize that. Their words, their dirty jokes, and whatever was eating them up inside—those observations helped to mold my sense of *normal* when I was young. Beep's issues were somewhere in the mix, perhaps more subtle than some. But that day, it was

Collin Jefferson's final act on earth that brought Beep to the trail to ponder his own end.

"I couldn't help Jefferson," he said. "I worry for you and Zach, that's all."

"You mean because of you?"

"Sure. I am the crazy one in the family. Normal as I try to be, it doesn't always stick to me too good, not in my own head, anyways."

I knew then he was indeed pondering an end, considering it for its viability, communing with the same demons that drove Collin Jefferson to the woodshed. Perhaps Jefferson had mistaken them for God. What Beep was hunting was a place between light and dark, between pain and numbness, the place Collin Jefferson finally found. This time, the behavior perplexed me. Beep's life was a happy life. He had us. He had Mother. He had a home.

"They've been here," he said. "They've been watching me, the same demons that fooled ol' Jefferson into leaving this world to search for his son in another . . . maybe in heaven, if that's where he went. They must come up the trail." He gestured with a toss of his head. "I've seen their footprints near the teepee."

For a moment I was frozen to the rock, listening while he struggled to detangle his thoughts. In his mind, demons arrived to put his very life under siege. And then there was Jason Lipton, once again stoking my fears. Time had passed. The torment had diminished little. Yet there he was, standing near the teepee, leaving his footprints in the soft earth, watching my window. Was that what Beep saw, a demon as real as Jason Lipton? That's what crossed my mind in that moment. Were Beep and I stalked by the same predator?

There was daylight, but it had changed color in the late afternoon, going from soft yellow to gray. Shadows were profuse in the undergrowth. Beep's eyes still searched, but he seemed less committed than when I first arrived. He allowed his gaze to escape to the treetops, to watch the movement in the soft quiet of the forest.

I heard voices coming up the trail through Jolly's woods. Beep heard them too. The shotgun jerked to the ready. One eye clenched shut. The other swept across the trail below.

I put my hand on Beepah's shoulder. I slid from the mossy rock and landed in damp leaves. "It's Zach and Booger Sullivan," I said with almost breathless caution.

Zach saw us just then. "Don't shoot!" he hollered, and he raised his hands above his head to surrender. He and Booger laughed at that even though there had been at least a chance of them getting shot only seconds before. "Did you guys see Tilly?" Zach hollered up again. "We followed her up here. She took out after a big buck."

Beep broke down the shotgun and removed the shells. He breathed a heavy sigh and handed the gun to me. "I could have shot my dog," he said.

I was relieved to have control of it finally. I wrapped both hands around it and stepped out onto the trail. "I'll put it in the barn locker," I said.

"Hey, Syd," he stopped me. 'I'm sorry I said those things." He shook his head in full contrition. "I'm still troubled about Jefferson. That's what it is. It gets to me sometimes, that's all."

It was a rare moment. He had allowed me to see the most vulnerable piece of him. It frightened me. I did my best to understand. There had been glimpses. There had been stories throughout my life. They were amusing stories, many of them. They were borrowed from a time when he was a much younger man. He had survived them once, years before. There was always an ounce of gratitude in his telling of the tales. They exposed his fragile nature in one clever way or another. But still, he was paradoxical, outwardly amusing, while on the inside he was seeking forgiveness for whatever truly tortured his soul.

"I believe you, Beepah," I said. I headed back through the ferns and crossed the creek on the stones. Tilly came bounding down from the meadow, sprinting across the trail between Beep and the boys until she caught up with me. She slowed and rubbed one burr-covered ear against my leg. I felt the spines of it sting my skin through my pantleg and I gave her a nudge. "You're a bad dog, Tilly girl," I said.

CHAPTER FOURTEEN

The day arrived as the clearest of mornings in the middle of May. Zach was to turn fifteen. After the birds were turned out to fly, I went into the backyard with my basket. Beepah had backed the pickup near the barn doors. There were four bales of straw in the truck bed. He pulled one off and dropped it just inside the barn, out of the way of any approaching weather. I kicked along through grass heavy with dew. It cleaned my boots left muddied by the coop floor.

Beep looked my way and smiled. "If you're going for eggs, you're heading in the wrong direction."

"Nope. I'm going to the meadow to check on bellyachers," I said of the meadow apples. "I can't think of anything better for Zach's birthday than bellyacher pie with worms."

Beep chuckled. "You're a thoughtful sister, but it's way early, Syd. Maybe apple blossoms. That's about it."

"Lots of blossoms means lots of apples," I said. "Besides, I've seen plenty of 'em hold on right through the cold. If the deer can't reach 'em, they're still hangin' there, and if they're not, I'll bring you some fiddleheads."

"Take Tilly with you."

"I didn't hear her moving in Zach's room."

Beep tossed a bale. "She came out with me. She jumped right in the truck and we headed out for straw." His eyes took a quick sweep of the tree line in search of the big yellow dog. "She wandered off someplace. She's chasing deer in the meadow. She thinks it's her job."

He pushed his hat up and scratched his knot of hair. He gestured to the shadows where the creek took a brief swing toward civilization. "Ol' Jolly took at least one deer every spring. Sometimes he was standing at his bedroom window without pants. I bet his salt lick is still out there." Jolly's salt lick always stood in plain view from his upstairs window. "He bragged about shooting a buck in his underwear, then he'd laugh. I'd take it upon myself to thin the herd, but I'd be inclined to wear pants. The buck can wear whatever he wants," Beep mused, offering up Ol' Jolly's tired joke yet again.

I scoffed. "It's a barbaric practice. Pants should be optional . . . maybe a breechcloth to cover your manly man." I spun and headed toward the trees, hoping to end the silly exchange on a winning note.

But no. Beep's cheerful yelping continued. "You didn't get that mouth from me, Syd Bowden!" he crowed. "And for the record, you ate your share of Jolly's deer meat in your day!"

I went out into the deep grass and circled the teepee to the creek. My feet found their footing on the slippery rock bridge, and I stepped off onto the soggy forest floor. Up ahead was the path, and when I crossed there and passed through a heavy bank of shadow, I was standing at the edge of the meadow. Sunlight pierced the treetops to the east, leaving the undergrowth untouched and dark. In the middle of the meadow stood the scraggly apple tree, its arms twisted and knotted with age, each branch straining to bear its own weight. Beep once said the tree was old, like Johnny Appleseed old. We bought into that tall tale, of course, like most things Beep told us when we were little.

The ground was spotted with last year's fruit. Even rotting, most had been devoured by the deer herd during early-morning visits. The branches were rich with pink and white blossoms, promising a bumper crop of hard green bellyachers by late summer.

Along the meadow's south edge, the forest diminished into mountain laurels and other low growth rising just above a rocky mezzanine. A doe stepped through the underbrush and into the clearing, then vanished abruptly when Tilly came bounding through the grass. She ran to me, her muddy club of a tail wagging against my knee. I tucked a sprig of apple blossoms behind my ear and spanked Tilly on her flank with my open hand. "How'd you get so dirty, huh? How'd you get so dirty, Tilly girl?" She rolled on her back over the rotting apples. I had to concede, "Dirty girl," I said.

I crossed in the wet grass with Tilly out front. Ferns were clustered in the deep shadows. Fiddleheads flourished there. The deer herd quietly retreated as I approached, their white tails dancing like fog lights over the rough terrain. They disappeared deeper into the forest mist and into the silence there.

The sun splashed down into the meadow. I remember the first time I discovered fiddleheads. I was five years old. I rode on Beepah's shoulders through the tall grass and into a sea of fern fronds. He dropped me down right into that very patch of ferns. I found a fiddlehead and pulled it loose and held it up for Beep to see.

"It's a lucky thing to run across these fiddleheads," Beep said. "Fiddleheads don't last long in springtime. Fairies steal off with them to make their music. The next time we sleep in the teepee, you listen. You'll hear them."

I remember sleeping in the teepee on that night, back when it was a pleasant time for me. We had a campfire and Beep's stories to entertain us. Mother was off to Singapore or Neptune. I wiggled into Beep's sleeping bag when the fire burned down low. Lying there in the dark, nestled into Beep's arm, I heard the fairies play their music. All along the stream and in the tall grass, their beautiful noise rose up. That night I became a true believer.

Beepah met us at the bus as usual. Even as I stepped off, things seemed amiss. Tilly was not sitting up front panting and licking her chops at the sight of me. She was always there on the days Beep collected us from the bus, ever since Zach's sixth birthday, nine years' worth of welcome-home kisses. Back then she was little Tilly, a moniker that lasted short of five months, until she began filling out into a big, happy, slobbering member of the family.

It was Zach who showed the first hint of concern. "Where's Tilly?" he asked Beep through the open truck window.

Beep shrugged. "She took out after something," he said. "It's almost always a deer that gets her going. She runs for a while and gets all tired out and sleeps on the back porch or the barn floor most afternoons." Beep scanned the road and the trees along the river. "I thought she might be down here waiting for you two."

We tossed our backpacks, then climbed up into the truck bed. The pickup slowed at every front yard on the hill. Our eyes surveyed from the right side to the left. Zach and I leaned out over the road, searching the familiar landscapes for the big yellow dog, expecting her to recognize the truck, expecting her to catch a powerful whiff of Zach or me on the breeze and come bounding from the shadows.

It wasn't worry, not in those first few moments. After all, tracking down Tilly was more routine than surprise. When the pickup pulled into the driveway, she was not there to greet us. Zach and I hauled our backpacks through the foyer door and dropped them to the floor. We went through the house and out the back. There was no sign of Tilly, and her absence left the backyard eerily quiet. Hens in the kennel yard exhibited only the slightest curiosity at our arrival, and ol' Cowboy, who had squirreled himself into a leafy depression in the cool earth to pass the day, barely moved.

All of that was about to change. A cloud bank rolled in to fill the sky to the southwest, ominous in its approach. It turned day to night as it moved above the treetops and devoured the sun. The first thunderclap signaled doom enough to stir Cowboy from his hole in the ground. He hurried past the hens and banged his way through the swing door. The flock of clucking females followed him.

"I'll go down to Nanny Jolly's," I said.

Beepah came out through the screen door. "You better stay with her, at least until this thing passes." He nodded toward the clouds rumbling in to shadow the barn and leave the teepee in utter midnight blackness. "You can't do much out there," he said to Zach, nodding to the southwest. "The best thing you can do is wait here. I'm guessing she'll show up."

"It's already dark as night out there," Zach said. "I'll take the flashlight and go out to the meadow. At least I can call for her. I might hear something. Maybe she's hurt. I'll stay in the teepee until the storm is over. At least I can listen for her."

I took off at a run, past the kennel and the coop. I crossed the sloping yard to the Jolly's back steps. I went in, just beating the rain, and I let the screen door slam behind me. I closed the inside door more quietly and shook off a sudden chill.

Nanny Jolly was in the kitchen adjusting the flame under her tea kettle. She peered over her glasses and smiled. "Isn't it odd, dear?" she said. "I was just expecting you."

"I came to check on you, Nanny. The weather is getting bad, and Tilly didn't come home. Have you seen her?"

"Oh no, dear, not for days," she said. She went back to the burner and twisted the knob back and forth. When she straightened again, she cocked her head as though she had hit upon a simple truth. "Isn't it odd, dear, when you know somebody so well you put the tea on to boil only moments before they arrive unannounced?"

She laughed her little endearing laugh. "Matty was like that," she said of Ol' Mathew Jolly. "Of course, he was a coffee drinker."

The hail started up. I pulled the door open and switched on the porch light. Hail the size of chickpeas battered the metal roof above the porch door. It was painfully loud. I thought of a train passing over loose tracks on a mad dash for the station.

Nanny Jolly covered her ears. "Oh, but that's an awful racket," she said.

"I don't think it's big enough to break windows, but it sure could hurt." I instantly thought about Zach out in the weather. He would be at the meadow or on the trail up the mountain. I had been out in it before, when a flash flood overwhelmed the trail, gouging out rocks and mud to fling downhill toward Esopus Creek. "Zach's out in it," I said.

Nanny chimed in just as the kettle began to whistle. "Oh, the poor dear," she said.

We sat at the kitchen table and sipped tea. I squeezed honey into my cup and stirred it until it dissolved. All the while Nanny seemed preoccupied with recollections of her fifty-year love affair with Ol' Jolly. She regaled me with anecdotes I found amusing. I was always aware of the photograph on the mantle. It was ancient by my accounting—sepia, enough to declare it old. Mathew Jolly raised a much younger Nanny in his arms, the two of them so very happy. "Matty and Me," it read.

"We got caught in a rainstorm just like this once," she said. "It was right after Matty began work on the big house. We lived an entire year in that little shed where the pigpen is today. We had a bed that was too small for Matty, and that was when he was more muscle than fat." She laughed at that, as if her words conveyed an unintended insult. "He said I stuck to him like a tree frog to a cattail. Over that year I got used to sleeping in the crook of his arm. We slept that way for fifty years." Her smile fixed in place. She said nothing more about their rainstorm adventures, but I got the gist of her tale.

The hail lasted only a few minutes, and after twenty more minutes, the clouds passed overhead and the sky brightened a little. Even the rain slowed to a drizzle. I said goodbye to Nanny Jolly and went back across the yard beneath a spattering of rain. Just as I rounded the kennel, Zach was returning from the woods. He was wet to his bones, walking stiff-legged from the icy rain, and seemed desperate to stand in a warm, dry place.

He stopped abruptly. "I didn't find her," he said. "She didn't come past the teepee or no place."

"Are you going back out?"

"Of course," he said. "I'm going down the trail, at least to the Esopus."

"Beep won't want you out there."

"Too bad," he said. "She's my dog."

"I'll go with you."

We went through the back door and into the kitchen where Beepah greeted us with a towel slung on his shoulder. The worry on his face slackened. Zach pushed the screen door open and went back to the porch. He stepped out of his boots and kicked them on their sides to let the water empty out. When he came back inside, his face was white with cold and his body racked by shivers.

"If you go back out there, you'll be sick. This rain ain't over. I saw it on the Weather Channel. There's a big black cloud working its way across Long Island Sound. It could get worse before it gets better," Beep warned us, already certain of Zach's intent.

Zach's teeth rattled uncontrollably. "Sorry," he said. "She's my dog."

"You went to the top?"

Zach nodded. "Part of the beaver dam washed down the hill. I couldn't see anything in the storm, but Tilly knows her way home from there . . . if she's not hurt."

Beep's lip curled with indecision. He gave Zach a long study. "It's too soon to call the sheriff, Zach, or the dog catcher. It's only been a few hours. They'd likely think we were overreacting. It's not like I lost one of you guys in the flood. She's a dog."

"I got a feeling, that's all," Zach said.

After a few moments, Beep finally relented. He took the towel from his shoulder and handed it to Zach. "Here. Get some dry clothes. We've got an hour of daylight. We'll go down the trail for a ways."

We searched that hour, and even the next, stumbling along in the faint light, and then in near darkness. The volume of rainwater cascading toward the river had diminished very little. The entire trail was a rolling torrent of mud and stone, spilling into the swollen creek. An ooze of red clay washed up from the bedrock, and black silt churned from new earth on the forest floor. They met in an angry swill at the bottom where the culvert extended beneath the road and emptied into a swelling Esopus Creek.

We clawed our way out of the deep ditch and followed along the road to the intersection at the bottom of Trumpet Hill. We turned uphill into the darkness and went past the school bus stop and the long Lipton driveway. Zach slowed there, stepping behind the hedge to survey the entire property. I could see the back of Emily Lipton's Bronco from the road, and there in the shadows was the blue mustang. I knew in that instant what Zach was thinking. I knew it in my gut.

Even Beepah seemed to know. "Let's give it tomorrow," he said, shining the flashlight toward Zach. "I'll let the Sheriff's office know she ran off someplace. She's easy enough to spot. If she doesn't show up at home, we'll find her."

Zach let his anger dissipate with some reluctance, but without a word. He stepped back onto the pavement and we walked the mile home, checking both sides of the road along the way. The ditches gurgled with rainwater, but the rain had slowed yet again. The storm we battled during our harrowing descent down the mountain was passing to the north, leaving a clear strip of dark blue sky over Trumpet Hill. There was no sign of Tilly. There was nothing that even raised suspicions she was hurt or worse . . . except, she was missing.

We took up the hunt the very next day. Cowboy crowed while I lay awake in bed. I hurried out ahead of Zach and Beepah to spring the flyway gate. Even without a wet and hungry Tilly waiting on the back porch, the early morning felt warm with promise. When Zach emerged from the kitchen, we went out. Out back, the stream remained swollen with rainwater, but the trail down the mountain had cast off most effects of the flood and returned to its rocky, muddy self. We found an acrobatic way to cross both without incident and in minutes we were standing in the wet grass at the edge of the meadow.

"We're looking for a dead dog," Zach said.

"You can't say that."

"I don't want to, but if she was alive, she'd come home," he said, his heart breaking visibly right before my eyes. "You know, when I got Tilly, I figured my life was filled up enough to last forever, like I didn't need another thing." A tear rolled down beside his nose and he wiped it away with his sleeve. "She was my best friend since I was six . . . except maybe you on a good day."

We weren't big huggers, not with each other, anyway. The occasions always felt awkward to him. But, if there was ever a moment Zach needed a hug, the moment had come. I knew how much he was hurting. I slipped my arm under his and gave it a tug. "Do you want to go up the trail? We've got time before the bus."

"No," he said. "I don't want to find her, Sydney. If I don't find her, she's still alive. There's a chance, at least. I lay awake all night remembering her." He pushed his hands into his jeans pockets and kicked at a clump of grass at his feet. "I figure someday, maybe after a summer or a winter, when I'm in the woods, I might come upon her bones. She'll be long gone by then. There's a tag on her collar that says Tilly, the one with our phone number on it, so I'd know her, even if she's only bones by then. I might not die if I find her then. I might not drop right down on my knees and die."

———

Two days after the flood, there was still no sign of Tilly. The Sheriff's office had been alerted, and in turn the dog catcher and the pound, and still no Tilly. Then, on the third day, Grace Campbell stood on our front porch. Grace was one of the neighbors Beepah alerted to Tilly's disappearance. All said, she was a good neighbor. We did favors and returned favors, but judging by the look on Grace's face, she wasn't here in the early morning to deliver a dose of cheer.

Beep greeted her with his coffee cup salute. "Gracie," he said.

"I might have found your dog, Ben." Her voice strained with discomfort. "I was out walking this morning and I might have come across her."

"It already doesn't sound good," Beep said.

"No, Ben, it's not . . . if it's her."

I pushed past Beepah. "Where, Grace?" I asked her, my heart in absolute freefall.

"In the ditch, down along the creek where the culvert comes through. Lots of water. The road even washed out not five miles south. Still passable, but it's dicey down there is what I heard."

"Get Zach," Beep said.

"He's on the mountain. He was gone before it got light out."

We went in Beep's truck, down along the creek where the culvert emptied. Beep pulled the truck far over on the shoulder, just above the churning water. He stepped out into the gravel and let the door go shut. I came out the passenger-side rear door and hurried around. The surging water had diminished its ferocity since Wednesday, revealing a tangled nest of brush that accumulated during the flood. Uncovered, just barely, was a patch of yellowish hair.

Beep skidded down the slope and found his footing at the edge of the swirling pool. He tore away the brush, pitching the tangle into the torrent destined for the river. Tilly was there finally, uncovered, half of her head barely above the water, lying stiff against the lesser torrent. The weight of her discovery must have hit Beep like it hit me. Just knowing he would have to deliver the news to Zach when he came down off the mountain crushed him almost to his knees. The hurt settled on both of us. Even Grace might have felt it.

"Gracie, I should drop you at home," he said.

"Can you get her out? I'll stay with you."

Beep got hold of Tilly's front legs and pulled her along the wet ditch to a place a few yards away, where the bank was less severe. From there he found a way to slide her onto the gravel shoulder. He went back to the truck and climbed in behind the wheel. He put it in reverse and inched the truck backward. I raised my hand to offer him direction but found myself barely able to summon the strength. Tears gushed out of me just as the truck tailgate put poor Tilly in its shadow.

I wiped my eyes and crept nearer, mustering courage enough to look at her lifeless body. I had never seen her so spotless. There were no burrs tangled on her ears. There were no rotting apples mashed into her hair. There was not a smear of blood nor a streak of mud. The only visible wound was a deep slice across her spine just in front of her haunches. Even the wound was clean. Three days of cold and rushing water had emptied poor Tilly of blood and scrubbed her hair to the purest pale yellow.

We dropped Grace Campbell at her front door. Beep mouthed the word "thanks," but his throat had tightened and no noise came out. Grace offered a conciliatory nod. There was no sign of Zach when Beep backed the truck to the place behind the barn where we buried dead animals. Thumper and Bumper were buried there with headstones. There were others, many others over the years. Beep would turn over a patch of turf and toss in the carcasses of chickens killed in a weasel raid. The tractor bucked its way over the little sinkholes on days Beep cut the grass. "Dead critter craters," he called the neat row of depressions in the field. There would be no such irreverence to describe Tilly's final resting place.

By the time Zach came down from the mountain, Beepah had dug a sizable hole in the earth. He was leaning on his shovel. His eyes kept watch on the open spaces beyond the teepee until he caught sight of Zach crossing the stream. Their eyes met across the expanse of tall spring grass in the field. Zach's pace slowed. My heart broke for him again. He must have known in that instant Tilly had been found.

"Mrs. Campbell found her when she went out for her walk," Beep said. His arm went over Zach's shoulder when he arrived at the pickup looking forlorn and fighting total anguish at the sight of poor Tilly stretched out in the truck bed. "She was down along the Esopus where the culvert empties. We must have walked right past her in the dark a few nights ago. Hard to say for certain, but it looks like she got hit by a car."

Beep had laid Tilly on an old blanket in the truck bed. Zach took her collar off and pushed it into his back pocket. The two of them folded the blanket over Tilly and gave it a little twist at both ends. They lowered her into the hole and folded the blanket ends over her.

It was in that moment Zach offered his only audible grief. A sob burst out of him. "I'll cover her up," he said.

"Okay, son," Beep said. He handed Zach the shovel and put his arm around my shoulder. "Come on, Syd. We'll give him a minute."

Zach was there an hour, pitching dirt into Tilly's hole in the ground. When he came back to the house, Tilly's soggy collar was double wrapped and buckled around his wrist. He was silent. I had almost stopped crying by then. I wanted nothing more than to comfort him, but he was stoic and completely withdrawn. He took an apple from the basket on the table and went to his room. I heard his door in the upstairs hallway click shut. I knew Zach, more than anybody knew Zach. I did not see him the rest of the day, nor did I attempt to. Fate can be the cruelest master. It serves up elation and misery with equal fervor, the same simple twist without prejudice.

That week passed into the next and Mom came home from Singapore. I had related the entire story over the phone two nights before, how poor Tilly had been run over by a car during a hailstorm, and how we risked death ourselves searching for her up and down the mountain, and how Beepah rallied the neighbors in the search, and how Mrs. Campbell found her in the ditch by the river. The truth is, she was likely killed long before the hailstorm even began, but it came together so nicely in my telling of it, and a detail or two out of place didn't seem to matter much. I wrote it all in my notebook. It got better each time I scratched out a word and wrote in another, and I cried less with each new version of the tale. Mom arrived home after midnight. I lay in bed and heard the commotion of doors opening and closing and suitcases dropping to the floor. I could picture my parents hugging ever so briefly, and they talked, with little bits of laughter strewn in for effect. Their words came up the stairwell or through the floorboards in mumbles. Most were impossible to decipher.

"Oh, it's good to be home," I'm sure I heard her say.

And he responded, "Good to have you."

I threw off the blanket and crept down the hallway to the front window in time to see the limo back out of the driveway. The front porch light clicked off. The limo rolled noiselessly down the road, taking its light with it until only the streetlamp near the Jolly's overcame the blackness to spread a dreary ashen-yellow glow against the pavement out front.

I hurried back to my room as they came up the stairs. By the time I slipped back into bed and pulled the blanket over me, they were talking in whispers. I turned my eyes to the window. For whatever reason, I was content enough knowing I would see my mom in the morning. She went by Zach's room. She must have stopped there and pushed the door open a little. She did the same at my door. "Such a sad thing, Tilly," I heard her whisper. Then I heard them moving in the hallway again. They went to the room with the big bed and closed the door.

It occurred to me in that moment, Alexandra Su Bien might have been in the limo when it pulled away. I imagined their kiss when they parted company after ten days together. I wondered if it was a kiss on the cheek, but I quickly decided it probably wasn't. There would be little excitement in a kiss like that.

I went out early the next morning to turn the birds out to fly. I sat on the rock wall as the sun came up, and I wrote what was to be the last draft of Tilly's story. When the morning shed all remnants of night and the sunlight crept down the length of the tree trunks to the west, Zach and Mother came out the back. Both her arms were locked around one of his when they descended the steps from the porch.

I shouted at her, "Mom!" and I jumped from the wall and scampered through the kennel gate, across the grass and into her arms.

"Oh, my girl," she said. "I missed you both so much."

We went together out to the grave behind the barn. Mom walked through the wet grass with her nightgown hiked almost to her knees and her slippers soaking up the morning dew in buckets. I could tell she regretted not dressing for the short trek across the yard to Tilly's grave. She was apprchensive to boot. Her lips quivered a little when she stepped near the fresh grave with Zach leading the way. He had raked it smooth every morning, and then again before darkness settled. Each day there were signs small critters had visited. It didn't seem to trouble Zach. He retrieved the rake from the side of the barn and passed it over the loose earth.

I had not visited in days and the occasion had me tearing up again. Zach fashioned a headstone from a piece of pine lumber. It was pushed into the ground. It was a grander tribute than any of the other small markers he had fashioned over the course of his childhood: Thumper and Bumper, a guinea pig named Jane. There was a baby crow Zach insisted could talk. There were others he might have never shared with me.

"I'll carve her a headstone," he said. "Right now, it's just magic marker."

It read simply, "Tilly."

Zach missed school for days after Tilly was discovered in the ditch by the swollen creek. Beep understood and said little. Zach was mourning the loss in his own way, but he did not closet himself like a grieving widow. He was keen to the goings-on up on Trumpet Hill. So, when Booger Sullivan brought news of a deer strike near the creek, Zach quickly concluded a driver had mistaken Tilly for a deer.

The very next day, Beepah pulled the string on Zach's truancy. "Sorry, Zach," Beep said. "Get out of bed. School misses you."

We rode down to the bus stop, me in the backseat behind Beep, Zach up front where Tilly always sat. Zach was sullen, realizing yet another day would pass him by without any sense of purpose, or any cure for the sadness he felt. School would do nothing to improve his outlook.

Booger had taken notice of Tilly's collar wrapped around Zach's wrist. The next day he showed up at the bus stop sporting his own collar on his scrawny wrist. It once belonged to a Rottweiler named Rascal who got taken out by a garbage truck almost two years back. Booger said he wore the collar as a sign of solidarity with Zach and Tilly. It went around Booger's scrawny wrist three times and still hung loose.

"You remember Rascal, don'tcha?"

"Of course, I do," Zach said, inspecting the big wad of leather wound around Booger's arm. "He had a big neck."

They raised their wrists in the air and rattled the collars draped with rabies tags and ID tags and all the other trappings. It was a light moment. There had been so few since Tilly was killed. Everybody at the bus stop joined in the wrist-rattling celebration.

Just then, Emily Lipton pulled the Bronco out of the driveway, and it rolled slowly down the middle of the road near Beepah. She stepped out onto the pavement while the engine added an unhealthy clang to its otherwise rhythmic purring. There was no hiding the damage. The grill was caved in and the headlight on the driver's side dangled like a dislodged eyeball.

Beep appraised the damage, walking out front, his lip curling with concern. The prominent clanging proved intense enough to draw the small gathering of curious school kids to the curb.

"Your radiator is pushed up against your fan," Beep identified the cause of the clanging, then he joked in typical Beep fashion. "Please don't tell me you ran over a crossing guard."

"Jason hit a deer." She muffled her words with a hand to her mouth. "The night of the storm." She shook her head. She was still bristling over the episode that left her car so damaged. "His battery was dead, and of course, he just had to go out. That boy . . . I swear."

I heard it. Booger heard it. Beep looked at Zach, and he knew Zach had heard it too. Jason Lipton ran over Tilly down by the Esopus, and he did it in his mother's car. Zach was suspicious on the night of the storm, but there was no proving it, not then, maybe never. We saw the mustang on the hill the day after Grace Campbell discovered Tilly's lifeless body under the brush pile. We watched the mustang roll past with Jason at the wheel. The car was clean. We could see no damage, and to Zach, that meant Tilly's death was truly an accident. Even if the driver was Jason Lipton, case closed. Suddenly, here was Emily Lipton, without an ounce of prompting, revealing an entirely different sordid tale. Zach's head dropped.

"I guess I can count my blessings," Emily said. "He could have been killed. He said it was a small deer, poor thing. Probably lost in the storm. The kid had to drag the animal off the road in the middle of all that rain."

Upon hearing that, Beep and Zach's eyes locked. They both

realized the very same thing at the very same time. If someone hits a deer with a car, that's one thing. It happens. It's tragic for the deer and usually the car. But if someone drags the poor creature off the road, even in the middle of a hailstorm, he or she will know whether they're holding a hoof or a paw. My mind was not churning out probabilities as rapidly as Zach's, but even then, I still thought Tilly's death could have been an accident.

Beep stepped over the curb and walked near Zach just as the school bus crested the rise. It rolled to a stop and the door folded open.

Beep put his hand on Zach's shoulder. "I know what it sounds like," he said.

Zach's sudden anger was bringing him close to tears. "What about the brush pile? Syd told me Tilly was buried under a brush pile. Who put her there?"

Beep gave Zach a squeeze on the shoulder. "Let's let this go," he said. He stepped back off the curb just as Emily was about to climb into the Bronco. Beep pointed at the little green river in front of the Bronco. "You're bleeding antifreeze!" Beep warned her.

"I'm taking it to Lowdy's Autobody!" she shouted over the rattle.

"You won't make it!" Beep shouted back. "You should have it towed!" He slid into the pickup and started it up. "I'll follow you!" he shouted through her open window when she wheeled the Bronco around the pickup.

I took Zach by the arm and led him toward the bus. I knew Beep was right. I knew nothing good could come from it. Even solving the riddle of Tilly's death would lead to no good end. There was no way to prove her death was malicious. Tilly would be just as dead, and Jason Lipton would forever go unpunished. I tried to feel what Zach was feeling just then, the confusion of it, common sense battling the rare impulse to take revenge. He allowed me to lead him away. We climbed the steps and landed three seats back from the driver.

"Jesus, that was something," I said. "What just happened?"

"Beep thinks more of the Lipton woman than he thinks of Tilly, that's what," Zach said, still shaking with anger, suddenly feeling the sting of Beep's betrayal. He leaned in close and cupped his hand near my ear. "I'm not going to class. When we get to school, I'm not going to class."

"Why?"

"I'm going to Lowdy's Autobody. I need to see the Bronco for myself."

After hours of worry and wishing I had gone with him, I ran into Zach in the hallway late in the morning "Where the hell, Zachary . . . ?"

"It's a long way to Lowdy's," he said. "It took me half the morning to walk there and back. I got detention again." He gave me a wry smile and pushed his hand into his pocket. He pulled out a fist and carefully relaxed his grip enough to allow the slightest bit of light inside. Whatever he was holding cupped in the palm of his hand was the grail, and he was treating it with gentle reverence. He slowly pushed it near my face to give me a better look. There it was, a small hank of yellow hair attached to a scrap of leathery skin.

"Where'd you find it?"

"Under the front bumper."

I examined it, but I could not be certain. "It's got dried blood on it," I said finally.

"It didn't get washed in the flood waters like the rest of her," Zach said. "It's Tilly, Sydney, a little piece of her anyway."

CHAPTER FIFTEEN

All things considered, it quieted on Trumpet Hill for a time in the early autumn of my fourteenth year. Nanny Jolly was holding her own against insidious dementia. She knew enough to know winter was approaching and winter meant mittens. She knitted them from muscle memory alone, and when true memories were enlivened, she could barely knit a stitch. Many days after school I stopped by to brush her hair. She would drop the mitten to the yarn pile at her feet and let invading pleasant thoughts pass over her. She smiled and let her eyes go shut for a time.

Zach exhibited some satisfaction in discovering the likely truth about Tilly's death, but Jason Lipton remained a glaring aggravation. Only once did he slow the mustang long enough to speak. "Hey, Bowden, at least I ain't seen your ugly dog around!" Jason laughed and thrust a vulgar gesture out the window while the mustang screeched its way toward the cul-de-sac. He swung it around at the top and aimed the beast downhill toward Zach and me. He revved the engine three times, then came screaming down the hill leaving a smoking black track in his wake.

Zach's expression barely changed. The mustang blew past, missing him by inches. It was the one time since Tilly was killed that I truly expected Zach to lose it, but when it did not happen, I even warmed to the idea my brother harbored a gentle soul. At some level my perceptions were wishful, of course. I knew him. He was fearless and clever. What I had never seen in him was patience.

That alone surprised me. Still, I felt in my heart, retribution in some way, shape, or form was coming.

Mom was preparing to make her annual autumn pilgrimage to Geneva for all things work related, unless she allowed time for a rendezvous with John Goff or Alexandra Su Bien. I never knew for certain what her plans included unless she decided to be completely candid in those matters, which happened out of the blue at times. As for our planned trip to New York to bra shop, it had yet to be discussed in depth. Work was so demanding. She rarely had time. I was certain I would be sporting melon-size knockers long before I got anywhere near the train to Grand Central.

"Alexandra is coming along this year," she said, and there it was, out of the blue. "I'll be so happy to have her. She's become my righthand man."

Of course, I was surprised by her bold revelation. "I haven't seen her all summer," I said.

"Nothing but work," she said. "We did steal an afternoon at the shore." She cocked her head to summon the memory. "That girl's skin is like brown butter. It tans so beautiful. I have to get burnt and peel like a crawdad to turn this blotchy shade of orange."

She never bothered to say which shore. It could have been on Neptune, for all I knew. The closest I came to the shore the entire summer was when I stretched out in the tall grass down along the Esopus to watch Zach fish for trout. I had not heard about their time at the shore. Now that I had, it stung a little, just knowing there was never an invitation offered to me. If the truth be known, I was not certain I was prepared to allow Alexandra a barely fettered viewing of my body, although I thought often about hers. "It's your Irish skin, Mother," I finally offered my appraisal. "I've got Beep's, so I stay rusty-looking all the time."

I watched for Alexandra the very next morning. The limo

pulled into the driveway beneath the cherry trees, and her bare feet swung gracefully to the asphalt. I was enraptured at the sight of her. She stood and softly brushed the hair over one ear. I took up my spot under the cherry branches. She said hello to me cheerfully, and I said hello back. I was frozen until Mother came out with Beepah right behind. She was wearing traveling clothes like Alexandra, except Mom wore flip-flops. Beep dipped his coffee cup toward Alexandra, and she offered a casual wave. Mom kissed Beep on the cheek. I heard no words exchanged. She came down the two steps and the limo trunk clicked open.

Martin stepped out of the limo and smiled toward the porch. "Nice day," he said.

Beep was just then admiring the bright September morning. "Beautiful," he replied.

Mom came around the cherry tree and kissed me on the cheek. She stepped into the driveway near Alexandra and they shared an anxious laugh. "I hope you brought shoes," Mother joked playfully.

Alexandra held up her own pair of flip-flops. She looked down and wiggled her toes against the asphalt. "It's cool under the trees. This feels good," she said. Her hair moved in the faintest breeze. A sliver of sunlight pierced the cherry branches and fell on her. Her sleek black hair gleamed in the dappled sunlight.

Mom stretched to kiss Alexandra on the cheek. As near as I could tell, everybody in or near the driveway got kissed on the cheek, except for Martin, which would have been weird. Zach had long since ditched driveway goodbyes. He was up early to escape the event, prepared to disappear for the entire morning if need be.

"Bye to Zach," Mom called out. She gave a wave and disappeared after Alexandra into the back seat.

That was it. Even Martin looked pleased. He offered an approving smile after he closed the trunk. He slid in behind the wheel and buckled his seatbelt. Departures from the Bowden driveway had become sterile affairs. Not one foul word was muttered, not a gripe nor a parting groan. There was not a squabble to be had. Lessons had been hard taught, but over the years, we learned them. There was Beepah on the porch, composing a biting inuendo he would never get to use. There was Mother, rolling up the blackened windows, no doubt giving Alexandra Su Bien a proper kiss. And there was me, canopied and silent under the cherry tree branches.

———

The lesson for that Sunday morning, just as Mother departed for a scheduled ten-day visit to Geneva, was that quiet could be short-lived. Beepah and I visited Nanny Jolly in the late afternoon. We removed an old daybed from a neatly cluttered bedroom upstairs and set it up in the front room. We dressed it up with clean sheets and pillows from her upstairs bed. There was a quilt Nanny made in celebration of her fiftieth wedding anniversary. She was lucid in describing the years before Ol' Jolly died. She was quick to recall pleasant memories. "Matty was so pleased with that quilt," she said of it. "Of course, he watched me stitch it together for years." I guess she meant the quilt was no surprise by the time it was completed. She laughed her endearing little laugh.

I made tea, and when Beep left, Nanny and I talked for a long while. She seemed pleased by the daybed addition, although it was squeezed into a corner up against the television, which was on continually and set to the same channel since Ol' Jolly died. Nanny did, on occasion, adjust the sound simply for the pleasantness of voices.

"I haven't seen your mother, dear," Nanny said. "I believe it's been a year. Is that possible?"

I had to shrug that off. "She travels a lot. She left for Geneva this morning."

"Oh, that's nice," Nanny said, and sipped her warm tea. "Matty and I never traveled much. There were always animals to tend to. I never liked to leave this place. You know, I never even liked going downtown to church. I can't bear to be away from this place for so long, and poor Matty can't go that long without his breakfast. I've always been too willing to fatten up that man. Isn't that awful?" She cupped her hand to her mouth and leaned my way. "Don't tell the ladies about church. They'll stop coming for tea."

"Grandmother found God in the natural world," I said. "She never thought much of church either."

"I do miss the dear woman," Nanny recalled.

I leaned in and cupped my hand like Nanny had done. "If they prayed to the Tooth Fairy at that church, I'd be more inclined to go."

That got her laughing devilishly, although she assured me she was frightened for my soul. I found a fresh nightgown and helped her dress for her first night in the daybed. I retrieved all things I deemed essential from her upstairs bathroom with little help from her in the process. She giggled incessantly whenever she thought about the Tooth Fairy, and she talked about Daryl, a nephew she had not seen in years. But, she said, he might find need of the daybed should he return. I found a toothbrush and a hairbrush and a glass for her plastic teeth. In the end I left with the full knowledge that there was no easy way to transfer a life so long lived, from one resting place to another.

Near twilight, I was scooping a pail of cracked corn from the bin in the barn for the next morning's feed. Zach showed up. He leaned his fishing pole against the barn wall and set his tackle box on the work bench. I glanced up with my hands in the feed bin. He was wet and muddy and without shoes. He had a string of trout. There were three of them of good size, and he was waiting for me to notice.

I gave him the required approving smile. "You've been scarce," I said.

He held the string of fish at arm's length. "Booger scored Grace Campbell's biggest watermelon," Zach said. "She'll be pissed."

"You can get shot for that . . . legally, I think."

"Gracie Campbell doesn't have a gun," he said with mock certainty. He clipped his string of fish to the edge of the workbench and dumped a can of foul-smelling bait worms into the grass outside. "Besides, we were starving to death," Zach said and laughed a little. "I've been watching that melon all summer . . . just sitting there getting fatter and fatter. Anyway, I thought it was damn good of Grace to donate her prize melon to the cause. So, we busted it on a rock. I ate half of it before Booger told me he stole it. How did I know? Near as I knew, he was digging worms in the woods back of her garden."

"We could have used your help." I set the full feed pail on the concrete at my feet and wiped my dusty hands on my shirt. "Me and Beep moved a daybed downstairs for Nanny."

"How is she?"

"She's sweet, like Grandmother before she died."

Beepah came to the side door. He saw the trout and smiled. "Get those fish cleaned, Zachary," he said. "We'll put them on the grill." He stepped inside with the shotgun pointing toward the floor. He walked to the gun locker and set it in place with noticeable confusion creasing his brow. "I shot a big tom turkey," he said. "I'll be damned if I could find him."

I heard a single shot an hour before while I was inside the kennel. It sounded like it came from the woods near the meadow. I remembered it distinctly. I stopped what I was doing to once again think of Beepah sitting alone on the trail, holding the shotgun at the ready, all the while contemplating something deadly.

I rarely ventured into the woods when the shotgun was absent from the locker. I thought of Ralph Lauren tumbling from the sky a few years back. I watched Ralph crash into Jolly's pond. Gunshots from somewhere in the trees terrified me at times, by the noise they made or the silence they threatened to leave in their wake.

"It was getting dark," Beep said, closing his eyes to get a fix on the bird. "It couldn't have been a shot more than twenty yards. I walked the meadow front to back, and not a sign of that bird." He gave the locker door a half-hearted slam and twisted the key. Then he hung the key on its nail nearby. "I could have used Tilly, that's for sure. She would'a sniffed him out." He pushed his hands into his back pockets. "I'll have to go out in the morning. The bird might not be ruined if it stays cool, unless a bear gets to him first." Beep headed for the big door. "I'll find something to go with those fish," he said on his way toward the garden.

Trouble stirred the tranquility on Trumpet Hill just near sunrise Monday morning. A dog came up the trail pulling a cop on a short leash. The dog was a black shepherd going along without barking, eagerly skirting the trees along the trail to the south. The forest was still drenched in shadows. The shepherd's nose swept the forest floor out in front of a posse of sheriff's deputies and police. Someone was leading a pack of hounds. A yelping, yapping crescendo rolled up Trumpet Hill, rousting me from the kitchen table to the back porch.

I could see the dog leading the way, the shepherd, straining against the leash just inside the trees near the far end of Jolly's pond. He pulled a man in a baseball cap who disappeared behind a clump of trees, then reemerged when the scant sunlight found him. Sounds were amplified, but on sight, the pack of hounds turned out to be two that were yelping like the fox was just loosed. Three men in plain clothes followed them.

Behind that gaggle came Micah Nash. I recognized him from that far distance only because of his blackness. Even though he was more brown than black, the sun caught his face just so and there was no mistaking him. He said hello to me just that once, the morning I saw him leaving Emily Lipton's house. He even knew my name that morning, not enough familiarity to declare a connection, but the man was instantly likable to me back then. I could see his khaki uniform shirt through the trees as he clawed his way up the rocky trail.

Beep came out on the porch. The screen clapped shut, throwing its echo into the mix. "People in the woods," he said. "I slept in the big bed. I could see them from the upstairs window. They're right out back."

"Micah Nash is with them."

"They're looking for somebody."

My brain began to ponder the events playing out in the woods, although I knew nothing about them. Part of me could not imagine any Bowden complicity in whatever was unfolding. Yet for some reason I felt vulnerable in the very instant I heard a shout from the meadow out back.

"Sheriff!" a cry went up. Then another, "Sheriff Nash!"

The forest began to buzz. Beep scratched his head with his cap. "God knows what, but they got something," he said, then added quickly, "maybe they found my turkey."

I looked up to confront the concerned look on Beep. "What is it?"

"Did Zach go out last night?"

"You know Zach," I said, just as I felt the weight of it. "Oh no!" I gasped. "I don't know."

"Go see if he's in bed. Get him up. I'm going to check things out."

I went through the backdoor shouting for Zach, screaming for my brother. "Zach! Zach!" By the time I hit the third stair with my first step, Zach was rubbing his eyes at his bedroom door. I almost fainted with relief, collapsing on the stairway for the briefest moment. "The sheriff is in the woods!" I blurted out. "They're tracking somebody with dogs—a robber, I think! Maybe somebody escaped!"

He was stricken with disbelief. "Get out, Sydney," he said.

I jumped from the stairs. "Fine. I'm going to tell Beep you're alive. I'm sure he'll be severely disappointed."

I bolted from the house. The screen door rattled, and I went across the yard at a gallop. In my haste, I had forgotten boots. The wet grass was cold on my feet, but I never slowed until I got to the barn. I turned the corner and went through the big door. Beep was staring into the gun locker, and his face was ashen.

"He's okay!" I said. "Zach's okay!"

I didn't know what caused his tear, but there it was running on his cheek. I tried mightily to put myself in his head, to find what he had unraveled, but I could not. Zach was alive. The horrifying thought of anything else might elicit enough relief to produce a tear.

Zach came running, turning the corner at the big door, and almost skidding to a stop on the concrete floor. He had on wrinkled jeans, and he swung a wadded sweatshirt in one hand. "What the hell?" he said.

Beep spoke with as much calm as he could muster, "Where's the shotgun?" He was still staring into the gun locker.

With all the dog yapping coming from the trees, with voices, urgent and loud, Zach's response revealed utter dismay. "I didn't take it," he said, instantly feeling put upon by an accusation of complicity in one nefarious deed or another. "I wouldn't take it . . . not without asking. We always had a deal about that. What the hell! You barely lock the locker anyways! Anybody could take it!"

I looked into the gun locker. True enough, the shotgun was gone. Beep stood for a long moment, leaning against the workbench, trying to reassemble details that had left him in the dark. He shot the tom turkey. He put the shotgun back into the locker. He opened the locker at sunrise and the gun was gone. Where was the glaring omission in that chain of events?

Beep could not solve the riddle. Instead, he closed the locker door quietly and hung the key on the nail. "I'm going to see what's going on out there," he said finally.

"I'm going too," Zach said.

Beep held up a finger. "No talking. No running. No getting in the way."

Zach led out through the deep grass and across the creek. We went up the steep grade to the trail. A few yards up the hill the meadow opened in sunshine just inside a line of trees. There was a gathering. I could see men milling about. Two of the men had a hold on the dogs. The hounds had quieted, lying in the tall grass amid whatever excitement was afoot.

Grace Campbell came up the trail, plowing ahead with her walking stick stabbing at the rocky terrain. Her movements betrayed arthritic joints, and her face grimaced with each step. She stopped every five feet to survey the path ahead and behind. Grace looked up when we arrived. She offered a shaky greeting and steadied herself with the use of her stick. She drew an uneasy breath and stumbled two more steps over the loose rocks and stopped. "I can't go any farther," she resigned openly.

Grace poked at the shifting stones with her stick and leaned in toward Beepah as if there was an encroaching crowd of eavesdroppers at her hip. She looked around to find the trail empty except for her and us and an occasional yelp from a hound. "The Lipton boy didn't come home last night," she said. "For some reason, there's a lot of panic." Grace leaned in even closer and cupped her hand to her mouth. "The sheriff has been spending time with the Lipton girl. And I mean nights."

We knew about Emily and Micah Nash. Beep said it was gossip, not news, and Beep would know. He suffered for it since Emily's arrival, back when they became fast friends, if not more for a time. Gossip about them ran its course and eventually ran out of juice. Grace Campbell led the way, gossip-wise. She fancied herself the lead messenger whenever new rumors began to circulate. "She's the missionary of gossip, if not gospel," Beep once said of Grace Campbell. "Either way, she's bringing the good news."

"We're going up to see what it's all about, Gracie," Beep said. "It looks like whatever it is, it's pretty close to my property."

Grace did a shaky about-face. She set off on her trip back down the mountain, stabbing at the rocky terrain. She slowed to holler back over her shoulder. "Stop by and bring me up to speed, won't you, Ben?"

We climbed the last few yards up the trail to the meadow. We went through the row of maples guarding the opening and stepped out finally onto trampled grass. A few curious people were milling at the meadow rim. More were gathered into a close half-circle out past the old apple tree. It was easy to see they were the ones in charge. Micah Nash appeared to be leading the operation. His arms directed attention here and there while his words crossed the meadow in an uneven hum. Every eye in the group studied whatever lay in the center of their half circle.

"Maybe they found my tom turkey," Beep continued to obsess over the bird. "No license. Out of season . . . I'll have to pay a fine. That's for sure." As if a wayward turkey poacher warranted a posse and a pack of hounds on his heels.

There was a man standing just off the trail peering through a clump of maples. He had a baseball bat slung over one shoulder and he propped his other shoulder against a maple trunk. It was Joel Maris, a neighbor who lived a few houses down from the Jolly place. He ran a fishing tackle shop about three miles up the road toward Kingston. Joel Maris had secured a curious cache of knowledge by arriving at events ahead of local law enforcement. If there was a swarm of cop cars, Joel Maris was probably leading the way. "He uses the bat for swatting bad guys," Beep once said with a laugh.

Beep walked over. "Morning, Joel," he said with a twist of his cap. He ignored the old Louisville Slugger at the ready on Joel's shoulder. "Who they got up there?" he asked instead.

Joel turned his head and gave a jerky nod. "I was up here before Nash and that bunch," he bragged about the race up the mountain. "I walked right past the kid," he said, pointing with the bat. He dropped the fat end into the damp leaves and leaned on it. "He's right there in them ferns. He's dead all right, shot in the face by the look of it. The dogs found him. Maybe he's gettin' ripe already but doubtful. It's cool . . . only been a few hours."

Gracie Campbell's news had the foul flavor of gossip. What Joel Maris said must have rang truer to Beep. The revelation almost took him to his knees. Joel's delivery was crass, to be sure, but his words must have stirred frightening thoughts in Beep. He reached out to support himself against the maples, bracing for whatever came out of Joel's mouth next. I was struck numb.

Jason Lipton was found where he lay in the tall ferns about fifty feet off the trail. There was a 12-gauge shotgun lying at his feet. By Joel's account, the kid was unrecognizable. He took a shotgun blast to the face. According to Joel, Micah Nash found two shotgun shells in his pocket, and in his wallet, two dollars and a student ID. There was a photograph. "Jason Lipton," it read.

"Nash gave me the ol' heave-ho after that," Joel grumbled, still stinging from the sheriff's impertinence. "What do I care? The tackle shop opens at seven anyways. I'll be late to my own funeral." He turned to go.

Beep braved the question. "Is that all they found?"

Joel rapped the baseball bat against a maple tree and let out a bold burst of laughter. "Jesus, Bowden, ain't that enough raw meat for one morning?" He stepped off into the stones and snickered his disbelief at the query.

A young man came up the trail at a full trot. He was dressed in a yellow fireman's slicker, and he carried something rolled under his arm. As it turned out, it was a body bag, and when he had crossed the meadow, he handed it off to Micah Nash. The party in the ferns began to reassemble while they rolled out the bag alongside the body. Jason Lipton was suddenly in full view, his body slumped backward over a rotting tree trunk. The left side of his face was blown away. Flies and yellow jackets had assembled into a ravenous swarm above his bloody corpse.

"Yup, time to go," Joel said, stopping long enough to watch the arrival of the body bag. "They're taking him out of here anyway."

Joel Maris said nothing more of consequence. He went back down the trail, tapping maple trees along the way. Every few steps he kicked a loose stone off the path or stepped into an old rain wash and growled one cussword or another. He disappeared around the bend in the trail while going along, tapping trees and cursing.

Micah Nash stood up and barked at Palmer Willoughby, the kid in the yellow slicker. "Wilby! Let's move these folks back down the hill. Put some crime tape across the path! We got crime tape, don't we? This boy has been out here long enough!" Nash waved his hand to encourage the steadfast bunch along the tree line to get moving. "Please, folks, go home," he said.

Micah recognized Beepah and crossed almost the entire meadow toward him before Beep took a few steps in his direction. "Ben," Micah greeted him when the two stood face to face.

Beep returned a nod of acknowledgement. "Micah," he said.

The sheriff gave a look to Zach and me, and I knew immediately he didn't appreciate our presence at his crime scene. "I wish these kids weren't here, Ben," he said, his voice not restrained enough to conceal his annoyance.

"We heard the commotion from the back porch," Beep explained.

"Awful thing. Awful. Emily called me a couple hours ago," Micah said. "It took a while to get all these men together. Tell you the truth, I thought she was acting hysterical. Mother's intuition, I guess you'd say."

Beep pushed his hands into his back pockets. "Yeah, who would've thought this?"

"All these folks coming and going, I'm sure she knows by now," Micah said. "I'm doing my best to speed this up, but the camera just got here. Emily will get here, and this is a pure heartbreak. Maybe you could slow her down a little, Ben. I heard you two were friends."

Beepah nodded.

Micah turned to go, then turned back. "Another thing, Ben," he said. "We're going out through your property with this boy. It's closest."

Beep nodded again.

We watched Micah walk back across the meadow while the woman with the camera sidestepped around the body as she snapped photographs. By the time he got near, the woman had taken pictures from every angle, but Micah wanted one more. He pointed toward the shotgun, describing the position of it with his arm outstretched. The photographer leaned in and snapped a couple more.

Beep was sending us back to the house then. He was gesturing and talking, but his words barely registered. What was happening was so completely incomprehensible to me, I was not certain I was awake.

"You two get to the bus," was what I thought Beep was telling us. "If you miss the bus, you'll have to walk to school. There will be a lot of noise about this today, plenty of wild rumors. "Don't talk about it. We're awful close to this, like it or not."

Seconds later, four men were stuffing Jason Lipton into the body bag just as Emily Lipton came clawing her way up the trail. Her gray sweatshirt sagged from the weight of the muddy water it had soaked up during her frantic climb. She was on all fours, plowing her way through the stones and mud, scrambling under the fresh crime-scene tape Willoughby had just strung from tree to tree. When she saw the commotion across the meadow, she straightened and her hand went over her mouth to muffle her cry.

Beep stepped out front when Emily cleared the trees. He reached her and put his arms around her, but she would have none of his comforting. She pulled away with a loud, "No!" and she went racing over the flattened meadow grass. By the time she got to Jason, only his head had not been zippered shut inside the body bag. She dropped to her knees and put her hand on the small patch of his face almost recognizable.

"I want you two to go now," Beep said, suddenly fighting tears of his own. "It's a lot to take in before breakfast."

We went back, Zach and me, over the stream and through the tall grass. I tried hard to understand what had unfolded in the woods. The nearest I came to Jason Lipton's body was the fifty or so steps across the meadow where he lay dead among the trampled fern fronds. From there I could see what remained of his face. It was blackened and bloodied. It was hard for me to reconcile, thinking of that face and the one that so brutally crushed against mine, now months in the past. I could not be certain how to feel.

I stepped into my boots on the porch and went to the coop to throw scratch feed for the chickens and send the pigeons out to fly. They peeled away over the barn and into the sky above the meadow. Men milling in the trees must have felt strange and threatening to the flock, and when the birds whirled to the north, an ambulance and a train of cop cars flashing red and blue lights hogged the curb along Trumpet Hill Road. The birds swung to the east over Jolly's pond and into the warmth of the brightening sun. I watched them from the safety of the aviary, and I contemplated the death of Jason Lipton. I was done with him at last . . . perhaps I was done with him . . . perhaps.

CHAPTER SIXTEEN

Even as Trumpet Hill remained in an elevated state of alert, Zach was quiet on the way to the bus that morning. A sheriff's car moving at a crawl came up the hill toward us. Lights flashed like it was leading a parade. The deputy pushed his hand through the open window and gave us an enthusiastic wave and smile. I fully expected he might throw candy like it was the Fourth of July. Zach barely noticed.

So much of my history with Jason Lipton had never been told. With his dying, perhaps there would no longer be nightmares to relive. I could only hope. There would be no eulogizing him, not from my lips. Any pretense might only reveal my elation and relief at his demise. Silence was my safest option. Perhaps Zach felt the same way. He never expressed hatred, not outwardly, except perhaps when Tilly was killed. But on the way to the bus, I saw complacency on his face and it took me by surprise.

I began to struggle with a question looming up inside me. I appealed to Zach, feeling my own personal sense of dread. "Where's the shotgun from the barn?" I asked.

He turned to me with the purest indignation. "Search me, Sydney," was all he said.

The ambulance siren screeched once from high above to announce it was rolling. The bus waited for us at the bottom of the hill. The ambulance went past, coasting along with brake lights pulsing red then dark. It came to a stop near the school bus, their collective tangle of flashing lights dancing in the air reminded me of the lights above a carnival teacup ride. The ambulance inched out in front for the trip to the morgue. The bus driver, Mr. Tobin, waved it through.

I've seen plenty of ambulances in my life. How an ambulance behaves says plenty about the condition of the cargo stretched out in the back. It was Zach who told me that a slow ambulance announces, "Stiff on board, and the slower they go, the stiffer the stiff." I'm certain Ol' Jolly rode in a slow ambulance. I know Grandmother did. This one was hauling Jason Lipton, dead as dead can be. The sheriff's car slid in as a rear guard, and the little caravan was moving mighty slow when it rolled onto the low road down along Esopus Creek.

We went up the bus steps and scurried along the aisle to slide into the seat right behind Booger Sullivan.

Booger spun around immediately. "What the fuck," he said. "Who died? And don't lie."

Zach shook his head. "You already know. It's all over the hill by now."

"I heard a hitman came from Philadelphia and shot Jason Lipton in the face," Booger said. "My dad says it sounds far-fetched. There was something on the news already, but it was sketchy. They said somebody got shot while he was out hunting, but they weren't naming names."

Zach rocked forward. "It was an accident. Micah Nash as much as said it himself. He said we shouldn't talk about it until he figures it out for sure."

"You saw it? Damn! You saw it?"

"He said we shouldn't talk about it, Booger," Zach said again. "Anyway, we didn't see much. It was out back by the old apple tree. How the hell did you find out so much? Don't tell me . . . Grace Campbell."

"Yeah, yeah, ol' lady Campbell came by when I was eating

breakfast. She got really pissy about her prize watermelon gone missing." Booger gave Zach a punch to the shoulder. "Damn good, wasn't it?"

Zach shook his head in disbelief. "You didn't admit to it?"

"Oh, fuck no. I buried the evidence by the creek in case she went all Dick Tracy on us," Booger snickered. "Anyway, she was talking to my dad. I heard it all. She said she got close enough to see the whole dead guy. It was Jason Lipton clear as mud and all shot up. Even if he took one to the face, she could tell it was him. She said it might be some kind of blood feud because Jason's father shows up once in a while and he's some kind of lowlife from Philadelphia."

Zach waved him off with a smirk. "Blood feud, my ass. That's a load. Listen to your father, dumbass."

Booger's thirst for the details was almost unquenchable. He kept up his grilling for the entire ride to school. With Booger it was never easy. Yet, if he was prepared to believe an ounce of Grace Campbell's version, Booger already knew more than I knew. I was certain Gracie never made it to the meadow, which meant she never got a glimpse of Jason Lipton. Even in my rather confused state of mind, I remember her spinning around and descending the mountain. She likely composed her murder mystery along the way, a story rife with details to fill any holes in the tale. And Micah Nash never did call the killing an accident, not that I heard. Yet, Zach was pushing the accident theory as the likeliest truth.

Zach's assertion clued me to a deeper concern. There was more at play than Jason Lipton tripping over his own gun and shooting himself in the head. Zach was worried about eventualities I had only begun to consider. There was Beepah, and there was the gun missing from the locker in the barn. If Micah Nash determined Jason Lipton shot himself, so be it. Otherwise, I might be forced to embrace the "hitman from Philadelphia" version.

That day in school, rumors spread like measles and almost all of them bordered on the sensational. The sheriff did it because he was jealous of the kid. The father did it by accident. Then of course, there was the hitman from Philadelphia. Booger Sullivan helped stir the pot with that bogus theory. Everybody expected Sheriff Nash would be looking for a patsy to hang for the killing, and after their conversation, Beep expected it too.

All that day, until the bus dropped me back at Trumpet Hill, I pondered the events of the morning. My feelings of relief did not last as long as I hoped they would. Instead, logic began to play on me. I felt oddly vulnerable. In the very brief aftermath, I feared for us all.

I stepped off the bus in front of Zach and the Sullivan boys and one of the Campbell grandchildren. We headed up the hill at a near dead run until we were all puffing from exhaustion. We slowed near the Lipton driveway. I counted four cars. There was the mustang parked far over near the fence. Emily's Bronco was pulled into the semicircle in back of the house. Right out front was the sheriff's car with blue lights flashing. The lights suggested the visit was official business. And parked closest to the porch was the big, red Monte Carlo convertible I had once seen. I assumed that would be Jason Lipton's father up from Philadelphia.

We went up a little farther and the Campbell kid peeled off, then the Sullivan boys, although Booger promised to meet us near the apple tree to investigate the crime scene. We stopped on the road in front of the Jolly driveway. An unfamiliar pickup truck had made a wide circle in the long grass and pulled up near the Jolly garage. There were cardboard boxes in the truck bed and ropes thrown over a loose tarp. By the look of things, unpacking had already begun. Zach was quick to identify its origin by the plates. "Maine," he said.

The strange truck was remarkable only because nothing

had changed at the Jolly farm since Ol' Jolly's passing. All of his machinery remained right where he left it when he died. His big green tractor was settling into the earth under a tarp-covered shed. And after twenty years of bearing the load of Ol' Jolly's enormous ass, the springs on his rusty flatbed lost their will to resist. The old truck listed badly, collapsing almost to the ground on the driver's side. It poked its front end through an open barn door and its back end into the dirt track that circled the barn.

The grass was not mowed, not since Ol' Jolly departed, and the salt block Jolly used to bait deer had been licked all the way down to the peg that secured it. Not a shot had been fired. Not a deer had been killed. There was no growl of a tractor nor the bleating of goats. Zach and I had delivered Buddy and Beebo down the road to Grace Campbell the week after Ol' Jolly died. Things became deathly quiet after that. I had fed them and pleaded with Beep to save them. "They'll eat us out of house and home," he said. In the end, Gracie Campbell made a benevolent first offer.

It's not like we missed the hooligans, as Beep affectionately called them. Buddy and Beebo continued their raids on neighbors up and down the hill. "They're worse than the James Gang," the Sullivans declared after finding their gardens ransacked. Our own gardens and feed bins were in their crosshairs more than once. After a year or two of that, Gracie Campbell was forced to hire Beep to build an enclosure suitable to house the head-butting marauders. Beep made a sign and hung it over the door. "Fort Knocks," it read. Gracie liked it.

There was a man circling the truck from Maine. He crossed the driveway and headed toward the barn. He resembled Ol' Jolly, but much younger. Nor was he as tall, but he sported the same broad girth. He saw us standing at the end of the driveway and his pace barely slowed. His eyes held a suspicious gaze on us while he continued tromping along toward the barn. He disappeared through the big doorway and into the darkness.

"Lots of strangers on the hill," Zach said.

I knew he was referring to the cars at the Liptons, and now this curious visitor at the Jolly farm. I knew what he was thinking. Suddenly, Trumpet Hill felt crowded, like we no longer had control of this place that had always been ours. "It might be coincidence," I said finally.

Zach kicked at the gravel along the ditch. "Might be more trouble. This one doesn't look too friendly neither," he said of the fat man in the driveway.

"Nanny said something about a nephew," I recalled. "I saw his picture on the mantle. I think it was a high school picture. This could be him."

"He'll take over the place, just our luck," Zach said. "Everything changed when Jolly died. There's nothing left here but an old woman and two old ducks on the pond."

We hurried up the hill, lest we be taken for interlopers. The house was empty when we arrived home. We dropped our backpacks and went out through the back door with the screen slamming open, then shutting with a screech and a slap. Beep's truck was half hidden behind the barn, and we went across the grass in a rush to find him. It had been the oddest of days for me, worse than Christmas morning for the waiting. But unlike Christmas I expected nothing good, only profound and certain dread.

When we came around the corner of the barn, Beep was on his knees by the entry door. When we got close enough, we could see he was installing a lock.

"Never figured we'd need one of these," he said. He didn't look up, not right away, at least. "Now with people creeping around the place and shooting themselves in the face, I might have to hire a night watchman."

I suspected he was stewing over the events of the day, much like Zach and me were searching for explanations, diabolical or otherwise. Beepah's mind was vulnerable, often plagued by shadowy misdeeds. To him they were indiscernible from the truth. Some days he suffered guilt for them, even remorse. His worries almost always troubled me because of his odd sense of culpability at times.

"I just spent two hours with Micah Nash," he said. "He had plenty of questions, and I didn't have too many answers." Beep fiddled with the lock to see if it latched properly. He gave it a squirt of oil and rattled it back and forth. "I'm not sure if I'm supposed to feel guilty because the kid died behind our house." He twisted the lock back and forth again to see if it clicked. The entire time, he continued to wipe his eyes with his sleeve as if they were filled with pollen. "They found my turkey," he said, finally turning his concerned look toward Zach and me. "I was right about that, at least. They bagged the bird for evidence. Maybe they plan to check the shot size or something, maybe turkey soup."

Some of Beep's psychotic episodes were documented. The VA said they were brought on by the war, but few of the psychologist-types were ever clear in the matter. Mom told me about them when I was years younger. She was careful in her descriptions of Beep's curious way of thinking. "It happened a long time ago, most of it before we met," Mother once said. "He was charming back then. I was young. It was easy to forgive his quirks."

I began to realize in the natural course of things that Beep was not so much like other fathers. He picked us up and dropped us off. He went to the grocery store and he sometimes made dinner. Except for building a barn or an aviary on our little farm, he never kept a job for long. Mom said she trusted him to take care of Zach and me. In a child's mind, Beep's tales were clever fables, and yet the day came when I began to recognize the ones that hinted of great tragedy from long in the past. I began to realize they had been borrowed from a darker place.

After that, whenever he concocted a tale and wrapped it in his mind, I held the moment close and rarely spoke of it lest I stumble upon some terrible truth that only Beep should know. I was eight when that epiphany occurred, when I realized losing Beepah to one of his dark places was the biggest fear of my childhood. It had always been there, simmering, even in the bluest of nights. It came to me then that the darkness I feared might have settled over his mind in the meadow while he searched for the turkey he shot, and in that dark place, Jason Lipton died.

When he turned to us, his eyes were damp and red with worry. I could tell he was struggling to untangle the events that occurred at dusk the day before. He went back to work on the stubborn lock. "I heard the kid's father came up from Philadelphia. That has to be awkward, since Micah Nash has been seeing the woman socially for a while . . . and now all this."

"The sheriff car was at the Lipton place," Zach said.

"I expect he's talking to everybody, and he's doing his best to comfort the poor woman," Beep conceded without any show of malice. "The kid's father has a reputation. I don't know if he deserves it or not. Emily doesn't speak well of the man."

Beep was right about Jason's father. He had a reputation for shady dealings. It was also true the sheriff's car was often seen at the Lipton home over the past many months. However the relationship between Emily and the sheriff was perceived by the locals, it never felt like a bad fit to me. I always liked Emily Lipton, although I saw little of her after Sheriff Nash came on the scene.

I could read the worry on Beep's face, so I asked him, "Did you tell him you were in the woods?"

"Of course," he said. "I had to, but I wasn't so sure about the turkey. I said it got too dark to see." Beep got off his knees and stood in silence for a long moment, wiping his hands incessantly with his shop rag. Finally, he pushed it into his hip pocket. "The sheriff asked me if I took any shots, and I swear, just then I wasn't sure. I told him I couldn't remember." His expression revealed his disappointment. "I don't think that was a smart thing to say. I'm sure it wasn't."

One last twist of the key and he appeared satisfied everything was working properly. He stepped inside and hung the key on the nail next to the gun-locker key. When he stepped back out, he was smiling about the useless lock and the useless key. He pulled the rag from his pocket and wiped his hands again. "It's a good thing I don't have a horse," he said, explaining his sheepish smile.

I got it, as far as barn doors go. To enlist words Beep might employ to further muddy the water, why install a lock once the horse has flown the coop? Of course, in this case it was a shotgun, mysteriously departed from the barn.

Beep took a few steps across the grass toward the house and stopped. When he turned back, his mood seemed to brighten a little more. "Did you meet your new neighbor?"

"We saw the guy," Zach said.

"He looks like a Jolly, but he's not as friendly as his uncle," Beep said. "I didn't see him at Jolly's funeral neither. He must have skipped that soiree. I met him a few months after. He came down from Maine to case the joint. He spent a year fighting it out in probate. I guess he owns the Jolly place now."

Whatever the outcome, to me it sounded grossly unfair. "What about Nanny?" I asked.

"Yeah, I guess he had her declared incompetent," he said with a shrug. "I went down to the Kingston courthouse one day in the spring, but as a neighbor, I held little sway in the matter of rightful ownership. I did manage to raise his back hair a little, so I doubt we'll ever be friendly." Beep found a dry spot on his rag and mopped his brow, then stuffed the rag back into his pocket. "As far as Nanny Jolly, if he sees to her needs, it could work out in the end."

Beep headed off toward the house at a tired pace. I realized then not every good thing Beep did was shared with me. I found out soon enough the man's name was Daryl Jolly, a nephew, a sole survivor... except for Nanny, of course. She was declared incapable of running her own affairs. In all of my visits with her, she had said nothing about a court fight or a ruthless nephew scheming to steal her farm. I suspect in that regard alone she was addled. Beep tried to protect her in his own simple way, but in the end, Daryl Jolly won the farm.

We caught sight of Booger Sullivan through the trees near the south end of Jolly's pond. He was making his way up the trail toward the meadow at an energetic lope. I heard the screen door close and Beep disappeared inside. Zach and I headed out back to meet Booger. We went over the trampled grass and past the teepee where much of the commotion took place only hours before when they hauled out Jason's bloody body. We crossed on the stones where the gurgling stream was loud enough to drown out other noises in the woods.

At the trail, Booger shattered the eerie quiet with his typical chide. "What the fuck, Zee-man? Is this where it happened?"

Suddenly, in the wee distance there was the recognizable sound of a shovel at work, stabbing at the spongy forest floor, creating a rhythm that was slow and methodic. Zach put his hand up to silence Booger, all the while peering through the stand of maples along the trail. I could see a man through the trees. He was dressed in jeans and wore no shirt. He appeared to be middle-aged. He was not a big man, but lean and muscled. He was hard at work on the far side of the meadow, right where Jason's body lay sprawled on a rotting stump in the chilly morning. By the look of it, the man was covering the stump with the soft earth from the meadow.

He paid us no attention for the longest time until even I began to question the purpose to our presence there. At best, we were intruders. The man straightened finally, looking down at the mound he had created. He ran the shovel over it to smooth the surface, then he bowed his head and leaned on the shovel handle. When he said his prayer, he looked across the meadow in our direction, twisting a little to find us through the tree trunks.

Once his eyes settled on us, he did not hesitate. He took a few steps across the trampled fern fronds to retrieve his shirt from the ground. He flung it over his shoulder and pinned it there with the shovel. He came across the meadow at a confident pace. When he reached the nearside, he cocked his head to catch another glimpse of us through the trees. His eyes fell on me in the shadows, and he engaged me with a bit of a smile.

Suddenly and without the slightest equivocation, I was certain of one glaring truth. Here was the man who drove the red Monte Carlo up from Philadelphia. It had been two years and then some since we had first laid eyes on the man . . . the same day the mustang arrived on the hill. I turned to Zach and Booger, and they turned to me. We all knew him! Here was Willie Lipton . . . the killer from Philadelphia! He spoke as though I was alone on the trail. "Did you know him?" he asked me.

I was frozen for a long moment. His was a voice filled with Philadelphia influence, even more than Jason's had been, much more than Emily's. "Yes, of course I knew him," was what I expected myself to say. But if I said that, I might have to admit that ours was never a happy acquaintance. I felt no compulsion to say something comforting, if comforting was needed.

"He told me about a girl he liked," the man said. "I thought it might be you."

His words shook me. I didn't want to believe Jason Lipton's obsessions began and ended with me, even though I had little reason to believe otherwise. "We all knew him a little," I said finally, turning to Zach and Booger to make the admission more inclusive.

"He was my boy," he said, stabbing the head of the shovel into the ground and pushing it in with his foot. He put his hands over the handle and rested his chin there. "I didn't get to see him much the past few years. I blame his mother. It's a long way from Philly to here, and I got work. She's the one who made the fight. If he went to juvie, he'da been out two years ago and still living in Philly where he belonged."

We had heard stories or invented them ourselves. He was a small-time hoodlum from Philadelphia who stole cars and got his son into the business. That was what we heard. He was also an embezzler, a wife beater, and a killer, if we were to believe the stories coming from Grace Campbell or any number of her acolytes.

"I came up here to find the place where he was killed," he said. "His blood was on that stump over there. I went back down and got this shovel. Blood is blood," he said, nodding toward the stump across the meadow. "It doesn't matter how much is left, blood is blood. So, I came up here to talk to Jesus, and bury this little bit of my son."

We all turned to go. I kept my eyes to the rocky trail. It was the best I could do, departing in silence. All of us must have felt the same because there was not another word from us. Even Booger held his tongue. There was only a gentle wind in the trees and the clicking of rocks on the path where we stepped. We heard nothing more from the man. He must have watched us depart. I searched for sympathy in my heart but found it incompatible with my severe dislike for Jason Lipton. Still, no matter what imperfections directed this man's life, it was clear he loved his son. In that moment, I felt empty.

———————

That evening at the table Beepah told us Mom would try and cut her time in Geneva short. "She might be home on Friday, but she wouldn't swear to it," he said.

He fell short of telling us he asked her to come home. He never suggested he told her he needed her, but this time I suspected he told her that very thing. In all my life, even during episodes that left his judgment clouded, never had I witnessed anything that affected him so deeply. He had no memory of the events in the meadow when he shot the turkey, and I could tell he was struggling desperately to fabricate a story out of thin air, one he could live with without complicity or guilt.

"I told her a neighbor kid was killed in the meadow behind the house. She asked who and I told her. I must have woken her from a dead sleep because she didn't know Jason Lipton." He shrugged and stirred at his chili bowl with a spoon. "The poor woman works too hard," he said. "She never gets to spend much time at home, and then something like this happens."

Those days dragged before Mother came home. I spent much of the time in my room writing in my notebook about the collapse of civilization on Trumpet Hill. Almost two years had passed since Ol' Jolly's demise, and months since poor Tilly was discovered under a brush pile along the river. On cool nights I would peek through the shade of my window, and if the light was just enough, I might imagine a puff of cigarette smoke roll into the night air near the teepee and my discontent would be rekindled for a time.

In the few nights since Jason died, my anxiety in the matter of window watching was heightened rather than relieved. Finding that puff of smoke in the night air could support any number of scenarios, beginning with my own sanity. There remained the possibility that Beep's demons had returned to ply his mind and his soul with all manner of irrational thought. Given his present state, he was ripe for a visit.

Beep let us stay home from school on Thursday. I headed out early to let the birds out to fly. They lingered over the meadow as if there remained a presence there. Then they headed north, dipping low over Jolly's pond just as the sun was changing black water into gold.

I pitched dirty straw into the scratch yard and covered the floor with a fresh layer. Water was refreshed. The chickens scrambled out on Cowboy's heels. His cantankerous entrance was proof enough the day was off to a predictably fortuitous beginning. He bounced aboard his favorite rock on the wall and craned his scrawny neck for his first bellow of the morning, letting the entire Trumpet Hill population know they were lazy assholes if they lay in bed for one more minute.

I headed for the barn swinging the empty feed pail. Zach was sitting in the sunlight on the bank of Jolly's pond. His arms were locked over his knees and his head was resting in the fold. The pigeons passed overhead and began to drop down to the aviary hard deck. Zach looked up into the morning sky. When I crept toward him, he must have felt my presence. I could see a smile tug his cheek. I dropped down beside him on the wet grass and gave him an elbow. "You're up early," I said.

"First time I've been up before you in ten years," he said. "It feels like a Saturday."

"Why's Beep letting us stay home from school?"

Zach pulled a clump of grass and pitched it toward his feet. "He's scared to be alone," he said.

"Scared? Really?"

"You've seen him. He's messed up over Jason Lipton's bloody farewell. I'm sure the sheriff is figuring out what happened in the meadow. He might be figuring Beep into the whole mess. Beep was in the meadow. There's no denying that anymore, and everybody on the hill knows there was no love lost between those two."

I pondered Zach's words for a long moment. "You're right," I said finally. "Beep doesn't know what happened. I bet it scares the heck out of him. Whatever memories he has didn't all happen in the meadow. They happened in Vietnam, some of them, and now they're all twisted together. The same memories that have him jumping off bridges, and now his gun has gone missing. If that doesn't make Micah Nash suspicious, what does?"

The early-morning dew had drenched the grass and left my jeans wet to the skin. I pushed myself up and tried without success to slap some of the wetness from my backside. "My ass is wet," I grumbled.

"Not my problem," Zach said with a snort.

I stood looking across the pond into Jolly's field where I had tagged along so many mornings with Ol' Jolly himself. Much of my memory resides in that place. The pigpen stood empty and leaned badly against a tool shed that leaned back. Down the way and just short of the trees where the stream ran through, Jolly's empty saltlick stood askew and barely recognizable without a heavy block of salt on the peg.

I remembered those days running out in front of Ol' Jolly all the way to the lower field just to run my tongue up and down the salt block. I'd have a good lick before he arrived out of breath to shoo me away. "That's for the dang deer," he cursed at me a little. Of course, in those days, not a year or two after sharing my morning bottles with a suckling pig named Panfry, a little deer drool wasn't about to kill me.

"I'm hoping Micah Nash comes by and tells us it was an accident. Jason Lipton tripped over a rotten tree stump and shot himself in the head. Case closed," I declared. "People can say what a tragedy and the whole thing will dry up in a few days." I turned over the feed pail for a drier place to sit, and I lowered my wet bottom to it. "That's too simple, isn't it?"

"Loose ends," Zach said. "Was there a shell in his gun? Was it spent? They found the bird. Who shot it?" He shrugged. "You know . . . things like that."

I found myself recalling events from far in the past while I pitched rocks to the middle of the pond. Zach tossed a rock and our ripples collided. "I remember going with Beep to see Dr. Campion. I was only three or four. I wouldn't even remember the man except I have a drawing of him in my room. I made him into a cartoon character—a chipmunk, I think. Anyway, it wasn't flattering. I was cruel as a child."

Zach's response was slim praise. "There's still hope for you, Sydney," he said with a laugh.

I jabbed him on the shoulder, and he fell back in the wet grass. "Oops, my bad," he feigned an apology. "Campion had a candy bowl in his waiting room. I remember that much. It put me on a sugar rush for the ride home." Zach laced his fingers together and stared at the brightening sky. The flock passed overhead, then dipped low, disappearing for a moment beyond the barn. "Something bad happened to Beep and a judge said he had to see a shrink. Nobody ever said it to me. I might have overheard it or figured it out for myself. I think Beep got nabbed for driving drunk."

That surprised me, not because of the likelihood or otherwise, but I had not heard it and it felt like a slight. "You never told me that."

Zach shrugged. "You were little. It took years before I knew, and by the time I knew, things changed. Campion died. After that Beep stopped going to shrinks. I heard Campion say once we were well-behaved kids. Beep puffed up over that until I found a plastic truck in the waiting-room toybox. I didn't want to leave without it. I threw a big shit fit." Zach laughed and squirmed a little in the wet grass.

"I remember," I said. "Of course, who knows which one of your shit fits I'm remembering. You flipped out plenty of times before you became the sweet, introspective guy you are today." I laughed, rolling a little on my upturned feed pail to deliver a punch to his shoulder .

"Ah, thanks, Syd," he said, gushing playfully. "I bet that changed Campion's mind about our behavior. Anyway, he said things like 'prolonged' and 'debilitating psychosis' when he talked to Mom. I didn't know those words, but they sounded like a death sentence. I listened for them after that, and I'd go into panic mode. It was years before I realized Campion was talking about Beep and not about me."

"You and me never talked about any of that," I said.

"When Campion died, most of that junk died with him. Anyway, Mom thought Beep was cured. Even I know you don't get cured from what he's got. He got it in the war. It messed up his head like the rest of those looney tunes at McCutchen's, Louie King and that bunch."

"Louie's not loony," I said and shrugged. "He just talks dirty all the time."

A slapping screen door pulled our eyes from ripples on the pond in time to catch our new neighbor, Daryl, standing on the Jollys' back porch. He stretched a little as if he had just rolled out of bed, and he scoured the entire backyard with a slow sweep of his head. His gaze found us and settled there with apparent indignance. I waved to him cautiously. He hiked his sizable pants to the middle of his belly and clumped down the steps, heading off across the gravel toward the barn.

A few minutes later, Ol' Jolly's small tractor engine growled and sputtered. The little John Deere rolled around the corner of the barn and plowed its way through the deep grass pulling Ol' Jolly's small trailer. He was packing a load of loosely wound hoses. As he drew closer, we could see his cargo included Ol' Jolly's gas-powered pump.

Zach had already assessed the man. "What's this jerk-off up to?" he said, pondering.

"He's coming over here."

Daryl wheeled the tractor down along the pond bank where the ducks clambered for feed in years past. Since Jolly's passing, they venture down to preen and wait for the occasional handful of pellets. The two old birds came waddling down from their pen just as the little tractor rolled to a stop in the thick red mud. Daryl pulled his big body out of the seat and his boots began to settle into the ooze. He reached across and cut the engine and the little tractor sputtered, then fell silent.

Big Daryl waved at us, but it was hardly a friendly wave. "You kids can't be here!" he hollered across the water. "If kids get hurt here, I'll get the blame! So, no offense, but I'm closing it down!"

I got up from the feed pail and retrieved it from the soggy ground. I almost didn't believe what I was hearing. No more pond for chucking rocks? No more fishing? And for Zach, the message must have been doubly offensive. No more turtle hunting. After the age of four or five, he had devoted entire summers to outwitting the big snapper. Daryl, by his declaration, put an end to the annual turtle hunt.

Zach watched the two old ducks cutting trails through blankets of dandelion puffs blown from the bank. The pond water snagged the puffs like flypaper and the ducks made a game of it. Zach pushed himself up from the wet grass. "Can't hunt snappers forever," he grumbled.

He headed back through the maple trees toward the barn. I followed him. His jeans and sweatshirt were drenched by the morning dew. I realized just then, tagging along behind, I had failed to watch him grow. He would be seventeen come one more summer. He was tall and he carried himself like a man. He had said nothing to Daryl in retaliation, a silence that might have defied his younger nature. He had grown wise enough to realize there would be nothing gained by casting an idle threat across the pond. I saw Beepah in him, all the strengths and all the good. Perhaps that is why he walked so tall. To my mind, that was reason enough.

CHAPTER SEVENTEEN

Mother came home Friday in the evening. I was sitting on the front steps thinking it might be hours before her arrival. I vowed to stay awake to greet her. The light was fading when the sleek limo pulled into the driveway just beneath the cherry trees. The trunk immediately clicked open. Martin killed the headlights and stepped out. He closed the front door quietly.

"Hello, Sydney," he said with casual familiarity.

I offered him my friendly face, which was often the best I could do. I realized then how long the ritual went on: Martin waving goodbye, Martin saying hello. My lifetime, at least. He went to the back door and opened it for Mom to swing her legs out to the asphalt. I came off the porch and walked to her while Martin retrieved her suitcase from the trunk. She threw her arm over my shoulder, and we headed toward the porch.

"How's your father?" she asked.

"He's struggling," I said.

Martin met us at the porch with Mom's bag. He set it near the front door and nodded. "Have a good evening, Angela," he said, and he went back down the steps. On his way to the limo, he let his suitcoat drop from his big shoulders. He folded it over an arm, and when he got to the limo, he laid it flat on the backseat. He gave one more obligatory wave and slid into the driver's seat.

I could not know what Martin knew about the latest Bowden family crisis, or if the two of them even engaged in conversations about such things. I remained silent until Martin pulled the door shut and eased the limo backward out of the driveway.

"You know Beep. He's not telling us much," I said. "He talked to the sheriff. I don't know how that went exactly, except it's got him pretty worried."

"I talked to him on the phone two nights ago," Mom said in a labored voice. "He sounded confused."

I suspected she spent the entire trip from the airport on the phone talking business with her team in Geneva. She had likely put Beepah out of her mind until her arrival home where she would have to confront the crisis. She gave me a tortured look. "He sounded very confused," she said again, and she wheeled me toward the door.

"Will you take this to my room, dear?" she begged after a long exhale. "Oh, and where's your father and that beautiful boy?"

"Zach's with Beep. He's driving the truck. He's taking driver's ed, or did you know?"

"Of course, dear," she said, as if she was always finely tuned to the intricate workings on the Bowden farm. She barely slowed on her way to the kitchen. "I need a drink."

For the biggest part of it, her world was foreign to me and far more expansive, but I always did my best to inject myself into it, with or without her help. There were few times she was willing to open up to me. There was John Goff. She spoke of him often with both whimsy and affection. During my developing years, my fantasies revolved around him until I actually met the man and severed all romantic ties and fantasies. I was ten at the time John Goff was at last revealed to me, more fossil than functioning male, as if I could discern the difference at ten.

I took the suitcase and made the first few steps to the landing. She had disappeared into the kitchen, and I could hear the faint rattling of ice into a glass. "Dog hair," I muttered, and climbed the remaining steps to the hallway. It was dark and the house was quiet. She added little to the hum of silence that infused the space, and I felt strangely lonesome.

Unbeknownst to her, I had felt that way much of my life. I had few friends either by choice or by chance, and my earlier years became a competition with my mother, not that she was aware. I resented her most intensely at times. Yet I convinced myself those days offered an accurate accounting of her life ... that, and my suspicions of a love affair with Alexandra Su Bien. The vision of Alexandra I also usurped for my pleasantest dreams.

With my father it was easy enough. We were much the same. At least that was how he explained our common genes. "We're cut from the same cloth, darling," he once said to me. "Storytellers, the both of us. Although, I'm the bigger liar, and even that is sure to be more practice than raw talent. Lies are invented. The truth is not."

Beep's words settled on me over time. I came to recognize silence as a most perfect lie. So, quite naturally I went about it quietly, putting pencil to paper in my stories, filling a void in the absence of flesh-and-bone companions. There was always a graceful elegance to Mother's deceptions. She managed them with the rarest amount of guilt. Of course, there would be no demand for recompense should her treachery be discovered. Beep could never achieve such guile. Guilt clung to him like soot to a chimney sweep, and it burned in his soul.

I flipped on the light in her bedroom. The bed was made, but there was evidence Beep had slept there once or twice during her absence. After the incident in the meadow, he retreated to the basement once again. I believe he slept very little in the days that followed. I dropped the suitcase to the floor on her side of the bed and tipped the candle jar on the nightstand. I pulled out the photograph of her and Alexandra near the beach in the Canary

Islands. I often visited the photograph when Mom was away. That meant Mom still held it dear, and the realization stirred a longing in me.

Mother was on the couch with a glass of dog hair when I arrived in the front room. She kicked off her shoes and beckoned to me with a wave of her hand. "Tell me everything," she said. "You'll have to bring me up to speed before the boys get home. There was nothing on the news in Geneva about the murder on Trumpet Hill." She laughed a little, finding her own remark clever, even amusing. "I wasn't trying to be glib. Well, maybe I was. Come sit here, dear." She patted the cushion beside her.

I sat on the couch where she directed. Immediately, by her expression, I could tell she was not prepared to admit to knowing anything about Jason Lipton. That meant I would have to spoon-feed her from his arrival on day one if I wanted the entire story told. I decided quickly that would not be my mission. Instead, I told her about the Lipton family down the hill, who had lived in the old Smoron house for at least seven or eight years. Even I remembered that the subject of Emily Lipton had been broached in years past, during the time of the great disposal fiasco. She finally admitted she had heard of Emily Lipton, an attractive single woman, she recalled.

"Your father seems to like her," she said, raising her feet to the coffee table and crossing her legs. "I never met the woman."

Her apparent disinterest surprised me a little. I was already aware of her penchant for pretty faces, given Alexandra's, and Emily Lipton's was definitely a pretty face. Then I considered John Goff, and I had to concede she had a penchant for homely faces too. Only once had I heard her describe John Goff. "Rugged," I believe was her word for him. I tried mightily to reappraise my vision of the man, but I never could. The contrasts had me smiling, and of course, she could not have known why.

I decided speaking ill of Jason Lipton would serve no purpose. Instead, I launched into an explanation of the events I witnessed in the woods on Monday morning. "It was early," I said. "I hadn't even gone out to the birds yet, and then all this commotion starts up out back. There were dogs and cops and sirens on the hill. What a racket."

I told her about Micah Nash leading the way, and how word got out quickly that the Lipton boy did not come home from hunting the day before and his mother was concerned. "Everybody knows, Micah Nash knows Emily Lipton. His car is always there, and it's the official sheriff's car too."

I told Mom that by the time we got out to the trail, a few regular people were there milling around. Grace Campbell convinced most everyone she confronted that the posse was a big joke. Some of them made an about-face and headed back down the mountain. "Grace Campbell called the whole production a charade. Grace reminded us that Jason Lipton was almost a grown man, and nobody goes looking for a grown man just because he went to the woods for a couple hours."

I took a deep breath. "Emily Lipton must have had a premonition because she convinced Micah Nash. He rounded up every dog in town to make a big show just to impress Emily. Gracie's story almost held up until Micah Nash found Jason dead in the meadow."

"Isn't he the Black man?"

"Of course, he's the Black man," I scoffed. "He's the sheriff."

"I always liked him," she said, rolling her eyes a little. "He came up here one morning when I was just leaving for a day trip to Atlanta. His lights were flashing. Thank God there were no sirens. He was very friendly and polite. He had a complaint about a crowing chicken. He acted a little embarrassed by the sudden urgency to investigate a loudmouth rooster."

"That's ol' Cowboy," I said.

"Is that bird still alive?"

"We hear him every morning, Mother. He's setting a record for longevity. Beep says he's over thirteen, and that's more than ninety in dog years." We both laughed a little at Beep's apples and oranges. "Anyway, every now and then the sheriff shows up way too late to catch him. He'd have to go on stakeout to catch ol' Cowboy squawking. No cop is willing to sit in the bushes all night to nab a scrawny rooster. It's pretty funny when you think about it."

Mom swirled the ice in her glass and tipped it up. When she set it to the table, the ice rattled in an otherwise empty glass. It was another half hour before the pickup made the turn at the side driveway and bounced up into the backyard. Five minutes later, Beepah and Zach came in through the kitchen door. They were still making small talk and laughing a little. I had not heard it for a few days, and it lightened me some. Beep came into the front room first. His eyes found Mom and he smiled.

"Look who's here," he said, the relief at her arrival settling on him visibly. He took the few steps and kissed her on top of her head. "I'm not sure why, but I didn't expect you until late."

"Martin makes everything so easy sometimes," she said, reaching out both arms. "Zach," she beckoned him.

We talked for another hour together, as a family, like it seldom was in those days. A kid I knew from school only as Josh delivered the pizza we ordered, sausage on one side, pepperoni on the other, with onions and peppers all around. I went to the door with a twenty-dollar bill and a few singles Beep gave me. "Keep it," I told the kid. He smiled and waved and called me Syd like we were old friends. I watched his car through the front window. It backed out and tore off down the hill.

Beep said little after he confessed for the hundredth time that he was in the woods that night. It nagged at him incessantly. He had no idea what happened in the meadow. In almost a week's time he could not manage a reasonable explanation for the blackout in his memory, but his calm demeanor was evidence enough he felt safer with Mom home.

As far as rumors and innuendos go, Mother was at least the third or fourth person removed from the entire calamity. She had spent most of her week sprawling sleepily in a Geneva hotel bed or pushing huge numbers across a conference table. There was nothing visual she could call upon, and most of her questions sounded trivial. She wanted to know why Jason Lipton was hunting turkeys in the dark, and she wanted to know what ignited the massive manhunt even though I had explained its inception in detail only an hour before. I reminded her it was Micah Nash and his insatiable desire to accommodate Emily Lipton that inspired the wild events that morning. Of course, it might have been her third dog hair that triggered her amnesia in the matter. She let us know again how much she liked Micah Nash.

"Nobody expected to find a dead guy in the meadow, but Sheriff Nash sure made a show of it," I said. "I bet there was a dozen people standing around in the meadow watching the whole circus, and now they all have an opinion."

Questions loomed without answers. What happened to the shotgun from the locker in the barn? And how convenient was its disappearance the night of the killing? What evidence will the turkey carcass yield? Beep had not admitted to killing the bird to Micah Nash, although he was certain he had gunned down the gobbler when he confronted us in the barn that Sunday night. It was Monday morning when all hell broke loose.

"I made more trouble for myself when I talked to Nash," Beep said, shaking his head over his memory lapse. "I was sure I shot that bird. I lay awake all night and by morning I wasn't so sure.

Nash won't believe a thing I say anymore, if he ever did." He pushed his cap up and gave his head a scratch of bewilderment. "To top it off, I fell out of bed. I was crippled all week, and you'd think Nash might ask me about my more pronounced limp." He continued grumbling more about the sheriff's line of questioning and the certainty Nash would never believe him again until his ramblings began to sound nonsensical and he must have realized it himself. "Damn, that concrete floor is a bitch to bounce off," he groaned finally.

"Falling out of bed is a poor defense, Benjamin," Mom said. "You might want to rethink that part of your story."

"Hey, the truth is the truth," he said, stung by her insensitivity in the matter. "I might not remember much, but I sure as hell remember that."

The conversation began to drag. Zach and I had said little for the better part of an hour. The pizza was down to scraps of crust. Mom's eyes drooped and Beep had all but spoken his piece, what he could recall of it. Suffice it to say the entire Bowden family was feeling besieged despite the absence of a single accusatory word. But, like Beep said in closing, "Micah has a job to do. He'll get around to me, if he ain't there already."

I climbed the stairs, giving a silent goodnight with a wave. In my dark room I slipped my fingers through the blind over the window. The blackness far out beyond the barn filled the hollows deep into the trees. It covered the teepee in darkness and quiet. Yet I could hear it all when my eyes closed, the fairies playing their music, the stream pouring over rocks on its way down the mountain. They all spoke to me. There were no smoke clouds exhaled into the chilly air to trigger foreboding premonitions. There were no demons huddled to spring their evil. I tried desperately to feel the peace there, but I could not.

Zach came up and shuffled in the hallway. He pushed his door shut and I heard nothing more from him. Mother and Beepah never came upstairs, not while I lay awake. I heard the basement door open, then click shut. I heard them on the basement steps. I don't believe they talked well into the night. A humming, undecipherable dialogue continued for a time. I suspect they slept. My hope was Beep slept in her arms. I prayed to the Tooth Fairy that Mom rekindled her capacity for that much kindness toward him.

I went out to the birds just as the sun cracked the treetops to the east. I opened the flyway trap and out they went. I sprung the latch on the swing door and Cowboy tumbled out with a big grouchy attitude. He speared my leg with his broken beak. He beat his wings and came at me again until I dismissed the half-feathered fossil with the edge of my boot. He collected himself enough to cock-walk his way to his favorite rock in the wall. He hopped aboard. He was shaken by my boot to the head. He quickly recovered enough to mount a victory crow. He was in good voice, as it turned out. Out strutted a parade of females in his wake.

An hour later Micah Nash came calling. I saw the blue lights breaking through the trees that lined Trumpet Hill. Two official sheriff cars crept along as if leading a funeral procession. Micah Nash wheeled his big car into the driveway. Tires popped on the scattered gravel. That was the only noise to announce his arrival. Right behind him came the second car with two deputies on board.

I heard the popping tires and knew the second car had made the turn. I came from the aviary at a full run, rounding the corner of the house in time to see Micah Nash step onto the asphalt and straighten his big frame. I stopped there and watched, afraid of their purpose. Micah rested his hand on the gun strapped high on his hip. He surveyed the front of the house, and when his eyes found me partly hidden behind a holly bush, he smiled. I quickly determined he was not there to arrest a loud-mouthed rooster for crowing. It was Beepah, and I was certain of it.

"Morning, Sydney," Micah greeted me in his friendly tone. He waited, and when he heard no response from me, he came right out with it. "Your dad up, is he?"

I had no idea if Beep was up. It was well after six. Under normal circumstances, I would have simply answered yes, but life had not been normal for the past many days. Beep and Mom were asleep in the basement bed when I slipped out to feed the birds and write a passage about Mom's return home from Geneva. I prayed her presence in the basement bed had comforted Beep. Micah's arrival shortly after sunrise felt more like I had been betrayed by whatever deity was fielding my calls.

"No," I said.

I swear, before the word cleared my lips, Beep stepped out the front door. He walked the three paces to the porch post and leaned against it. His demeanor was calm. Oddly, he exhibited relief at seeing the big man standing in the driveway. He took a sip from his coffee cup and tipped it toward the sheriff. "Micah," he said.

"Ben."

"Too early for coffee for your boys?"

"We've been up a good long while."

I went along the flower garden until I got to the front steps. I went up and leaned against Beep. He bent a little to kiss me on the head. I listened for Micah to state his business, to say he was closing the book on the incident in the meadow, to say there were no guilty parties. Jason Lipton's death was a tragic accident. All the while I felt my world imploding. My knees began to wobble, and I could feel the fear twisting at my gut.

"We need you to come downtown, Ben," Micah said. "We uncovered some disturbing evidence. We're hoping you can help us get a better handle on it. Sorry to disrupt your Saturday so early. Can you come along? It sure would be helpful."

I felt a hand on my shoulder. "Maybe you should get your mother," Beep said.

Zach passed me in the doorway. "What the fuck?" he whispered to me.

Minutes later, we all stood on the front porch in various stages of dress, me in my coop boots and Mom in a bathrobe. Zach was naked but for his cutoff jeans and his usual tangled bedhead. Beep was dressed for Saturday farm work.

"What's this about, Sheriff?" Mom asked, although to the rest of us, the question sounded inappropriate for its lack of depth . . . unless of course, she had just dropped in from Neptune.

"Just loose ends, Mrs. Bowden. Ben might help. We're hoping so, anyway."

"I could go," Zach said.

Micah offered a conciliatory smile. "Maybe next time, Zach. For now, we think your father might be able to give us what we need." Micah turned to Beep. "You can ride with me to my office. You've been there. It's not far. You ready?" He made a vague gesture toward the back seat of the sheriff's car.

Beep still appeared perfectly calm, much more at ease than I'd seen him during the entire week following the shooting. He even appeared to welcome the intercession into whatever nightmares he'd suffered. At last, I suspected, he felt he would hear the truth about what happened in the meadow and his worry and guilt would end.

"Are you ready?" Micah asked again, this time, with some impatience.

Beep looked down at his crusty boots and ragged work clothes. "I guess, if it ain't black tie," he joked, attempting to signal us there was little to fear.

———

Micah Nash called later that same day. He informed Mother his office would be keeping Beepah until a hearing scheduled for Tuesday of the following week. "You can bring him some toiletries, if he has some favorites, and you can bring him some clothes suitable for a court appearance," was somewhat how he worded it. We were certain Beep had been Shanghaied by Micah and his polite words and hauled off in the wee hours to a dark and dank dungeon. Mom even said she could not imagine what she ever saw in Micah Nash. She stopped liking him on the spot. She made that clear enough.

We spent the day alone on Sunday. By then, word of Beep's arrest had spread to all of Trumpet Hill and into neighboring towns, if not the whole country. Mom held us close a good part of the morning. She even scrambled eggs and served them with wheat toast and peach jam. I was certain she had not slept, pacing the floor in the big bedroom, consumed by worry. When I came in from the birds, she had already packed a small bag for Beep. Just before noon she said she would not be long and left.

Zach and I retreated to the barn. The shed roof on the backside kept the rain off the split wood we mostly used for teepee fires. The big extension ladder reclined across the wood stack. The contraption must have measured twenty feet when it was stretched out. We only needed half that length to get well above the shed roof.

The ladder rattled when it fell against the overhang. Zach climbed the first eight rungs and stepped off onto the shingles. I followed him. We walked up the sloping roof and sat with our backs against the barn wall. From there, we had a clear view of Jolly's pond.

Zach said nothing for a few minutes. We both studied the pond and realized it had changed. There was more red mud visible above the waterline. Even the ducks seemed perturbed by it, skirting clumps of vegetation adrift in the middle of the pond. But all things were still and quiet and had been that way throughout the morning. Jolly's big gas-powered pump rested idle in the grass atop the far bank. A heavy hose climbed the muddy slope to the pump, then exited the backend and crawled the entire width of the field until it disappeared somewhere near Jolly's saltlick just into the trees.

"He wasn't lying," Zach said. "He's draining it."

"Why?"

"If I didn't know better, I'd say Micah Nash has something to do with it."

"Beepah's gun?"

"That's where I'd toss it if I wasn't thinking straight, and that's where I'd look first too."

We heard Jolly's tractor start up far off in the distance. Moments later, around the corner of the barn came Big Daryl straddling the little John Deere, plowing his way toward the pond. He had beat down a road through the deep grass in his many trips. This time he was hauling two big gas cans in the small trailer. He caught sight of us sitting on the shed roof. He appeared unshaken by our interest, pressing forward until he pulled to a stop near the pump.

"I haven't seen Nanny since he showed up," I said to Zach. "I saw her almost every day before things went crazy on the hill. Now it's been a week. I feel like I should keep an eye on her."

"Are you sure she's still alive?"

"That's not funny, Zachary."

Big Daryl managed to muscle one of the red cans from the trailer bed. He opened the pump's gas cap and tipped the heavy can, slopping gasoline over the grass until he found the hole for the nozzle. The fill-up only took a minute, and when he retrieved the nozzle more gas slopped out. He moved the can away and fumbled with the choke and the on-off. He finally got around to the pull rope. He gave it four mighty yanks, then stopped to catch his breath and tinker with the choke again. One more pull and the pump sputtered and coughed to a start, steadying finally to a punishing, hammering racket.

Suddenly, I had to raise my voice to nearly a holler. "I can't imagine what the world thinks of us," I yelled in Zach's ear.

Zach gave a wry laugh. "Ha! I'm pretty sure I don't give a flying fuck," he shouted back.

After a few hours Mother came home. She had visited with Beep and talked to Micah Nash. She was quick to assure us that Beep was in good spirits, although Nash only allowed her to speak with him through the bars. And only after the deputies had pawed through it was she allowed to give Beep the small bag with socks and underwear and a clean shirt and pants. She tried to shield us from the cold, hard truth, but her efforts proved futile. She could not keep the reasons for Beep's incarceration out of the conversation.

"Nash gave him a lie detector test. Your father had to agree to it, of course," she said, rolling her eyes. "That was a couple of days ago and we're just finding out now. You can't be a criminal and a trusting fool too. They're not compatible. Pick a side, for chrissake!" She threw up her hands, utterly bewildered. Her head dropped for a moment. "I hired a lawyer right away. I should have done it sooner. Ian Finley. Your father knows him. He's going to meet with Beep tomorrow morning. The court date on Tuesday is a competency hearing."

According to Mother, Nash found out nothing from the lie detector results. In fact, he was only frustrated by the effort, listening to Beep's stories about jumping from bridges into rivers of raw sewage or meeting with the boys at McCutchen's for therapy. To top it off, he blamed any future catastrophes on the loss of his dog, Tilly, some months back. Mom even laughed a little, appreciating the hair loss Beep's responses must have caused.

"That's your father," she said. "Every answer was deceptive, and yet, every answer was the gospel truth. I don't know how we're going to defend against this. Do they really think he killed that boy? Is that what they think? This is your father. This is normal for us. Since we came here twenty years ago—and then you guys were born—this has been normal for us. We've been safe and happy, am I right? How do we defend that?"

We sat on the back porch with Mother between us. She held our hands in hers and fought tears. I could tell she felt personally under attack after the meeting at the jail. As frightened as I was for Beep, I found it refreshing to see her worry turned outward. She was part of us, and although she rarely let it be known, she feared for Beep and bore the insufferable burden of suspicion Nash leveled against him.

"How can they keep him locked up? It's not right," I said.

Zach was incredulous. "They had to charge him with something. You can't just chuck a guy in a hole and leave him there. This ain't Calcutta."

Mother put her hand on Zach's shoulder. "They've got this obstruction thing hanging over his head . . . either that or tampering with evidence. Your father told the sheriff the shotgun was stolen. Of course, Nash doesn't buy that. They came on Wednesday to ransack the barn," she said. "Your father let them walk right in without a warrant."

She looked to Zach and then me, back and forth until she was certain we knew nothing of the barn toss. "He didn't even tell you, did he?" she asked anyway, convinced she had hit upon at least one glaring omission to Beepah's daily ramblings. Even so, she was left stunned by our silence. She gave her knees an angry slap. "That so figures," she conceded, letting her own wry laugh escape.

Zach found his voice. "They might as well open their cold cases and pin the whole mess on him. He's such a willing suspect, so ready to confess to something."

Mother's frustration continued in small bursts while she pondered the dilemma of Beep's incarceration. She turned her eyes to the kennel just as a straggler dropped to the flight deck and pushed his way through the trap gate. He fell into the blackness inside. "It does sound like the old fool is dying to confess to something, doesn't it?" she conceded.

———

On Monday, we went to school. Mother insisted, even though delivering us to the school bus was almost a new experience for her. She stepped out of her car and said hello to Grace Campbell, who she vaguely knew. By Gracie's reaction, word was out. The Bowdens were killers. Not wanting to encourage the remotest suspicions of complicity, Grace returned a chilly, "Good morning," and left it at that.

And on Monday morning the school fell inches short of closing for the entire day. It was the day of Jason Lipton's funeral. The autopsy was completed and the coroner released the body for burial. Nearly the entire population of nearby earth was bound to attend out of little respect and plenty of curiosity. I doubted there were many who knew Emily Lipton well. She entertained very few visitors aside from Beep and Sheriff Nash at the old Smoran house during the years since her arrival.

Near as I could tell, Emily otherwise kept to herself. In the grocery store and around town, she was recognized as the attractive dental hygienist from Dr. Manny Lapeer's office. And, according to Beep, no men around town were skipping teeth-cleaning appointments once they scanned the depths of Emily Lipton's cleavage. "Yep, they're all smiles, those guys. It's like starin' into a box of Chiclets," was how Beep gauged the grins among patrons departing Lapeer's office after a thorough hygienist tooth scrub. Of course, I often labored long and hard to grasp the full meaning, if there was one.

Everyone on Trumpet Hill had been affected by the screeching tires up and down the road while Jason was alive. Some residents, I suspected, would show up at the Episcopal Church simply to experience a silent reverie in the matter of Jason Lipton. He was always trouble. He was always angry, and near as I could tell, he was always without a friend in the world. I myself was often alone, so there might have been the basis for a rare kinship. But, if ever it was companionship he craved, he went about it badly.

The Bowden family would not be in attendance, but much of the nearby world showed up. Our boycott proved to be a virtual admission of guilt to the locals—that, and the fact that I sat in most of my classes alone but for a distracted teacher. Absent the pomp, Jason Lipton's funeral was like a night at the Oscars but in mid-morning.

To end my torture the superintendent closed school at noon. Zach and I exited the bus and began the climb up Trumpet Hill in the midst of a very cold world, it seemed. The big, red Monte Carlo convertible rolled past and turned at the Lipton driveway. The top was up, but I immediately caught sight of Emily Lipton in the passenger seat on the far side. The big car jerked to a stop and the driver-side window rolled down. I recognized the man pointing his finger at Zach and me. It was Willie Lipton, Jason's father.

We had met in the meadow the day after the shooting. He quickly recognized us from that first meeting, but his cordial demeanor had since vanished. "I know you two! I know you two!" he spit the words. "I know what you done! My son! My son! You son of a bitches!"

Willie Lipton's words shook me to my core, and I began to circle the big car to escape his wrath. Zach put his arm out and stopped me in my tracks. He stood as calmly as he could, holding me back until the window rolled up and the big Chevrolet spewed gravel into the road, churning up the driveway in front of a dust cloud.

"Don't ever walk behind a car when the driver's that pissed off," Zach warned.

"He scared the you-know-what outa me, Zachary. I've never been so scared."

Zach hurried past the driveway pulling me in tow.

Indeed, the world had changed, spurred by the vaguest suspicions alone. What had been a peaceful existence began to feel like a potential killing field, and all because Beep had difficulty remembering the simplest pieces of his life. What was described as a tragic accident in the meadow one morning had all the markings of a perfectly planned ambush by sunrise on the third day, and it appeared Willie Lipton was more than eager to embrace the popular suspicions about Beep.

We found Mom in the kitchen when we arrived home. "I made egg salad," she said.

We could see Booger Sullivan through the door windows. He was sitting on the back porch with his chin in his hands.

I slowed enough to ask Mom, "Any word?"

"Mr. Finley came by after he talked with your father," Mother said. "He's going to petition for his release tomorrow morning in court."

"The Tooth Fairy hard at work," I said. My pace quickened as I charged on through.

Booger must have heard us through the closed door. He rolled his head over his shoulders to greet us when we came through the back. The door all but rattled off its hinges when Zach pulled it shut.

"Thank God I didn't have to go to school," Booger said. "What the fuck was that like?"

"Like water torture," Zach said, dropping down beside Booger. "You were at the funeral?"

"Yeah, me and my mom," Booger said. "What a load. That goes to show you, if you want to get the whole town together, shoot yourself in the face. That's what I'd do."

"You shouldn't be here, Boogerboy," Zach said. "It's your death warrant. We saw Willie Lipton at the bottom of the hill and he's gunning for us. We're lucky he didn't shoot us dead on the spot."

"He said that?"

"You would have shit yourself."

"Oops, too late," Booger said, rolling one butt cheek from the porch floor to complete the gesture. "Anyways, everybody knows we're friends."

"We ain't that good'a friends," Zach said, and he delivered an elbow to Booger's ribs. "Keep a low profile . . . that's what they say. If you're real lucky, you might dodge the bullet."

"Ha! Funny." Booger cocked his head toward the neighbor's. "What's the noise?"

We all listened. Just like the day we first heard it, Ol' Jolly's pump growled out an almost unbearable racket on the far side of the pond. We had blocked out the noise until Booger called us on it. My first concern was the birds. No doubt, they had listened to it all day, and Cowboy, assuming the old crower could still hear, must have been crazed to the brink of convulsions by the noise.

"It's the new guy over there, Big Daryl," Zach said. "He's draining the pond."

Booger slapped his knees. "Fuck no!" he protested.

Zach had a sudden idea. "Let's go to the barn. We can see how much water's left."

We ran across the yard and scampered up the ladder to the shed roof. The sun was to the west by then, leaving the asphalt roof cooling in its wake. We parked ourselves in the shadows up along the barn wall. There before us was a sight none of us had ever fully anticipated. What had been a shoreline was now high above the water. Red mud was exposed the full depth of it. Wilted clumps of buttercups clung to steep walls of drying clay.

Zach jumped to his feet to survey the destruction. "It's down a good two feet," he said, just as something even more provoking caught his eye. "There he is! There!"

Booger and I jumped up and our eyes followed the direction of where Zach was pointing. Sure enough, the giant snapper had not found a way to escape the perilous pond purge. At the far end, almost to the trees, the area Ol' Jolly referred to as the San Andreas Fault because of its rumored bottomlessness, Zach's one great lifelong nemesis clawed against the soft red clay. Time and again the big snapper rattled his breast plate against the great wall of rock and mud. He could neither scale it nor move it, and he appeared exhausted by the effort.

"Look at him," Zach said, sharing the turtle's desperation. "He can't get out!"

"We could lasso him," Booger said.

"Yeah, sure."

"No, really, listen up," Booger kept on. "If he doesn't go for the bottom again, maybe we could get a rope around his neck."

Zach studied the water. It was red and soupy from the churned-up clay. "You could be right. Most turtles like mud, but this might be too much mud, even for him."

We went down the ladder, first me, then Booger, then Zach. We slipped into the barn through the side door and found Zach's turtle rope. Zach said the mission was strictly rescue, and we would not need his high-tech, turtle-catching, bait-basket contraption that had been refined over the course of the past decade. He quickly removed it and dropped it to the floor. The rope was bare, and Booger fashioned a lasso at the end. Then he fastened it to Beep's seven-foot walking stick in a series of loops designed to peel off after the turtle was snared. They examined it for flaws, and Zach put it through several dry runs, snaring a shovel handle and holding the rope tight against the walking stick before he declared it perfect . . . until the big snapper went for the bottom.

We went back out and through the maples, crouching low to conceal ourselves from Big Daryl, who was surely lurking somewhere on the farm. We crept to the far end of the pond where the big turtle still frantically pawed at the steep bank. Zach pulled us aside and we all went to our knees on the soft earth.

"Here's how we'll do it," Zach began in a whisper, then raised his volume to accommodate the noisy pump. "Sydney, you see that tree there?" And he pointed. "Get three or four loops around that tree, and leave a little slack for us to work with. Once we get him, hold on tight. I'll drop the loop on, and Booger, when I give the word, pull like holy hell."

"Gotcha," Booger said.

"Remember, Booger, if he goes down and sticks to the bottom, we'll be raising the fuckin' *Titanic* with a fly pole."

"Gotcha," Booger said again.

I got to the tree and found a place with good footing. I threw the rope around four times, like Zach said. Then I took another six wraps around my right palm. I figured if the snapper took the rope off the tree, he was likely to take half my hand with it. And, I figured further, it would be worth the pain rather than suffer the wrath should I fail in my assigned mission.

They shuffled in close, right to the very edge, and Zach peered over the bank. The turtle must have been oblivious because Zach took one step back and gave us a silent thumbs-up. He eased the walking stick down along the mud wall. Seconds passed. My heart was in my throat. Everything was about to go black just as I heard Zach's command, "Booger!"

Booger leaned on it with all his might, falling backward into the weeds. I didn't pass out after all. Instead, I found myself working as fast as I could to take out the slack. I went around the tree, ducking under the rope, pulling along with Booger! Pulling along with Zach!

"Hold him!" Zach howled, leaning over the edge to get a better fix on the situation. "He's halfway up! His mouth is open! He might be choking! His face is turning blue!" he said, exhilarated and horrified all at the same time.

I held on, leaning into it, pulling out the slack, exhausted as much as the turtle. At last, I saw the big snapper's head poke above the wall. One more herculean tug and the turtle flopped down in the grass, disoriented and bone tired. He took a few labored steps before Zach corralled the monster, taking hold just in front of his hind legs and lifting him off the ground. The snapper flailed while his cavernous mouth searched for something to bite.

"This took ten years!" Zach said, excited and out of breath.

The pump motor sputtered to a stop. Across the way and high on the bank stood Big Daryl. "You kids can't be here!" he hollered, cupping his hands around his mouth. "Get off my property and stay off before I call the cops!"

Zach turned in Daryl's direction. He raised the snapper over his head to give the big man a look. "I came for my turtle, like it or not!" Zach shouted across the pond.

Booger used a stick to loosen the snare from the turtle's neck. I pulled the rope into a tangled wad, and the three of us headed back through the maples. Zach lowered the snapper into the bed of Beep's pickup truck. The exhausted reptile pulled his head into his shell and lay still as a stone.

There he was, this creature that had enthralled and occupied Zach for the better part of a lifetime. After all of the battles, all of the scheming, there he was, delivered by a most unfortunate twist of fate, risen up and out of the red primordial ooze like the very first of his kind . . . if you believe in evolution and the Tooth Fairy and such.

Booger studied the exhausted creature, then trained his smirk toward Zach. "Really, Zee-man, his face is turning blue?"

Zach shrugged. "I was talking about you, Boogerboy," he said.

We laughed about it.

CHAPTER EIGHTEEN

When darkness fell, we made our way out again. Without a breath of breeze nothing moved on nearby earth. The encroaching stillness raised goose bumps on my skin and forced us to speak in whispers so as not to disturb the night or anyone in it. We had a plan and slipped across the open ground to the pickup that was parked at the back of the barn. Big Daryl had shut down the pump. That kindness brought a moment's peace to the world. Fairies took full advantage, filling the night with the sweetest music.

Zach shined the flashlight. By the look of it, the turtle had not moved, but when Zach touched the big snapper on the nose, the beast pulled his head deeper into the safety of his shell. He was indeed alive. We had not strangled him in our efforts to save him from the thick, red swill of the pond.

"Did you talk to Mom?" Zach whispered.

"She's asleep on the couch," I whispered back, pulling the passenger door open and sliding quietly into the seat. Zach went around and did the same on the other side. We eased the doors closed with barely a sound. Once inside the truck, whispering was no longer required. "She's lying there with her cell phone thinking Geneva might call. I tried to tell her it's the middle of the night in Geneva. I think she had a few dog hairs," I said with a shrug. "Anyway, I told her we were taking the turtle to the river."

Zach turned the key and the pickup engine revved, then slowed to a purr. "How'd that go?" he asked about Mother.

"She smiled and nodded. I guess she was happy for the turtle."

We both laughed a little. Zach made a big circle in the open field without headlights burning through the heavy air. He managed to put the truck in the proper tracks along the dark side-yard driveway. We took a right at the end and rolled out onto Trumpet Hill Road.

Zach put the pickup in neutral and we coasted clear past the Jolly's driveway before he turned on the headlights. We went past the Sullivans' place, then all the way to the long Lipton driveway. Zach touched the brakes and we slowed. The porch light splashed a bright yellow circle out into the gravel drive. The Monte Carlo was nestled near the steps. The blue mustang, always faithful in its location along the fence, was gone.

Zach stepped on it, defying fear, laying down a patch of rubber along with a loud screech. He regretted it instantly, easing up on the gas, rolling to a complete stop at the end of the road. "That wasn't too smart," he grumbled at himself, then shook it off just as quickly. "We'll go to the canoe launch. We can park close to the water. There won't be anybody there, unless it's kids making out and stuff."

Minutes later we rolled over the gravel parking lot with our headlights shining out over the moving water. Zach wheeled the pickup right down to the edge of the Esopus. He turned off the engine and left the lights shining across to the far bank. In early autumn the creek was low, and Zach stood looking out over the water cascading gently over and around scattered boulders in a steady trek toward the Hudson and the open sea.

He said finally, "This is a good spot . . . if he finds a new mudhole before he lands in New York City."

He went to the back of the truck and picked up the snapper. He walked to the front and stood right between the headlights. He stooped down to touch the turtle's bony belly to the cold water that rolled over the gravel in little slapping waves. Immediately the turtle responded, waking from his coma well rested, his long neck emerging to strain against Zach's grip. His legs quickly gathered strength enough to take flight in the moving water. Zach let the beast loose. "There you go, buddy."

The turtle made one big splash at the surface, and in two frantic strokes with his powerful legs, he disappeared in the current. Zach straightened. "Good luck," he said.

We were silent until we got to the bottom of Trumpet Hill. Zach was pleased. I could see it on him, but there must have been sadness there too. He had battled the turtle for so much of his life, and the battle was finally over, ending in a draw, a fait accompli.

"You didn't say anything about the mustang," I said when we went past the Liptons. "Do you think they sold it?"

"Maybe," he said. "Either that or crazy Willie had somebody take it back to Philly, or he's driving it around town." We sped up the hill to the back driveway and turned under the trees on the uphill side. The pickup bounced over the dirt road until we made it to the back field and went across to the barn. Zach pulled into the same track we'd left only a half hour before. "I wish I didn't squeal the tires," he admitted. "I don't want to start a war, unless it's already started."

On Tuesday morning Mother dressed for court. Coffee was made before her slippers shuffled to the bottom of the stairs. When she arrived in the kitchen, she appeared tired and completely put off by the whole court affair. "Oh, thank you, dear," she said when she shuffled into the kitchen and heard the coffee pot gurgling to a finish.

We sat at the table where she spent the next hour telling me about the lawyer, Mr. Finley. She recounted their visit on Monday.

As it turned out, Finley had defended Beepah a dozen years prior, just before he began his visits to the psychiatrist, Dr. Campion. Mr. Finley said he was uncertain if any of those early psychiatric records would be admissible in court, but if so, they could be incriminating.

Mom said it was a fine line. "On the one hand, they could charge your father with evidence tampering," she said. "They could even find him incapacitated. Finley says it's a lose-lose. Either way, your father goes away, and for what?" She lowered a spoonful of sugar into her coffee and gave it a distracted stir. "I thought he was cured. Those were good years between then and now. He drove me crazy with his barn building and chicken farming, but all said, he's been a good father to you and Zach."

She said there was a third option that Finley assured he would pursue. Finley was certain—unless he grossly neglected some aspect of the prosecution's flimsy case—it was far too soon for a competency hearing in the matter. No charges had been brought. Autopsy results only determined Jason Lipton died from a shotgun blast to the face, which might or might not have been self-inflicted, accidental or otherwise. Finley insisted that any accusations, absent malice or evidence, could only be overreaching by a prosecution and a sheriff bent on finding a patsy who fit the crime.

"In fact, Mr. Finley said he would ask Micah Nash that very thing," Mom said. "Why the bum's rush regarding your father's guilt?"

Mom became quiet then. I could tell she was stewing over the impossible predicament Sheriff Nash had created. She tipped her coffee cup and sipped it while I polished off my orange juice and set the glass in the sink. I heard Cowboy, still crowing well past sunrise. The court hearing downtown was not scheduled to commence for three hours, and Cowboy's crowing was not likely to let up until I made an appearance.

"I have to go out to the birds," I said, and I headed for the door. "I'll be back, Mom. We can talk more."

She set her coffee cup down and stood up, then twirled a full pirouette in her slippers. "What do you think of this, dear?"

I gave her outfit a quick once-over, black slacks, a sharp-fitted jacket. She was always striking in her attire. Under normal circumstances, she exuded confidence. By my estimation, this outfit should have encouraged similar results. "Power suit," I said without hesitation.

"I'm not sure how it plays in court," she said. "Finley was no help. I actually asked the man what to wear and he said something like, 'It's not about you,'" and she mimicked the man in his gruff-lawyer voice. She even laughed at his unmitigated gall in the matter. "I thought his remark was insensitive," she said.

"Lawyers," I offered, if only to share in the insult she was reliving. I was hoping it was the last word in the wardrobe critique, but to no avail.

"The sympathy card," she stewed. "Something frumpy maybe."

"Pick a card, any card," I said, then dredging the depths of sarcasm, I added, "Do you own something frumpy, Mother? Feel free to borrow something of mine," which meant I was offering a closetful of baggy flannel shirts for her perusal.

She dropped back into her chair and retrieved her coffee cup. I put my hand on her shoulder, and she reached up and covered my hand with her own. She was suddenly reflective and near tears. I knew in my heart none of it was about power suits and flannels. She was afraid. She was truly afraid for Beepah and for us.

"They can't keep him," I said. "They can't. It isn't right." I went out then, and almost made it to the kennel before I cried.

In the end, Mother insisted on going to the courthouse alone. Zach and me both raised holy hell over her decision. At the very least, I felt betrayed. I made her coffee and shared an hour with her before I turned the birds out to fly. In all that time she did not reveal her decision to us. She must have already been regretting the eventuality.

"I won't ask you to go to school," she said. "I know that would be difficult, given the gossip. Believe me, I could use your hands to hold during this horrible thing. Like Finley said, it isn't about me, and if it isn't about me, it isn't about you either."

Zach stomped to the back door. "What does that asshole know?" he said of Finley.

"Zachary!"

Zach pulled the door open and kicked at the screen. "He better get it right!" he shouted back. "He sure better." He pulled the door shut with a bang and went down the steps and across the grass toward the barn. Moments later, he appeared on the shed roof overlooking Jolly's pond, just as the pump grumbled and sputtered to a start. Zach slid down against the barn wall. He pulled his knees up and dropped his head over his folded arms.

Mother smeared black eyeliner across her cheek with a tissue. She dabbed at it without the aid of a mirror. She stood at the backdoor watching Zach while a lump grew in her throat. "I'm sorry, dear," she said, straining to get the words out. "This is the very thing Finley was afraid might happen, and it's a good thing if it doesn't happen in court."

She returned from the bathroom after removing all of her makeup. She tied a print scarf around her neck and tucked it in at her jacket collar. "How do I look?" she asked me.

"Like a traitor," I said.

She pushed her arm through her purse strap and stuffed a pack of tissue in the bag. "Yes, I feel like a traitor," she said, her eyes spilling over again.

I hurt for her. As angry as I was, I hurt for her. I searched for something to soften the moment, something that didn't hurt quite so much, and something that didn't suggest complete forgiveness. "The scarf's a nice touch," I said.

"Thank you, dear."

Hours passed before she returned home alone. As it turned out, they did keep Beepah. They kept him for what turned into another nine days on a contempt-of-court charge that caught Lawyer Finley completely off guard. The prosecution requested the charge after eliciting what were called "nonsensical answers" from Beep.

Judge Leonard Testa tried to assure Beep his answers were crucial in establishing competence. Mom said Beepah tried mightily to defend himself, but each response was met by an ambush question from Prosecutor Sylvia Dumont. That's what Finley called them, "ambush questions."

"I told you he's an asshole," Zach reminded us. "He should have seen that coming."

Mom said Dumont asked Beep if he ever killed anybody, and Beep answered, "Not in recent memory." Dumont said, "What about children?" And Beep said, "I have two." Mom said Dumont's questions went on endlessly, or at least until Judge Testa asked a bunch of questions of his own. Testa asked Beep if he suffered from post-traumatic stress syndrome, and Beep answered him clearly. He told Testa he didn't suffer from anything. He said he had a good life.

She lined us up across from her at the kitchen table and revealed everything that had happened, everything she could recall, everything cruel and accusatory. "I don't think you could have taken it, Zach dear," she said. "I don't think even his lawyer was prepared for the manipulating questions Dumont asked. They hurt your father, and it became clear that was their intent. I always knew your father had quirks. I didn't know any of them were punishable." She put her hand across the table, but Zach refused to touch her. "I hope you'll forgive me," she said.

In the midst of the extreme sadness she was feeling, Mom laughed quietly. "Can you believe he told Testa he jumps off bridges almost every night? I guess that takes crazy to new heights," she said.

CHAPTER NINETEEN

To paraphrase a great paraphraser, Beepah once said, "Those days moved slower than a sawdust milkshake, unless of course, you're a termite." As far as slowness goes, Beep might have been talking about Zach on his way to school, or me on my way to dance class, which was a pursuit short lived from its inception. The truth is, Beep spent much of our childhood baiting us with ridiculous vocabulary enhancements. "Slowness," Beep insisted, could be easily remedied by a swift boot to the tail socket. It was a threat—an idle one most often—but it did teach us the precise location of the anatomical feature known as the tail socket.

Mother went back to the office. We skipped school and watched the pond empty. It was a slow process. In fact, four days after Big Daryl first started the pump, the entire undertaking had become a full-blown comedy of errors. The pump ran out of gasoline every thirty minutes. Dust in the carburetor, red mud in the fire hose, and across the field came Big Daryl aboard the little green tractor to troubleshoot the problem.

We were on the shed roof when a deputy sheriff showed up on the rise beyond the pond. He had his hands on his hips as he scanned the full length of the red mud across the way. His eyes found us, and he shaded them with his hand to give us a long look. Eventually he used the same hand to acknowledge us with a less than exuberant salute.

When the pump sputtered to a stop, an almost deathly quiet

might have settled over all of Trumpet Hill, except for the little John Deere growling its way across the field. It pulled up beside the deputy, and Big Daryl shut down the engine and dismounted. The two men began to talk.

We heard nothing, strain as we might, not until the deputy raised his voice a decibel. "It should have been a one-day job!"

"Get the fire department!" Big Daryl barked in protest. "I can't afford a new pump!"

The deputy put his arm over Big Daryl's shoulder and led him down into the field. We heard little else of substance, only a murmur of words that accompanied the flies hovering in clouds over the tall grass in the field. Big Daryl stood with his head down while the deputy talked into his ear.

Zach gave a gentle elbow to my ribs. He directed my eyes cautiously to the far end of the pond, right where we had pulled off the great turtle rescue only days before. "You see it?" he asked me in a whisper.

My eyes searched along the rim, then at the waterline. The water level had dropped only a little, but I found it. It was black. Draping from the visible four-inch section was a ragged clump of weeds, limp buttercups, and red sludge. "I see it," I said, suddenly feeling a great foreboding.

"It's right where it's supposed to be," Zach said. "I almost figured as much. If it's not in the barn and it's not in the house, it's probably in the pond. At least that's the story Micah Nash is spreading around."

"Wait a minute," I snapped. "You think Micah Nash has been in the house?"

"Of course, he has," Zach scoffed. "Christ Almighty, Beep practically invited him into the barn. The gun locker was empty. The key was sticking out. That's all Nash needed. Who knows? Maybe he walks right into the house too."

"But there's nothing in the house."

"So what, Sydney? Nash wouldn't know that without looking. He would have to rule it out."

"Maybe he went in the house on the day of Jason Lipton's funeral," I said. "Everybody was in church. Mom was gone. We were stuck in school all morning."

"Sure, why not? Just to make it official. After the search, Superintendent What's-his-fuck closes school for the day. Willie Lipton threatens to shoot us in the head, and now they've got Big Daryl, all the way down from East Bumfuck, Maine, draining the pond to find an old shotgun so they can finish framing Beep for murder. What a fucked-up circus this has turned into."

"Does Micah Nash really believe Beep did this? Does he really?"

"Course not," Zach dismissed the idea. "For all we know, Nash set the whole thing up himself. Beep's an easy mark. Everybody knows he's a little quirky. And Nash—he's got the hots for Emily Lipton. Maybe he didn't want the pain-in-the-ass kid around messing things up. He could be way ahead of the game. He could have snatched the gun any time during the night. He shoots the kid, walks into the barn, takes Beep's gun, and tosses it. The perfect crime."

Zach pushed his back against the barn wall and walked his shoulders up the clapboards until he was standing. He folded his arms and leaned against the barn wall again, watching as the two men returned from the field to the edge of the pond.

Zach kept on. "Now all Nash has to do is convince the town, and he's done a pretty good job of it too. What would you rather have: your run-of-the-mill, self-inflicted shotgun blast to the face, or a grizzly murder? Face it, Sydney. People want a killer."

"I want Beepah back."

"I didn't get to see him in court, thanks to your mother," Zach chided, still angry enough to disown the woman. "I can read Beep pretty good. I wish I'd seen him. Anyway, if they don't have a confession yet, they're squeezing him. That's all I know."

My head fell and I couldn't help but cry. "I was afraid he would hurt himself," I said. "He told me about his leprechaun friend who shot himself in the woodshed."

Zach must have heard a version of Beep's sad tale because he nodded vague recognition. "Mr. McGregor . . ." he said.

"Mr. Jefferson," I corrected him. "I had a nightmare about Mr. Jefferson shooting himself. It was the same night Beep killed the turkey and said he couldn't find it in the dark—the very night Jason Lipton got shot in the meadow. I got out of bed sometime in the night. I was frightened by the dream. I came out to the barn. I walked out through the wet grass into the coolness of night. The moon was blue as Neptune. Everything the blue light touched was clear as day to me. It was Beep's face in my dream, and it seemed like the dream never stopped."

"That's creepy," Zach said. "It was a pretty ordinary day, if you ask me. Mom left for Geneva. Me and Booger went fishing. I mean, it was ordinary until the next morning when all hell broke loose. It feels like a year ago already, but things can sure change in ten days."

I admitted it finally . . . a secret that weighed heavily on me. But in that moment with Zach, I knew I couldn't hold it in any longer. "I went into the barn and took the gun from the locker."

Zach's chin dropped. "You did this?" he asked in a moment of pure confusion. He spent a full week building his own personal case against Micah Nash, and now my admission blew a big, fat hole in his perfect-crime theory. The revelation tumbled in his head while he decided whether to be angry or relieved that I was the culprit. He issued no loud outburst. Instead, he slammed his fists backward against the barn wall and slid down to put himself right beside me again.

"I should have known, Sydney," he said. "I thought Beep tossed it . . . then I thought Nash. Of course, finding it still fits his story. It doesn't really matter who tossed it. If he gets his hands on that gun, Beep's toast."

Zach dug in his shirt pocket for a joint. When he pulled it out, he gave it a lick at one end and put it between his lips. "You asked me about the gun on the way to the bus that day, like you were blaming me for tossing it. The whole time it was you. That's what I can't believe." He fished in his jeans for his lighter and flicked it a few times. "Am I the only one with a memory around here?"

I touched him on the arm. "I thought it was a dream, the night the moon was blue. When I woke up in the morning, there was red mud on the sheets. I was twice as confused. In the blue of my dream, I tossed the gun to end the nightmares and premonitions about Beep. I was hoping you would admit you tossed it, so I could be certain it was a dream and I wouldn't have to carry the memory around with me the rest of my life. Who knew this would all happen?" I began to sob. "We're losing Beep," I sputtered. "I did something I can never fix."

Zach sat for a long moment without attempting to console me. Instead, he studied the gun barrel and its precarious position in the mud against the bank. "You throw like a girl, Sydney," Zach said finally. "You missed the San Andreas by twenty feet. Good thing too. We'd never find it down there, not before the sheriff's boys, anyway."

My sobbing jerked to a stop. "Can we get it out?"

"We have to," he said.

Only a moment before, Zach's fist-banging had drawn the attention of Big Daryl and the deputy across the pond. They looked up, mildly put off by our presence; either that or they were simply curious. They watched while Zach made a show of the ceremonial joint lighting. He took a deep drag and handed the joint to me. I mimicked him and took a long hit. I held the smoke in until I began to turn purple. I exhaled a big white cloud that encircled my head. The deputy gave Big Daryl a slap on the shoulder and headed off across the field toward his car parked near the Jolly barn.

Another hit and I was quickly heading deep into the throes of a mellow high. Both of us started laughing at Big Daryl while he tinkered with the pump. We put our heads together at our knees and blew smoke out between our legs, and each time we did it, we giggled helplessly.

"I don't blame you, Sydney. But it does create quite the conundrum," Zach said, then added, "There's a word I don't use too much . . . conundrum. I don't think I ever used conundrum before."

That started us laughing again, not yet rolling on the shed roof, but close.

"I'm telling you, I was living in a strange dream that night. I went through the maples and stood on the grass in the moonlight wearing white pajamas." Even that description was enough to keep me laughing. "White pajamas, like camouflage, only brighter."

Zach did nothing to quell the laughter. "Bright white camouflage—it sounds like something Beep would invent. Ghost wear for the paranormal, hiding in plain sight."

So finally the secret was out. "It's not like I meant to hide it, Zachary," I said. "I wanted to take the gun away from Beep. That's all. He scared me with it. I was afraid he might hurt himself," I said, admitting it all with a shrug. "I might have told him if he'd asked me, but he never did. He only asked you. Besides, I was never certain I tossed it. Until this very moment, I was sure it happened in a dream. You can't go into the woods with a gun ever again—that's what I would have told Beep, end of story. Then Jason Lipton got killed, and it got really complicated."

"That's the conundrum."

"I tossed it right there," I assured him. "I watched it slip into the black water with hardly a splash. I was hoping it would go straight to the bottom and get sucked up by the mud. I was certain Beep would never find it there. That's all I wanted. How did I know it was the crime of the century? How did I know they would drain the pond to find it?"

Zach smiled and pushed the hot end of the joint against the shed roof until it cooled. "We better put this away," he said of it. He tapped me on the knee. "Tossing the gun might be the best thing you ever did, Sydney."

———

It took another hour to craft a plan. We were both buzzed up on marijuana, and with Big Daryl as comic relief, the laughs kept coming. In the midst of it, Zach referred to my version of the midnight gun toss as "karmic." He even said it might have stayed that way for eons, buried in the mud, holding true to my best intentions but for Jason Lipton's untimely demise. If Nash and his posse found the shotgun at the bottom of the pond, my story would be little more than a flimsy fabrication designed to secure my father's freedom. Beep would be ten times guiltier, circumstantially speaking, of course.

After midday, it was too hot on the shed for roof sitting. We went down the ladder and into the coolness of the barn. Zach was certain Big Daryl would forever be watching. We would need stealth to recover the shotgun. In fact, he said, the deputy likely gave specific orders not to allow us near the pond. Without planting himself on guard duty with his own shotgun across his lap, the best Big Daryl could do was be watchful. Zach knew that much.

The pump growled, and Big Daryl went back across the field on the tractor. Zach continued to stew over the gun rescue. As long as the pump ran, the water level dropped, and if all went well for Big Daryl and the lawmen, by the end of one more day, much of the gun would be exposed.

Zach studied the scene through the back window in the barn. Suddenly, he cocked his head to the north end and then to the south. "They can't see it," he said. "Look at that." He waved me to the window, and I pushed my head against his to get a look while he wagged his finger to the south. "The banks are too high and steep. They can't see it from over there."

Sure enough, Zach was right. The steep bank jutted out to support a stand of birch trees. "I can crawl right up behind that and reach the gun," he said. There was no line of sight to the shotgun from the mound where the pump churned out its monotonous clamor. Zach studied the terrain until he came to the conclusion there were only two places near the pond that allowed clear views of the clump of weeds and mud concealing the gun barrel. The shed roof provided the best vantage of the southeast corner of the pond. We had occupied that lofty vantage throughout the morning, obsessing over the gun rescue while getting stoned and progressively more paranoid.

There was only one other place Zach identified. He pointed again, this time at the duck ramp, a gradual slope Ol' Jolly graded out years ago, back when there was a bigger population of ducks and geese. The ramp ran from the duck house to the pond. It was notoriously slimy, covered and caked with the greasiest duck swill imaginable.

"If you stand right there, I think you could see the far corner," Zach said.

I laughed. "That's how Booger Sullivan got his name, boogieboarding on the duck ramp."

"The water was green by then. It was that time of year," Zach said, striking a clumsy surfer pose. "Here comes Booger, riding a goose-shit tidal wave down the duck ramp. We made a mess of it by the end of the day. Ol' Jolly was pissed." Zach straightened again. "Booger . . . what a dumbass," he laughed. "I don't think Big Daryl will stand in that slime pit. It's a sure way to end up in the drink. I might die laughing before I can toss him a line."

Zach found the turtle snare he and Booger fashioned the week before. He reassembled it and practiced by snagging a shovel handle. "How hard can it be? I caught a giant snapper with this thing. The shotgun won't put up much of a fight. Let's do this."

I nodded and went through the cool midday darkness inside the barn to raise the overhead door. Warm air and light rushed in to fill the space. I went to the old tractor and checked it for gasoline. It was almost full. I jumped aboard and pushed the lever to let the seat slide closer to the steering wheel. My part was simple enough. Cut the grass. Put the tractor on a track to pass back and forth across the open yard, and keep an eye on the pond and Big Daryl all at the same time.

"Don't let him see you watching. Just act natural," Zach directed. "I can keep an eye on him from back there." He thumbed over his shoulder toward the small window at the back where we had just stood surveying the pond. "Maybe he'll get the idea we lost interest. I'll be happy if his truck leaves. Either way, we have to get that gun today. The pond could be empty tomorrow. We'll be up shit's creek."

I pulled out the choke and gave the key a twist. The tractor sputtered. I threw it into drive, rolling out into thick, deep grass. The tractor noise mingled with the rattling pump motor, and I closed off the world with a pair of earplugs from the workbench in the barn. The mower deck dropped into the tangle and off I went, first around the entire yard, then back and forth, near the garden, then out toward the teepee, all the while stealing looks toward the Jolly farm for signs of Big Daryl.

My surveilling continued for half an hour before the pump chattered to a stop and Big Daryl made an appearance astride the little John Deere. I continued to pass back and forth across the yard, giving Zach a thumbs-up when I rolled past the big open door. He acknowledged me with a subtle nod and walked toward the rear window.

Big Daryl maneuvered the tractor to a stop right near the pump. He cut the engine and slid his two big hams out of the seat and straightened. His eyes searched the vacant shed roof before fixing on me only for a moment. He bent and opened the pump's gas tank and emptied the last from a five-gallon can. He dropped the empty into the trailer.

Big Daryl put the cover on the gas tank and straightened once again. He looked across the pond, and his steady gaze followed me until I made the turnaround at the garden-end and headed south toward the trees and the teepee. He bent finally and took hold of the pull rope. Out of the corner of my eye I saw him give the rope three mighty yanks before the pump sputtered to a jerky start yet again. I took one more look when I made the turn. Big Daryl was back astride the tractor. He swung it around and headed back across the field.

I wheeled the tractor through the open barn door and cut the engine. Zach was standing there waiting. "He emptied his gas can," I said. "He might have to fill it. That's our chance, maybe."

"There's plenty to worry about," Zach said. "The pump's running better. That means the water goes down. I don't want to wait until dark, but come morning, if we don't get it right, that gun could be high and dry, lying on the bank like a carp in a bikini."

I had to laugh at his fish reference. "That's a Beep-ism . . . maybe Louie King. Take your pick. Except Louie would have said, 'a carp in a fucking bikini.'" I shrugged. "It's a subtle difference."

Zach's plan was simple enough. He would head for the trees, out past the teepee and across the stream to the trail. From there he would come in south of the saltlick, staying in the cover of the trees until the time was right. The saltlick was visible from the upstairs window in the Jolly house. The shed roof was not, nestled behind low-hanging maples. I was to go up to the shed roof. From there I was to stand watch for Zach.

"Keep an eye on the driveway down there in case Daryl heads out for gas." Zach pushed his jackknife into the side of his boot. "Use the hand signals, like when we were kids. Remember, there's somebody watching. You can be sure of that—maybe that deputy is sitting out in the trees waiting for us to screw up."

Zach went out over the fresh-cut grass, kicking along like ol' Appleseed himself, out for a stroll. His walking stick rose and fell in a cadence. He went past the teepee and crossed the stream on the stepping stones. I watched him through the south window. I lost sight of him there. I went to the small fridge and took a bottle of water and snatched the cushion from Beep's rolling chair near the workbench.

I went out into the sunlight and turned my eyes to the sky. A small contingent of pigeons, truants from the morning fly around, made a turn out over the meadow and spun north toward Trumpet Hill Road. I looked to the shadows for Zach. All was quiet after the birds winged north. Zach would be on the trail by then, most likely strategizing, seeking the perfect place to step off into the trees.

I went around the barn and over the graveyard where Tilly had spent the past few months. There was a stone there; Zach had found it near the stream and hauled it up in his wagon. He had yet to chisel her name into it. "It doesn't matter," he said. "I'll always remember her."

I sidestepped the hump in the ground where she lay. Her passing still pulled on my heart, but I realized finally, after weeks and months of fervent prayer, there would be no resurrection. I was never again to catch sight of Tilly bounding up from the meadow covered in briars and rotting apples. The Tooth Fairy had done nothing to intercede.

I scaled the heights to the shed roof and went across the hot shingles. The barn wall was in shadow by midafternoon. There was a foot of roof cooling in the shade. I dropped the cushion and slid down to settle on it, hoping my scrawny butt didn't start to sizzle like bacon in the heat. From there I could scan all the open spaces. There was no movement near the Jolly's barn, and when I looked toward the saltlick and into the trees, all was still.

Twenty minutes later Zach had not appeared, and the pump sputtered to a stop. It seemed I had gone deaf. My ears had been barraged by the rattling pump for days. When it stopped, quiet came in a senses-numbing tsunami. It all but left me adrift in the ether, not touched, not anchored. I might have drifted from the shed roof without the weight of the noise holding me down. I might have floated on a cloud had there been one. My brain emptied out and then infused itself with a peaceful moment, a perfect pot high.

In the quiet, a seagull dropped from the clear sky and lit on the grassy mound across the pond. He appeared lost, corkscrewing his neck in all directions to identify anything familiar. I figured he winged in from far to the south, down around New Jersey or someplace, then followed the Hudson north. He stayed but a moment once he caught sight of me. With a three-step running start, he launched himself to the east to retrace his journey. I watched him go, circling high above, then disappearing finally near the creek far below.

In that brief moment, my mind drifted off. When I looked to the south end of the pond, my eyes found Zach crouching among the ferns at the edge of the trees. In the same moment I caught sight of Big Daryl making his way up the beaten trail on foot, marching along like he had a purpose. A shotgun barrel was in his hand and the butt of it rode along on his shoulder. I calculated quickly. He was halfway to the pond and his eyes were fixed on me! Something had to be done and done fast!

I pushed myself to my feet just as Zach turned his eyes to me, expecting a signal. I gave him a clenched fist. In the apple wars, a clenched fist always meant stay put and be still. It was quickly apparent Zach's interpretation was different. He dropped to his belly and began snaking his way toward the steep mudbank.

I knew that within minutes Big Daryl would crest the mound and have a clear look at Zach, and once he found Zach, he would find the gun and the clumsy game Louie King once referred to as hide-the-pickle would be lost—and maybe Beep's freedom too. My mind tumbled over options, bad ones, mostly, but I had to do something fast.

There was no way to alert Zach. He would know soon enough. I went across the roof and shinnied down the ladder. In seconds I went through the maples. Seconds more and I was standing on the bank above the red clay staring at the duck ramp and all its slime. I raced the four steps and launched myself into the swill like a belly slider into second base. The ramp took me, pulling me slowly but certainly down into the red water. I quickly found the muddy bottom with my boots and stood neck deep in the rust-colored soup.

I forced the panic. "Help! Help me!" I cried out. "Somebody, help me!"

I braved a glance to the south end where Zach was already snare fishing for the gun barrel. He craned his neck. Our eyes locked for an instant. He must have understood quickly. The commotion was a ruse, and that meant Big Daryl was nearby. He went right back to work with great urgency, looping the barrel, pulling it upward carefully, freeing it from the mud inch by inch. Losing his grip meant it would go even deeper. It would be lost to us. It would settle to the bottom and wait for Micah Nash to find it once the pond was dry.

"What are you doing there, girl?"

I spun around in the water. Big Daryl was standing near the silent pump. "I slipped! I can't get out! Help me!"

He slung his shotgun to his other shoulder and studied my predicament. "I can't come down there," he said finally. "I might slip in there and drown myself for sure. Can you swim?"

"A little," I blurted out quickly even though I could hold my own in the water. "Every time I get near the bank, my boots get stuck in the mud."

"Maybe we should get your turtle-snatching brother," Big Daryl said.

"He's fishing," I said, praying my pleading voice would keep him engaged. Every second he amused himself at my expense meant Zach was that much closer to success and escape. "I wanted to see Nanny," I said. "I haven't seen her in weeks, ever since you came here."

"Oh, you mean my auntie? You're the one she asks about," he said, rolling his big melon of a head from one shoulder to the other. "You can see her. I never stopped you. All I said was don't go near the pond. Look at you, bobbing around like a cork out there in the middle."

"You're not friendly," I said. "You scare people."

He swung his big arm to point the butt of his shotgun toward the shed roof. "You sit up there all day, watching me, laughing," he said, instantly perturbed. "You call that friendly?"

"Sorry," I said, pulling at my boots to keep from sinking deeper.

"I don't have a rope. I got a coil of hose," he said. "Maybe you can tie it around. Maybe I can pull you out. How much you weigh? Eighty pounds?"

"More than a hundred and something," I said.

"We're like twins," he joked, patting his belly like Ol' Jolly.

Big Daryl leaned the shotgun against the pump and came to the edge with his hose. He tossed an entire armful of coils into the water. It splashed down like a tight-wound slinky and began to slowly uncurl. I grabbed the hose and put it around my waist and gave it a loose tie.

Big Daryl started pulling. As soon as I felt tension on the hose, I worked my way back toward the edge near the duck ramp. I found footing at last and pulled myself up without allowing the maneuver to proceed without his help. With one giant step and one herculean tug from Big Daryl, I was up and out at last, flopping to the grass above the red clay.

Lying there with my face pressed against the good earth, I caught my breath and laughed. There was much to acknowledge, relief without question. I had survived the ordeal, and it came close to fulfilling Zach's ridiculous and nonsensical prophesy: a carp in a bikini indeed, absent the scanty swimwear, of course.

And after those few moments of mutual struggle, Big Daryl had made the giant leap from a person of suspicion and distrust to a potential friend. I didn't even look to the far end. I figured with those few minutes Zach could have crawled a mile, let alone back into the trees, with or without the shotgun. I slogged up the mound and dropped my bottom to the ground. I pulled off one boot and then the other, dumping the muddy water into the tangled grass. "Look at this," I said, smiling up at Big Daryl. "We saved my boots."

Big Daryl smiled back. He picked up his shotgun and laid it over his shoulder. "The sheriff said I should keep an eye on you kids," he said. "This pond is a crime scene or something, in case you didn't know. Crime scene or not, I can't get this old pump to suck anymore mud. They'll bring the fire department up here next."

I jumped to my feet. "I'll be on the roof for that one," I said. "I might make popcorn and have you over." I collected my boots and went down the mound, then raced through the grass and around the duck house. It was safe to cross through the trees there without another ramp-skidding catastrophe. Once I got to the Bowden side of the maples, I turned back to find Big Daryl watching me. There was still a smile on his face, an undeniably friendly smile.

I had never witnessed such a transformation in a man, especially not a man the size of Daryl. But then, saving a drowning damsel from certain death will change a man. Big Daryl was living proof that even an ogre could change for the better. He was reluctant at first, but in the end, he saved me, whether I truly needed saving or not. By falsely asserting my vulnerable predicament in the mud, I found a way into his heart, and in doing so, I had pulled off the perfect ruse.

I felt no guilt in the matter, none whatsoever. After all, declaring my intentions honestly would have served no good purpose. Big Daryl might have left me there to drown, and Zach would have been discovered, and Micah Nash would eventually find the gun and . . . well, it's easy to imagine all the best-laid plans exposed if I failed.

I admit, Big Daryl was an easy mark. He was sour on the world. A week of observation was enough to see the man was devoid of friendships. But now he had a friend—me—and it didn't matter so much that I lied my way into his good grace. I smiled back at him to clinch the deal. I had accomplished the impossible, maybe even the miraculous. Even dripping with mud and duck shit, it was one of the most exhilarating moments of my life.

"Tell Nanny I'll come by!" I hollered to him from across the muddy pond.

And Big Daryl waved to me.

CHAPTER TWENTY

I poked my head through the big door when I went past the barn. There was no one there. I went out toward the teepee and the stream to wash away the bad and hold onto the good. The stream was sure to be icy cold. The mountain gave up its water from deep in the rock where it had cooled almost to freezing. When I was near the teepee, I heard the soft gurgling of the stream, and I felt the icy chill of anticipation on my skin.

Zack stuck his head out of the teepee. "That was some performance, Sydney," he said, laughing a little. "Did you mean to do that?"

I could tell by his mood he had the gun, but I asked him anyway, "Did you get it?"

"We have it," he said.

He waved his hand at me like he was shooing flies, and he grimaced his full-blown disgust at the foul smell of me. I hadn't the luxury of a mirror. I'm sure my hair was pasted to my head by whatever goo resided in the wallow of the pond.

"How good does that feel?"

I laughed. "It feels like chicken shit, only duckier."

I walked out to the stream and dropped my boots on the soft bank. I stood in the water until my feet turned blue. Then I lay down in the place where we had often bathed, where the water fell over the rocks like they were the bubbling jets in a turbo tub. There was room enough for both of us when we were children. I realized how much I had grown, stretching the length of it, my toes pushing at the rocks below. There was always a challenge:

who could hold their head under the longest. Zach always won. I put my head under and counted to thirty, and let the icy water rinse the red mud from my hair.

On the way to the house, I asked, "Where'd you hide it?"

"I'd tell you, Sydney, but I'd have to kill you," he joked. "When Micah Nash starts stabbing bamboo shoots up your toenails, you'll sing like Old Mother Hubbard." He laughed at that. Retrieving the shotgun had eased our fears and lightened our mood so completely, at least for the moment.

I chided him about the Old Mother Hubbard reference. "I didn't know the woman could sing. She sure didn't have much to sing about, dirt poor as she was, and not a bone for her dog either, poor old thing."

"Believe me, Sydney, my silence is for your own good."

"You'll tell me," I assured him. "Sooner or later, you'll tell me."

"I'll sleep on it," he said, as if that in itself was a clue for me to ponder.

On Thursday, Mother took the train to New York. She needed to get away for a few days and give Beepah's situation the proper attention. She was feeling besieged, she said. Besides, in her words, John Goff had always been a comfort to her. "He's been my friend for so many years now. And his health isn't so good. He has a pacemaker. His heart could stop at any moment. I'd hate to be off in Singapore or someplace when he breathes his last. I'd never forgive myself."

There were times I had to take a step back, speechless, if only to assess the woman's humanity. This might have been one of those times. "What about Beepah?"

"I can only tell you, dear, nothing will happen this weekend." She sighed painfully. "According to Mr. Finley, they're seeking temporary residence in a psychiatric facility. They want to hold your father for observation."

I'm sure my chin dropped. "You are fucking kidding me!"

"Sydney! Must you?"

I stood near the table looking down at her, trying to peel back the past few minutes of my life. Cowboy had rousted me. Sunrise was barely breaking. I imagined Beep's footsteps on the basement stairs and Mother at the kitchen table early. I even imagined for a moment they had spent the night together, embracing each other in Beep's basement bed. I was heartened by the image. The world was closer to normal for an instant until I fully woke and found myself listening to plans for a train trip to New York City.

I stomped to the back door and pulled it open. "Mother, I'm going to talk to Mr. Finley today," I said, more restrained in my delivery. "I don't think much of him, letting all this happen to Beepah, but there must be something me and Zach don't know and nobody is telling us . . . not even you."

"I'm keeping the lines of communication open," she said. "We've always known your father needs help sometimes. This could be a blessing, believe it or not."

"A blessing? A blessing? A blessing for who? You and John Goff? Do you even know what's happening? They're draining Jolly's pond!" My frustration was finally spilling over in the form of rage. "They're looking for a crime that never happened! They're blaming it on Beep! Don't you see anything?"

"That pump will rattle your marbles," she said, ignoring me. "I had to go to the office yesterday to get away from the noise."

"And today it's the 8:10 out of Kingston. Your boyfriend waits there while my father gets a gurney ride to shock therapy. Why is that all right?"

She was annoyed and hurt. "That's clever," she said. "You're so much like him, you know."

"I hope so, Mother. I'm a genius, or did you forget?"

"I'm reminded. An evil one, it seems."

"My clever brain should help me understand you, but it hasn't. They have yet to introduce the course, 'Understanding Mother.' I've taken every other class they offer except auto-mechanics. I'll be taking that in the winter," I tossed in as cruel sarcasm. "I'm still going to graduate two years early. I'll barely be sixteen, then what?"

"College," she said. "I often talk to John Goff about your future."

"John Goff, my ass! I want my father back!"

I went out then, pulling the door shut in teeth-clacking fashion. The air was cool. I had felt the gentlest of breezes through my open window. I had fought the urge to wake, but the effort was futile. I had done it all for so long, pulling on pants and a flannel shirt and making my way down the back stairs. Yet, it was not until I crossed the yard and went through the iron gate was I even certain all things I just heard from my mother were actually true. I don't mean true in any moral equivalence, not in the manner of cosmic realities, but true only in the sense I had indeed heard them. None were imagined, although I would have preferred them to be.

Cowboy was pacing when I arrived. I let the old stumblebum loose in the kennel, and I stepped into the aviary. There was a carcass on the dirt floor, defeathered partly, beheaded and half eaten. Even with that much destruction, I knew right off it was one of Beep's favorites, if in name only. Chloe Corn Tits had orange markings on both breasts, and the colorful portions of her anatomy once compelled Beep to intone, "Jessica Rabbit in a strapless gown." Cowboy crowed, shattering the moment of silence. It always amazed me how, during the ten or so years of the cranky rooster's existence, he had managed to dodge the weasel.

"Sorry, Chloe," I said, pitching her carcass to the scratch yard near the gate. I opened the flyway. Out went the entire flock in a mad dash while I looked overhead for more signs of carnage. It looked peaceful, no blood dripping from the rafters, nothing but a few pinfeathers put adrift by the flock's hasty exodus.

I scratched the hard earth with the rake until Chloe's blood disappeared into the dirt floor. I threw down fresh straw and opened the swing door. The girls all hopped from their nests and made their way to the scratch yard. One or two stopped by Chloe's carcass to express their curiosity with a cautious peck. When the sunlight began to slip through the hemlock branches, I threw down fresh cracked corn. I washed the water trough and collected eggs into one nest.

Zach came out the backdoor just as I was heading toward the barn with Chloe's carcass in one hand. He trotted across the yard and slowed to match my stride. "Who got it?" he asked.

"Chloe Corn Tits," I said.

"Who did it this time?"

"A weasel," I said with a shrug. "They almost always kill more than one. I guess we got lucky." I swung the headless carcass toward Zach's face to give him a good look.

He raised a hand to swat it away. "Come on!" he protested, then quickly asked, "Where's her head?"

"It must be somebody's favorite part. You like drumsticks, so you're off the hook." I snorted a little laugh. I let Chloe's carcass swing down to my boot tops again. "Did you see Mom?"

"Sure. She came in to kiss me on the cheek and tell me I'm her favorite," he said, returning my laugh. "Then she left for New York, I think."

We went through the barn and Zach snagged the shovel. He peeled away a small patch of sod under the maples, and he dug down another foot until he began to see the bones of victims past. I had stood countless times in that very place watching as Beep dropped a carcass or two into a fresh hole. Sometimes I clung to his leg and cried. "An aviary can be a safe place, Syd," he once told me. "But if a weasel gets in there somebody is probably going to die. It's a cruel fact of life."

I dropped Chloe Corn Tits into the hole on top of the old bones. Zach pitched in dirt and smacked it down with the shovel. He got on his hands and knees and laid the sod on top and straightened it perfectly. For a moment I was wishing I was small again. I was wishing Beep was nearby so I could hug his leg and cry a little and listen to his voice.

———

We agreed we would not go back to school until one of our parents showed up at home to boot our scrawny asses to the door. We sat on the shed roof and watched the sun climb over the treetops to the east. We told the saddest jokes, jokes about orphans and jokes about abandoned children. We made a plan to surrender. We would walk into Sheriff Nash's office with our wrists extended for shackling and high hopes of seeing Beep. We eventually scuttled the idea. Too risky, we determined. Sheriff Nash might throw a dragnet over Greenwich Village and discover our dear mother huddled in John Goff's paint locker, complicating the entire investigation. We laughed about that, as silly as it was.

"She might not forgive us for that one," Zach joked while holding an early-morning joint pinched in his fingers.

Somewhere near eight o'clock, a firetruck backed into the Jolly driveway with lights flashing. Two men stepped out. Big Daryl came out the back door and crossed the porch. He came down the steps and walked over to meet them. He shook one hand with little enthusiasm. They talked, and Big Daryl nodded several times before all three men turned and strolled up the path.

They walked to the mound to get a look at the pond. The pump didn't run throughout the night and the red water was still. Daryl pointed to several access points, at the duck ramp and the south end where the water was deepest. All three men quickly found us sitting quietly on the shed roof. Big Daryl offered up a cautious wave and smile, and I smiled back. The smaller of the two firemen leaned toward Daryl's ear. Then the big man pointed toward our house beyond the maples. I'm certain he explained our presence. He might have even called us by name. "The Bowden kids," he might have said.

The smaller fireman kept his eyes on us for a long while, then I heard something like, "Ah, those delinquents," but I won't swear to it. I considered attributing my interpretation of his words to creative hearing, but I was quick to quash that idea. I blamed it instead on my newly established state of paranoia, fueled by the last toke from Zach's joint and the public bloodlust leveled at us before and after Jason's funeral.

It took nearly two hours to back the firetruck into the field and string hoses and get the big pump ready to suck the last of the red water from the pond. What took Big Daryl and his little pump a week to accomplish, the big pump managed in just under forty minutes. The firemen got their shoulders beneath the big hose and pulled it free of the mud. They wrangled it onto the truck spool while the long snake of a hose puked out gobs of red clay as it crawled back across the field.

In the end, all that was left was mud and pools of barely navigable thick water filled with small fish desperate to catch a breath. Zach said it was no use trying to save them. Even if we could scoop them up, their gills were coated in mud. They wriggled helplessly, propelling themselves across the shallow pools, mouths gulping mud in one last feeble search for clean water to inhale.

I jumped to my feet. "There's hundreds! If we get them to the stream, they might make it down to the river."

"They're suffocating, Syd. They're dead already," Zach said.

"Anyway, it doesn't matter." He got to his feet and watched as the deputy's car came up the driveway and stopped near the barn. Zach kicked his boot heel against the barn wall and nodded his annoyance toward the deputy. "They're not going to let us take anything, not even a bucketload of dying fish, and that's all they're going to find."

I shook my head. "All this fuss for a shotgun that's not even there," I chirped.

"There's no evidence on that gun, anyway," Zach said, a little disgruntled. "But if the gun's in the pond, they make a case against Beep. Beep says he shot the turkey in the meadow, but who knows? It doesn't even matter who shot the bird. Then what happened? Beep shoots Jason Lipton in the face and chucks the gun in this nearby pond?" Zach hooked his thumbs in his pockets and scoffed at the simple chain of events. "Some people might call that open and shut."

I dropped my butt to the hot roof and quickly bounced back up, feeling the burn. "It doesn't seem like enough," I said. "Do you think it's enough?"

"Well, there is Beep's weird storytelling," Zach said. "Only God knows how he's entertained those police guys. And Nash can twist it however he wants. Nobody's calling it an accidental shooting. The dumbass shot himself in the face . . . end of story."

Big Daryl and the deputy came up the path just as the firemen finished stowing the big hose. The firemen waved to the two on the path and climbed up into the truck. They pulled the doors shut and gave the siren a quick burst as the truck rolled from the field, then down the driveway to Trumpet Hill Road. Halfway down the hill they blasted the siren one more time just to annoy the world.

I headed for the ladder. "I got eggs to get," I announced, giving my scorched ass a cautious rub. I shinnied down and waited for Zach at the bottom.

"I don't believe any of it," I said finally. "No matter what, I don't believe any of it. I keep thinking there's got to be more. Willie Lipton gets chased back to Philly by Sheriff Nash . . . that's if you believe Grace Campbell. Beep is locked up for life, or until he's not crazy anymore, whichever comes first. And good ol' Micah Nash spends most of his time sniffing around the porch at Emily Lipton's house. Can't somebody find a motive in there some-place?"

"People believe what they hear, Sydney. And if they hear it enough . . ." Zach shrugged. "Right now, Micah Nash is spinning a yarn and everybody's listening." Zach threw an arm over my shoulder. "We did a good thing. Whatever happens, we did a good thing."

***

If Grace Campbell was to be believed, Micah Nash left his wife and children. Word was, he was putting most of his energy into building a case against Beep. Whatever the urgency, there was little doubt Emily Lipton figured into his plans. The amiable sheriff had dropped a bug in enough ears in the two weeks since Jason Lipton's death, the entire citizenry was ready to pronounce Beep guilty.

The truth is, I always liked Emily Lipton. I admired her good looks and cheeriness, although I never understood how a woman with such a pleasant disposition gave birth to a son with such an unpleasant one. In life, Jason Lipton was cruel and unhappy. Though I had rarely considered it, Emily must have suffered greatly over his remarkable misery.

Inside the coop, I found half the girls had returned to the nesting boxes to lay more eggs. Mornings were often like that. I collected the eggs into my upturned shirttail and took them to the kitchen to wash. Zach came through the back door. I washed up and scrambled eggs and shredded cheese on top. I buttered toast and slid a plate across the table toward him.

He gave me a nod for the breakfast. "You know there's nothing we can do," he said. "Anything more only makes it worse. They have no evidence, and without evidence, there might not even be a crime. But all Micah Nash has to do is wait for Beep to confess to something."

My head fell. I knew he was right. Beep was caught up in a tragedy that might never reach a rational end. Retrieving the shotgun should have dismissed the only scintilla of evidence, no matter how circumstantial. Yet, Beep was about to be transferred to a holding facility for observation.

We returned to the shed later in the morning, but we decided not to climb to the roof. Our hearts were not in it, although there was plenty of comic relief had we chosen to be amused. Sheriff Nash showed up to inspect the waterless hole in the earth. He arrived with two men with metal detectors. Zach called them beachcombers, like they were seeking out expensive rings or gold teeth. These two descended into the empty abyss after donning waders. They stumbled in the mud, sweeping their wands back and forth over the slimy bottom, hunting landmines, or shotguns, or whatever evidence gurgled to the surface of the drying red ooze.

Right away they discovered a hinge still attached to a rotting gate post. One of the men did manage to strike gold. His trophy set off mild excitement. It turned out to be a roll of rusty wire fencing. And there were other nuts and bolts that had accumulated in the abyss over the years. Zach said it was like finding a finger bone from a T-Rex and building an entire dinosaur from wild speculation alone.

"Maybe they can make a shotgun out of all that junk," Zach said almost loud enough for Micah Nash to hear. "Booger's ditching school. We're going fishing."

I would remember that morning for the profound sense of finality it left with me. I was destined to spend many days in my room chronicling all of the sad events. I fought with Mother just before she ran off to Greenwich Village to visit John Goff's bed. I felt completely in the right doing so. Yet, I spent that morning feeling deep regret. We buried Chloe Corn Tits, who lost her head to a weasel. To top it off, I watched while hundreds of little fish choked to death on mud at the bottom of Jolly's empty pond. There were innocents dying all around, it seemed. But then, the weasel lived. Even he was innocent enough, innocent as weasels can be.

The beachcombers did not return on Friday. In fact, other than a huge color photo of the empty red gouge in the earth, it appeared all interest in the pond and its hidden booty were about to be abandoned by the sheriff and his treasure-hunting specialists in rubber waders. "The mystery still lurks below," the headline in *The Kingston Freeman* read. The only evidence to support their efforts was two small piles of rusty spikes and rusty hinges and a rusty muffler, filled with mud and barely identifiable. Not a single gold doubloon. Not a nickel's worth of scrap.

On Friday I called the lawyer, Ian Finley, from Beep's bench in the barn. A woman's voice came on the phone after two rings, an elaborate recorded message telling me where she was and when she would return. Before she completed her apology-spiel explaining her absence and the reason for it, a man's voice took over.

"Ian Finley—"

"Mr. Finley, I'm Sydney Bowden."

"Oh yes, Sydney," he said after a pause. "We've not met."

"I want to see my father."

"We've been open to that, Sydney, but your father would have to agree. He has rights, too, however you look at it. So far, he's been stubborn," Finley said. "It's all part of his sickness, you know. I believe he thinks he's protecting you."

I was incensed. Suddenly, my father had a sickness. Suddenly, I had to be protected from the one man in my life who I understood fully. "If anyone needs protecting, it's my father!"

"I talked with your mother only moments ago to inform her of a special hearing scheduled for Monday morning. I believe they've found a place for your father. In the long run, that could be good news. He'll get good help there."

Ian Finley, a card stuck to the refrigerator identified him. I pictured him in that moment as a rather fat fellow sitting at his desk with his feet up to prevent ankle swelling and probing the gap in his teeth with a floss stick, all the while working me over with comforting blather about my father's state of mind. To top it off, I was convinced he was cajoling with the prosecutor at every turn, with Nash, and even with my mother. The dear woman was keeping abreast of things from a studio flat in Greenwich Village. Those three, at least, must have been the "we" Finley referenced when he spoke of the collaborative efforts to put Beepah away. "We think it's for his own good in the long run," was how Finley phrased it.

I realized in those few moments, I was no match for Finley, seasoned as he was after years of lawyering. My perceptions were emotionally driven, and the man soft-pedaled his answers to all of my concerns in words that were coddling, given my age. It became clear to me that whoever was greasing the wheels of justice was seeking a long stay at the noodle factory for my father. Finley spoke as though a good compromise had been struck.

The truth is, I heard little else after Finley informed me of the court hearing on Monday morning. I sat in the coolness of the barn in Beep's roll-around chair, pushing myself back and forth over the concrete floor. I caught the buzz of insects out over the tall grass and the less steady rhythms of the breeze in the trees. Blue jays in their crass, ungentle way taunted each other from the thickets, encouraging stiff retaliation for the words they chose.

For the first time in my life, I found myself wishing for a real Alexander Graham Bell telephone that actually worked, one of those black phones prominent on dark desks in dark offices in old black-and-white movies. Beep's phone was on the workbench collecting dust with no wires attached. I needed a big, black phone to slam down, if only to express my emotional discontent. Back in the day, at the turn of one century or another, the phone set the mood. The phone did the talking. Somewhere along the way, the phone lost its nerve, and with that, its character.

"I'll be there," I said of the Monday morning hearing. I ended the cell call with Finley abruptly. I reached across the workbench to pick up the receiver on Beep's defunct black relic. I said good-bye and slammed it down. *Slam! Slam! Slam!*

What troubled me as much as anything was there was no mention of Jason Lipton during my brief conversation with Finley. Was it possible an entire population accusing Beepah of everything from waiting in ambush, to poaching turkeys out of season, had suddenly lost its taste for blood? Word leaked that Ben Bowden was the killer of an innocent young man, and he had finally pleaded guilty to one crime or another.

"I told you!" Zach said. "I told you they'd get to him!"

It was quiet on Sunday morning once the wind died down. I sent the birds out to fly and raked the scratch yard to make cracked corn easy pickings for the birds. Then I went to the top of Trumpet Hill Road with my drawing pad. There was a curious-looking scrap truck parked at the curb and abandoned, at least for a time. It was an old truck, twice as old as me by the look of it. It was covered in rust. Orange paint nicely complemented the formidable tarnish. I sat on a rock near the edge of the cul-de-sac and drew a picture for Beepah.

Mother arrived home after midday Sunday. I heard the screen door slap shut, and I caught sight of her from clear back at the stream. Her eyes found me there. She stood for the longest time, folding her arms to express a rather passive impatience, expecting me to give in and make the long walk to greet her. I waited. She came as far as the barn and stopped. I gave in finally, wringing out my shirt and throwing it over my shoulder.

I went through the tall grass, skimming the tops with my hands, hoping she could detect my annoyance and the prolonged anger I truly felt. She watched me approach with her same impatience, and when I got near her, she unfolded her arms and gave me a quick look from head to toe. She pushed her hands into her pockets. She must have perceived by my demeanor that I was not expecting a hug, nor was I preparing for one.

"I never could get you to wear shoes," she said.

"Hello, Mother," I said back.

"I can see your nipples, dear." Her eyes examined my breasts pressing into my wet tank top. "You have to be careful," she warned me in her own nauseating kind of way. "It's how things are these days," she kept on, as if the woman had actually been mothering me for the past many weeks. "Anyway, didn't I buy you a half-dozen bras on our last trip?"

"I hate those contraptions. Besides, that was two years ago, Mother. My tits are bigger now."

"Who would know, dear. You're always in a flannel," she said, giving her head a disapproving shake. Her eyes went shut for a moment. "I didn't like your choice of words, is all."

"I speak frankly, Mother." I shrugged. "I get it from you," I said, even though I knew I could never win a lengthy pissing match with the woman. "The water is cold back there. It makes my nipples poke out. How was New York?"

"Believe it or not, quiet." She pulled a hand from her pocket and took the two steps to get near me. She put her arm over my shoulder. "I'm sure you don't believe I missed you, but I did."

"It has been an enlightening few days," I said. "They finally emptied the pond." I pulled my twisted shirt from my shoulder and whipped it open. Then I draped its cool wetness over my head to shield me from the afternoon's heat. "Zach and I watched the whole clumsy operation from up there on the roof. They didn't find anything . . . just some of Ol' Jolly's junk."

"Yes. I talked to Finley."

"Me too," I said. "I really don't know whose side you two are on."

The innuendo caught her by surprise and it must have stung. "You can say all those mean things, dear. I only want what's best for your father."

"Mother! They almost charged him with murder!"

"That should be off the table now, thanks in part to Ian Finley."

"I told him I'd be at the hearing tomorrow."

"That might upset your father," she hedged.

"He'll get over it," I said.

We cooled off, the both of us. Mother once referred to it as mutually silent forgiveness, and it eventually became our own personal method for settling scores. That way, neither of us had to apologize. We talked throughout that late afternoon, about Ian Finley and the goings-on at the Sheriff's office. I told her how Finley tried to browbeat me into staying away, per Beep's insistence. "He talked on and on for nearly an hour," I grouched, dropping down in the grass just beneath the maples.

"Oh, great. There's a billable hour I'll never get back," she grumbled.

"I spent the whole time reciting from *Alice Through the Looking-Glass*." I turned a smug face toward Mother. "One of my earliest reads," I boasted and laughed. "It got in my head, and I couldn't get it out."

I cleared my throat, preparing for my voice to climb an octave. I leaned toward Mother. "Contrariwise," I said like Tweedledee. "If it was so, it might be . . . but it isn't, so it ain't." I clutched my knees and rocked in the cool grass. "It's only logic," I concluded the nonsensical quote. "Anyway, that's how Tweedledee explains Mr. Finley, the contrarian, if he is one."

Mom laughed. "Are you sure it wasn't the dumb brother?"

I admitted I had no clue. "I swear, those two look like twins," and we both giggled. "Anyway, whatever Mr. Finley was saying, all I heard was one of the Tweedles giving me his twist on it."

"He's a straight shooter, I think."

"Dee or Dum?"

"Ian Finley."

"Oh, him. I pictured him fat."

"Nothing like the Dee-Dum boys," she joked. "Anyway, it was simply poor mothering on my part. That book was declared inappropriate reading for toddlers."

"I was seven."

We sat on the grassy bank, looking out over the deep trench once known as Jolly's pond. Tragic as the cracked and drying wasteland appeared, our hearts were lightened by our silent forgiveness and our silly conversation about the Tweedle boys.

Big Daryl came up the trail on his tractor. For an instant I considered dubbing him the lost Tweedle triplet. But then, as Beep was likely to say, we had beat that dead horse into a coma.

Besides, Daryl was my new friend. When he cut the engine and dismounted, we waved to each other. He threw a coil of small hoses into his trailer. He stood on the opposite bank where the mound rose up. He passed his eyes back and forth over the deep crater in the earth.

There was little evidence of the perished fish population. In dying, they had sucked the last of the thick water from the lowest pools. They settled into the earth with barely a sunbaked tail fin wrinkling the red clay from below. Zach had weaned himself on adventures there, catching the little fish and hurling them back to the middle of the pond. The stark reality of the pond's demise proved too much for Zach. He spent most of that Sunday off with Booger Sullivan working on an old car.

Big Daryl put his hands on his hips and gave us a cheery look from across the pond. "Maybe I'll fill it up again!" he shouted. "If they let me!"

Mom leaned near my ear. "That's our new neighbor? He looks like Jolly himself, back when I first met him years ago."

I joked about Big Daryl's girth. "Beep said they share obvious genetic markers. He's my newest friend," I said, beginning a count on my fingers. "Let's see, there's Daryl, there's Zach and Booger, and there's the Tooth Fairy, and that's about it. And lately, I haven't heard much from the Tooth Fairy."

———

Monday mornings were busy in the Kingston Courthouse. Briefcases were the tote of the day. Long black pants were at least part of the uniform for both women and men, and walking fast was an exercise regimen—either that or they were all late, and every one of them had a cell phone stuck in their ear explaining why.

There was a high ceiling and a grand staircase heading for a second floor, and there was an information desk in the middle of the lobby. Mom stood behind us appearing less than interested in the pedestrian grandeur of the place.

In my hand was a paper-towel tube that contained the rolled-up picture of the scrap truck I had drawn for Beep in the cul-de-sac on Sunday morning. The woman manning the metal detector looked me up and down, dismissing politeness as a requirement. "Empty your pockets," she intoned.

I pulled my phone from my back pocket and laid it on the conveyor.

"That's fine. I'll have to have that," she said, speaking strictly to the paper tube.

"It's a picture," I said, as if the woman had asked. I dropped it on the conveyor and watched it disappear under the imager.

"Step through."

When Zach came through, I held up the paper tube. "I forgot the hack saw," I joked, and I was instantly struck by an acute unease at my own suggestion.

Zach collected his wallet and his phone. "Don't get me in trouble here, Sydney," he warned me, his face going almost ashen. "I wouldn't do well in solitary, especially with you."

It was a Beep-ism, and it caught me off guard. The tiniest laugh squeaked out of me, which I quickly squelched. Solitary, the two of us . . . really?

Mom knew the way. She ushered us to the stairs. We climbed steps to the second floor and went down a broad hallway to Courtroom Three. Zach held the door, and Mom and I entered, then Zach. I had recognized a few people in the hallway, most of them, not by name. It was much the same inside the courtroom. A few townspeople were scattered about. Joel Maris was there, absent his baseball bat. Grace Campbell sat three rows up from the rear. She smiled at me when I caught her eye, then quickly jerked her gaze to the front of the courtroom where things were slowly coming to life.

Sheriff Nash sat on the aisle behind the prosecutor's table. Emily Lipton sat inside of him. I recognized her by her auburn hair. It was pinched at the back, much like she wore it to the bus stop in mornings past. She was quiet with her head down.

All of that went for nothing. It was little more than a ripple in the ether. During the first second of my arrival my eyes found Beep. He sat right where I expected to find him, at the table up front and to the left, like almost every courtroom scene ever staged. His eyes locked on me, then Zach. He had not wanted us to come out of shame or some other primal urging. Upon seeing us he could not contain his joy. His smile broadened to the brink of splitting his cheeks.

My lips formed an exaggerated "Beepah" that I tried to deliver in silence.

It proved to be loud enough to get heads to turn and elicit a whisper or two. I walked to the long seat, two behind the defense table. I slid along the bench until I could almost reach out and touch Beep on the shoulder. Mom followed, and then Zach. It was a church pew, except there was no place to kneel, a slight to Catholics. Everything else was the same. There was a man in a black robe up front, and I was expected to remain uncomfortably silent and pretend to pray for dead relatives.

According to Mom, the man in the black robe was Judge Leonard Testa. She told us, in the opinion of Ian Finley, Testa was a reasonable man. And there he was, Finley himself, sitting beside Beep. Mom was right. I had mischaracterized the man. He was not at all portly. He was smallish, with hair plugs clearly visible when he leaned toward Beep for a word. The man was so slight in his physical stature, I was driven to contortions just to see if his feet actually touched the floor as he sat.

Beep twisted in his chair and gave us all a brave look and a wink. I held up the paper tube so he could plainly see it. Judge Testa clapped his gavel and scanned the courtroom over his glasses. He called the bailiff over and the man approached. Judge Testa leaned far across the bench and whispered something to the bailiff. The next thing I knew, the man was heading in my direction.

He reached his hand out. "I'll have to have that," he ordered.

I reluctantly held it out to him. "It's a picture," I said.

"I understand," he said, taking it. He held it to his eye like a spyglass and looked through it. "I'm sure you'll get it back." He delivered it to Testa, handing it to him across the bench.

Testa gave the apparently mysterious paper-towel tube the same once-over. He held it to his eye, searching for anything nefarious. He even took off his glasses and held it up again. Finally, he shook the tube and removed the drawing. Testa rolled it out and gave it a long look, and nodded his head with approval. He looked up at me. "Is this for your father?" he asked me.

Oddly, the gravity of the moment got hold of me. A chicken egg of a lump settled in my throat. I could not swallow. I could barely breathe. I could not even hold back tears. Mom put her hand on my knee, and I managed a nod of admission for Judge Testa.

Testa took a moment to consider. He rolled the picture carefully and pushed it back into the paper tube. "I'll make sure he gets it," he said, placing it gently to the side. He looked over the courtroom and gave the gavel one more gentle rap. "This court will come to order," he said.

During the next hour I was to learn little about Beep's fate. When Judge Testa asked about charges regarding the unfortunate death of Jason Lipton, the prosecutor answered simply, "Not at this time, Your Honor."

As it turned out, when they truly got down to business, it became increasingly clear most of the business had already been conducted. Papers were pushed from one side of the courtroom to the other, seeking signatures or checkmarks verifying what they were reading was remarkably identical to what they read in preparation for the hearing. It was little more than a performance for those of us bored to near death in the cheap seats.

When the papers stopped drifting back and forth, Judge Testa dropped his glasses to the bench. "As to the contempt charges levied on you a week ago, Mr. Bowden, I prefer to believe what I perceived as belligerence on your part was a misunderstanding on mine." Testa leaned far over the bench. "I apologize for my haste in the matter, and I dismiss you from that charge," he said.

Suddenly, there were no charges against Beepah. By any number of accounts, he should have been a free man. He was not. As it turned out, all the bigwigs had gathered in a judicial mosh pit to determine Beep's fate: Judge Testa, Nash, Ian Finley, and the prosecutors. They were all in cahoots—that bunch plus the entire staff at the Weeble School. Beep had undergone observation there in the past, before Dr. Campion died. That was way back when Zach and I were kids, and we named the place in honor of the strange student body wobbling around the grounds in bathrobes and penguin pajamas.

"You understand, Mr. Bowden, this is an open-ended order?"

Beep nodded, and Ian Finley said, "We do, Your Honor."

"Once you're settled, you can arrange visitations. Is that understood?"

Beep nodded again.

"Sheriff Nash, you'll arrange the transfer and protection order?"

Micah Nash rose to his feet. "Yes, Your Honor," he said.

"Bailiff, have the guards remove Mr. Bowden from the courtroom," Testa ordered.

Beep stood up. I could tell he was ashamed of the handcuffs he wore. They were anchored to a belt around his waist. I watched his hands fumble for an uncomfortable moment, but he could not conceal the cuffs. He turned and gave us all an assuring smile when they led him out. "See you," he mouthed the words to us.

Testa stood up and rapped the gavel. "This court is adjourned," he announced.

CHAPTER TWENTY-ONE

I visited Nanny Jolly in the afternoon. I could not remember the last time. It had been months, by the feel of it. I lost all sense of chronology in my day-to-day life. There was a hailstorm one night. I remember that. Tilly got run down and killed. I recalled the night plainly. I was with Nanny that night, listening to the hail on the tin roof. So much had happened since then, so little of it good. During my absence from Nanny, Jason Lipton shot himself in the face, or at least, some said so. Others preferred the even more ghastly version and continued to blame Beepah. To some at least, Zach and me were his evil spawn. Whatever the truth, Grace Campbell helped stir it into a murder mystery destined for reruns decades into the future.

I could tell Nanny had barely disturbed her knitting pile in all that time. I recognized the thumbless snow-white Christmas mitten still occupying the top spot, and still unfinished. I gave her a kiss on the cheek that she received with a little giggle. It took a moment before she even identified me.

"Oh dear!" she said.

Beyond that, we talked little about anything of substance. I talked about the hailstorm the night Tilly was killed. She seemed to recall that night, although I could not be certain which hailstorm she remembered. It was clear her mind was failing. She talked about Matty Jolly, good Ol' Jolly. I considered talking about the drained pond but thought better of it. I doubted she realized the commotion out back signaled the undoing of Ol' Jolly's creation.

The very idea, no matter the purpose, was bound to upset her. I went behind her chair and bent to touch my cheek to the top of her head where the hair was thin and tangled. I recalled one of my fondest and earliest memories, how gently she reacted the morning she discovered little Panfry and me sharing a bottle. "There's a fine way to catch your death," she'd said, that or some such thing. I'm sure she giggled. That was her nature. To this day I don't know if she was talking to me or the pig. Perhaps both. I found her hairbrush on the lamp table and began passing it through the tangles.

"That's so nice, Matty dear," she said. "That's so very nice."

My eyes welled with tears. I had lost her almost completely. It left me empty, to lose her along with all that had departed.

———

It was another ten days before I heard the slightest noise about visitation. As it turned out, we were all signed up to see Beep on a Thursday, and I confess to a certain apprehension. Thoughts of Beep left me feeling that way sometimes, when I was uncertain where his mood would take him, challenging the demons of his imagination who often threatened to remove him out of this world. I should have felt some comfort just knowing he was a proud member of the Weeble School student body. I could only hope he felt safe there, no doubt learning to walk like Charlie Chaplin in penguin pajamas.

Zach was to drive the forty miles and I sat up front. Mother was quiet in the back until we were halfway there. It was raining, and even Zach, with his penchant for speed, kept Mom's Mercedes throttled to a crawl. I turned to catch her fumbling in her purse for a tissue. For some strange reason, I assumed she was preparing for a cry.

"Did you know, my dears, you once had a sister?"

"Oh, Mother," I said, overcome in an instant, without a moment to calculate, or even consider the weight of her words. I twisted completely backward in my seat. "We never talked about this."

She understood my confusion. "Not me, dear," she said. "A girl in Vietnam, not much older than you, I suspect. She had a baby that died in a fire." Mom dabbed at her eyes with the tissue, and when she spoke again, she choked on her words. "A baby girl . . . your father's," she struggled.

"Sophie," I said out of the blue, speaking a name I had heard many times while he slept and held me close in the big sleeping bag in the teepee. I was little then, maybe three or four. It was a name that felt harmless to me, a fantasy, the good dream we all wish for each night. I never asked him. How could I know he was missing a child from forty years past? All at once I felt oddly protective, and tears quickly spilled over for this dear little sister I had only known from Beep's dreaming.

Zach heard it all. He wheeled the Mercedes into a rest area and pulled it between two white lines in front of the utility building. There were a few other cars and a few travelers scampering through the rain to find bathrooms. Zach put the car in park. He watched the windshield wipers slap back and forth. He shut them down to slow and let the pouring rain conceal us inside. In a moment, the rain diminished to a sprinkle. In a few minutes more it had stopped completely and the sun broke through the clouds overhead.

"How'd you find that out?" Zach finally spoke.

"I came over on Monday with Ian Finley," Mother said. "Believe it or not, I had papers to sign. We talked to a Dr. Peete. He related some highlights of his early sessions with your father. Sophie was one of those revelations, and according to Peete, Campion had barely scratched the surface before he died."

"We never knew any of that," Zach said.

"I found out much like you, dear," Mom said. "I heard it in his dreaming. He spoke the name Sophie many times in his sleep." She dabbed at her eyes with the tissue and laughed a little ruefully. "I was even jealous in the early years. I only asked about her once. I expected he would lie, but he said nothing. I never once gave any thought to the idea Sophie was a child. It wasn't long after that he started sleeping in the basement. Isn't it strange, the things we assign so little weight? You remember Dr. Campion? Well, it was Campion who exposed little Sophie. She was mentioned time and again in Campion's records, which, by the way, the attorneys petitioned for release."

Mom went on to describe some of Campion's own struggles from ten years past, referring to Beep's condition as borderline schizophrenia, even though he said it was far from a classic case. According to Campion, the opinion was observational and less than diagnostic. "He referenced borderline as a catchall afflictive category," Mom said. "I believe those were his words."

Zach put the car in reverse and maneuvered the Mercedes out. "See that, Sydney," he said. "Beep's not normal, not even for a schizoid."

Even in the depths of that moment, Zach made me laugh. "You said a mouthful," I managed, still overcome by tears.

Mom leaned up. "You think that's a mouthful, here's one," she said. "Dr. Peete gave Beepah some kind of intelligence test. You might be pleased to know your father is at least partially responsible for your genius. I always figured him to be off the charts, just not that chart."

I laughed again and slapped Zach on the leg as he wheeled us back onto the highway. "I often suspected you were no fool," I gave him a dig. "Clever you, hiding it so well all these years."

"Stuff it, Sydney!"

Upon first take, the Weeble School had changed little over the years, although it took a few minutes to dredge my memory of the place. Blue paint peeled around all the windows. The glass panes were streaked in the emerging sunshine of the day. Every window was covered with iron grates anchored into the brick veneer on the outside. On top of the big main building, a tripodal antenna reached almost to the clouds. Satellite communication apparatus clung barnacled to any attachable surface, giving the wobbling student body in one-legged pajamas direct access to the more stable alien worlds beyond.

The lobby was brighter than I recalled. Murals of children playing sports ran along the front and back walls. The colors were vivid. We passed through slow-moving people traffic on our way to the receptionist. The inmates were most curious about our presence there, and they rubbernecked their way toward the day room. The name plate at the reception counter displayed the name Arnette Button. She was a Black woman, round, with a face forever at the brink of a smile, but she seemed disinclined just then.

"Your name."

"Angela Carmichael."

"Who are you here for?"

"Ben Bowden."

"These are his children?"

"Yes."

"Your name."

"Zachary Bowden."

"And yours, sweetie."

I was a sweetie, and very much put off by it suddenly. I considered answering Sweetie Bowden, but I beat back the urge. "Sydney Bowden," I said instead.

Arnette went down a list she clearly knew by heart. "Any firearms, blades, weapons of any kind?"

Mom responded with a similar lack of enthusiasm. "That would be a no, no, and no," she said.

"Any medications, prescription drugs, drugs of any kind?"

"I have aspirin, which I often need . . ."

Arnette showed the first sign of a bubbly nature and smiled. "You'll have to leave that with the guard," she said, and she extended her hand toward the metal detector.

The guard threw a switch and the conveyor started without noise. Mom put her purse aboard, then my phone, then Zach's. We went through without any additional fanfare and the guard beckoned us to follow him toward the dayroom.

Beepah was there, standing in pajamas and a bathrobe. His eyes found us the instant we turned the corner. By then the sun was streaming through the dirty windows and caught him completely, standing within a single frame of light. His arms came up and his smile broadened. I broke clear of Mother and Zach and ran to him. My arms went around him like I might never let go.

"Syd, my beautiful Syd," he greeted me. "I wasn't sure I'd know you."

I cried with joy, and I hurt for him all at the same time. "It's only been a few weeks, Beepah," I said. "I hope you don't forget me after a few weeks."

Zach caught up with me. He pushed his hand out, and Beep took it and pulled him into our tight embrace. "Hi, Beep," Zach said.

Mother and Beepah touched cheeks. The gesture appeared to comfort both of them. We found a table and we all sat down. Beep wanted to hear everything. We talked about the birds, about who had lived for the past month and who had not. I told him the sad news about Chloe Corn Tits, and how Zach buried her back of the barn. We talked about Big Daryl and how the pond got emptied by the firetruck, and all the fish died. We told him about the big snapper, and how we saved him and let him go in the creek by the canoe launch. We told him nothing was the same on Trumpet Hill when he went away.

"Some of us kick up a rat's nest when we show up . . . some of us, when we leave," he said. "Maybe I caused a little snafu." He touched us both on the hands. "Listen to your mother. Keep an eye on her until I get back. She's inclined to work too hard."

There was no mention of little Sophie. She was the part of Beepah's life he had not yet shared with us, nor had he reconciled her existence, not even in his sleep. It was Dr. Campion, years before, who had discovered little Sophie in the darkest depths. They were the memories Beep must have struggled to reclaim, resurrected at last, only to fuel his post-traumatic stress and corrupt his sleep for the remaining nights and years of his life.

The revelation of little Sophie's brief existence was far too fresh and complicated for me to delve deeply. Yet I found it easy enough to accept her and take her into my heart. There were moments during the many days that followed when I found myself choked by grief at the loss of her. She had truly lived for a time. Campion found Sophie adrift in a mind fragmented by war and hurt. Hers was a life and death belonging to an eternity that existed in the world long before I arrived in it, and I had scarcely begun my own struggles to imagine what part she played so many years ago.

———

Within the passage of two months, Big Daryl managed to trickle enough water into the giant crater in the earth to refill it, turning it back into the glorious mudhole it was meant to be. Big Daryl even installed a small gaggle of geese into the duck house and went about the business of refurbishing the place with fresh straw and nesting places. I could watch the half-grown goslings from the shed roof while they chased down food pellets on the slippery duck ramp.

I learned to drive in the course of that early winter. Zach quietly reveled in the teaching process. I took out Grace Campbell's mailbox when I skidded right instead of left. Zach and I replaced it with a temporary, guaranteeing a permanent post version once the ground thawed. Grace was gracious in accepting our offer to revisit the mailbox repair come spring. But then, in true Grace Campbell fashion, my reputation ballooned to include reckless driving among my many foibles.

I got my driver's license near Christmas, the same day Nanny Jolly died. I missed her by minutes, me traversing Trumpet Hill for the first time as a legal driver only to interrupt an ambulance just then departing with Nanny on board. It was moving very slowly, so I knew. Later that day I opened a small package she had wrapped for me. It contained a pair of thumbless white Christmas mittens. In return, I prayed to the Tooth Fairy to allow Nanny immediate access to a spot in the earth next to Ol' Jolly and not yet frozen. Go right in, no waiting in the dark in the chilly brick building.

And come spring, Zach and I graduated together. For me it was time. I had long since concluded that the brain bank in charge of the high school had seen enough of me. I began to believe the entire schoolboard was scheming behind my back to unload me to one high-powered college or another. I spent much of the year ensconced in the guidance office, speaking with representatives from the Ivy Leagues: Harvard and Yale and others. As much as possible, I took it in stride. I had always been a bit of a freak. The attention only ensured that popular opinions of me lived on.

When graduation was driven indoors by torrential rains, I challenged Zach to shed his shoes for the ceremony. I kicked off mine and went barefoot across the auditorium stage, leaving damp footprints on the hardwood. I meant it to be playful, if not symbolic, daring to go barefoot into an uncertain future. When I looked back for Zach, I saw my own footprints cool and disappear in my wake. I raised my gown enough to expose my ankles. The gesture drew scattered laughter and applause. Zach followed and did the same, hiking his gown in can-can fashion. Even our dear mother might have broken into smiles. It was complete. We were graduated.

I spent weekends that summer making the drive to the Weeble School in a car Mother bought for Zach and me to share. I carried news, as much as possible. Beepah wanted to hear everything. I did my best to screen the headlines. Mom was in the Caribbean with Alexandra Su Bien—on business, by some reports. The trips happened twice within a month, although the second getaway took them to the Canary Islands, so perhaps they had unfinished business there as well.

"Tenerife is wonderful in summer," she said upon her return.

Beep had his own take, and of course, "The woman works too hard," came out of his mouth.

Zach accompanied me often and carried news of his own. One such visit Zach informed Beepah he was considering enlisting. "I'm thinking US Army Airborne," he said boldly. "I don't like leaving you . . . stuck in this place, I mean."

"Don't sweat over me," Beep said, leaning toward Zach in a gesture more candid than usual. "You were thinking I might try and talk you out of it. I know how steadfast you can be, Zach boy.

Besides, I'm hearing they're springing me from this fruitcake factory come Thanksgiving," he said, rocking back in his chair. "They've managed to scramble my brain enough to render me harmless to the natives. They'll stamp my ass and declare me safe as rat poison, and they'll boot me to the curb."

Beep did come home the Monday before Thanksgiving. I was in the scratch yard the morning the car came up Trumpet Hill. I heard a car door close, then another, and I watched the black sedan depart. Beepah came around the corner of the house and caught sight of me with my head poking out past the iron gate. He walked toward me, and his pace quickened. He dropped his little suitcase on the kennel stoop and threw his arms around me and pulled me close.

Zach was gone by then, off to army bootcamp. I alerted Mother that Beep had finally arrived. She left work early and came straight home. Later that day we managed to arrange a brief FaceTime chat with Zachary. Beep insisted that as a veteran, he deserved some privilege. The army conceded, allowing us to squeeze out a few precious minutes. It was a glorious exchange, all of us together as much as could be.

CHAPTER TWENTY-TWO

Cowboy crowed at sunrise. An hour later Beepah came to the kennel, walking out on a cool and cloudy morning to find me sitting on my stone with my notebook. The birds were out to fly in the pale light. I watched them swoop low over an aging teepee that drooped in folds filled with pine needles and crumpled leaves. The birds climbed toward the clouds and out over the meadow, then swung north toward Trumpet Hill Road.

I wrote in my notebook that morning, "Beepah arrived in the aviary just after dawn. It's a Tuesday." I never considered it remarkable. I was only seeking to find normal once again. He reached above the door and switched on the radio. There was Spriole spewing news about yesterday's stock market. Beep stood for the longest time filling his lungs with aviary air and reveling in it. In that moment, all was as it had always been.

We talked only a little about his time away. There was talk about my future. I was young, not yet seventeen and in no rush to be educated. I talked to him about the art school in Greenwich Village where Mom's friend John Goff was already pulling strings on my behalf. I told Beep I would consider the art school as a curiosity more than anything. I was afraid I would lose my individual approach to art if I stayed too long. Beep had no opinion, not really. In all the years since John Goff became an occasional subject at dinner, Beep had not uttered the man's name. I always suspected he knew nothing of Mother's frequent clandestine meetings with the man. I was no longer certain how much he knew, or how much he forgave.

Those conversations, as inconsequential as they might have been, lasted a week or two. In the middle of them Beep would simply remove himself, walking off to the basement or to a straw bale in the aviary to sit and ponder one new fear or another. There were further inklings of his unease. There were sluggish footsteps on the basement stairs, and it became instantly clear that the distance between Beep and Mother had grown vast. She never visited the basement to share his bed and hold him in the dark to ease the new loneliness that returned home with him. It was not easy to determine if his year at the Weeble School damaged him further, or if it was an expected progression to his complex mental state.

One morning he came to the kennel with a pail of kitchen scraps. It was foggy and damp. The sun was reluctant. I sat on the stone wall bundled in winter clothes, and I watched as he tossed lettuce and carrot peels and eggshells over the churned-up earth. Chickens scrambled for the treats. When the pail was empty, he dropped it near the coop door. Beep did not meet my eyes. His back was to me, and he said nothing for the longest time. His eyes wandered off into the hemlock branches overhead and he appeared to pray.

"I was afraid they would cancel my visitation if I didn't say what they wanted to hear," he said. "When I complained, they said it was pure paranoia." He turned toward me, and I could see his eyes glisten with tears. "It's impossible to fight paranoia when you're accused of it," he said. "I'm not sure they ever got their confession. I find it strange these mornings, to have the freedom to speak."

I assumed he was referring to the Weeble School interrogators. I knew through our conversations during the year, he saw them that way, Dr. Peete and the rest. He even leaned in and told me as much on more than one occasion, referring to any one of them as "comrade" and expecting severe reprisals. In Beep's mind they were desperately trying to get inside his head, to unravel deep secrets, to get him to confess to one high crime or another.

"Little Sophie had green eyes, much like yours," he said, pushing his fingers through the chicken wire and dropping his head against the back of his hands. "Mai Li was sixteen. Her father, Sinjin, didn't trust me much. But he figured if I got out alive, maybe I could get Mai Li out." Beep sobbed a little against the back of his hand. "I couldn't get her out. Even after she got pregnant with Sophie, I couldn't get her out. So, I reenlisted, and Uncle Sam never let me forget I owed him two more years."

There was a huge regret he could barely contain, and he choked out the words. "I should have moved Mai Li closer to the base," he said. "She wanted to stay with her family. I was gone so much. Sophie was six months before she began to recognize me. Her little round face brightened like the moon when I held her. I looked into her eyes and promised her everything."

He turned his head and smiled. I could tell he had caught a flash of Sophie's face. He remembered the color of her eyes and compared them to mine. That memory—had it been the only one—might have left him whole, but his face turned quickly dark again. He dropped his head against his hands and began to sob openly.

I slid from the rock wall and went across the kennel. Tears distorted my vision and spilled onto my cheeks. They were a torrent by the time I reached him. I put my arms around him and cried into his shirt. Listening to him, I could tell he had pieced the story together over the past many months, no doubt with Dr. Peete's prodding. He managed to rescue it from his nightmares, out of the dark and into the light where his hurt and guilt became almost tactile.

Beep let loose of me and turned away. "It was a week before I got back," he confessed, forcing his words past the tightness in his throat. "There was barely a soul—only an old man sitting cross-legged in the road. I dropped down in the dust and asked him if everybody ran away. 'Dead,' is what he said. 'They're all dead.'"

Beep recounted those scraps of his memory as best he could, all the while fighting to keep the horrors of those days buried deep in darkness. The old man told him Sinjin lived. Some others might have scattered in the jungle, but it had been eight days and only a few came back to bury the dead. "The old man said Mai Li and Sophie were among them, in the ground forever."

Beep looked off toward Jolly's pond, where the fog over the water remained a shroud in the cold air. The sudden clarity of his recollections must have surprised even him. The pain appeared on his face just as a scant breeze began to twist the fog and lift it. "Sinjin buried his family," Beep said, "and when he was finished burying them, he no longer wanted to live." With that memory Beepah's knees began to crumble. He pushed his fingers into the chicken wire to hold himself upright. "The old man showed me how he covered his eyes, and how his hand shook when he shot Sinjin in the back of the head."

Beepah turned and took me in his arms again and held me desperately. "I was nowhere," he admitted. "Stoned," he said. "That's how I was in those days."

He held onto me for a long while after admitting his failing. I expected him to squeeze me until I relented and offered him absolution, as if I had the power. He was not there when they died horribly. In his mind, that sin alone was monstrous enough to be absent from his memory for more than forty years. Perhaps he felt forgiveness at last, and throughout the balance of the morning, I could tell Beep's heart was lightened, if only for a time.

An hour later we were bucking along the road near Esopus Creek in the old pickup truck on our way to get straw bales for the aviary. On our return, I listened to him growl about the price of straw. "What the hell? It ain't gold and I ain't no Rumpelstiltskin," he grumbled.

It made me laugh. The fairytale imp Rumpelstiltskin could spin straw into gold, but he was bargaining for the life of a firstborn child. I decided not to go there. Instead, we toyed with the idea of getting a pig. We even considered naming him Panfry in honor of the bottle-snatching porker of my early childhood. Remembering Panfry's eventual fate compelled me to nix the idea.

I swept out the barn later in the morning while Beep spoke about the day the army no longer considered him fit for duty. "They stamped me safe as napalm and kicked my ass to the helipad," he said. He equated the sudden discharge from the army to his hasty departure from the Weeble School. "I must have said the right thing for once," he joked, mystified. He fully expected them to realize their mistake and come looking for him again. We laughed at that, but I could tell it had become a genuine concern to him.

Six weeks had passed since his release from the Weeble School. What took him to the brink was a question to ponder for a lifetime. When the birds went out to fly in the crisp January air, Beep did not arrive in the aviary. Spriole was silent that morning, and the aviary was cold. I searched for him in his basement bed. He was gone. The sheet was barely pulled back. He had not slept, perhaps for many nights. What drove him away must have consumed his thoughts until fears and his awakening mind compelled him finally to go, to spare us from one approaching calamity or another, or simply because he could no longer put one day in front of another without confusion.

Mom left for work a few hours later, dismissing Beep's absence as barely a deviation from normal. "It's Beepah, for chrissake," she said.

After she had gone, I went out and scraped the ice from the windows of the trusty car Zach and I drove all summer for trips to the Weeble School. I had not driven it since Beepah's return. It was reluctant to go in the cold. It started, like I was stirring thick mud. I let it run for twenty minutes until it was almost warm, and I drove the roads that entire day, even searching the ditches and the shoulders where snowplows heaped the fresh snow to bury any trace of him.

McCutchen's Bar and Grill was open for business as usual. I swung the old Chevy against the snow drift overflowing the curb and clumped my way across the street and up the concrete steps. When I stepped inside the open door, the familiar smell of the place returned to me. It was warm inside. The wood stove gave off more heat than the small place could efficiently disperse, and the doors were propped open the entire winter, unless there was a blizzard.

I pushed the parka hood from my head and looked around the place. Two of the boys were sitting at the big table. They smiled and nodded their recognition in my direction. It had been well over a year since my last visit to McCutchen's, back before the world grabbed me by the head and tail and snatched normal out of my life. At McCutchen's, little had changed since then. Dust and ashes covered the floor, and an old man sat hunched over at the bar. Above the whiskey bottles in the back hung my drawing of the leprechaun Collin Jefferson. The memory of that day brought a brief smile, and I harkened back to the days Beep, Zach, me, and Mother were all happy. Then I thought of Collin Jefferson dead and Beep lost in the snow. I feared those happy days would never return.

"You must be looking for your father," someone said.

The other at the table quickly added, "Why else would she be here anyways?"

I could not remember their names, although I was certain I had met them both some years back. One might have been the guy Beep dubbed Mr. Glitterman because of his preference for costume jewelry. This one wore a cluster of turquoise glass beads around his neck and a single peacock feather earring, but his accessories were so understated, I was not certain he was the original Glitterman. I decided not to address either by name.

"Have you seen him?" I asked. "He walked away last night in the snowstorm."

"Most of us didn't even know he was home," the glittery one said. "Not until he rolled in here a few days ago. He hasn't been back here since. We've been watching for him. He seemed a little spacey . . . you know, out of it. Whatever clover they fed him at the bunny ranch didn't agree with him. He's not the same ol' Ben Bowden we once knew."

"A few of us have been there," the other one said. "We know the drill."

By the time I left McCutchen's that day, I had spoken to almost everyone in the place. They all knew Ben Bowden. Most had not seen him in well over a year, let alone the past twenty-four hours. Many of them had not forgotten the Jason Lipton killing. Some still accused Beep, and others never would. The tragedies of the killing in the meadow, his incarceration, the poking and prodding that exposed a great darkness in his past, all left him diminished in his capacity to reason, to communicate in the joyful discourse we had come to recognize as Beepah.

Some days later we alerted authorities to his disappearance, uncertain what to assume, hesitant to describe the man we knew as Beepah as anything more than a man afflicted by a troubled soul. Even Sheriff Micah Nash conceded we should have reported his absence sooner. Nevertheless, Nash issued the all-points bulletin. Weeks passed . . . then months. There was no word of him, not a single credible sighting according to Nash.

There were mornings I sent the birds out to fly and returned to the house just as the sun began to brighten the hemlock, and crotchety ol' Cowboy barked out evidence of his survival yet another day. I would descend the basement stairs into the dim light only to find empty sheets, untouched. I wept at the loss of him.

Zach came home for a visit before deploying to Afghanistan. Six more months passed without a single word of Beepah's whereabouts. Then, in late spring, on a Wednesday, an official letter arrived with the Department of State seal stamped into the envelope. It was addressed to Angela Carmichael Bowden. I scrambled to open it in Mom's absence. The message came from the US Ambassador to Fiji, of all places.

My father was found sitting upright at the base of a banyan tree on the outskirts of the town of Savusavu, on Fiji's north island. There were few details about his death, though foul play was barely considered. He carried one identifying paper—no passport, no tickets of any kind, only a discharge order from the Weeble School. To Beepah, I suspect the paper alone was enough to legitimize him.

There was no recent history, no hint about where he had been or where he was bound. No tramp steamer captain came to collect a missing crewman. He had not escaped pirates, by any rational accounts. For lack of a more plausible explanation, he had dropped in from Neptune and landed in Fiji. The ambassador's office was kind in its remarks, avoiding the word *vagabond*, although there was little doubt, in his travels, Beepah had achieved that lofty station and little more. Officials found two Fiji dollars and two nickels in his pockets. In his hand was a crinkled photograph of

Zach and me taken from across the fire in the teepee during the last autumn we were truly together.

I will likely never know how he died, or if he just got tired and sat down under a tree to embrace the long sleep. I will likely never know if he was on his way to Vietnam, or if he searched for a way back home to us, and I will likely never know if he found little Sophie, or if Sophie was even part of his wanderings. Perhaps he found her buried in a field near a village that appeared in his dreams. I can only hope whatever he discovered softened the pain he felt at losing her.

Mother and I spent much energy in the weeks and months that followed seeking a way to bring Beepah home again. Negotiating with the state department proved a maddening affair. But when the red tape ran out, a cannister containing a clay urn half filled with ashes arrived via courier. Secretly, I questioned the validity of the contents. Filling clay jars from a busy crematorium was likely not an exact science, and I suspected a fair number of Fijian vagabonds found their way into the same crowded urn.

When Zach arrived home on leave, we scattered the ashes in the scratch yard just outside the aviary. To me it seemed fitting, and Mother did not protest. I could talk to Beep there, like I talked with Grandmother. In conversations from my stone in the wall, I could keep him abreast of Zach's successes, and my own.

We were alone with Beep that morning, me and Zach and Mother . . . until Louie King showed up with a couple of boys from McCutchen's. How they got wind of our quiet farewell, I may never know. They talked about Ben Bowden in bold tones. They recounted stories passed between them in the years since Vietnam. They laughed quietly at some of them. They were stories only they could know, every story infused with gentle epithets we recognized as integral to the tale. Louie touched his hand inside the clay urn and held it in the breeze. He rubbed his fingertips over his bib overalls to capture a swipe of Ben Bowden's ashes. He confided to us he would carry him back to the world.

Zach spent the following morning chiseling a stone that identified the man who taught me fiddleheads and star counting and goodness to others and the freedom of birds. Zach hauled the stone in the trailer from the barn. He set it slightly askew into the earth across from the kennel gate.

In my dreaming, the night is blue, truly blue, thanks to the moon, or thanks to the sun on the far side . . . or maybe thanks to me just for standing in it. I feel safe in white pajamas turned blue by the light, conspicuous like fairy music, or Neptune above the meadow. I am standing at the teepee door, soaking in the blue. There is a freedom here these days, hard fought, now cloaked in blue and safe.

I am walking backward in time, pushing my toes into soggy holes in soft snow where his heels touch down on his return trips home. Even birds in the aviary feel safe roosting there as the blue pours in all around. Weasels stay put on such glorious nights. Birds, with their eyes aglow as moonlight catches them just so, watch me standing silent in the blue. They do sleep well, assured I have not come there to eat them.

For Zach and me, our inheritance is grand enough to last a lifetime. We were left a Fiji dollar and a nickel each, and there is a chiseled stone, soon to be riddled in moss and years. I can touch it on cool autumn mornings. It is solid, everlasting by its nature. It reads simply, *Beepah.*

ABOUT THE AUTHOR

If not for his ten brothers and sisters, Richard Quinn might have been an only child. He grew up near Lake Superior in Michigan's north. He joined the Navy during Vietnam, then attended Michigan State University with hopes of being a doctor. Instead, he became a carpenter. He's been told it was a decision that spared lives.

For many years, Quinn worked as a journalist, chasing hard news in a sleepy Connecticut town, and scratching out satirical columns designed to lighten the hearts of local citizenry—an enjoyable pursuit that won notice from the New England Press Association. He was also noticed by the *Hartford Courant* for a lengthy fictional piece celebrating Mark Twain's *Connecticut Yankee*. Twain was one, transplanted like Quinn, a century apart.

Quinn lives in Unionville, Connecticut.